A
Bitter
Rain

ALSO BY JAMES D. SHIPMAN

Constantinopolis
Going Home: A Novel of the Civil War
It Is Well

A Bitter Rain

JAMES D. SHIPMAN

PUBLISHING

Published by Lake Union Publishing, Seattle
www.apub.com

Amazon, the Amazon logo, and Lake Union Publishing are trademarks of Amazon.com, Inc., or its affiliates.

ISBN-13: 9781477819807
ISBN-10: 1477819800

Cover design by Shasti O'Leary Soudant

Printed in the United States of America

I dedicate A Bitter Rain *to all the victims of World War II. As the world again trends toward nationalism and even fascism, may we never forget the consequences of modern dictatorship.*

PROLOGUE

Königsberg, East Prussia, Nazi Germany
August 1939

Greta giggled as her fingers slid down the razor-sharp blade.

"Careful," warned her father. "That has a bite to it."

She ignored him, brows furrowed, concentrating as she traced designs on the mirrored steel.

He grasped the hilt and drew the blade swiftly to her hair, plunging his thumb downward and slicing through a yellow lock.

"Daddy, stop it!" she protested.

He returned the knife to the nightstand, glancing to see if his wife had noticed. She hadn't. He tucked the lock in his pocket, his eyes never leaving his daughter.

"Erik, get that thing away," ordered Corina, peering up from her ironing in irritation. "Honestly, I don't know who's the bigger child."

He reached out tenderly and wrapped both hands around Greta's. She resisted for a moment, laughing again before she let go. His daughter sprang from the bed and out of the room as if the dagger would hunt her, a lace and platinum blur.

"You indulge her too much," complained Corina. "She won't behave herself if you let her do whatever she wants."

"Don't worry, Corina, soon enough you will have all the time there is to correct her bad habits."

A cloud blocked the sunshine of their morning. "Did they say how long you'll be gone?" his wife asked.

He moved behind her and answered her only with his arms, lifting her in the air to twirl around. She batted at his wrought-iron limbs, but he wouldn't let go. She jerked her whole body and drew herself back to the floor, her glare flickering molten fire.

"I have to finish the ironing, Erik!"

He flinched and released her. She adjusted a scarlet scarf at her neck and smoothed her sweater before resuming her task. She roamed critically over the fabric with her iron. "You didn't answer."

"There's no way to know. It depends on many things. Have you heard from Karl?"

"Not a word. It's likely too late now. I didn't expect all this so soon, or I would have called him earlier."

"There may be time still. Who knows?"

He tried again to swallow the fear resting leaden in his throat. *I'll think of other things.* He stood over her, watching her labor. He admired her skill as she pressed out each wrinkle, drawing the scorching metal along the cloth as she traced a razor edge in the creases. Soon she was finished, and she drew the warm fabric over him. He let her dress him. Silence choked the room.

He tucked the shirt into his trousers and tightened his belt. Erik wandered to the aged wardrobe standing guard in their bedroom to remove a gray tunic. After he worked his arms into the material, he buttoned the front. He drew himself up, laboring to look the part. Corina materialized behind him, her fingers tugging and smoothing the fabric until she was satisfied. She placed the cap on his head, making fractional adjustments. "There," she announced at last.

He examined himself again in the mirror and shook his head. "I look like a fool."

"You look like a man."

He shook his head. "I didn't want this."

"You needed it—we all did."

"Maybe we'll hear from Karl," he said.

"We still might, but you have to be prepared for the alternative. He's very busy."

"Too busy for you?"

"Perhaps even that."

Greta reappeared and squealed when she saw her father fully dressed. She flew into his arms still giggling. He twirled her around. She weighed no more than a feather. He held her tightly, closing his eyes for a moment, fighting back the tears.

"Where will you go?" Corina asked.

"Wherever they tell me, but to the barracks to start."

"Will you be able to come back before your first assignment?" She moved past him, lifting the collapsible ironing board and placing it on a nearby hook. She eyed it for a moment and then straightened the board slightly.

"I don't know," he answered, pausing a little at the thought. "I hope so. It depends on how rapidly we move."

Greta was still squirming and laughing, and he tossed her on the bed, willing a smile down at her. She jumped up and demanded that he throw her again. "I'm sorry, sweetheart, but I have no more time today for games, even for my little princess."

"Where you going, Daddy?" she asked, a serious expression crowding her face.

"You already know the answer," he said sadly. "Remember what we talked about last night? I must go away—but just for a very little while." He looked at her with mock sternness. "You must obey your mother. She will not put up with your antics as I have."

"Don't say that," snapped Corina. "She already sees me as a tyrant." His wife shooed Greta off the bed and whisked over to smooth out the wrinkles in the fabric.

Greta ran to him again. She held him tightly with her tiny arms. "I don't want you to go. Why can't you stay here with us?" She disengaged and picked up the dagger, dropping down on the bed with the weapon on her lap.

Absently he took the knife away. He might never see her again. The idea choked him, and he jerked his head back to study the ceiling. He drew a sharp breath before the words stumbled out. "I don't have a choice. You must be my brave girl while I'm gone."

"Don't worry her so," said Corina, busying herself with the pillows, turned away from him. She finished and moved close, taking his hands, her gaze softening. "You must be careful. Promise me?" He drew her near, kissing her. Her smell of starch and soap, and an underlying sweetness, intoxicated him. He relished this moment of closeness. She withdrew, staring out the window.

He nodded and steadied himself, his mind assembling hasty barricades to the encroaching grief. He glanced again in the mirror, trying to gather his courage, but the reflection mocked him. What did he know about being a soldier? He'd had a sniff of training. He must stay strong. Karl might still intervene. He raised his hand and fingered the lightning-shaped *SS* on his collar. He was out of time. He had to go.

CHAPTER ONE

Königsberg, East Prussia, Nazi Germany
August 1939

Erik leaped down from the train to the crowded platform, his gaze a lighthouse sweeping the sea of bodies swirling past him in the twilight. He waded through the human current, ceaselessly scanning the crowd. In the distance he spotted a diminutive white fairy darting in and out among the jostling figures. He quickened his step. There she was—his angel! She saw him, too, and he heard Greta's musical laughter as she sprang up in his arms. He spun her around. She giggled and her flaxen curls danced.

"That wasn't long." The voice froze him. Erik set Greta gently down.

Erik faced Corina. She swam under a flowered dress, a white lace scarf cutting into her neck. He smiled and moved methodically toward her, reaching an arm out to cup her waist. He could have wrapped it around her thrice. She'd never regained her weight after the illness, he realized. She pecked his cheek briefly, but he pulled her closer, kissing her firmly on the lips.

"Erik! Stop now! There's too many people around us." She smiled briefly and looked him over. Her forehead furrowed. "Where's your uniform?"

"I took it off on the train," he stammered.

She frowned. "You shouldn't have. Be proud of who you are." She gestured at the mass of bodies. "If you had it on, we wouldn't be treated like this by the mob." As if the press of people was too much for her, she glanced around sternly. "Look at these people. This is no place for a reunion. Pick up Greta and let's go." She spun abruptly and pressed through the throng.

Erik lifted Greta, swinging her around as they followed. Her legs flailed wildly as he spun her, nearly toppling an elderly man who scampered out of the way with a grumbling complaint. Erik didn't care. He was home.

"Daddy, I knew you would come back soon!"

"I will always return to you."

"Do you promise?"

"I do." *Should I deceive her like this? No matter. If I don't return, a broken promise will be a drop in an ocean of grief.*

They arrived home shortly at their town house, crowded among the unending rows along the Yorckstrasse, in the northern portion of the Sackheim District. Erik was greeted with warm embraces by his *Mutter und Vater*. Anna, Erik's mother, pinched his cheek and smiled through her cracks and creases before tromping back inside to resume her post in the kitchen. He watched her fondly from the hallway. She stood a gray-haired pillar amid a whipping wind of delicious aromas and clanging dishes.

Corina rushed Greta up the stairs to change clothes, and Erik's father motioned him into the narrow sitting area. Mementos huddled on a mantel beneath framed family pictures too small for the dark breadth of paneling. The walnut flooring was immaculately scrubbed but worn and peeling. Peter Mueller eased himself into the folds of a high-backed chair that engulfed him. His frown was buried in a peppered moustache that matched the thatched forest above his eyes. He watched his son for a moment, scrutinizing Erik as if searching for the proper words.

"So, it didn't begin."

"Not yet at least," said Erik.

Peter took a deep breath. "Maybe we have nothing to worry about then."

"Perhaps, but I doubt it; they aren't backing down."

"They will. Who are these Poles but a whole nation of *Untermenschen*? The Führer thinks they'll give in, and he's been right about all the rest."

Erik chuckled, surprised. "Praising our glorious leader, now are you? That's not something I thought I'd ever hear from you."

Peter crossed his arms, his hand forming a thoughtful crutch beneath his chin. "Perhaps I've been wrong about him. I've been wrong before." His face seemed to darken.

"Now, Vater, let's not talk about that."

"You're right, no point in stirring up the embers of the past. There's trouble enough right now."

"You were saying? About the Führer?"

"Maybe he's right after all. Nobody took him seriously when he came to power, with promises to restore Germany's place in the world," Peter said.

"He's done that."

"He's achieved military greatness at least," observed Peter. "At the cost of our social programs, the opposition parties, and the press."

"We still have a legislature, and the courts," said Erik.

"Hah!" His father laughed, slapping his knee. "And you call yourself a historian. Rome kept their senate right through the empire. That didn't make it a republic. The forms don't make the substance."

"You might be right, Vater, but here we are."

His father grunted in agreement and changed the subject. "Enough of the past. Tell me, honest son, do you think the Poles will fight?"

Erik hesitated, turning the thought over. "I don't know. I would have said no, but England and France have steeled their resolve."

Peter scowled and took a violent puff on his pipe, coughing and sputtering through the smoke. "That band of robbers," he stammered. "We're in this fix in the first place because of them. If they'd treated us decently after the last war, there'd be no Hitler."

Erik shifted in his seat. He ached from days of drilling. He wanted to go upstairs and sleep, but his father needed to talk.

"A lot of good it did them. Only twenty years and Germany is back where it should be. Strange that they sat back and watched us do it. *Gott* knows why they want to interfere now—when it's too late. They had a dozen chances to stop us, but they did nothing," Erik posited.

"Don't underestimate them, especially the French. Wild animals in war. They froze us for four years on the western front."

"That was then. They've no fire now, even if they'd really help the Poles."

Peter leaned forward. "You have a little time now. Are you going to meet with Karl again?"

"This is a day of surprises. First the Führer and now Karl."

Peter spat into a garbage bin near his chair. "I don't like Karl a bit, and I trust him less. Still, if there's a way he could maneuver a transfer . . ."

Erik bristled, shocked at his father's words. "You don't want me to serve? You were in the army. The whole war."

"That's different. That was a long time ago. We didn't have a choice. Besides, it's a miracle I survived."

"You're afraid you'll lose me?"

"What father wants his son to die?"

"I suppose being a coward would be better?" Erik answered defiantly, or was it with fear?

Peter removed his pipe from his lips. "Not a coward. You'd still be serving, but you'd be on a staff, away from all the blood and death." He shook his head. "Bah. Just answer me: Are you meeting with him?"

Erik shrugged. "Corina made an appointment for next week. There's no guarantee he has anything, you know."

"It doesn't hurt to try."

Corina stepped into the room, carrying a porcelain tea set she placed on a table between them, removing a cloth from her pocket to swiftly dust beneath the tray before she set it down. Erik noticed she'd changed clothes.

"I see you've won over a convert," he said, addressing his wife.

"What do you mean?" asked Corina, looking up sharply.

"Your Karl plan now meets with Father's approval as well."

She handed him his tea with a stiff gesture, the hot liquid sloshing over the brim to flood the saucer. She frowned, swiping quickly with the cloth until the saucer gleamed again.

"I'm sure you meant to say *our* plan, not just mine," she corrected. "I knew Peter would come around just like you did. What could possibly be wrong with a promotion, and a station right here in Königsberg?" She straightened up, anchoring her fists against her hips as if preparing for a battle.

"I don't understand what you want from me," he said. "You pushed me to join the military. Now a war is coming, and you want me to desert my men?"

Her cheeks kissed scarlet, and she fixed him with a steely glare. "I didn't push you into anything. You didn't have a job. We can't *eat* your history degree. After your father lost the store and they moved in here, we were on the verge of starving. I had to do something."

He felt hot humiliation bubble up, but he choked back his retort. "Many people have lost their livelihoods, not just Father. This damned depression—"

"Which is why you joined up. Karl helped us then, and he wants to help you again now. That way you can avoid the fighting."

"Fighting indeed," snorted Peter. "You're not even in the real army. What is this SS-Verfügungstruppe? The damned party playing at war."

"The SS is every bit as capable as the *Heer!*" snapped Corina.

"Would you two stop your squabbling? I'm exhausted and I need to think," Erik said, massaging his temples.

"Of course, dear, how forgetful of me," said Corina, her voice tinged with iron.

"Always the little martyr, aren't you, Corina?" observed Peter.

She fixed her father-in-law with a venomous stare, fangs set to strike. "What do you want to say to me?" she hissed.

"Dinner!" The call from Anna in the kitchen was a clamoring bell that disrupted the moment. Peter and Corina glared at each other, coiled to pounce. Sighing, Erik stepped between them, his expression a pleading prayer. She stared at him for an instant before storming down the hallway.

"A fine woman you have there," said Peter.

"Quiet, Father. You've said enough already."

A smothering silence engulfed the meal. Even Greta seemed to sense the tension and was quiet. Erik tried to catch Corina's gaze, but she refused to acknowledge him. He knew he had a long evening ahead. He shook his head. All he had wanted was to get home, to see his family again.

His thoughts swirled amid the ringing quiet. He didn't know what to think about Karl or this offer. He was terribly afraid of the coming storm. Still, could he truly leave his platoon on the verge of war for a safe job at home in Königsberg?

After dinner, Erik and his father settled back into the study to resume their conversation. Peter filled his pipe without a glance, his hands instinctively drawing the nutty tobacco out of a leather pouch and tamping the dried leaves into place. He lit the pipe and drew a few deep breaths, filling the room with a rich, smoky aroma.

Erik fiddled with the radio, searching amid the static for any news. Through the fog of background noise, a sharp voice emerged. He could tell immediately something important was happening from the excited tone of the announcer. He listened, stunned, as a detailed report came in, followed as always by a playing of "Deutschland über alles" and "Dem Horst-Wessel-Lied."

"What is it?" asked Anna, who materialized and filled the doorway, trailed by Corina.

"We've signed a treaty with the Russians," said Peter, his voice cracking.

"That can't be true," said Corina. "They're our worst enemies. The Führer would never allow that. They are criminals, a seething barrel of communists and Jews. What a disaster!"

"Not so fast. Maybe it's a disaster, but then again maybe it's a stroke of brilliance," Peter said. "If we don't have to fight the Russians, the French and English will think twice before they come after us. I'll give our Führer credit; he knows his politics. He just took away our nightmare from the last war: a war on two fronts."

"Then there won't be fighting after all," said Corina. "The Poles must back down now."

"Or we just signed Poland's death warrant," predicted Peter. "If we don't have to worry about the Russians, then we can gamble on a war with the Poles."

A knock at the door disrupted their speculation. Anna tramped woodenly over to unlatch the lock. She opened the door and greeted someone outside, returning a moment later carrying a bulky brown package. "It's for you," she said, handing it to Erik.

Erik took the hefty envelope and scanned the front. The letter was an official communication from the SS. He opened it quickly and browsed the contents. His heart sank.

"What is it?" asked his father.

"Orders. I'm to report back to our headquarters in forty-eight hours."

"But you were just given two weeks' leave," protested his mother.

"All leave is canceled," he said, flashing the first page. "We are on emergency alert."

"Oh no," said Corina. "What about Karl? You are supposed to meet him next week."

"Too late. I'll be long gone by then."

They stood in silence at the news, like willows holding a soundless vigil over a midnight meadow. Erik looked from one to another. There was no time left. No chance for the miracle his wife so desperately wanted. War was coming.

<hr />

Erik slept fitfully that night. Shadows chased him. He dreamed of the war and fire and death. He woke sandy-eyed with his mind in a fog.

Corina was already up with Greta. He could hear their voices echo up the stairs. He splashed cold water on his face in the washroom and stumbled groggily down the wooden steps to the kitchen. His mother was there, as she always seemed to be, working away at their *Frühstück*. Hearty sausages sizzled and crackled in a charred iron skillet so heavy it required two hands to move. She labored through this morning ritual in deliberate, never-ceasing movement. He watched her, feeling a wave of peace wash over him. She was a cornerstone. Always present—carrying the weight of his life.

Eventually she noticed him and gave him a smile and a wink. He stacked some sausages and a hard-fried egg on a plate and plopped down at the cramped table. His father joined him, smoking his perpetual pipe and scanning the morning headlines while he munched on a piece of toast.

"The papers are full of this treaty," he mumbled.

"That's no surprise," said Erik. "Any news about the Poles?"

"They haven't said much yet. Of course, the story just broke last night. Nothing from the French or English yet, either." His father chuckled. "They must be stewing in their own pudding." Peter reached for his lighter and drew the flame through the half-burned tobacco in his pipe until scarlet embers glowed and smoke bellowed from his lips.

Erik looked around. "Where's Corina?"

Peter snorted. "I'm not your wife's keeper."

"Now, Vater, you're not still mad about last night, are you?"

Peter shrugged. "I'll get over it. I always do." His stare bored into Erik. "You're off to war then, is it?"

Erik felt an electric jolt. Despite his nighttime torment, he'd forgotten about that. "I suppose so. I don't know what else my orders could be about."

His father shifted in his seat, pressing his hands together. "I thought I'd have more time. I can't tell you much . . . about the fighting. You must live it. I don't wish combat on any man, especially my son. But listen to me, boy. Don't do anything stupid; there are some things I can teach you. Don't be a damned hero! The men that go out there trying to win medals end up in bloody bits." He pointed a shaky finger. "You be smart. Keep your head down. Follow orders. Stay with the men. You'll be all right. I pray you will." He leaned back again, exhaling deeply. "When you're home on leave, we'll talk about it. More to say when you've seen it yourself. In the meantime, I hope for a miracle, that this is just a drill. That it won't come to a real fight."

"Not much we can do about that," said Erik. He was surprised by his father's speech.

"Your mother and I are proud of you." The words stuttered out of Peter's mouth in a halting jumble. "I've never really thanked you for taking us in after—"

Erik reached over and squeezed his father's arm. "You don't have to say those things. You're always welcome."

"Never thought I'd have to accept charity from anyone, let alone my own boy." He seemed to wither in his chair.

"Times were tough. Everyone suffered. You did your best. We all did. Don't forget, I lost my job, too."

"But you found another."

"No. Corina found me the job—or I'd still be looking."

"She and her friend Karl. Now even he can't help you."

"To be honest, I'm not entirely sure I'd accept the assistance if it was offered."

"I know that, too. But you need to reconsider if you get the chance. You're like every boy facing war. You're afraid to go, but you're drawn to it like a moth to fire. After an hour at the front, you'll never wish to be there again." His voice rose and hardened to a flinty edge. "You listen hard, boy: if by some miracle Karl still comes through, you take the transfer—do you hear me?"

"I see you two are talking away the morning," observed Corina, emerging with Greta in tow, both dressed for what promised to be a warm summer day.

"Morning," mumbled Peter, not looking up.

"Good morning." She closed in on Erik. "It's going to be beautiful today, and I'm not going to spend it roasting in this trap. Get dressed. Let's go for a walk."

Erik nodded and rose without a word. His father watched him intently all the way out of the room. After he dressed, he returned downstairs.

"Where's your uniform?" demanded Corina.

"I'm not on duty," he stammered. "Besides, it's too hot to wear that thing out there today."

She shook her head in apparent frustration. "You would think you're ashamed of it. You're in the SS, Erik. Be proud of who you are. People will admire you—they will fear you."

Erik laughed. "I'm a history teacher. Nobody's ever feared me, unless I scratched the chalk too hard down the board."

"You're not a teacher anymore. You're a soldier, and a party member. You are somebody now. Don't hide that from the world. We deserve respect."

"Did you hear the 'we' in that last part, Erik? That's the spot," said Peter, chuckling to himself.

"Laugh away," Corina said, turning on her father-in-law. "Your old world is gone. You surrendered to the French and the Jews. We will never lose again. Erik is part of the new Germany—we all are. The world will see soon enough, starting with the Poles." Corina turned and stormed out, tugging Greta along behind her.

Erik raised his hands, but Peter waved him off. "Go after her before you get yourself in any more trouble. Thank Gott it's you and not me, that's all I've to say."

Erik followed rapidly out of the kitchen and met his wife and child at the door. Together they strolled outside and down the Yorckstrasse. Bright sunlight shone through the trees and danced off the rooftops up and down the street. The day was fine and warm. The shadows of gloom melted away from Erik beneath the dazzling sky.

They walked quietly toward a local community *Garten*, taking their time while Greta skipped forward and back, laughing and shouting.

"Are you afraid?" Corina asked him, breaking the silence between them.

"No." But he was, and they both knew it.

She slid an arm through his and drew him toward her, pressing her warm lips against his cheek. "You're a brave man, Erik. I knew that from the moment I met you. You have great things before you. You must focus on your duty and do your best. If you win a promotion, you will help us. We are so close to everything we've always wanted."

As Erik started to formulate a response, he was distracted by a woman and child coming their direction. She seemed familiar, a person from the past who was out of place here for some reason. Then it struck him.

"Guten Morgen, Trude," he called out.

The woman looked up in surprise and abruptly stopped, squinting through the sunshine. She had a daughter close to Greta's age, he noticed, but with raven-colored hair that hung straight down her back, in sharp contrast to his child's bouncing golden curls.

"Erik, is that you?" she asked.

"Yes. I haven't seen you in years. What are you doing here? You're not from this neighborhood."

"We moved here a year ago. My husband and I." She turned her attention to Corina.

Erik realized he hadn't introduced his wife. "How rude of me. Trude, this is Corina. Trude and I knew each other at the university."

Corina nodded politely but said nothing in response.

"Trude was a wonderful musician, one of the best. You should have heard her. Do you still play in the symphony?" he asked.

The color drained from her cheeks. "Uh . . . no, I don't play in public anymore."

Embarrassment washed over Erik as he realized why. "Oh, I'm sorry. I shouldn't have said anything."

"That's quite all right." She turned to Corina, who was watching Trude's daughter and Greta begin to play together. "Do you live nearby?"

"Just a block away," answered Corina, not looking up. "What a fascinating toy your child has there. What is it?"

Erik glanced down and saw the object, a diamond-shaped wooden top painted in alternating black-and-white stripes. Greta had the toy in her hand, turning it over and over in wonder.

"That silly thing. My husband made it for her. He is brilliant with his hands—and his mind."

"I'm sure," said Corina. "Come now, Greta, we mustn't delay them. Come to Mother."

Greta smiled and returned the toy to the other girl.

"What's her name?" asked Erik.

"Britta."

"Ours is Greta," said Erik. "So close."

"It's been nice to meet you," said Corina, nodding again slightly.

"Nice to meet you as well." Trude turned to Erik, her eyes dancing. "What a nice surprise to see you."

"You too, Trude. Farewell."

They parted and continued their walk in silence until Trude was out of earshot. Corina turned abruptly on him.

"How dare that Jewess walk down our streets!" she hissed.

Erik was shocked by her comment. "How do you know she's a Jew?"

"Her hair, her nose. She can't play her music publicly anymore!" Corina looked around. "We shouldn't have even talked to her. And you let her child touch Greta!" His wife hurried forward and began scrubbing Greta's fingers with a handkerchief.

"You don't believe that propaganda about vermin, do you?" asked Erik, his mind racing to catch up to the scene before him. Corina didn't answer but kept scrubbing away roughly.

"I need water. Don't touch anything, Greta. That little girl is full of disease."

His daughter's face paled, and she looked up at Erik. "Will I get sick, Daddy?"

"You're just fine." He turned to Corina. "Don't fill her head with that garbage," he whispered. "She has enough to worry about with the war and my departure."

Corina ignored him and whisked their daughter up in her arms, turning around and walking briskly back toward their home. The day turned frigid and dim, the sun losing its power over them.

"You're back early," observed Peter, standing at the doorway as they arrived. Corina pushed past him with Greta and disappeared inside.

"We ran into an old friend of mine and her daughter," explained Erik. "She's Jewish so Corina thinks Greta might catch something."

"She can't be serious," said Peter. "Nobody believes those stories, do they?"

"Apparently, she's bought into the whole party line. More maybe than I realized. I guess when you hear a lie told over and over, eventually it becomes the truth."

"You'd better do the same."

"What do you mean?"

"This came while you were gone. It's from Karl."

Erik stepped forward and tore open the envelope. The package contained a letter from Karl. Corina had apparently phoned him last night. Karl knew about Erik's orders and asked if Erik might come by the local party police headquarters tomorrow afternoon. Karl would be there, even on a weekend day the letter explained, because of a backlog in work.

"That's only a few hours before I leave. I'll have to decline."

"Oh no you won't," said Peter.

Erik protested. "I want to spend what time I have left with the family."

Peter shook his head. "If he can pull strings, you won't have to leave in the first place. I know you think you want to go to war, but remember what I said. This is your chance, Erik. Go see Karl, and see if he has a place for you here. The family needs you here."

Despite his show of resistance, Erik felt a vast relief mixed with nagging shame. What if Karl could transfer him? There still might be time after all. *Does it mean I'm a coward that I desire this?* He shook his head. He would let fate decide. If Karl had a job for him, he would hear him out and make his decision. Erik found himself whispering a prayer of thanks as the warring emotions within him struggled for peace.

The Muellers rose early on Sunday morning and made their way to a morning service at the Lutheran cathedral on Kneiphof Island in the Pregel River. They usually attended the Lutheran church in Sackheim, but Corina insisted today was a special occasion. Erik had visited the cathedral only a half dozen times or so. The majestic structure rose out of the wooded area below, a hand reaching up to the sky dominated by the tapered clock spire on the south end of the edifice.

Once inside, the family pressed in tightly with the rest of the crowd. Erik gaped in awe as always when he entered the medieval building. The roof rose high above, arching into a wooden spider web. Erik's gaze followed the spindly black maze as it worked its way along the ceiling and down toward a mountainous gilded altar crowned by a crucifix reaching over the congregation.

After the service the Muellers ate pastries and drank tea at a nearby outdoor cafe. The sun hid behind a torrent of clouds, in stark contrast to the perfect weather the day before. Now the company was as cold as the day. Corina remained cross and distant. Even the news from Karl did not rouse her out of her dark mood. She wouldn't tell Erik why. He couldn't understand. Could she still be so angry about Greta touching a Jewish girl? Was she jealous of Trude? How could she know?

After they made their way home, Erik maneuvered his father into watching Greta for a time while Anna went to work on the family laundry for the week. Erik steeled himself for the storm he knew must be coming and knocked on the door to their bedroom, where Corina was preparing his uniform for tonight's meeting. She didn't answer, but he knew she was there. He let himself in. She sat on the bed, a brush in one hand and a jackboot in the other. She was scrubbing the already mirrored boot with rapid movements. She didn't look up.

"Do you want to tell me what you're angry about?" He asked a direct question, hoping Corina would talk to him.

"Nothing. I'm fine."

He stepped cautiously toward the bed and then lowered himself until he was sitting next to her. He carefully placed his hand on her thigh, but she brushed it away instantly, scooting down the bed.

"You're not fine."

"No, I'm not," she said, her voice shaking. She looked up. "How could you embarrass me like that?"

Erik was baffled. "What do you mean? Are you talking about my vermin comment? I wasn't trying to be rude. I just meant I'm not sure we should take all of that so seriously."

Her anger flared, and he knew he'd somehow missed the mark. "I don't care a bit about that. I can handle my own child's well-being. I'm talking about the way you were mooning over that Jewess."

"What on earth are you saying?"

"Why haven't I ever heard of her before? You tell me all about your university days, but I've never heard of some dark-haired temptress who was a brilliant musician. Why did you hide that from me? Was she your lover? They are masters of seduction. You know that, right? They want our Aryan blood, and they will stop at nothing to get it. Did she steal some of yours?"

He reached out to her, but she sharply pushed him away. "Corina, you're being ridiculous. I hardly knew the woman. We had a class or two together. I remember her because she lugged around a violin case all the time. The university symphony played a few concerts for the student body. I saw her there. That's all there ever was."

She looked at him now, and her face was a scarlet maelstrom. "I don't believe you."

He reached for her again, and this time she let him touch her. He gently pulled the boot and the brush aside. She finally relented, throwing herself into his chest and sobbing, the lines of her narrow back rippling with each gasping breath. He held her there for a few minutes and let her cry.

"Promise me you never talked to her again after school," she stammered between breaths.

"I promise. I hadn't seen her for years until yesterday. I had to think for a minute before I could even remember her name."

She held him tightly now. "Oh, Erik, I'm so worried about you. So worried about us. I don't want you to go to war. If something happens to you, we will be left with nothing." She looked up at him. "You have to convince Karl to find you a position. We need that promotion and we need you here, safe and sound. I can't deal with your parents and Greta by myself."

He ran his hand up and down her back, trying to calm her. She was so thin and fragile. "There, there, my pet. I won't let anything happen to you. Don't worry, it is a very good sign that Karl has asked to see me. I'm sure he has something in mind. I'll be able to stay here in Königsberg and take care of you and the family."

"Promise me you will stay and take care of me! I can't do all this by myself. I can't take care of the house and your parents and our little girl. It's too much." She buried her head in his chest.

"I promise I'll do everything I can. It's in Gott's hands."

Early in the afternoon Erik dressed in preparation for his visit to Karl. He stood before their full-length mirror while his wife looked him over critically, fingers pulling and smoothing the material long beyond the time he was sure he looked perfect.

Finally, she was satisfied. "I guess this must do."

"You have outdone yourself," he said. "I couldn't look better."

"Remember to salute smartly and be enthusiastic. Karl is a friend, but he still must do his duty. He won't tolerate lukewarm devotion to the party."

Erik nodded and made his way downstairs for a brief good-bye with Greta and his parents. If things did not go well with Karl, he would have only a few minutes with them tonight before he had to depart for the train station and his unit barracks. *I won't think about that right now.*

He embraced each in turn and departed the house for the walk to Karl's office building—the headquarters for the party police and much of the SS in Königsberg. He raised an appraising eye at the clouds above but didn't sense rain. What a disaster that would be to his uniform!

He arrived at the building in less than half an hour, and after Erik identified himself an SS functionary led him to a waiting area to sit. The halls were deserted late on this Sunday afternoon. He'd just sat down when he heard an enthusiastic voice calling him.

"Mein Erik. Guten Abend!"

He looked up to see SS Captain Karl Schmidt, a blond-haired, black-uniformed recruiting poster in the flesh. Schmidt radiated the new Germany, and his chiseled features reinforced the theory of Aryan superiority.

Erik stood, clicking his jackboots sharply and thrusting his right arm out in a crisp salute. *"Heil Hitler!"*

Karl returned the gesture and looked him over, grinning warmly. "You look sharp, Sergeant. Your military SS uniform suits you perfectly, although I think you would look better in black than in gray. Yes?"

A good sign. A transfer to Karl's unit would mean a change in uniform. Would it also mean a promotion? That was what Corina desperately wanted.

"Come with me," said Karl. The captain led him up several flights of steps and down a long hallway. They didn't pass a single person along the way. Karl's office, a spacious corner unit with large windows, faced out over the *strasse*. Pictures adorned the walls. Erik noted a gilt-framed oil painting of the Führer, and next to it a picture of Karl with Heinrich Himmler, the head of the SS. The photo was signed by the *Reichsführer*.

Erik gawked at the ornate office. He'd never been here before. When Corina originally brought Erik to see Karl, the captain had occupied a modest space on the ground floor. He was clearly moving up in the world.

"Have a seat," said Karl, motioning to a straight-backed leather chair in front of his desk. Erik obeyed, removing his cap and placing it in his lap. His hands shook a little, so he moved them lower, hoping Captain Schmidt wouldn't see how nervous he was.

"How is our Corina?" asked Karl, arms folded on his desk and leaning forward toward Erik, looking him over again sharply.

"She's doing well," said Erik.

"She hasn't changed a bit since we graduated from the gymnasium. I was delighted when she contacted me about you. What was that, two years ago?"

"Just about, yes. We are eternally grateful for the opportunity you gave me."

Karl leaned closer. "And now you are looking for something different, yes?"

Erik felt uncomfortable. His emotions clouded his mind again. "I realize the timing is difficult. I have struggled with this because—"

"Because it makes you look like a coward?" Karl said shrewdly. "That thought has crossed my mind, too. Are you a coward, Sergeant Mueller?"

"No, sir. I haven't pushed this. Corina has. I'm satisfied with my position and ready to fight for my country, for the Führer."

Karl said nothing for a moment. His eyes continued to bore in. Erik tried to relax. He kept his gaze steady. Karl seemed to ease, sitting back and tucking his hands behind his head. "I believe you." He laughed. "So Corina has pushed this, has she? She's a strong woman. Still, the party needs men like you, Erik. Men loyal to the Führer and the party. Are you loyal?"

"*Jawohl.*" The word slipped quickly from his lips, rushing to escape his conscience.

"Good, good. I took this interview because I wanted to see you again for myself. I think your wife's faith in you is well founded." The captain sat back now, crossing his arms. "There is but one problem.

I don't have anything for you right now. I thought I had an adjutant position, but it was snatched up by one of Reinhard's favorites. Have you met Heydrich?"

"No, I haven't." Erik assumed Karl was talking about Himmler's number two, Reinhard Heydrich.

"Well, he has an older cousin in East Prussia, and that man wanted the job. What can I do about that? I'm only a medium fish in a big pool—for now."

"So you don't have a transfer for me?" Erik felt the fear fill him again, mixed with an equally powerful sense of relief.

"Not for now, my friend, but don't worry. I will soon enough. A tempest is coming, but you should weather it well. When it's over, come back to me, and I'll see what I can do." The last remark was a dismissal, and Karl waved him away, returning to some paperwork spread out before him. Erik saluted without a verbal response and stumbled out of the office in a daze. Before he knew it, he was standing on the street.

So, it was war after all. There would be no last-minute miracle from Karl. Erik would face combat—he might only last a day or two. Another part of him reveled. He wouldn't run away from his duty. He would fight like his father. But he felt badly for Corina; she had wanted this transfer so dearly. *Did I want it as well?* He knew the answer to this. Regardless, he felt peace wash over him. Now there was no uncertainty. Whatever the future held, he was ready. He turned toward home and the final good-byes before he departed for war. The raindrops were falling long before he reached home. A storm was coming.

CHAPTER TWO

Königsberg, East Prussia, Nazi Germany
August 1939

Trude Benshcim kneaded the dough between her fingers and pressed it into the pan, her narrow digits stretching the sticky substance along the greased metal until it felt right. She glanced at the clock. *I mustn't think about it.* She reached over and ladled a spoonful of sugared apple onto the dough, spreading the mixture along the length of the pan, making sure it was not too thick or too near the edges. With a brush, she painted on a layer of butter and a dusting of cinnamon.

Britta perched at the kitchen table nearby, thumbing through a picture book—oblivious to Trude's anxiety. *Thank Gott she is unaware of the danger.* God. She laughed at herself. She wasn't religious—her parents hadn't much use for the old traditions, Johannes had even less. She'd hardly thought of herself as a Jew until the Germans made this fact the center of her universe.

Trude moved to the oven and ignited the gas switch. Cooking kept her busy and calmed her nerves. She returned to the pan, taking another blob of dough and stretching it out over the top of the strudel. She looked down at the line of pastries laid out like soldiers—or like graves, she realized. She shook her head, attempting to drive away the ominous thoughts that invaded her waking hours and haunted her sleep.

Keys jingled at the front door. She closed her eyes. *He's home. Another miracle.* The hinges creaked, and she heard the wood slam back into place. Staccato thuds banged against the floor, and he materialized in the doorway, a brown-coated outline clutching an overstuffed satchel brimming with paper. His countenance, still in the shadows, lay featureless beneath a disheveled mop of curly hair—as wild and rebellious as he was.

"Guten Abend, Frau Bensheim," he said, bowing with a flourish. Britta looked up and pushed away from the table, yawning and stretching like a cat while she waltzed slowly over to her father.

He paused, watching them for a moment with raised eyebrows. "Such an enthusiastic welcome," he joked. "My two girls spring to life when they see me!"

Trude laughed in return. "Reading and cooking are serious business— and wearisome, too. You must let us work up to our welcome."

He kissed Britta on the head and embraced Trude warmly. He held her close for a moment and kissed her. Their eyes met. He winked. She loved when he did that. She felt an electric stir.

"I was worried," she whispered. "You're late."

"You're always worried," he said.

"One day I'll be right."

"Perhaps, but not today, my love."

"Is there news?"

He frowned and looked over at Britta. "I wonder if my little princess would be so kind as to retrieve her father's slippers?"

"Of course I will, Father," she said. She scurried out of the room, and the sound of her heels echoed off the stairs.

"Well?" Trude asked again.

"I have ten visa applications approved by the authorities. They will be ready in the next few days."

"That's a relief," said Trude. "I don't know how you've done it. You are brilliant."

"Each time's a miracle, and it's grown harder and harder, but I'm confident I can do it one last time after this."

She drew in her breath. "What do you mean?"

He turned away, scanning the ceiling. "All of them are spoken for, my love."

She pulled him back, forcing him to look at her. "You promised me we would leave."

He shrugged, his cheeks warming. "I know what I promised, and I meant it at the time, but there are important people who don't have a chance in hell of getting out of here. Dr. Krauz and his wife, for example. You wouldn't believe what the doctor has—"

"I don't care a damn about Dr. Krauz and his wife!" she said. "I care about us. I told you we should have left with our parents. You promised me we would follow them straightaway."

"And I meant it." He put his hand on her arm, but she pulled away.

"That was almost two years ago, Johannes! For all that time, we've rotted away in this town while the world crumbles. First my job, then yours. One by one they've taken away our rights. Germany first, indeed! We're as German as anyone else, but we've lost everything. We had to give up our home and move to this wretched neighborhood! Every day I sit here in the dark expecting I will never see you again, trying to make dinner or clean or do any dull thing to keep my mind off what might be happening to you. One day they'll come for us all."

He smiled and tried to reach for her again, but she crossed her arms, the tears spilling down her cheeks. Finally, she wilted, and he swept her into his embrace.

"Now, now. I know it's been difficult, but this is important work— essential. Who else has the contacts to work these little miracles?

Without the organization, how many more Jews would be stuck in this cesspit forever? We've saved hundreds."

"And damned ourselves in the process!"

"How so? Am I in jail? Have they taken us away? Are you unsafe?" His body hardened and his voice bristled in suppressed anger. "I dare the bastards to try. No, my dear, they know they can't touch me, and that means they can't touch you, either. I've already filled out the paper-work for three visas—just for us. They will be ready in less than a month, and we'll leave this wretched country forever."

"What if the war comes first? They'll never let us go."

"I've talked to my contacts about that. They all agree this squabble is between our esteemed countrymen and the Poles. They don't think the French or English will even get involved. How many times have these 'Allies' threatened to do something to Germany? They've no back-bone for a fight. No," he said, shaking his head, "there won't be a fight. The Poles will cough up Danzig and the corridor, and we will all go on with life."

"But what if they do fight?"

Johannes shrugged. "If they do, I'll get us out through Russia instead. I've already done that a time or two. From there we can catch a steamer to Britain. Don't you worry. We'll be walking through Hyde Park with your mother and father by October—probably freezing to death!"

She willed herself to believe him. He always seemed to be right. So many times, he had overcome her objections—forced her to trust him. He had always come through. He thumbed his nose at the party and got away with it. Somewhere deep in her soul, though, she was terrified. How many times could he taunt this beast before it turned and struck?

"Did you ever find out anything about Erik?" She had told Johannes about their chance meeting. Ever vigilant for a possible new contact, he had told her he would find out more about her former university friend.

Johannes chuckled. "I forgot to tell you. I found out about him indeed. Your old chum is in the SS now."

Trude gasped. "You're kidding me? I'm shocked he even talked to me."

"I am as well."

"Is that a good sign? Is he someone who could help you?"

Johannes shook his head. "He's far down the chain, unfortunately— and in the wrong branch. He's playing soldier with the rest of the SS-VT." He rubbed his hands together. "Now if he were in the Gestapo, that might be interesting. No, we can forget your old friend. He won't influence our lives."

Britta returned with his slippers, and he took a spot near her at the table. Trude continued with their dinner. She was surprised about Erik. Joined the SS? She didn't understand people. Johannes did. He could stare down their soul with a glance. Perhaps that's why she trusted him.

She enjoyed their dinner together and the rare family evening in the sitting room, playing games they made up as they went along. Britta grew tired and fell asleep near the fire. Johannes retrieved some work from his satchel and scanned the documents. He rarely rested. Her husband frustrated her so, but she loved him for it. He was his own man. She smiled and moved closer. She felt a lingering tension from earlier, and she wanted to set things right.

"Why don't I make a dinner for your friends from the organization tomorrow night?"

He looked up in surprise. "You never give them the time of day."

"I'm just jealous of the time they take you away," she jested, her lips brushing his ear. "But really, I would love to do it. Seven o'clock?"

He took her hand and gave it a little squeeze. "That would be wonderful, my love. With the visas set, we don't have as much work for the next few days. A celebratory dinner would be *wunderbar*."

They fell asleep early, and when she awoke in the darkness before dawn he had already departed. She spent the day at the market, purchasing food for the dinner and meeting with another Jewish mother in the neighborhood about school plans. Since November the year before, Britta had been banned from the public schools, along with all the other Jewish children. The few remaining families in the area worked together to create a home school. Trude taught music theory once a week.

She returned home in the early afternoon, weighted down with groceries. Britta carried a bag as well, but she was so tiny she couldn't share much of the burden. With great relief, Trude reached the front door and leaned against the wood as she fumbled for her keys. To her surprise, the door opened on its own. She sucked in her breath and looked up quickly. Johannes was there. His face was ashen.

"What's wrong?" she demanded.

"Something terrible."

"What?"

"Britta, go upstairs. I need to talk to your mother."

Their daughter protested, but after he jabbed a pointed finger toward the steps, with lips in a pout she complied. He waited until they heard her door close.

"Something's changed."

"What, Johannes? You're scaring me."

He sat down, his head facing the carpet. "The bastards refused all the visas."

"What do you mean? Some kind of delay?"

"Not a delay, a denial."

She drew in her breath sharply. "That's never happened before."

He rose and paced past her into the kitchen. She followed. He leaned over the sink, splashing cold water over his face. His breathing came in spurts. She'd never seen him like this before, and she felt fear's icy grasp clinging to her ankles and climbing her calves—threatening to drag her down.

"Did they say why?"

"No. I asked Helmut, and he wouldn't answer me." Johannes reached a hand out to turn her chin so she was facing him. "He wouldn't even look at me, Trude. I've known him a decade. My father knew him in the army—even before the war. A lifetime. He wouldn't tell me what was going on."

"But what does this mean?"

"I can't get them out. Not through Helmut at least."

"What about us? Johannes, you promised me there was still time."

He didn't answer. He stared out the window, his expression glazed and distant.

———

They stood there in the kitchen for long moments. It seemed an eternity. She'd never seen him like this.

She closed her eyes, remembering the first time they'd met. He'd shone with confidence and strength. There he was, arguing hotly with a group of young privileged Junkers at the university. He, a young Jew. A nobody, a nothing to them. He'd stood up to them, shouted them down with logic and force of character. She'd been drawn to him, metal to a magnet—attracted by his power.

Now he was silent, distant, shaken. She tugged at his arm. "Johannes, what are we going to do?"

He didn't answer, as if he couldn't see her or hear her. She waited, the minutes stumbling by. She heard Britta clomping around above. A bird landed in a tree outside their window, hopping along a branch. She tried to watch it, labored to be patient.

"Johannes," she whispered. This time he responded. She watched the color return to his cheeks, a tide washing up the shore. The shade transformed from light pink to angry scarlet. His arm trembled beneath her hands. His eyes were bloodshot, staring through her.

"They won't do this to me," he said, his voice shaking.

"What will you do?"

"Helmut is one man. I know others. I will go to them. If he's turned coward, others won't abandon us. I'll talk to Gunther."

"But he's a Nazi! A real one," she protested.

"Who isn't these days? He's a friend of the family. Besides, he has better connections than even Helmut."

"You didn't go to him before because he joined the party."

He took her hands in his. The fire was back. "Desperate times, my dear."

"What if he turns you in?"

"He wouldn't dare. None of them will. That worm Helmut wouldn't. He might deny me—might refuse further help—but he would never do more. My father . . ."

"Is gone."

"His honor isn't—nor is his reputation."

"How long can that protect us?"

"A while more. It must."

He pulled his hands away, turning from her. He started toward the door.

"Where are you going?" she asked.

"To see Gunther."

"Don't do it now!" she pleaded. "I'm scared. Please stay with us today. You can see him tomorrow."

"I have to go. There's no time. I have to secure thirteen visas."

"Thirteen? Then you mean . . ."

"Yes, my love. It's time for us to leave."

Her heart sang with relief. She threw her arms around her husband, holding him tight. She felt his hands stiff on her back.

"Will you be able to get the visas?"

"I must go and see. My father saved Gunther's life. He owes us. He may be a Nazi now, but he has one favor in him—at least I'll wager that."

"Oh, Johannes. Thank you! I love you so much."

"I love you, too." He kissed her on the cheek. "I'll be back tonight with better news. You should start thinking about what you will take. We can't bring the furniture. Only necessities. A suitcase or two apiece."

After he departed, she remained in the kitchen, standing dazed and unsure. They would finally leave this terrible place. But could he secure the visas? He'd always done so in the past, but she could sense their time was running out. The storm clouds were amassing over Europe.

Trude spent the afternoon in the house, cleaning and keeping Britta busy. She began a list of what they might need to take with them. The hours limped by. She visited the clock too often. As her mind flitted through images and thoughts, she found her lips muttering a prayer. She shook her head. Why bother? What had the father of Israel ever done for his people except keep them in bondage and suffering?

When she did not believe she could take it any longer, she heard the familiar jingle of keys at the door. Johannes had returned. She searched his face for answers as he clambered into the kitchen, Britta clinging to his waist. Something was wrong. That expression. What was it? Defeat? Not quite, but not triumph, either.

"Britta, take father's coat upstairs, please." He tossed his jacket over her. The material nearly buried her, but she held it over her head, giggling at this game they'd never played before. She waddled down the hallway and started up the stairs.

"He said no," she said, sure she was right.

Johannes shook his head. "He said yes."

"Then we are safe."

"For a price."

"What price?"

"He wants ten thousand Reichsmarks."

"What? How dare he! But—we should be able to come up with that."

"Ten thousand each."

She gasped. "He wants 130,000 Reichsmarks. We don't have that. We can't raise that."

He nodded. "It's quite a sum."

"What about thirty thousand? We might be able to come up with that." She felt terrible when she said it. Selfish.

He looked her over, his eyes appraising her. She saw the flicker of disappointment. "Do you mean save ourselves and leave the others? Never."

"What difference does it make? We can't rescue everyone. At what point do you protect your family?"

"I won't go without the others." He shook his head violently, as if driving the thought from his mind.

"Why?" she demanded. Her heart pumped the guilt through her veins, but she didn't care. This was her family. Her daughter. "If you save those ten, how many more remain? A thousand? Ten thousand? They have no way to leave. You've done as much as you can."

His back stiffened. The scarlet washed over his cheeks again. "There are fifteen hundred or so and I won't leave them!" he said, his voice molten iron. She wilted. She knew he would never change his mind.

"What are you going to do then? How are you going to save us?"

"Is that all you care about? Saving only us?"

He stabbed her with shame. "No, that's not all. But this is our daughter, Johannes. This is our family. I've waited patiently. I've kept my faith in you." She stepped closer, grabbing the front of his shirt. Her hands were shaking. "You have to get us out. You promised me."

He drew away. "This is bigger than us. Greater than you and me. You told me you understood that, but you obviously didn't." His expression dripped disdain. "Don't worry, my love. I've never failed you. I'll get us out, but I won't leave the others behind. They've put their lives in my hands." He marched out.

"Where are you going?" she cried. Fiery tears burned her cheeks. She felt wretched. He was right. She cared only about their family. She wanted to feel more, but at the end, it came down to the three of them. She knew there were no more chances. They had to leave now.

"I'm going to go get our Reichsmarks. I'm going to raise the money and get us out of here. All of us."

He stormed out the door, slamming it shut behind him.

"What's wrong, Mutter?" Britta stared up in concern. "Where's Father? Did you have a fight?"

"No, dear. Vater had to run some errands. He will be back soon."

"Why were you yelling at each other?"

"We weren't yelling. We were just talking about a few things."

"Then why are you crying?"

Trude ran a hand over her cheek, wiping away the tears. "I'm not. Everything's fine. I promise."

Britta ran into her mother's arms. "I'm scared."

"I know. It's going to be all right. Do you want to play a game?"

"What kind?"

"Hide-and-seek?"

Britta giggled in delight. Trude envied her daughter. Oh, to be young and without the cares of the world.

"Hurry up and hide now. I'll start counting."

Britta tottered off, scrambling up the stairs. Her voice shaking, Trude began counting slowly: *"Eins, zwei, drei, vier, fünf."* She labored to pull herself together. *He's always come through. Every time. He's right, this is bigger than just us. He will find a way to raise the money, and he will save us all.*

They played for an hour, then Trude turned to making dinner. She was thankful for the distraction of preparing their meal. The familiar, mechanical duties kept her busy and passed some of this endless day. She and her daughter ate dinner in silence. The clock was her enemy again, clinging to each minute stubbornly as if she were willing the hands to advance. She cleared the dishes and read Britta a story, a crackling fire flicking across the worn pages of the book as she muttered the wooden words. Nine o'clock. He still wasn't home. What if something had gone wrong?

She put Britta to bed and turned on the radio. The news was awash with rumors of war. The commentator lashed out at the Poles, the French, and the English. Absent was criticism of the Russians and communism. After years of constant attacks by the Nazis, now apparently the Bolsheviks were their friends and worthy of praise. How could the German people not see the hypocrisy of their leader and the party? The Nazis repeated their lies until the people believed them. The truth was what the Führer willed it to be.

The door jingled again and her heart stuttered. A flash of gray material. Johannes was back, this time striding in with triumph etched on his chiseled jaw.

"You've done it," she said.

He nodded.

"How?"

"I've pulled every string. Every favor from every German I know, high and low, neighbor and Nazi. I've sold everything, promised the future, but I've raised the money."

"What do you mean you sold everything?"

"Our estates. My father's property, everything we had."

"But you don't own that property. That's your father's to sell."

"He's never coming back, Trude. Neither are we. Germany is dead to us forever."

She was stunned. His father was worth millions. He had land all over Prussia. She wanted to argue further, but she knew there was no point. Johannes was right; they had to leave and they would never be coming back.

She ran into his arms, holding him, sobbing anew.

He patted her back. "Everything will be fine, my love. Didn't I tell you so?"

"Where are the visas?"

"I don't have them yet. Gunther will deliver them tomorrow. He wants to pick up everything first."

Her heart froze. "What do you mean?"

He gestured around him. "All this. We can't take it with us. I sold as much as I could directly to him. He's sending movers over tomorrow to retrieve it."

She looked around at their furniture. They had only brought what was most precious to them when they'd been forced to move here. But they'd brought the best. Handcrafted pieces from all over Europe. Some of them hundreds of years old. Family heirlooms. She shook her head. All of it was going away. Still, what did she expect? When they left, they would be able to take only a few items. Clothes mostly. A few pictures, their jewelry. All the rest would be in the hands of a grubby little middle-class Nazi whom she wouldn't have glanced at on the street a few years ago.

She closed her eyes and breathed. None of that mattered. They would be leaving. They would have visas tomorrow. She imagined boarding a ship bound for England. In a few days, they would be with their parents. Safe. She held him closer and whispered a prayer again. She was thankful. If there was a God, she owed him one. And she owed her husband, who always came through.

The next morning Trude was awakened by a sharp banging on the door. She clothed herself quickly and hurried down the stairs. She was greeted at the threshold by four burly men, dressed in gray overalls.

"You are the Jew Bensheim?" asked one of them, looking her up and down appraisingly.

"I'm Trude Bensheim," she responded, taken aback by his tone.

"You mean *Sarah* Bensheim, don't you?" he asked. He was referring to the requirement that all Jews add the name Sarah for a woman or Israel for a man.

"I'm Trude," she answered defiantly.

"We're here for the furniture," he said, ignoring her response. "You need to leave while we're here."

"Why?" she asked. "I need to see what you're taking."

"We're taking all of it," he said, laughing while he stroked his stubbly cheek with fat fingers. He looked her over again with a leer. "So you should leave. Unless you're part of the goods."

The men laughed, and she felt hot humiliation. "There are things I need to take. I'll need a few minutes."

He shrugged. "Help yourself, but all the big stuff stays."

The men pushed their way in and started moving furniture around in the sitting room. She wanted to throw them out, but she knew she didn't dare. She'd never felt more violated. She wondered if she should try to somehow contact Johannes, but she knew he had so much to do. She decided not to do anything and instead went upstairs to their bedroom. She closed the door to make sure nobody was watching her and pulled open the bottom drawer of the dresser to fish underneath the clothing, keeping her attention on the door. She found a lumpy item surrounded by cloth and drew it carefully out. It was a bag, tied at the top by a crude leather thong. She untied the strings and poured the contents on the bed. Five gold coins tumbled out along with diamond earrings and a large pendant. She looked everything over and returned the items to the bag. She placed them into her purse and started packing clothes and a few pictures into her suitcase.

As she finished packing, a nerve of terror struck her. Where was Britta? She'd awoken so suddenly and focused on packing their essentials. She raced toward Britta's bedroom a meter away. The door was open and her bed was empty. Panic rose and she felt her heart beating out of her chest. "Britta!" she called. There was no response.

She leaped down the stairs and into the sitting room. The sofa was gone along with the mahogany end table and several of the lamps. The men were not there, but she heard a sound in the kitchen, the voice of the man who had leered at her earlier. She found him sitting at the table, Britta on his lap. He was spooning pudding into her mouth and telling her a story.

Trude gasped. Britta looked up and smiled. The man did, too, although his grin looked maniacal and crude. "Come here right now!" she ordered.

"Hello, Mommy," said her daughter.

"Get over here!"

"Come on now," said the man. "Britta and I are getting along just fine. Why, I have my own little one, almost the same age. They could be friends under other circumstances."

She ignored him and called her daughter again. Britta hesitated and then finally dropped down to the floor and came over to her. Trude grabbed her arm hard and jerked the girl away, keeping her focus on the man. "Go upstairs right now, and don't come back," she whispered to her daughter.

The man's eyes moved along Trude's figure again. Britta departed and Trude took a step back. "Where are the rest of your crew?"

"On break, I suspect. I sent them away for a little while. I came into the kitchen looking for you but found your little girl instead." He started to stand up, and she took another step away. "Now where did we leave off?" he asked.

She felt her panic rising. She'd thought his crude humor earlier was harmless enough. Now they were alone. She turned and started walking away down the hall, calling out loudly to him as she made her way to the front door. "I'm sure your men will be back soon."

To her relief, she saw a figure at the front door. When she adjusted to the light, she realized it was Johannes, along with Gunther. She hadn't seen Gunther in a few years, but he looked the same, a little plumper now and wearing the uniform of the SS. His slumped, slovenly form made the sharp black uniform look dumpy and unkempt.

"Trude, my dear, it's been too long," he said. He bowed slightly and stepped forward to kiss her on both cheeks with cracked middle-aged lips. He fought to catch his breath. He removed a handkerchief and wiped it over his forehead and the bald patch that extended to the back of his head. His eyes darted here and there, hungrily appraising their belongings.

Behind her he heard a murmur, and she turned back to see the mover filling up the hallway, his face a mottled red. She moved past Gunther and stood behind her husband.

Gunther, oblivious to the situation, mistook her movement. He waved his hands toward the sitting area. "I'm sorry it's come to this, Frau Bensheim. These are brutal times."

She felt her anger flare. "Thank you for helping us, Gunther—for a price."

He started to respond, but Johannes interjected.

"My wife apologizes. We both realize how much risk you take obtaining these visas for us. It's no more than fair that you should receive a small gift from us in return." He glared at Trude and turned away from Gunther as he uttered these words.

Gunther smiled as he raised his hands. "It is nothing. I'm happy to assist you." Trude watched as Gunther's eyes flickered through the sitting area. He was looking over their possessions with an eager, greedy gaze. He turned to the mover. "Where is everyone else?"

"I gave them a break," the burly supervisor responded.

"Well, they've had it," snapped Gunther. "I want everything else moved out of here no later than three. Is that understood?"

The mover stood at attention and clicked his heels. "Jawohl."

Gunther turned back to them. "I'm sorry about them. So hard to find professionals. Everyone is in the army now." He clapped Johannes on the back. "Well, my friend, I will have your visas tonight. I'll drop them by your organization office at six. Will you be there?"

"Yes, I can make it there by six."

"All right then." Gunther watched as the movers returned and carried out the dining room table and a few of the chairs. He lingered, shouting suggestions to them as they went, laughing with Johannes and seemingly oblivious to how much this affected the Bensheims. Gunther departed after another half hour.

Trude thought of telling her husband about the mover but decided against it. He would confront the man, and there was no telling what might happen from there. That would do no good. They were so close to escaping. Instead, Trude begged Johannes to stay, and he agreed. They sat on a couple of chairs in the front room, Britta at their feet, drawing. They sat in silence, watching the material items they had collected, that represented so much of their life, pass piece by piece out of the front door. The movers finished at four. They left the two chairs, a small kitchen table with some bare metal seats, the master bedroom mattress, and piles of clothing. They had taken the art, the tables, the sofas, even the pots and all but one of the pans. Virtually everything of value.

The process was an agony for them. Trude could tell that although Johannes acted indifferent, the loss of their possessions affected him deeply. He appeared drawn, gaunt.

With the movers finished, Trude and Johannes made their way upstairs, carrying Britta, who had long since fallen asleep on the floor. Johannes placed her gently on some blankets next to their bed, then he lay down to take a nap. Trude fell exhausted next to him, her arms around him, clinging in silent comfort, trying to heal from the wounds they both felt from this day of defilement.

When she woke, she sat bolt upright. She felt disoriented, her head groggy. They had slept too long, and her mind fought to remember why that was important. She looked at the clock. "Johannes!" she yelled, pushing on his back. "It's already past six. You're late!"

He groaned and blinked several times to try to wake up. He realized what she was saying and he sat up quickly, fumbling for his shoes. "I have to go. I'll be back in an hour. Make us some dinner as quickly as you can. I don't care what. Anything. We will eat, and then we will leave." He turned to her, held her close for a moment, and kissed her forehead. "I love you."

"I love you, too," she said.

He turned and rattled down the stairs. She heard the door clang closed below. Britta was sitting up, rubbing her eyes. Trude helped her up and led her downstairs to the kitchen, where she fumbled through the icebox, searching for anything to eat. There was a little ham left over and some cheese, along with a slab of bacon and a few eggs. She searched the bread box and found some stale rolls. She took a knife and cut crudely at the crusty bread, making rough sandwiches for the three of them. All day she had possessed too much time, but now it seemed she didn't have enough. She heard a loud crash, and the front door was thrown open. Johannes was there, already returned.

"You scared me," she said, starting to take a step toward him. He reached his arm out and grasped hers, pulling her toward him. He motioned for their daughter.

"Britta, go upstairs."

"But, Daddy, I want to show you something."

"Upstairs now!" he shouted. Trude was shocked. She'd never heard him speak to their daughter like that.

Britta stepped back, and her face drained of color. She burst into tears and flew up the stairs.

"Johannes, what's going on? You're scaring me!"

He moved quickly to the window and peeked through the curtains, straining to see to the curb.

"They arrested everyone," he said.

"Everyone? What do you mean?"

"I arrived at the office at about six fifteen. Thank Gott I was late. The Gestapo was crawling all over the place. They were pulling my people out and shoving them into cars. I hid behind some trees and watched the whole thing." He balled a fist. "I shouldn't have watched. I should have done something."

"What could you have done?" she demanded. "They would have taken you, too. Oh, Johannes, what are we going to do? They will come here any moment!"

"We have to leave. Are you packed?"

She nodded, but it was too late.

A sharp banging on the door echoed through their home. They were here.

CHAPTER THREE

East Prussia
August 1939

Erik rode along in the jarring truck as twilight dimmed the evening sky. They'd driven for hours, bumping along in an endless line of vehicles starting and stopping, the exhaust filling the covered canvas like a suffocating balloon adding to their misery. Erik oversaw the group, but he didn't know what to say. What orders do you give to men jostling down the road? Nobody was misbehaving or even speaking for that matter. Every man's head bobbed, lost in his own thoughts.

Erik was thinking of home. He'd left only a few days ago, but he missed his family terribly, especially his darling Greta. He glanced at his watch, straining to pick out the dials in the dim light. They would be finished with dinner now, he realized. His mother would be doing the dishes while his father puffed at his pipe and skimmed the paper. Corina would be straightening up or getting Greta ready for bed. Perhaps she would come down and pick a final evening fight with Peter before turning in for the night? He smiled to himself. Those domestic conflicts seemed so trivial now.

He was headed to war. He wasn't sure when or where it would start, but it seemed clear now that his unit was going into Poland. They'd been issued rifles and ammunition, along with rations. His SS Deutschland Regiment was combining with other party units and some Heer regiments to form Panzer Division Kempf. They'd never drilled together. The SS units hadn't even worked as a larger unit before, let alone functioned at the division level with regular army commanders and soldiers. Most of all, they were unused to maneuvers with tanks. In the past few days, as Erik had sat on the fringes of some of the command meetings, he'd seen firsthand the confusion as the leaders of various units tried to work out logistics, supply, and communication—to elbow for control. He'd hoped they would have a few weeks to sort out the kinks before the unit went into the fight, but time had run out.

Combat. That word lanced through his thoughts again like hot fire. He didn't know anything about real fighting. Sure, he'd drilled, marched, shot rounds. He'd even participated in some war games. But none of that experience added up to anything more than playing at war. When they were in training exercises and people were "killed," they stood up at the end and started over. Erik and the men around him had never experienced live fire or real casualties. So, each man juddered along at present, lost in his own thoughts, grappling with this same notion: *How will I handle myself when the shooting starts?*

Maybe the Poles wouldn't fight. The hope flared through Erik's mind for the thousandth time. The Austrians hadn't. Neither had the Czechs. With the Russians gone over to the German side, nobody could come to their aid in time. Certainly, the French were a worry, but what could they do to help the Poles, who were hundreds of kilometers away from them on the other side of Germany? He prayed the Poles would give in, that a last-minute miracle would stop all of this from happening. He would be home in a few days, perhaps promoted, ready to take the job Karl was striving to arrange for him. He would never have to face these fears again.

He shook his head. He was deluding himself. They'd never been this close to a real fight. The Poles were stubborn. They had the French to back them, and even if that meant no immediate help for the Poles, it meant the Germans would have to fight on two fronts. No, this fight was coming.

Finally, as darkness surrounded them, the trucks ground to a jolting halt. Shouts of *"Raus!"* filled the night air, and Erik motioned for the group to hop out of the back. He rose to his feet and jumped, his legs on fire as he hit the ground. He stretched his back, trying to straighten. His joints were stiff. Some way to prepare for a fight. They would be worn out before they even moved out for the front. If there was a front.

"Sergeant, get your group together and then assemble with the rest of the platoon and company. We're over there!"

Erik recognized the voice of the company commander, Dieter Vogel, in charge of Second Company, Third Battalion, SS Deutschland Regiment. He saw the captain standing near a Panzer II light tank. Vogel looked like an old man among all the kids running around, although Erik doubted he was much past forty. The captain smiled at Erik and waved him over, placing a hand on Erik's shoulder as he approached.

"How are the boys?" he asked.

"Good so far. A little rattled from the ride."

"Is that all? I bet they didn't talk much."

"Not a word."

Vogel assumed a serious expression. "They're worried, and so are you. Nothing to be done about it, Erik. You can't prepare for combat; you just have to experience it. You'll be all right. They all will. Just remember what they've trained you to do, and stick together. You'll be fine."

"How am I supposed to lead when I've never been in combat myself?"

"Don't let it trouble you. The men like you. You're a good man. When it starts, just follow orders, make sure the boys are with you. Nothing to it."

"What about when people start dying?"

"It will happen. You'll lose some of your people. Maybe a lot of them. Just keep going. You can't save everyone. Your first duty is to accomplish your orders. But don't let anyone be a hero, either—quickest way to get killed. Just remember the basics: lay down some fire, then move fast to the next cover."

Erik drew comfort from his captain, one of the few with real experience from the last war. So many of the officers had none. Even the senior ones. He noted, too, that the advice echoed his father's from not more than a week ago.

"Mueller, don't you have your men together yet?"

Lieutenant Reinhard Sauer, his platoon leader and immediate superior, strolled up. Sauer spotted Vogel and clicked his heels in the Hitler salute. *"Guten Abend!"* he intoned, a sly grin creasing his lips.

"How is the platoon, Lieutenant?" asked Vogel.

"In good shape and all together, except for Mueller's group here." Sauer turned to Erik, and his eyes sharpened. "Sergeant, gather your men and get them over to the platoon. I need to talk to the captain about a few things. Get some hot food in them and be ready to move out in the next few minutes."

"Do we know where we are headed?" asked Erik.

"Now, Sergeant."

Erik stiffened and shot a salute to the lieutenant. He turned crisply and strode away, barking commands at his men to form up around him as he led them to where the platoon was gathered around a steaming pot of stew. A cook ladled the hot liquid into mess tins while the men waited greedily in line. There was fresh bread and tea as well.

"Eat your fill, boys," ordered Erik. "This might be the last hot food we'll have for a while. When you're finished, check over your gear. If anything needs to be repaired or replaced, now is the time to do it."

He felt like a hypocrite. What did he know about leading men into war? Still, having a command, even a small one, forced him to dig deep for courage and gave him something to worry about besides just the coming bullets.

He stood last in line, waiting for his turn to eat. Eventually Lieutenant Sauer returned, and he motioned his way. Erik didn't want to leave the line, but he couldn't refuse. He just hoped there would be something left for him by the time he got back.

The lieutenant watched him with eagle eyes as he approached, a stone statue frozen without emotion. "You and the captain seem to get along," Sauer noted.

"I don't know if that's true. He seems a good man, though. He's stopped to talk to me a couple of times."

"Just remember who your commander is. You take orders from me, not directly from Vogel. Do you understand?"

"Jawohl."

"I can't wait to get into these Poles," said Sauer with unexpected relish. "They've never experienced anything like the SS. They hid behind the Russians in the last war. This time they will face our steel storm without any help. These Untermenschen Slavs have no right to our lands. We will take back what is ours."

Erik nodded without comment.

"What's wrong, Sergeant? Don't you believe in our destiny?"

"Of course I do, Lieutenant."

Sauer's eyes narrowed. "Make sure that you do. You were privileged to join the SS. I'm aware of how you received your position: a friend calling in a favor. There are many others who *earned* their rank here. Make sure you merit yours as well."

"I will, Lieutenant."

"You're dismissed."

Erik saluted again and made his way back to the mess area. The stew was gone, and he had to satisfy himself with the butt end of a roll and some lukewarm tea. Sauer's words stung him. More so because they were true. Erik hadn't worked his way through the SS ranks. He wasn't sure he even believed half of what they stood for. He *had* received his rank through Karl's personal influence, attained through his wife's efforts and connections. He'd hoped that was not an issue, but apparently it was—at least with his commander. He would have to work doubly hard. Sauer was not a man to be crossed.

He was summoned to a company meeting a few minutes later. Captain Vogel addressed them with a face as white as the klieg lights illuminating his command tent. He began his briefing with only two words: "It's war."

———

Erik spent the rest of the evening and the early morning hours of September 1 getting his men ready for battle. They checked and then double-checked their equipment. They counted ammunition, made sure canteens were full, and confirmed that they had three days of rations. He looked through his field mess, which was composed primarily of coarse bread and a pasty sharp cheese in a tube. His head jerked back when he sniffed the stuff. A little after midnight, Captain Vogel appeared. He talked to some of the men and then approached Erik. "Ready, Sergeant?"

"Yes, sir," Erik replied.

"Remember what I told you. I've been through this. I know your type, Mueller; you'll do fine."

"Thank you, sir." He wished he felt as confident.

"I have something to help you." He motioned for a nearby guard, who retrieved an MP 40 machine pistol. Vogel gripped the weapon and handed it to the sergeant. Erik was surprised and delighted. He'd only fired the MP 40 a dozen or so times in drills, but the lightweight submachine gun would give him a decided advantage over the unwieldy standard-issue bolt-action 8mm Mauser in close combat. He also had a P38 pistol and a bayonet for hand-to-hand combat.

"Thank you very much, sir."

"A good leader needs a good weapon. You take care of yourself this morning. We'll have coffee in Warsaw."

"Sure thing, sir," said Erik. Vogel reached out and shook his hand, giving it a hard squeeze before he evaporated into the darkness. Erik returned his rifle at the depot and was handed six clips for his machine pistol.

When he returned, he pulled his group together to review their initial orders. The company was to provide infantry support to a platoon of Panzer I light tanks as they rolled into Poland.

"Those are the ones with a couple machine guns, not a cannon, right, Sergeant?" asked Franz Messer, a private from Königsberg.

"That's right, Messer," he said. He liked the private, a devout Lutheran who spent his leave at church instead of at the bars and brothels.

"Why can't we have some of them cannon tanks?" asked Corporal Heinrich Hensel, his second-in-command. Hensel bit down on an unlit, half-consumed cigar that slurred his words.

Erik laughed. "Do you think they tell me anything? Cannons would be great, but I'd rather be running along behind a tank than nothing at all."

"Can we trust these regular army types?" asked Hensel.

"They are well trained and equipped. Perhaps more than we are, to be honest."

"Didn't help them in the last war," noted the corporal.

"They just needed the SS to help them get the job done," joked Erik. That drew a laugh. "I do wish they would have given us more time to train together."

Lieutenant Sauer appeared and ordered them to gather their equipment and follow him. Erik motioned to his group, and within a few minutes they were connected up with the entire platoon, fifty men making their way as silently as they could through the darkness that was already starting to fade from the eastern sky.

For hours, they marched down a dirt road. Always toward the southeast. They were forced to stop and wait at times, and at others they were required to trot to keep the next platoon of the company in view. The tanks were nowhere to be seen. They must have either been behind them or prepositioned at the front, Erik realized.

Finally, they reached a village on the road south of Neidenberg. They were informed they were near the Polish border. The sun was well up by now. Erik noticed among the houses there were Panzer I tanks, part of the Second Battalion of the Panzer Regiment, the armored component of Group Kempf. He looked over one of the tanks. Two MG 13 machine guns poked out of the upper turret. He'd seen them operate in drills a couple of times. They were short and narrow, fast but lightly armored, and without the punch of the bigger tanks. Still, they would be a comfort to have along when the fighting started.

As he looked over the vehicles, he realized he could make out a dull thudding. He strained his ears: artillery. The war had started. As if in answer to this awareness, a droning buzz out of the west grew in volume. He looked up to see a flight of six Stuka dive bombers rumbling slowly past above him, heading southeast toward the sound of the fighting.

He pulled out a set of binoculars and followed their exhaust trails as the planes disappeared in a cluster of trees over the horizon. Erik scanned this forest, which must lay across the border in Poland. He couldn't see anything. Either the area in front of him was bereft of Poles, or they were too well concealed to spot. Well, they would know soon enough.

Erik assumed the attack would begin immediately, but the morning labored by without any orders to advance. He checked in with the lieutenant, who knew nothing more than he did. The tension grew minute by minute. He wanted to push forward, to face whatever was in those trees and get it over with. Orders came down, but not what he'd expected. Erik watched the cooks break out their pots and begin to prepare a hot breakfast. So there was no command to go forward—not yet.

They broke their fast amid the booming clatter of invisible giants in the distance. An occasional airplane streaked across the sky, too far away to identify. Otherwise they sat there milling around, a boiling cauldron of stress and anticipation.

A new noise erupted as morning faded and the sun began its slow descent in the sky. First one tank rumbled to life, then another. Soon the village was awash in roaring engines, the diesels purring in unison and coughing up a sickening cloud of exhaust. Still there were no orders. He didn't know how much more he could take.

"Sergeant!" He heard Sauer's sharp bark over the clamor.

"Yes, sir!"

"Come here."

Erik moved over to the lieutenant, who stood with the other group leaders. Sauer towered over them, his icy glare freezing each of them in turn. "We've got our orders. We are moving out with the tanks." He turned to Erik, his thin lips twitching. "Mueller. You are in the lead. You will follow the first tank, directly behind. We're crossing that field into Poland. Keep right behind the panzer. If you see any flashes from the trees, then spread out and return fire. I want the other groups in reserve, coming in behind the second set of tanks. I have mortars set up and zeroed in on the trees as well. We need to cross that field as quickly as possible. *Verstehen Sie?*"

Erik nodded. He felt his heart racing. He understood all too well. They were going into combat, and he would be in the lead. Whatever was in those trees, he would face it alongside a single tank. They were bait to ferret out the enemy, and he knew it. Had the lieutenant picked him on purpose?

Erik gathered his group and told them their orders. When he asked if there were any questions, nobody responded. He looked from face to ashen face. This was *his* group. They'd trained together, and now they would fight together—perhaps die together.

He led the men through the village and toward the fields on the outskirts of the cluster of houses. He identified the lead panzer and waved at the black-uniformed commander. They didn't speak over the hum of the engine, but they understood each other. This tank would be going in first, and Erik and his men were in support.

Erik scanned the trees again, looming five hundred meters away. He still couldn't see anything. He prayed the forest was empty and that they would make it to the other side without incident. He looked back up at the tank commander, who was on the radio. The man set the receiver down and saluted Erik. It was time.

The Panzer I's engine spit out a plume of grayish smoke and surged forward, rumbling over a gravel road and down a slight incline into the field below the village. Erik raised his hand and began walking, motioning for the group to spread out directly behind him. He soon had to jog to keep up with the tank, the exhaust nauseating him, his heartbeat throbbing in his ears.

The tank advanced, crushing the chest-high grass in front of them. The forest was still. Erik could only hear the engine and feel the bouncing clatter of his equipment. He gripped his machine pistol so tightly that his hands became ghostly pale.

The panzer lurched sharply in front of him and slammed to a stop. Angry smoke and flame belched out of the turret. Erik stared in horror as he realized the commander's body was still in place in the top of the turret, but his head was missing. A blaze licked out of the top of the tank, consuming the body in fire. Erik motioned to his group to hit the ground. Several had rifles raised and were firing at the forest. Hensel shouted at him, pointing back at the village. A string of holes appeared across the corporal's chest, and scarlet liquid plastered the grass around him. Hensel stared down in surprise, and then the field swallowed him. Erik dropped into the grass, closing his eyes, his hands gripping the earth. Explosions and thudding claps screamed around him. He waited for the bullets to come.

CHAPTER FOUR

Königsberg, East Prussia, Nazi Germany
August 1939

The pounding at the Bensheims' door increased. Trude and Britta clung to Johannes. He stood frozen. She could feel his trembling flesh. Her rock.

"What should we do?" she whispered.

He didn't answer. The hammering continued.

"Johannes. We have to do something."

He squared himself, hands reaching up to disengage from his wife and child. He smoothed his clothing and ran fingers through his onyx mop of curls. "Don't move," he whispered. He took a tentative step forward and then another. He marched leaning forward as if against a violent wind.

Trude pulled Britta to her. She looked around at what was left of their things. So strange that violence and danger were coming to this home where they had lived in relative tranquility. She'd heard terrible rumors of the Gestapo jails. Starvation. Torture. Rape. So few who went there ever returned. Especially the Jews. She would fight them to keep

Britta with her. Whatever else, she would die before she would let go of her little girl.

Johannes took another step. The pounding continued. He raised a shaking fist and placed his fingers tentatively on the handle. He turned the knob slowly and opened the door. A figure in a black uniform flung the door open and stormed in, pushing Johannes roughly out of the way.

"Are you mad?" demanded the figure. "Leaving me out there like that for all to see."

Trude was flooded with relief. The SS officer was Gunther. He was huffing and puffing, his uniform wrinkled and disheveled.

"What's going on?" demanded Johannes. "You betrayed us."

"Shut your mouth!" ordered Gunther. "I did nothing of the kind."

"What happened then?"

"It was Helmut. I heard about it at headquarters. He turned your organization in to save himself. It seems he finally realized the risks he was taking and decided to preserve his own skin."

"That can't be true. Helmut would never betray me."

"Really? You're so sure?"

"I've known him my whole life."

"I saw the paperwork myself. It was him."

Trude felt overwhelming shock. For Helmut to refuse to assist anymore was understandable. To turn Johannes in was another thing. She watched her husband. He seemed to shrink. His back curved and his shoulders bent forward. He shook his head slowly back and forth.

"It can't be true."

Gunther slapped him across the face. The sudden violence stunned Trude. Britta screamed and ran up the stairs.

"Listen, you little Jew. Who the hell do you think you are? You think your father will save you now?"

"I know times have changed," Johannes muttered.

"More than you know. Your father's war service and his money won't save you anymore. The Jews are finished in this country. Do you think things will get better with this war? They will get worse. More terrible than you can imagine."

"What are we to do?" The words dribbled out in a slur.

"I'm good for my word. I told you I would get you the visas, and I will. I still have a connection that can produce them for me, but it will take all of tomorrow."

"Tomorrow we will be in jail, or worse."

"I don't think so. I looked at the address that Helmut provided. He still had your old address in Mittelhufen." Gunther looked at him with an appraising stare. "Funny you never updated this great friend of yours with your new address. Perhaps you didn't trust him as much as you pretend you did."

"We had to register at this new address."

"Eventually they will find you. You better pray to that Gott of yours that I get back here before they find you."

"We're not religious."

He shrugged. "A Jew's a Jew. That won't save you, either." He looked up at Trude. "Make me something to eat. I'm starving."

Had she heard him right? This SS pig wanted her to make him food? She looked at Johannes, waiting for him to order the man out of their house, but he just nodded and stared at her blankly. She stood for a moment then stumbled into the kitchen, her mind in a fog.

She prepared the food in silence. Johannes and Gunther sat at the kitchen table. The SS officer had taken his boots off and was rubbing his feet while he sipped some tea. Britta returned downstairs, and he called her over to him. She was hesitant at first, but Johannes encouraged her, and soon she was sitting on Gunther's lap, her hands toying with her black-and-white top while Gunther told her fairy tales.

Trude cooked bacon and eggs in her sole remaining pan while her mind receded under what felt like layers of cotton. At any moment the

Gestapo could arrive and they would be taken, perhaps forever. Yet here she was feeding a Nazi who had taken all their possessions and struck her husband just minutes ago. During all of this he had no fear and sat smugly enjoying himself.

She finished cooking and served Gunther. The SS officer set Britta down and gripped his fork with a balled fist. He stared down at the food for a moment and laughed to himself. "Bacon? What kind of Jews are you?"

"We told you we aren't religious," said Trude.

"You might want to reconsider. You'll need Gott before long." He began shoveling the eggs into his mouth. He grunted and groaned, chewing quickly and reaching down for the next bite. He finished his plate in a flicker of minutes and demanded a second helping. Trude had saved the rest of the meal for the family, but with a nod from Johannes she served Gunther the remaining portion, and he consumed it as quickly as the first. Finally, he was finished, and he reached down to the tablecloth and drew a corner up, wiping the linen across his greasy chin.

"Good spread, my dear. Good indeed." As she approached to clear the table, he slapped her on the behind. Johannes pushed his chair back and flew to his feet, his face a mottled splotch. Gunther looked up passively. "Was there something else, *mein Freund*?"

Moments passed, and Trude could see the warring emotions in Johannes. She willed him to strike this Nazi bastard. To choke the arrogance out of him. She wanted him dead right here, right now. In this moment of fury and humiliation, she didn't care what the consequences might be.

"Please," she whispered. Her eyes begging.

Johannes placed a hand on the table and gripped harder. Gunther smiled. He reached his hand up and grasped Trude's bottom again, giving her a hard squeeze. His eyes never left her husband.

Johannes glared at Gunther a moment longer and then hung his head. Trude's heart was crushed. The shame burned through her. Gunther patted her a couple more times then chuckled and returned to his tea. "Good. Good," he said. "We are starting to understand each other better. You might live through this yet. If the police don't beat me back here." Gunther reached out and tousled Britta's hair. Their daughter had watched the scene indifferently, and Trude was so thankful she was too young to understand what had just happened.

After a few more minutes, Gunther rose. He flicked some crumbs off his uniform and stretched his body, wiping his greasy fingers on his wrinkled shirttails before tucking them back into his trousers. He stared at Trude a moment longer with a look of hunger, then he gave her a wink.

"Tomorrow I'll be gone all day arranging things," he announced. "Make sure you have everything ready to go." He looked around and chuckled again. "Well, whatever is left. You must travel light. They won't let you take more than a suitcase apiece." He shook a finger at Johannes. "And no valuables! You Jews always try to hide your diamonds and gold. You will be thoroughly searched. If they find anything, you'll be arrested, and all my work will be ruined. Do you understand me?"

"Jawohl," answered Johannes.

"*Ganz gut.*" He turned to Trude. "Thank you for a delightful meal—and for your entertainment."

She didn't respond. She wanted to spit in his face, but she couldn't gather the courage. Her husband's failure to act had shaken her core. How had they come to this?

Gunther nodded again and strolled down the hallway, whistling as he passed. A moment later the door opened and closed, and he was gone.

They stood there in the kitchen for a few moments, neither of them talking. Finally, Trude broke the silence. "How could you let him do that to me?"

Johannes didn't look up. His hands flexed and unflexed. He gripped the edge of the table again, and his knuckles grew white as if he sought to break the wood in half. He shook his head slowly over and over.

She was too harsh with him. She knew that. His calm had saved their lives. Gunther was their salvation. Their only chance at freedom. She stepped forward and put her arms around Johannes. He flinched at her touch, but she pulled him close. He fought a moment more and then fell into her embrace. He buried his head in her chest and sobbed. She held him there under the garish glare of a bare bulb, clinging together tightly for dear life.

Hours passed. Darkness gave way to morning and then to the day. The Bensheims sat huddled together in the living room where they had pulled in a couple of their kitchen chairs. Trude strained her ears to hear any sound at the door, but as the time ticked by it was silent. In the distance, they could hear what sounded like thunder, a strange noise, as the sun shone and the sky outside was blue. She didn't expect Gunther until evening, but the endless hours still pressed in on her.

They still hadn't talked about what had happened with Gunther. The first awkward moments had given way to the work of repacking their belongings. They had started with two suitcases each, along with a large trunk. After this morning, they had whittled down to one suitcase each for Johannes and Trude and none for Britta. Item by agonizing item they had been forced to choose what to take and what to leave behind.

Then there was the matter of the jewels and gold. If they were caught trying to take these, then they would be arrested. But they had to have them. Who knew what trouble might lie ahead? Without any valuables, how could they pay for food or the expenses of their travel? Worse, what if they had to bribe someone else? They weren't out of East

Prussia yet. They could be stopped anywhere along the way. They would need their valuables to assure safe passage.

Trude experimented with hiding the items in various places in the luggage. No matter what she tried, it was simply too easy to find them. Finally, she drew out a needle and thread, and laboriously sewed the items into their clothing where they could not be found except by tearing the cloth itself. In a way, she was glad of the time-consuming work. At least she couldn't think about what had happened in their very kitchen. The humiliation of letting a low-class middle-aged wretch fondle her in front of her husband and child. She realized there were worse things that had happened, that could still perhaps happen, but she felt violated at the deepest level.

And she was angry. Furious with her husband. She knew intellectually that there was nothing he could have done. If he had reacted, had struck the German or even worse, then surely they would have been arrested if not outright shot. Johannes had done nothing, his only course of action. Despite this, she felt betrayed. Not just because of last night, but because she had believed in Johannes. He was the God of her life. He had led her, pushed her, forced her to stay here far longer than she wished. He had promised that no matter what he would be able to get them out of Germany. She had believed in him implicitly. Now their future hung in the balance, and he just sat there and said nothing. Was her life a lie?

She realized he might be just another man after all. If he was wrong about this, he might be incorrect about everything. She had long ago laid her soul at his altar. She didn't want to let go. He hadn't let her down yet. Gunther had promised to get them out. He was a pig, but he was their savior now. By midnight tonight they could be on a ship heading out toward England. Johannes had arranged it. They would be safe after all.

The monster put his hands all over me—and my husband let him.

The thunder crackled in the distance.

"There must be a storm coming in," she said, breaking the silence they'd endured for hours.

"Yes, a storm," he answered, woodenly, mechanically.

She watched him. His eyes strayed back to the carpet. His hands absentmindedly traced designs in Britta's hair. She sat at his feet, a pile of lace and ribbons. Did she even know the danger they were in?

Trude wished they still had their radio. Gunther had taken it with everything else. Had the news reported the arrests last night? Was it mentioning Johannes and his organization? Even if the news contained nothing relevant, at least there would be music to fill the minutes while they waited for their rescue or their doom.

A light knock skipped against the door. Her blood froze. She recognized immediately that the sound was very different from what they had heard last night. A gentle scratching. Would Gunther have changed his knock? It was possible. He'd been a little frantic the night before. She might be grasping at a desperate hope. Still, would the Gestapo announce itself so meekly? Would they even knock, or might they just break down the door? "Johannes, someone is there."

"I know that."

"Aren't you going to answer?"

"I can't. You do it."

She looked over sharply. He was going to let her face the police by herself? She started to argue with him, but then she stopped. He just sat there staring at the carpet, still holding on to Britta. She didn't know what to do. The delicate knocking came again. She had to do something. Trude reached down deep and drew a breath. Whoever was there, they would not go away. She couldn't hide from the future by sitting silently. She took another breath, the air seeming to burn her lungs and throat. She coughed and tasted bitter bile in her mouth. Hesitating a moment more, she pulled herself to her feet with an effort and walked to the door. The scratch came again. She reached down and drew the door open.

She expected a storm of uniforms, but instead there was a woman, her gray dress merging with her hair, wispy locks running along the creased valleys of her temples. Frau Werner. A neighbor from a few doors down. They'd met a handful of times.

"*Guten Tag,*" Trude said, trying to fight down the lump that filled her throat and threatened to suffocate her.

"Hello," Frau Werner replied.

Trude scanned past her, expecting a trick. Waiting for the black leather trench coats, the torture and death. The street was empty. "What can I do for you?"

"I'm so sorry for bothering you, but I wanted to check in and make sure you were okay. There was a terrible banging at your door last night. I looked out my window and saw an SS man force his way in. I feared the worst."

"He was a . . . a guest."

Her eyes narrowed. "Some guest for you to have."

"What do you mean?"

"The neighborhood has many ears and even more mouths, my dear. I know where you came from and why." She looked out toward the neighboring row houses in disgust. "You caused quite a scandal when you moved in. As if they'd never seen a Jewish family before."

"We don't practice the faith."

"That hardly matters. Your husband's father was a well-known German and a well-known Jew. Now that those are two distinct things, you must know many petty people are more than happy to see you fall."

"I'm learning."

"And you still insist that monster last night was a friend."

"I . . . I won't say friend. But he's promised to help us."

"Don't trust him. They are a pack of thieves, the lot of them. Don't rely on him, and be careful with our neighbors, too. There are wolves all around you."

"Thank you for coming."

Frau Werner smiled with sympathy. "Of course. We haven't all lost our way. I'll check in on you again."

"We will be gone tonight."

Her eyes paled in sadness. "By the way, in case you haven't heard, the war's started. We invaded poor Poland this morning. What has been bad will grow worse."

She turned slowly and with great effort moved her legs down the stairs and back toward the street. Trude watched her leave but then, remembering her words, looked up and down the row of town houses. *There are wolves all around you.*

Trude returned to the sitting area, to her husband and daughter. Johannes didn't look up, didn't even ask who was at the door. She felt terribly alone. She sat back down and resumed her vigil. *We will be gone tonight.*

The hours crawled by, but Gunther didn't return. The thunder continued. The daylight faded into darkness. She stumbled wearily into the kitchen and cut them up some sandwiches, the last of their fresh food. They ate in silence and then resumed their endless waiting. Evening turned to night, and the time trickled by. Midnight came and went. In the early morning, she finally gave in and closed her eyes. He wasn't coming. War was here, and they'd been betrayed. They had waited too long; now the darkness would consume them. Today or tomorrow the Gestapo would come, perhaps led by Gunther. She would be arrested with her family, and they would likely never return. Another little light devoured by the storm.

CHAPTER FIVE

Neidenberg, East Prussia/Polish Border
September 1939

Concussive waves mowed the grass, and the zip and zing of bullets rained overhead. Erik held tight to the earth, his eyes fastened closed. His face sprayed with dirt from a nearby round. Time stood still.

This was combat. Burning bodies and dead friends. He didn't want to move. He would lie here until the inevitable shell tore his body apart. He would be at peace at last.

No! Another part of him screamed out in righteous protest. *You will do your duty.* Or was it: *I want to live?* He didn't know, but he wouldn't just lie here and wait for the end. He opened his eyes and rubbed the earth away from his face. He was surrounded by grass. He couldn't see anything. He could only hear the explosions and the high-pitched whistling of the rifle rounds.

Erik drew himself to his knees. His head was still below the grass line. Now he could make out billowing smoke in front of him. Likely from the panzer. He craned his neck slowly to see the forest again. The trees and the flashes of rifle fire. After a deep breath, he rotated his line of vision to behind him. Several more pillars of smoke kissed the sky in that direction. Two more tanks were out of action, but three in his immediate view were advancing and returning the fire to the trees. He couldn't see any of his group.

"Can you hear me?" he screamed, calling to his men. He heard nothing at first, and then, one by one, the muffled responses. There were many. He'd feared they were all dead, but miraculously most had survived. He crawled back toward the sounds and soon came upon a cluster of his men, hiding inside the smoldering indent of an artillery crater. He dropped down among them.

"Sergeant, you're alive," said Private Messer. "We thought you were killed by the first fire."

"*Nein.* Does anyone know what's going on out there?"

"There's artillery somewhere, and a bunch of Poles. They must have been waiting for us," said Messer. He fingered a cross around his neck, and Erik could see a silent prayer pass his lips.

"Where's the lieutenant?" someone asked.

"I don't know," said Erik. "I don't think we can wait for him." Finding his men gave him new courage. He felt the strange power of command again that seemed to spirit away his fear. He had to be strong for the men.

"What do you want us to do?" asked Messer.

Erik thought for a second. "Let's sneak through the grass up to the panzer. Once we get there, we will spread out on both sides right behind the tank. On my command, we'll all rise as one just above the grass level and start pouring fire into the trees. Pop up, pop down. Reload and repeat. I'll be to the right, nearest the tank. I'll keep up as steady fire as I can."

The men nodded. Erik pulled himself out of the crater and crawled forward in the grass. He looked back to make sure the other men were following.

Moment by agonizing moment he advanced through the grass toward the smoke. He expected a bullet to kill him any moment, but he kept moving forward. After what seemed an eternity, he made it to the tank. The vehicle still burned so hot that the heat seared his skin. Still, he remained as close as he could, knowing the panzer provided at least marginal cover. In short order the rest of the group was up, six men out of the original ten. He didn't know if the rest were dead, wounded, or in other parts of the field. *Except Hensel,* he reminded himself. He knew where he was.

He couldn't think about that right now. He split up the group. Three men moved to the left of the tank. Private Messer and another joined him on the right. The group watched him closely. Erik took a deep breath. He wanted desperately to stay here in relative safety behind the tank, but he knew he couldn't. He uttered a quick prayer and reached down to cock the bolt on his machine pistol. The metal slid neatly in and out. Another moment passed before he pulled himself to his feet, aimed the MP 40, and sprayed short bursts into the forest.

Very soon, he could see Messer next to him to his right. He couldn't see what he was aiming at, but it felt wonderful to fire back, to do something. His men popped up and down like jack-in-the-boxes, firing, reloading, and firing again. He remained above the grass, firing a few rounds at a time. Bullets ricocheted off the panzer, and he wanted to duck back down and hide, but he kept himself in position, firing over and over. When the clip ran empty, he extracted the long, rectangular piece of steel, throwing it behind him and reaching into his satchel for another. He slammed it into place and began the process over. He expected to be hit at any moment, but somehow the whizzing bullets continued to miss him.

Over his head he heard the deep roaring of aircraft. He looked up and saw a trio of friendly Stuka bombers, dots in the blue expanse. As he watched, they seemed to fall out of the sky, pointing their noses earthward and blazing toward the ground like eagles seeking their prey. A terrible screaming erupted. The Stukas emitted a high-pitched shriek that threatened to tear his eardrums apart. He dropped his weapon and pressed his hands over his ears.

The Stukas plunged angrily onward. They were headed straight toward them. The firing around them stopped. Or so it seemed to Erik. The screaming of the dive bombers was so intense he couldn't tell. The planes were close now; he could see the determined looks of the pilots in the cockpits. They seemed to be aimed right at Erik, and he would have fled if his body wasn't frozen with fear.

At the last moment, the bombers jerked out of their dive. Erik could see dark cylinders detach from the bombers and plunge toward the earth like black angels. The bombs sailed over him and struck the trees immediately ahead. A thunderous explosion blew him off his feet. He lay in the grass, stunned by the detonation. His ears rang and his jaw ached. He blinked a few times and forced himself back up, above the grass line. The forest was a fiery hell. Trees broken and bent in every direction. Flames licked the branches and chewed at the trunks. He could see bodies now, writhing in fire, arms waving, screams tearing the air.

He looked toward his men. Their faces bore the same dazed expression. His ears rang. His head throbbed. Private Messer's mouth moved as he tried to say something to Erik. He shook his head in return, and Messer seemed to understand.

They stood there for some time, watching the inferno while more men gradually advanced in support. The fire was too hot to advance for now, so the men and surviving Panzer I's clustered at the edge of the trees and waited.

"Sergeant, I see you made it," said Lieutenant Sauer. His voice sounded muffled, as if strained through cotton. The lanky blond arrived among a herd of moving gray. The whole company was coming up, and Erik saw it was largely intact. He nodded without speaking.

The lieutenant shot his arm out in a triumphant salute. "Well done, Mueller. I wasn't sure if you had it in you, but you led these men capably. Heil Hitler." Mueller saw Captain Vogel a few meters behind. He was pointing out directions to a man on a map. He finished and looked over. He grinned approvingly at Erik with a nod.

Erik turned back around and stood silently with his men. He watched the slow-burning fire without seeing. He closed his eyes. He wasn't dead. The relief washed over him. He'd made it. He'd led his men in combat. He'd survived, at least for today. He thought of Hensel and the others. He'd lost men today, but he'd kept his group together to push the Poles back—with the help of the Stukas, of course. He felt a glorious thrill. The sky covered him and the sun warmly embraced his face.

He felt a hand on his shoulder. Private Messer had come over. He looked at Erik with thankfulness and respect. Erik smiled back. He closed his eyes again and breathed the summer air, thinking it was a fine thing to be alive.

<hr />

Over the passing weeks, Erik's unit pushed farther into Poland. The Poles fought valiantly, he thought, but they were outnumbered and virtually without air cover. Panzer Group Kempf captured Mlava, then Różan, Łomża, and Klicym. Erik's group dwindled down to four men from the original ten, the platoon a bare fifteen, and the company seventy.

Lieutenant Sauer led the platoon bravely, Erik had to admit. Sauer might have been too zealous of a believer in the Nazi cause, but he was courageous and smart, and he was concerned about the men's safety, equipment, and well-being.

Captain Vogel had survived a brush with death when his command vehicle was hit by a mortar. His face sustained flash burns and part of his right ear had been blown off, but he refused to leave his men. He was patched up at a field hospital to return immediately to the front.

Now it was late September, and the division was nearing Modlin. Resistance had tapered off for the past few days; rumor was the Poles were calling it quits. Erik had heard still better news: although the French and English had declared war, they were sitting in their positions in France and Belgium and making no move to honor their treaty commitments to the Poles nor launching any attack. Best of all, the Russians joined the fight on September 17 and streamed over Poland's eastern borders.

Of course, this only mattered to the living. Erik focused on the here and now. On his little group. This morning they were moving down a heavily forested road, inching ever closer to Modlin fortress, seventy-five kilometers from Warsaw. The company was escorting two Panzer II tanks, with Sauer's platoon in the lead. Erik walked just in front of the lead tank, with Messer alongside him.

"Do you see anything out there, Corporal?" Erik asked.

Messer looked up surprised, then grinned. "I'm still getting used to the promotion." He strained to see down the road. "Not a thing. It's strange. They fought like lions, and now they've just melted away. Do you think they're done?"

"I don't know. Captain told me we're in Warsaw. The Russians met up with some of the boys as well somewhere down south and east. They won't last long."

"Still nothing from the French or British?"

"I guess not. I don't understand that, either. They went to battle on day one in the last war. Why would they wait until we kill off the second front?"

"Gott's will."

"You might be right about willpower, but I don't know about Gott. I think they don't have any spirit for another war."

"Do we?" Messer questioned earnestly.

"To make Germany great again? I think so. They took too much from us. My dad lost everything. His store, his savings, his world."

Corporal Messer nodded. "My father lost his job when the economy collapsed. He came home and drank himself to death. Hardly said a word to any of us for two years."

"We've all paid the price for that war. If they'd only left us alone when it was over, we wouldn't be in this mess today."

Messer looked around. "What about this other stuff? The Nazi talk. Do you believe all of it? About the Jews, and the Slavs, and our race should be on top?"

Erik was surprised. The corporal was taking a terrible chance voicing such concerns out loud. He realized the man was reaching out to him. After weeks of combat, Messer was trusting his life to him in yet another way.

Erik shrugged. "I don't know. I just want Germany back. I want my father to smile again, for us to be able to walk with our heads high in the world." Erik grinned and clamped his friend on the back. "Besides, we're in the SS; we better believe it all."

Messer laughed and threw his arm around Erik as well. "I guess you're right. We joined the wrong group if we still have questions."

"Plenty of us do. But be careful talking that way. You could be reported. Not by me, of course. Remember, though, there are ears everywhere."

The corporal nodded. "I understand, sir. Thank you for listening."

They came out of the forest and into an area of cultivated fields. Wooden fences zigzagged lazily across fields dotted with grazing sheep, apparently oblivious to the war around them. A shepherd stood leaning against a tree a few hundred meters away, watching the oncoming column with interest.

The lead panzer ground to a halt. Lieutenant Sauer strutted to the front, shadowed by two guards with machine pistols.

"What's the situation out front, Sergeant?" he asked, wiping his pale forehead with a white handkerchief.

"Not much to report. Village up ahead. No activity. Farmers are out in the fields. They don't seem to be expecting a fight."

Sauer nodded. He extended a narrow finger down the road. "Move out. We'll take lunch once we've secured that village. Keep a sharp eye out."

Sauer flipped backward and hit the ground hard. Erik stared down at him for a moment in surprise and then heard the echoing report of a rifle. He knelt over the lieutenant and saw he was hit in the upper shoulder, but only grazed. "Get the men into position for an attack and get me into that ditch," Sauer ordered with gritted teeth.

Erik and Messer grabbed the lieutenant and dragged him toward the side of the road. Bullets kicked up the dirt near them, and a roaring cascade of clamoring thuds rolled over them. An artillery shell bounced off the lead panzer. The tank's turret rotated and raised slightly, then fired a return round toward the village. Erik, head low, pulled out a handkerchief and applied it to Sauer's wound.

"Don't worry about me, Sergeant," the lieutenant grunted. "Get the men moving forward!"

Erik nodded and motioned for the platoon to spread out on both sides of the road. Bullets landed around them. So far they seemed to be from single-shot rifles rather than machine guns.

A medic started treating the lieutenant. Erik stayed a moment longer before he turned his attention to the fighting. He was amazed at what he saw: a sight from another age. Lining the village and for a quarter kilometer or so in each direction were hundreds of Polish cavalry, a long row of horsemen. Some of them actually had lances, with pennants flapping in the wind. As Erik stared they began moving forward slowly, and then broke into a galloping charge.

"Fire!" screamed Erik. "Fire, fire, fire!"

The platoon commenced shooting along with the lead panzer. Small gaps appeared in the lines, but the charge streamed forward. A second tank moved into place and laid down machine gun fire. More SS scrambled into position as the company came up. The horsemen took casualties now, but they still came on, closing the distance: first a kilometer, then a half kilometer.

The full force of the company and two tanks was now unleashed on the charging Poles. Shells chewed holes in the line, and machine guns mowed down vast arcs like a hungry scythe.

Still they came on. Erik felt the panic rising. In his weeks of fighting he'd never seen anything like this. He finished a clip from his machine pistol and hastily shoved in another, continuing to pour fire at the attackers, who were less than a quarter kilometer away now. He knew his weapon was largely ineffective at this distance, but there was little else he could do. He was struck by the strange and terrible beauty of the charge and the bravery of the Poles galloping through a wall of metal.

The horsemen's numbers dwindled. At two hundred meters, more than half the mounted assailants were down. Now as they reached the most dangerous range of the Nazi small arms, they toppled over like so many matchsticks. Still they advanced, closing the remaining distance. One hundred meters, then fifty. A few dozen reached their lines. A Pole charged in on Erik, saber raised. He shot the man with his machine pistol, spraying wildly; he watched a pattern of blackened dots dance down the soldier and his horse. The soldier still rode on as if nothing had happened, but frothy blood bubbled out of his lips. Horse and man crashed to the ground in front of Erik, a bare meter away. Neither moved again.

Erik stared hard for a few moments. He felt sorry for the beautiful animal—he realized the irony that he had become desensitized to the death of humans, that the loss of this majestic animal affected him more. He looked around. The charge had failed. The wounded lay all around, moaning or screaming. A dozen of the enemy were prisoners. They had stopped the Poles.

"Well done, Sergeant!"

He turned to see Lieutenant Sauer coming up. His shoulder was bandaged and his face was a ghostly white, but otherwise he seemed fine. His eyes shone a fiery blue. The wound seemed to fuel his passion, his speech coming in excited bursts.

"Where is the captain?" asked Erik.

"He stayed for the fight then went back to request reinforcements. Orders are to dig in here and wait for more men and armor. The Stukas are going to bomb the hell out of that village."

Even as Sauer spoke the words, Erik heard the rumbling of the dive bombers overhead. The rumble transformed into the now-familiar scream of the planes as they dived down in a near vertical plunge toward the cluster of houses a kilometer away. Percussion waves washed over them as detonation after detonation blew the village apart.

Corporal Messer came forward, prodding a couple of Polish prisoners. "You tried to attack the men of the Fatherland!" screamed Sauer at the prisoners. "Look what happens! Look what happened to you!"

Sauer struck one of the men, spinning him to the ground. Sauer drew his pistol and pulled the Pole back up to his knees.

"Lieutenant!" protested Erik.

Sauer fired. The Pole's head jerked back, blood spurting from the wound as the body collapsed to the ground. The second Pole broke free of Messer and turned, fleeing. Sauer took aim and fired, hitting him in the back. The prisoner froze, arms in the air. He turned slowly around, staring into the sky, a bloody lake forming at his chest. He grimaced, clearly in pain, and then fell face forward, his body writhing spasmodically on the ground. Sauer stepped up and fired at the man's head. The body bounced one more time and was still. Sauer spit on the man's back and then carefully returned his pistol to the holster. He looked up and winked at Erik.

Erik stood in shocked silence. His commander had just murdered two men before his eyes.

CHAPTER SIX

Königsberg
September 1939

The night wore endlessly on, but Gunther failed to reappear. All the next day and the next they waited, but nothing. Each moment the Gestapo might arrive. Aside from that shattering fear, there was the more mundane concern that there was little food remaining in the house. They had some soup and other canned goods, but this could only last a few more days.

Trude worried about Britta. Her daughter had never stayed indoors for this long. The girl grew impatient and agitated as she clamored to go for a walk or play in the park. Trude had to tell her no over and over.

Johannes was even worse. He had never recovered from the other night. He sat in his chair quietly, listlessly, staring out the window. She didn't know what to do. He was her strength, her guide, and now even though he was physically present, it was as if he wasn't here at all. She tried to draw him out, but he would merely nod or quickly answer, then return to his silent vigil.

She should have been frightened, but she felt only exhaustion and a crippling numbness. Her world was collapsing. She'd weathered so much already: the loss of her position with the conservatory, their home, their status. Their parents escaping while her small family remained behind. The stares and whispers when she would shop or walk down the street. Like she had a disease.

None of these humiliations compared to the situation now. At least before they'd had food. They'd been able to go outside. Most of all, she'd had her husband—her rock. He'd left each day, worked his miracles, defied the Nazis, and returned to her each night. Now he was a mere shadow, a hungry apparition draining her.

A knock at the door. She froze. Somebody was there. Familiar fears crowded the room. Would the Gestapo knock? She stood and made her way reluctantly to the door. She opened it and was relieved to see Gunther standing with a packet tucked under his arm.

"Guten Tag," she said.

He grinned at her and strode into the house toward the sitting room.

"Johannes, mein Freund, was machen Sie?"

Johannes didn't look up.

"What's wrong with him?" asked Gunther, registering alarm.

"He . . . he hasn't been the same since the other night."

"Since what?" His face was clouded for a moment and then broke into a sheepish grin. "Oh that. What is a little joking around among good friends?"

"Did you bring our visas?" she asked.

"It can't be done," he announced.

"What?" demanded Trude. "You promised us. We paid you."

His eyes flared. "Careful now, Frau. Don't forget who you are. Who *I* am."

She repressed her anger, lowering her gaze. "I'm sorry."

He grinned again and threw his arms into the air. "Your frustration is understandable. I did everything I could, but with the start of the war they've cut off all travel for Jews, particularly international. We will simply have to wait until all of this is over. Which won't be long if things keep progressing."

"What do you mean?"

He looked at her surprised for a moment. "Oh that's right, your radio was . . . taken. The Poles, my dear. They are falling back everywhere. Fifty divisions of them. You'd think they'd put up a better fight, but what can you expect from these Slavs?"

"Surely the French—"

"Haven't budged. They sit in their Maginot Line and wait for us." He moved closer, raising his hand to his cheek as if whispering a secret in a crowded room. "If you want my opinion, they never intended to fight."

She was shocked by the news, but she couldn't worry about it. Wars meant nothing to her. She was only concerned about the here and now. "We can't wait for a war to come and go. We have to get out."

He laughed. "I don't blame you. You should have left years ago. You had all the resources to do so." He looked over at Johannes. "Instead your young knight insisted on playing the hero. He thumbed his nose at us, thinking he was proving something." Gunther turned back to her. "Do you think we didn't know? We didn't mind letting the Jews go. Oh yes, we've been watching his little organization for a very long time. But they paid well, and we obtained a steady income of businesses, land, and savings from all these emigrants, all the while ridding ourselves of part of our Jewish problem."

"You knew?"

He laughed again, taking a step closer. "Of course we did, my dear. Did you think your little Jew husband pulled the wool over our eyes? Now look at him. A little trouble and he crumbles into himself. You people have no endurance—but I do."

"What do you have in the package?" she asked, trying to divert his attention. Her mind was reeling with what he'd just told her. They'd played a game with her husband all along. All this time he thought he was beating them.

Gunther looked down. "Oh yes. I almost forgot. I brought your passports back." He hesitated. "They've been revoked, unfortunately." He held the package out to her. She tried to take it quickly, but he grabbed her hand and wouldn't let go. She glanced at Johannes for support, but he continued to stare out the window as if nobody was there.

Gunther took a step nearer her. "Don't you worry, my dear," he whispered. "There may be another way."

"What do you mean?" Her skin crawled and she wanted to pull free, but she willed herself to remain still. This man could still save them—or damn them.

"There is more than one way out. So far we've only explored legal means, but there are alternatives, especially for someone like your husband, who has certain connections."

"What kind of alternatives?"

He moved his lips to her ear, his fetid breath sickening her.

"We are a port city. Ships of all sizes and descriptions leave here every day. There is no way to check all the cargo. Rats make their way on board all the time. Even Jewish rats."

"We want to go to England."

He laughed. "You'd never get to England. Not straightaway. You probably don't know this, but we're at war with the buggers, and with the French, too. But we trade freely with Russia, and Sweden and Norway are neutral. You're only a few hours from Stockholm."

"Could you help us get on board?"

He brushed his lips against her ear. "You might be able to convince me."

She shivered. She turned her head slightly.

"What are you saying?"

He grinned at her, his eyes slowly moving down her neckline and to her chest. She stepped back in disgust.

He laughed. "Don't worry, my dear. As charming as you are, that's not what I'm talking about. I'm not talking about what I want. I'm talking about what I need."

"What is that?"

"Money, and lots of it."

"We don't have anything else."

"Of course not," he said. "You already used up your resources. That's where your husband's connections come in."

"He already met with everyone we know."

"Oh, I doubt that. Clever boy like that. He'll figure out something."

"How much more?"

"Who's to say? I'll have to make certain inquiries."

"When will you know?"

He drew his hand to his chin and tapped it, considering the issue. "Some days, I would think."

"But we are almost out of food!"

He glanced down again, sweeping his stare over her figure. "I thought you'd lost some weight. It suits you."

"Gunther, please. What are we to do?"

"You'll manage. Rats always survive—even on crumbs."

There was that word again. "We're not rats."

He grinned. "I know that, my dear. I just refer to the party line—you're officially vermin, don't you know?"

"You don't really believe that."

He leered at her again. "Obviously, I don't."

She regretted her question. Then a thought occurred to her. "How am I supposed to reach out to Johannes's connections? Look at him."

Gunther followed her gaze. "Good question. I can't solve all your problems. You'll have some time." He turned to her husband. "Did you hear me? Be a good little Jew now and perk up a bit. Your life depends on it." Still, Johannes didn't stir.

Gunther turned back. "I guess you have your hands full. Now give me a kiss good-bye. I have to leave."

She was horrified. "I can't kiss you."

"Oh, but you must, my dear. That's the down payment for my services."

"But you said that wasn't part of it."

"I said nothing of the sort. I merely said you couldn't pay for my services fully that way."

She was terrified. What should she do? Should she refuse him? Spit in his face? But then what would *he* do? He would leave and come back with the Gestapo. He might do it anyway. Everything he told her might be a lie. What choice did she have?

"Well? What will it be?"

"Quickly then," she managed to mumble. She closed her eyed and pressed her lips tightly.

She felt his hands on the back of her head. She tensed, but he pulled her forward and pressed his lips against hers. She tried to pull away, but he gripped her tightly. He forced his tongue through her lips and into her mouth, moving it around for a few moments. She choked and coughed, finally managing to pull away. He laughed, his eyes brimming with mirth and something else.

"Thank you, my dear. That will do."

She didn't respond. He clapped his hands together. "Well, I guess that's it for now. I shall return." He bowed with a mock flourish and turned to leave.

"What if the Gestapo gets here first?" she managed to say.

He shrugged. "I wouldn't answer the door if I were you." He chuckled to himself, turned, and left.

<hr />

Days passed and Gunther did not return. The days turned into a week, and then weeks. Each day Trude woke expecting the Gestapo to appear and arrest them all. Each night she went to bed, thankful for another miracle, but wondering when or if Johannes's SS connection would ever return. Their canned food dwindled. Even with cutting their intake, first in half, then to a third, they were nearly out. They were now subsisting on the remaining few cans of stewed tomatoes. If they didn't get something to eat soon, they would starve.

Johannes continued in his stupor. He would respond to basic questions and commands, but the light of his spirit was gone, perhaps forever. The weight of everything fell on Trude. She felt her sanity slipping away with the stress and the worry.

As September faded into October, they ate the last of the food. Trude realized they would have to do something now. They couldn't wait any longer. Someone would have to go out and buy groceries, whatever the risks involved.

She walked into the sitting room where Johannes was perched in his traditional spot, staring out the window. "Johannes, we're out of food," she said.

He didn't respond.

"Johannes," she repeated.

He turned his head slowly. He was gaunt, having lost weight. His eyes were bloodshot, his curly hair greasy and unkempt. He stared at her for a moment, as if trying to comprehend who she was.

"We're out of food."

His eyes moved back and forth over her features. "Food," he repeated back absently.

"Yes, food!" she screamed. She slapped him hard across the face. He reeled from the blow. She struck again and his arm flashed up, catching the blow. He flushed red, and she could see a glint of flame in his gaze.

"Stop it," he said.

"I won't. We are out of food, Johannes! Do you know what that means? We are going to starve! Our little girl is going to die! We must do something! You have to do something!"

He looked at her a moment. "There's nothing that can be done."

She pulled her hand free and grabbed his shirt, jerking his head back up, pulling him toward her. "That's not an answer! You are the father of this family. We are dying. You've had enough time to sit back and sulk while I've been left with all the work, all the worry! I'm done!" She burst into tears, all the stress and fear of the past weeks washing over her.

"Mommy!" screamed Britta. She felt her daughter's arms wrap around her leg. She regretted her outburst; she'd thought her girl was upstairs. She tried to stop herself, but she couldn't. It had been too much, too long.

She felt another hand on her neck. A strong hand. She looked up in surprise. Johannes was holding her, conscious, looking at her intently.

"Johannes."

"I hear you. Food."

He had returned to her, at least a part of him. "I've been so scared," she admitted.

He looked around wearily. He rubbed his face and shook his head, as if waking from a nightmare. "We need something to eat."

"We do. And I need you. I can't do this by myself anymore. I can't take it."

He didn't respond. She wanted to strike him again, to scream at him for what he'd put her through, but she was afraid he would recede into his shell. She watched him, observing the first signs of life in her husband for weeks. She tried to suppress her anger at him and focus on what they needed.

"Johannes, I need you to go to the grocery store. It's a terrible risk, but we must take it. Do you think you can go?"

He looked at her again, pausing a long moment before answering.

"Food," he said again, nodding, understanding.

She rose and moved to her coat. She reached into the internal pocket and removed a stack of Reichsmarks, all the paper money they possessed. She walked back and pressed the bills into her husband's hands. He balled the notes into a fist. His hands started to shake. The tremors moved up his arms and into his legs. He squeezed the notes harder. His face grew scarlet. "Gunther," he said at last.

She thrilled at this response. She felt the old admiration and love—so damaged in the past two months. "Yes, darling. We can talk about that later. I need you now. I need you to keep us from starving."

He didn't respond. She thought she was losing him again, but finally he nodded. He stuffed the notes into his pants pockets and stood up. He nearly toppled over, and she realized how weak he was. He'd hardly touched his food this past month, and the lack of nutrition had taken its toll on what had once been a body hard with wiry muscle. He steadied himself and looked sheepishly at her, giving a slight shrug as if to acknowledge how foolish he'd been.

"I've left you with everything. I know that. I haven't been fair."

She drank another sip of relief. *He's coming back to me. I'm not alone.* "I know you're weak, but bring us back food and I'll make us a feast tonight to celebrate."

He smiled wanly. She wanted to rush to him, to bury her head in his chest and sob. To transfer all responsibility to him. She was afraid that would be too much. *Small steps.*

He left a few minutes later, a little unsteady on his feet. She collapsed into the chair after the door closed. Britta crawled into her lap and nuzzled her, falling asleep. Her girl was almost too big now to sit this way, but Trude clung to her, trying to keep her emotions in control. They sat that way for some time, Trude feeling the first relief she'd experienced since the terrible night of those first arrests. Her husband was returning to her. He was exhausted and weak, but she had seen a little ember of the old spirit. If she could rekindle his will, she was sure everything would turn out all right. He was the most courageous and resourceful man she'd ever known.

Now there was a chance. Perhaps they could even forget Gunther. If there were other ways out of Germany, surely Johannes—the old Johannes—could find them. She would wait in hiding a few more days while he arranged everything, then they would make their escape. She closed her eyes, imagining the three of them standing on the deck of a small ship as it drew away from Königsberg, headed to Stockholm or Copenhagen or anywhere but here. They would sell a piece or two of jewelry, check into a hotel, get ahold of their family by telegram, and wait for their rescue. They might even make a little vacation of it if there was a delay. No matter what, they would be out of Germany and safe. Together.

She thought of her parents, waiting at a dock on the Thames when they eventually reached England. She'd only been to London once as a child, but she'd found the city a delight. Johannes would find employment at a university—there were no barriers in England. She could return to her music. She shook her head. Why had they waited so long?

She flinched at the sound of the keys at the door. She'd fallen asleep. What a pleasant dream, and now dinner was coming, the first fresh food in weeks. She looked over her shoulder, smiling by way of greeting. She froze.

Johannes was there at the threshold, but his arms were empty. Where was the food? Perhaps he was having everything delivered. Of course, there would be too much . . .

"I couldn't get anything," he said, his voice shaking.

"What do you mean?"

"Cards. We don't have any ration cards."

"There aren't ration cards."

He looked at her with pain. "There are now. They came out while we've been here. I had a bit of work explaining to the clerk how I didn't know. He was very suspicious. I left without giving a name or any other information, but I had to get out of there quickly."

"Were you followed?"

"I don't think so." He looked at her. "What are we going to do?"

There it was again. This strange role reversal. He wanted answers from her. At least he was talking. "I don't know, my dear, but at least you've come back to me."

A cloud crossed his face. She could see his shoulders slumping, and he started toward his chair.

"Johannes!"

He stopped and stood a moment, as if a silent war was going on inside him. Finally, he turned to her. "You're right. Not that way. Still, we need food. I don't know what to do. For the first time in my life, I'm lost."

He looked at her, and she could see the fear and the shame spelled out on his face. She went to him, embracing him, holding him closely to her. "We're both lost, dearest. We will find our way together."

CHAPTER SEVEN

Königsberg
Early October 1939

Erik knocked. He hadn't called. He wanted to surprise them. His mother opened the door. A flicker of excitement showed and was gone, as if it had never existed. She extended her sturdy arms in silence, and he stepped into her embrace. She held him there tightly. He closed his eyes, fighting back tears. The darkness and the shadows of the past two months diffused beneath her oaken comfort.

"My boy has returned," she stated simply. Behind her a clatter of excitement grew and rattled toward the door. She didn't move. She looked him slowly over, as if making sure he was still in one piece. She allowed the sliver of a smile before she nodded slightly and then stepped aside, allowing the flood to pass.

Greta flew into his arms, a white blur of squealing delight. He drew her up, and she kissed his cheek and neck, snuggling in and holding him tightly. "Daddy, Daddy!" she screamed.

"Ah, my precious angel is here," he said, wincing at the weight. "Have you been a good girl while I've been gone?"

"She's been the best," said Peter, emerging from the dim shadows. "She's a brave little one."

Erik looked around. "Where's Corina?"

"She's upstairs cleaning," said Peter.

Erik called up to his wife. She didn't respond. He called again, and after waiting a moment, he started toward the landing.

"Let me take her for you," said Peter, motioning to his daughter.

Erik handed off Greta and started up the stairs. He could hear a thumping clatter from the bedroom. He knocked gently and the noise stopped.

"Come in."

He opened the door, and there was his Corina. She was midway through changing the sheets on their bed. Her face showed irritation at the interruption, but she brightened when she realized her husband was home. She dropped what she was doing and ran into his arms.

"You're safe," she whispered. She held him tightly and kissed his neck.

He delighted at her response. Feeling all the old warmth. "Yes, dear wife, I've made it home."

"Thank God." She pulled away, and her eyes sharpened. "Why didn't you call ahead so we could meet you at the station? And where is your uniform?"

"I changed on the train. I didn't want to call attention to myself." He braced himself for a tirade.

"You're impossible." She laughed. She pulled him close again, kissing his neck and cheek. "I've missed you so much. I'm so proud of you."

"There's nothing to be proud of. I did my job. I'm just happy I've made it home to my girls." He darkened. "Many didn't, you know."

"Where's your medal?" she asked. "We were all excited when we heard the news."

He fumbled with the interior pocket of his jacket and drew out his Iron Cross.

She took it and held it up, laughing to herself. "My husband: a real hero. I've told everyone. All the neighbors and our family. People can't stop talking about it."

He laughed. "I can't imagine why. They handed out plenty of these. It's hardly a Knight's Cross."

"That will come in time. What about your promotion? Any news?"

"Lieutenant Sauer mentioned something about looking into it, but I don't have any specifics."

"I'm so curious about him," said Corina, fingering a gold-colored silk scarf, her eyes dancing to the flicker of a candle. "He sounds so brave and wonderful."

"Wonderful? He killed unarmed prisoners," blurted Erik. He had promised himself he wouldn't say anything, but the words rushed out before he could gather them.

"What? Why?"

"I don't know. It was near the end of the campaign. We were in a firefight, and we took some prisoners. The lieutenant was wounded. I think he was angry."

She paused a moment and then pushed her hand out as if waving away the event. "What does that matter? They were Poles, yes?"

"Correct. Polish prisoners. I think I have to say something."

Her smile faded and a frosty cloud entered the room. "Don't you even think about it," she snapped, her voice shaking. "You are a decorated hero now, with a promotion on the way. If they make you a lieutenant, you will be an officer. An officer, Erik! It's everything we've ever dreamed of. Think of what it will mean for Greta's future. For our future. We can find a better house, leave this drab neighborhood behind. Doors we've only dreamed of will open for us." She stepped forward and pointed a finger. "You can't give all that away for a couple of dead Poles. This is war. They would have killed you if they'd had a chance." She reached out to pull his chin toward her until their eyes met. "You promise me, now. Promise me you won't say a thing to anyone."

He hesitated. Was she right? Certainly, it could hurt his future if he turned the lieutenant in. But Sauer's actions were murder, plain and simple. If he ignored that, what did it make him? "I will wait and see, that's all I can promise you."

That seemed to be enough for her. She pulled him back in and kissed him on the lips. "Oh, Erik, thank you! Thank you! Imagine when you are promoted. I can't wait to tell everyone. You have made all of us so proud. Karl will be delighted, too."

"Karl? You've seen him?"

She pulled away and started moving the sheets back into place. "No. Not really. I ran into him at church one Sunday. He asked about you, of course. He is always interested in your future. He was impressed with your medal. I know he wants to see you again as soon as you can."

"I won't have time now. I'm only home for forty-eight hours."

"Where will you go after that?" she asked.

"I don't know for sure. West, I would think."

"Surely the French won't really fight us?"

"They haven't backed down yet. Neither have the British."

"But they aren't doing anything, are they?"

"No, that's the strange thing. They sat back and let us roll over the Poles. I mean, what was the point of declaring war to protect them in the first place if they weren't going to fire a shot at us while we defeated their allies?"

"I'm sure they won't fight now," she insisted. "That's why it's so important that you don't say anything about your commander. There may never be a chance again to earn a promotion."

He watched her for a moment. She was busily straightening the bed. She was so petite and strikingly beautiful. She was probably right; he needed to take care of his family. Sauer had been wounded and under extreme pressure after all. Erik stepped back and closed the door. She looked up and smiled at him. "My hero."

He left the bedroom sometime later and returned downstairs. Greta was in the kitchen with his mother. Anna was showing his daughter how to mix the dough for a pastry. He smiled at the girl's fierce concentration. *Oh, to only have the worries of a child.*

He walked into the sitting room. His father perched in his chair, puffing away at his pipe while he thumbed through the paper. He looked up. "*Ach,* Erik. Come join me."

Erik took a chair opposite his father. "I was wondering if I could talk to you about something."

His father set the paper down, giving Erik his full concentration. "What is it?"

"Something happened while I was gone. I wanted to know if anything like this ever happened to you."

"Tell me."

Erik described the last battle and Lieutenant Sauer's actions. The color drained from his father's face as he finished.

"You've seen plenty of fighting and war now, son."

"Did you ever have something like that happen?"

"No, but I heard plenty of it. Prisoners sometimes didn't make it back to the rear areas. Even when the fighting was good and done. Think on it, Erik, you watched your men die. How did that make you feel?"

"Like nothing that's ever happened to me."

Peter nodded. "Precisely. Those emotions take a bit for some folks to recover from. Everyone handles combat differently. Is this Sauer a good man otherwise?"

Erik thought about that. "He's very brave. He's a party man, though. A true believer. He takes all of this propaganda much more seriously than I do."

"Well, there are plenty who do." Peter leaned forward. "We're in strange times, boy. I don't know if the party is here for good or for bad. Some of the stuff they say I figure they can't possibly believe. I certainly don't condone their conduct in every way. Still, they've made Germany great again. Greater faster than I would have ever believed possible after we lost the last war. I kept expecting the Führer to fail, but somehow he ends up on top over and over. He's some sort of genius, I guess. He's made a great many believers out of the hopeless. You can't blame Sauer and others for giving the man everything they have. You just have to keep your own wits about you."

"What should I do? I wanted to turn the lieutenant in, but Corina told me that would be disastrous for us."

Peter nodded. "For once I agree with her. He's not going to get into trouble over a couple dead Poles. It would probably be your word against his, and he outranks you. If it's bothering you, talk to him man to man. If he's as brave a soldier as you say, he won't mind speaking about what happened. He might even be happy to discuss it with you. He's probably haunted by what he did. None of us are proud of what we do in war."

Erik nodded in agreement. "Thank you, Father. That's just what I'll do."

Erik reported to his platoon after his brief leave and boarded a west-bound train. The men took over an entire passenger car, veterans taking the best seats for themselves and their equipment, while the new recruits brought in to replace the dead and wounded huddled together in a few cramped seats in the back.

Erik took no notice of these replacement troops when they'd reported to him, other than to briskly order them into their seats. As a platoon sergeant, he knew he should welcome them, but he wasn't ready to open up to them just yet. Let them sit and stew in fear for a few days. Hadn't he had to do the same? When they arrived at their new location, wherever that might be, then they would have a chat. For now, he wanted to spend time with *his* men. His companions through the Poland campaign who had shared the mutual terror, sweat, and death.

The fields and villages of Northern Germany whisked by the windows on either side as the men sipped hot soup and swapped stories from their visits home. Erik drew a flask out of his pocket and spun open the lid. He took a sip and then stared at the container. The schnapps burned his throat before he felt the liquid enter his stomach. A warmth filled the length of his body. He leaned forward, offering the flask to Corporal Messer.

Messer looked up and smiled, shaking his head slightly to decline. Erik didn't think the straitlaced Messer would take a sip, but he'd offered nonetheless. He chuckled a little to himself. The corporal had faced certain death. They were about to battle the French, who had killed millions of Germans in the last war. Messer had every right to indulge himself a little. His faith and integrity wouldn't allow it.

"Sergeant, what's the condition of your men?" He recognized the voice barking the query. Lieutenant Sauer leaned over him, hands on hips, an accusing scarecrow with straw-colored hair.

"All good, sir."

"Corporal, could you excuse us, please?"

Messer stood and saluted stiffly, then made his way down the aisle to the opposite side of the train. Sauer watched him go. Once they had a little more privacy, he eased himself down into one of the chairs, a grimace flashing across his cheek.

"Is it the wound, sir?"

Sauer grunted, ignoring the question. A flicker of pain flashed across his face. He breathed a few times, seeming to calm himself, before leaning in to address Erik. "The Poles are finished. What do you think about the French?"

"Not sure why they're even in the fight still, sir."

"They may not be. The rumor is the Führer is negotiating a face-saving peace for them—and the English."

Erik nodded. "That would be a relief."

"Are you afraid to face them?" Sauer asked.

"No, sir. But is there a point if we don't have to?"

"Very true. We've no use for France. What we want lies out in the east. Land, fields, space."

"Do you believe in all that Lebensraum propaganda then?"

Sauer looked up sharply. "It's not propaganda, Sergeant. It's our future. It's our destiny to dominate Eastern Europe. There is simply no reason that eighty-five million Germans should be bottled up in a tiny country while worthless Poles, Ukrainians, and Russians lounge around on land intended for our use."

"Is that why you shot those Polish prisoners? Because they were worthless?"

Sauer leaned forward, his cheeks filling with blood. "Something on your mind, Sergeant?"

Erik looked at the floor. "No, sir. Not really. It's just . . . they were unarmed prisoners."

Sauer snorted derisively. "Don't be sentimental. They would have slit your throat given half a chance. Besides, there are too many of them out there in our land. Gut them now or later; soon enough they must go."

"You can't mean we would kill civilians?"

Sauer's voice was like ice. "How did you get into the SS in the first place, Mueller? Haven't you paid attention to anything? We are going to take that land out east. We are going to farm it and rebuild the cities in our German image. Those Untermenschen are in the way. The future is for the strong, Sergeant. I had doubts about you from the start, but that changed in Poland. Do you know what I saw? I saw a brave young German fighting for his future. I recommended you for the Iron Cross and for promotion because I thought you were one of us. Was I mistaken?"

"No, sir. You were not."

Silence crept over them. Erik focused on the floor. The quiet chilled him. He felt a hand on his shoulder and looked up. Sauer was smiling.

"Don't you worry, Mueller. These are difficult times, and it takes a bit to get used to our new world. It's not for the weak of heart. Don't you fret about your part in things. You're a good soldier and a strong leader of men. Let others be concerned about the big picture. You'll be fine."

Erik nodded and stood as the lieutenant rose. They both extended a formal salute. After Sauer left the car, Erik sank back down into the cushions. He shouldn't have said anything. Corina was right. She always seemed to be. Had he ruined his future? Should he care? He couldn't have lived with himself if he'd never said anything. The lieutenant seemed at ease in the end. Perhaps things were indeed fine. He took a few deep breaths, closing his eyes.

"What was that all about?" asked Messer, returning to his seat.

"Nothing." He extended his flask again toward the corporal.

"No thank you, sir."

"Of course." He absentmindedly unscrewed the cap and took a deep pull, battling the demons in his mind.

The train traveled all night, sputtering to a stop now and again at a lonely station. At first Erik looked out with curiosity at all the little signs, but soon he lost interest. He still felt plagued with uncertainty, and as they drew westward a creeping fear spread through him. In Poland, he'd grown used to combat until he hardly felt the tension. Only when they'd left the front lines did the battle stress overtake him. Now, as he approached another combat zone, he could feel the uncertainty and fear again, almost as if he'd never seen combat at all. Almost.

He slept fitfully, his head lolling about as he nodded off. There was no room to lie down. He started with every lurch of the train or the blare of the lights at another stop. Near dawn the passenger car came to a final halt, and the rumble of orders thundered along the train.

Erik gathered his gear and shambled out with the rest of the platoon. Nuns served hot coffee and two slices of thick black bread per man. They were loaded onto open-backed trucks and were soon rumbling away from the platform, down a wooded dirt road that bumped and jostled the men. The nauseating smell of diesel filled their lungs. Men masked the stench with cigarettes and by holding their coffee to their nostrils.

They bounced along for a few hours down the winding road, always headed westward. Finally, when Erik felt his bones couldn't stand much more of the jarring vibrations of the truck, the convoy pulled into an open space filled with wooden buildings. Military vehicles were scattered around the compound along with a couple of tanks. SS officers stood in a cluster, watching the vehicles rolling in. Captain Vogel was there, standing among some majors and a colonel.

"Out of the trucks and into line," shouted a commander as their vehicle lurched to a stop. Erik scrambled out of the back double time along with the rest of the men. They assembled into their platoon and then formed a long triple line composing the full company. Captain Vogel walked to the front along with Sauer and the other platoon commanders.

Vogel called the men to attention. The entire line gave the Hitler salute. "Men, I trust your accommodations were comfortable for the trip?" Nobody responded. Vogel nodded and continued. "We will be joining the front lines. This front has been quiet for a very long time now." He glared sternly at them. "This could change at any moment. You are the SS! You may not know this, but the regular army doesn't want the SS to bear arms. They want to dismantle us. They have criticized our performance in Poland. The Führer will not listen to them. Instead, he is going to let us fight together as one full unit in France. I have the pleasure to tell you that we are now part of the SS-VT division. This is a new unit in the history of the world. We are the army of the party. We will perform with honor and courage. We will prove to the world not only that we are the match for the Heer, but that we surpass them! Do you understand me?!"

A tremendous roar came from the company. Vogel waited for the sound to die down. "There will be some new assignments, which will be discussed by your platoon commanders, but there is one I want to announce now. Lieutenant Althaus was wounded at Modlin and unfortunately will not be able to join us for the fighting here. I am pleased to announce that on the recommendation of Lieutenant Sauer, we are promoting Sergeant Jaeger to lieutenant of the platoon."

The men clapped again enthusiastically. Erik joined them, but he felt hot sand in his mouth and his heartbeat quickened. Sauer had promised him that promotion. There was no doubt he'd taken it away last night. The lieutenant stared at him for a moment. An eyebrow raised a fraction. He received the message: *Don't cross me again.*

CHAPTER EIGHT

Königsberg
Early October 1939

A few more days passed. Gunther still didn't return. They ate the last of their provisions. Trude watched Johannes carefully, concerned he would fade back into a fog. He didn't, but he wasn't entirely his old self, either. He was alert now. He played with Britta. He would talk to her and answer questions. But the fire was still gone. He approached nothing proactively, but instead merely reacted to her suggestions.

Thank God they still had water, but the situation had to be remedied. Finally, Trude could wait no longer. She broached the subject with her husband.

"Johannes, what are we going to do about our food?"

He looked up from his familiar chair, staring intently at her for a moment as if trying to understand what she was saying. Then he nodded slightly. "You're right; we do have to do something. I've been thinking about that the last couple of days. We cannot rely on Gunther. At least not entirely. What we need now is money. I still have some friends out there. People I haven't asked yet for their help."

"What kind of friends?" she asked.

"Gentiles. People my dad knew after the last war. People who know and respect him and who I think would be willing to help us."

"How can they help us get a ration card?" she asked.

"I'm not talking about a ration card. I'm talking about getting out of here. We need some money, and we need access to a ship. My father has an old friend, Captain Dutt, who retired from the *Kriegsmarine*. He lives up in the Steindamm District. After he retired from the military, he captained some merchant ships. I think he might even have an owner-ship interest in one. He is who we need to go and talk to. He would have both money and possible contacts to get us on a ship out of here."

"When would we go?" she asked.

He stared at her for a moment. "I can't go, you have to."

She was shocked by his words. "What are you talking about? I can't go by myself. Johannes, listen to me! I've been through enough. I'm exhausted and starving. Britta is going mad cooped up in here. I can't keep taking care of all this on my own. I don't know this person, and he doesn't know me. He's not going to help me; he will only help you."

"I can't leave the house again, Trude. Think about it. We took a huge risk when I went to the grocery store. I'm wanted by the Gestapo. They will have a description of me, possibly with pictures posted all over the city. Certainly, the regular police will be looking out for me. There's no way I can leave this house. You're going to have to do it."

She realized to her horror that he spoke the truth. If he left the house, there was every chance he would never come back. Then she would have no connections and no hope. She could just imagine Gunther coming back to discover that her husband had been arrested. What would he do to her then?

"You're right," she said finally. "I must go." She turned away to head upstairs, but he was there. Hands on her waist. Holding her back.

"Wait until after dark, my dear. I doubt they have a description of you, but it's possible."

She nodded, the fear embracing her.

They spent the next several hours in silence. Moments ticked by one after another as if each second desired to desperately cling to the clock a little longer. Finally, the sky darkened and the day faded into twilight and then darkness. In the meantime, they pored over a map of Königsberg. Johannes traced the route with his finger and forced her to repeat the directions over and over until he was satisfied she had them memorized.

Her hands were clammy. She'd never been particularly good with maps, and the captain's home was a long way off. It would take at least an hour to get there. An hour through unfamiliar streets where any police officer who might inquire about her papers would immediately arrest her. If that happened, she knew she would never see her family again.

Johannes drew out pen and paper and composed a long letter for the captain, explaining the circumstances and asking for his help. He carefully creased the note and placed it in an envelope for her to carry when it was time.

She reached out for it, surprised her hands were shaking. "I don't think I can do this," she whispered. "There has to be some other way. Couldn't you go? It's dark now."

He shook his head. "It's too risky. I'm sorry, but it must be you."

She nodded, understanding. She embraced him and her daughter and made her way out the front door into the night. The evening was cool and crisp. She was taken aback for a moment by the coldness until she realized she had not been out of the home for over a month. *It was summer when I was last out,* she thought, remembering their walks through the *Strassen* and *Gärten* of Königsberg before the war. She thought life was so difficult back then. The loss of their jobs. The hatred and suspicion from neighbors. Now it all seemed a pleasant memory.

I must pay attention, she chastised herself. There was danger everywhere. She scanned her surroundings. The street was near deserted—even of cars. She looked around carefully to make sure nobody was watching and then she made her way.

Each step seemed a miracle. She kept waiting for a voice out of the shadows. The stern command of a police officer materializing from the darkness to demand her papers. Here and there she passed a civilian pedestrian. She felt their eyes boring in on her but realized this was probably her imagination. They couldn't tell she was a Jew just by looking at her. Just another fair-skinned brown-haired woman walking along the streets of Königsberg.

The trip seemed to take an eternity. She was sure she would get lost, but somehow she kept the names and turns straight. She rounded a corner and realized she had arrived. Across the street, rising out of a forested hill, rose a towering stone house—almost a castle. A narrow cobblestone driveway wound up through the trees toward the voluminous structure looming above.

Trude scurried across the street, her head bent against a windy flurry of snow that threatened to blow her over. She climbed carefully up the driveway, slipping on the treacherous stones. She arrived at the front door winded and trembling. She was safe for now, but she walked into new dangers. There were no guarantees how she would be greeted here. What if this Captain Dutt was a friend of the new regime?

She turned a metal knob, and a shrill, trilling clang rang out within. A minute passed and then another. Nobody came. *What if he's not home?* she thought with panic. *I came all this way for nothing.* She rang again, and to her vast relief the enormous wooden door opened to reveal an elderly gentleman staring out at her curiously.

"May I assist you, madam?" he asked.

"I'm here to see Captain Dutt," she said.

"Hmm. And who might you be?"

"I'm Trude Bensheim. My husband is Johannes Bensheim. My father-in-law was a good friend of the captain."

The gentleman stared at her for a moment longer as if deciding what to do. Finally, he spoke again. "I will apprise the captain of your presence," he said. "Please have a seat here, and I will be back down in a few moments."

She stepped into the entry hall, and the gentleman disappeared through a side door. Trude took a seat on a high-backed hard wooden chair resting beneath several large paintings of what must have been the captain's ancestors. She glanced around while she waited. The wooden walls were adorned with these oil paintings of ancestors and what appeared to be the depictions of naval battles of the past. The walls were a rich cherry and the floors were covered in silk carpets. She couldn't imagine how much even one of them might have cost. She forgot herself there in the moment, lost in the detail and beauty of her surroundings.

"Frau Bensheim?" An elderly voice greeted her, mixed with age and power. A commanding voice. She looked up and there was the captain, every bit of seventy years old with iron-gray hair and powerful features. A pince-nez perched jauntily on the bridge of his nose as he watched her, scrutinizing her over the steel-gray ocean of his suit. He examined her curiously, as if not sure what to do with her. He clamped his hands tightly together. His posture was erect.

"I'm rather surprised to see you here this evening, Frau Bensheim. I had assumed you and your husband were wise enough to have departed our lovely new Germany long ago."

"We were supposed to leave in September, but our visas were revoked."

"I see. Well, you had better come in and tell me why you're here."

She followed the captain out of the entryway and down the long hallway to his study. His office was a cavernous room with floor-to-ceiling bookshelves. Intervening spaces were filled with antique swords and rifles. A massive mahogany desk floated in the center of the study like a dreadnought, dominating the room. He motioned her to a chair in front of this behemoth, and then he himself came to rest behind it, sitting stiffly with arms crossed and eyes piercing her.

Still she was quiet. She was unsure what to say, how to begin.

"Are you thirsty?" he asked. "Or perhaps you would like something to eat?"

At this suggestion, her hands shook and her mouth watered. In her fear and exhaustion, she'd forgotten just how hungry she was. She tried to answer him, but the words would not form so she merely nodded.

"I'll take that as a yes to both," he said. "Franz!" he called in a booming voice. Soon the elderly gentleman returned. "Bring us some tea and refreshments!"

He turned his attention back to her. "Now, please tell me why you're here."

She didn't know why, but this small act of kindness released the flood of her words. She knew she should've been more careful, but she found herself telling this gentleman everything about the organization, the arrests, about Johannes's collapse and Gunther's advances. The tears rolled down her cheeks, but she did not pause to wipe them. She stopped only when Franz returned with tea and food. There were biscuits, cookies, and finger sandwiches. She was ravenous, and they stopped talking for a half an hour while they ate. Throughout the meal he stared at her passively. She didn't know what he might be thinking; perhaps the Gestapo was already on its way. She didn't care anymore. At least for this moment, her stomach was truly full. After all these months she dared to hope that she had somebody who would listen to what was happening to her. Finally, she continued her story. By the time she related all the details, she had been there for hours.

He watched to make sure she was finished before he shifted in his seat. She still didn't know what his reaction might be. Had Johannes been wrong about him? Wrong to trust him?

He spoke, his voice beginning as a light breeze on the water but growing in strength until it had the force of a whipping gale.

"What you just told me, young Frau, is one of the more incredible stories I've ever heard," he said. "I'm not surprised by Johannes, for his actions were the actions of his organization. He is clearly his father's son. But what you tell me about my own people, about Gunther in particular, surprises and saddens me. I do not know what is become of our country. I served the kaiser. I watched our navy grow and our nation rise until it was one of the greatest in the world. Then our emperor embroiled us in that stupid, senseless war. We lost everything, and in the chaos that followed, we let this party of criminals and fools take over. They play on our fear—on our base emotions. Now there is no honor left in Germany.

"You come here for my help? You risk much to do so. Don't you fear, my dear, you shall have it. Your husband was right to expect my trust and my aid."

The captain leaned back, his fingers absently scratching the opposite elbow. "The tricky part is, what to do? I have money. Not endless amounts, mind you, but money enough. I can help you there. But a ship?" He shook his head. "I'm retired. I've sold my interest in the merchant industry. I do have some connections, but can they be trusted?" He shrugged as if considering the point. "That is something I must think on. For now, I will help you as I am most immediately able."

He rose and made his way to a cabinet. He opened the door and retrieved a heavy metal lockbox from within. Grimacing a little at the weight, he shuffled back to the desk and gingerly set the container down on the surface. He drew keys from his pocket and fumbled through them until he found the one he was looking for. He set the key into the lock and then opened the top, reaching in to carefully pull out several stacks of money. He thumbed through the notes, his lips counting silently, then returned a stack and brought the remainder over, extending his hand to her.

"Here are fifty thousand Reichsmarks. Hopefully this will be enough to obtain a ration card on the black market. Who knows?" He shrugged. "Perhaps that's enough to get you passage on a ship? Although I doubt it in these times. But never worry, I'm going to send you home with as much food as you can carry. I want you to come back in a few days. I will check with my connections and see what I can do about getting your family out of Germany."

She was so relieved. Trude stepped forward and embraced him. She could feel him stiffen beneath her arms, but she didn't care. She had to show him some gratitude. Tears washed over her again like waterfalls down his back as she clung to him. He patted her, gently repeating over and over, "There, there."

Before long, she was leaving through the front door, two bags of groceries in her hands and the money tucked inside of her coat, new hope in her heart.

The fresh groceries lifted their spirits tremendously, and a promising new atmosphere filled the Bensheim home for several days. Johannes almost seemed himself, laughing and playing with Britta and telling her stories of England and her grandparents. Trude whisked about the kitchen preparing meals just like it was the old days. Except for the fact that they could not leave their home, things almost felt normal.

The food supply quickly dwindled again, however, and Trude knew she would soon have to brave the uncertain streets to visit their savior, Captain Dutt. Still, the risk could be greeted with greater prospects because there was hope now. She could imagine their family steaming out of the harbor from Königsberg bound for a neutral port and freedom. She whistled childhood tunes as she thought of her parents smiling, waiting for them in England.

Finally, the day arrived when she could wait no longer. She decided to bring the Reichsmarks with her just in case. There was a chance that if she was detained by the police, she could bribe her way out of the situation with the money. It was also possible the captain would need the notes back if he had secured them passage on a ship. She dressed herself carefully and applied makeup, wanting to look perfect. It wasn't that she needed to feel beautiful for the captain or that she sensed that her attractiveness was important to him. She simply felt in some small way that he deserved her very best and that today could well be a momentous occasion.

The time came to depart. She embraced Johannes and Britta, clinging to her daughter for a moment. She stepped cautiously outside for the trip to the captain's home. The journey seemed much easier this time, and while the dangers were just as real, they felt less so. She traveled the familiar kilometers to the captain's home without incident. She kept her head down and walked with a brisk but casual pace. There was one frightening moment at a busy intersection where she encountered a police officer directing traffic, but he was intent on his duties and uninterested in the pedestrians crossing this way and that in the frosty evening.

Soon she was at the captain's home and again knocking at his front door. Franz answered, all smiles this time, and directed her to Dutt's study, where the captain soon joined her.

Captain Dutt seemed just as stern as the last time, but he did awkwardly pat her on the shoulder when he came in. He was dressed in a severe navy-blue suit, and he helped himself along with a long black cane topped by a silver handle. He wore highly polished jackboots that clomped methodically along the hardwood floors until muffled by a silk rug that dominated the center of the room.

"Well, Frau Bensheim, I see you've made it back here safely. I did not know if I would ever see you again. I'd hoped perhaps the money I've given you was sufficient for you and your family to make your getaway."

She shook her head. "We've heard nothing from Gunther," she said. "Not for ages. I don't know that we will ever hear from him again. I think he just took our money and went his way."

"That might be for the best," said the captain. "I do not know the man, but I trust no Nazi, particularly SS, and neither should you."

"I never wanted to," she explained. "He was Johannes's contact. A last resort really. He's crude and a letch. Nothing like you."

The captain blushed slightly. "Kind words. Oh yes, I'm glad I decided to help you. Although I must say with great disappointment I've not been able to do everything I had hoped."

"What do you mean?" she asked.

"Try as I might, I cannot secure passage on a ship for you. I contacted several of my partners and friends. Not, I must admit, without a little risk to myself. None of them are willing to run that kind of danger for a Jewish family." He leaned forward, his voice lowering to a whisper. "I don't know how much you know about what's going on out there, but they are truly cracking down on anyone who helps the Jews. The war has made everything much worse. The Gestapo is arresting people now for the most trivial of reasons. People are disappearing in the middle of the night and not coming back." He wagged a finger at her. "Not just Jews, mind you, but gentiles, too. I hear tell of neighbors reporting neighbors. Children turning in parents for making an unpatriotic statement or listening to foreign radio transmissions." Dutt shook his head. "These are terrible times."

Her heart sank a little, but she knew she mustn't be rude. This man had already placed himself in danger on their behalf. "Thank you so much for trying," she said. "You did so much for us, giving us the food and the money." She reached into her pocket and pulled out the stack of bank notes. "I have it here, if you would like it back?"

He put both hands in the air, pushing away from her. "Oh no, you keep those and I'll double the amount for the bargain." He reached into his desk and pulled out a thick envelope, extending his arm out to her. "A hundred thousand Reichsmarks should get you a long way on the black market, one way or another. I only wish there was more I could do for you."

She tried to resist, but he opened her hand and placed the envelope into it, forcing her fingers around it. "No time to be stubborn," he boomed. "Like I said, I only wish I could do more. I will keep trying, and if I find anything more out, I will come to you. That reminds me," he said, hobbling back to his desk to retrieve a pen. "What is your address?"

She hesitated for a moment, afraid to tell him for fear he might turn her in. But how could she deny this after everything he had done for them? She called out the numbers and the street while he scribbled down the information and read the address back to her.

He placed a hand on her shoulder, giving her a reassuring squeeze. "Thank you for trusting me with this," he said. "If I learn anything else, I will come to you. Do not put too much hope in me, however; I've already exhausted my best contacts. I do not hold out hope that others I know less well will be more accommodating, but perhaps Gott will send us a miracle."

She squeezed his hand tightly. Here was a real man. Somebody who did not owe anything to them. Here was a true German who was risking his own life to try to help. She rose and turned to leave, but he stopped her, calling for Franz and making arrangements for another load of groceries for her to take. They stood silently in the study for a few more minutes while the staff collected the food. Then she thanked him again.

"Go with Gott. And remember, do not trust this Gunther. No matter what he promises, he is your enemy."

She nodded silently in reply and turned to leave. She took a few steps down the hallway before she paused. Some force within her drew her back. She returned quietly to the entryway of the study and saw him, face buried in his hands, slumped over his desk weeping. Her heart was torn to see such a brave, wonderful man crying on their behalf. She raised fingers to her lips, blowing a silent kiss before she departed for home.

The trip back was the same as before, although her arms ached under the weight of the food. She didn't mind. She knew they would have something to eat. Their precious daughter would not go hungry, at least for a little longer. She worried that she might seem suspicious carrying sacks of groceries kilometer after kilometer through the darkened streets, but nobody seemed to notice. She reached the house, fumbling for the keys in the dark, but the door opened on its own, and she walked in excited to tell Johannes the news. She froze in the doorway. Gunther stood at the entrance. He had opened the door for her.

"Come on in," he said, grinning. "I was wondering where you had wandered off to. Johannes has been very evasive." He reached out to take the groceries from her hands, keeping contact with her body for a moment longer than was necessary.

He reached his hand up and pulled back the top of the bag, peering in with a show of interest. "What do we have here?" he asked. "Such a clever girl. You must tell me how you get groceries without a ration card. But then these are not grocery bags. Tsk, tsk, it looks like someone has a friend. Who might that be?" he asked, drawing his face even closer to her.

"Nobody of importance," she answered, looking quickly to Johannes, who was sitting in his chair watching the two of them impassively.

Gunther laughed, taking a step back, his eyes wandering up and down her figure. "Such a smart girl. I'll let you keep your secrets for now, but not forever, mind you." He stepped farther into the house, motioning for her to follow. "Come on in, please. Perhaps you can use your new-found bounty to make us a fine meal. I have important news for you. I was just about to tell your husband when you so pleasantly arrived."

Gunther took the bags out of her hands and carried the groceries into the kitchen. She stayed for a moment at the threshold, trying to communicate silently with Johannes. He looked past her, and she felt the sharp claws of fear piercing her again. What if he collapsed back into himself again?

"Are you coming?" Gunther called from the kitchen. She took a step toward Johannes, finally catching his attention. She nodded toward the kitchen, silently pleading with him to focus. To her relief he shook his head and took a deep breath. He nodded, rose out of the chair, squared his shoulders, and moved into the kitchen.

Gunther was busy putting the groceries away as if he lived there. He had rolled up his sleeves, and he was whistling contentedly to himself. He finished quickly, putting aside some sausages, sauerkraut, and a bottle of white wine. He sliced the sausages with a deft hand, chatting away about inconsequential matters as if they were all just old friends having dinner together on a Saturday evening. He poured wine and handed them glasses, clinking his own with them and then taking a deep drink.

"Well, my friends, I told you I have news for you, and the news is good." He reached into his jacket and pulled out a packet. "Brand-new ration cards and identification papers." He shook his head. "You have no idea how difficult these were to obtain. You would think the Gestapo could get anything they want, but times have changed." He set the package on the table and looked up at them, frowning. "What's wrong with the two of you?" he asked. He reached over and placed his fingers on the bottom of Trude's glass, pushing it up toward her lips. "Drink, drink. When you've finished the toast, come help me with the sausages. Johannes, butter the bread. We must celebrate."

Trude willed herself to move around the counter, starting the stove and pulling out an iron skillet. Soon the sausages were crackling in the pan as Gunther chatted away about the difficult job of obtaining the ration cards and the false identifications.

"These documents will get you by for now," he said. "You'll be able to obtain food, and if you're stopped on the street, these papers will identify you as good little Germans just like me." He looked at them and paused for dramatic effect. "That's not even the best news," he said, moving around the table to Trude. He stood close to her, making her skin crawl. "I'll tell you the rest, although you could show some more appreciation."

She stood frozen, waiting for him to touch her again. Thankfully he stepped back and turned to the table, reaching out to pour himself another full glass of wine. He shrugged slightly. "Oh well, I guess it doesn't matter," he said almost to himself. "I can understand the difficulty of thanking someone who has done so much for you." He snapped his fingers. "Where was I? Oh yes, the biggest surprise of all." He rang his hands together. "I have the best news. I will be able to secure you a spot on a ship soon. If you think the ration cards and ID were difficult, this was almost impossible. I've worked many days, but I have a captain who's willing to play . . . for a price, of course." Trude saw Johannes's face light up at this, and she felt even greater relief. He almost looked himself.

Her husband rose from the table. "Thank you, Gunther," he said. "Thank you so much." He grasped Gunther's hand with both of his, shaking it profusely.

The German warmed at this and smiled, taking another deep drink. He looked up at Trude. "What about you, my dear? Don't I get a proper thank-you?" He moved toward her again, but this time Johannes stepped between them. Her husband reached his arms out and grabbed Gunther by both wrists. The men struggled together for a moment, but Johannes held him firmly.

"That's enough of that," he said. "That's my wife you're speaking to."

Gunther's face flashed fire, and he stepped back violently, ripping his hands away. His hands clenched into fists, and Trude feared he would strike her husband. The German closed his eyes, taking a couple of deep breaths, and seemed to relax. He unclenched his fingers, raised his hands into the air as if in surrender, and laughed. "Fine, fine," he said jovially. "I'll knock it off. It was always just a little fun, mind you. You have a beautiful wife. I don't have to tell you that," he said, winking at Johannes.

Trude felt the gratitude washing over her. This was her husband, the man she had fallen in love with, risking his life for her. Afraid of no one. The sausages were done, and she quickly served each of them a plate, cutting up some bread with butter and refilling their glasses with wine. They took their meal in relative silence, although Johannes, out of politeness, inquired for more detail about the ration cards. He thanked Gunther again for everything he'd done for them. They clinked glasses with him in a toast to their future. After some time, the meal was over and Gunther rose to leave.

"How soon can we expect passage on a ship?" asked Johannes.

Gunther turned to them. "As soon as you're able to make the payment."

"What payment?" asked Johannes. "We've already given you everything we have."

"We used that money for strategies that unfortunately didn't work out," said Gunther, shrugging. "What can I say, my friend? This is war. I will need a bit more to make this new deal work."

"How much more?" asked Trude.

"Unfortunately, it's quite a sum," he said. "The price is one million Reichsmarks."

"That's impossible," stammered Johannes. He took a step toward Gunther.

The Gestapo agent raised his arms. "I'd be careful, my friend," he said. "I let the moment in the kitchen pass, but I won't let another. Don't forget who I am and who you are. I know it's a lot of money, but I don't need it all now. The ship will be there when you've raised the funds. Don't tell me you're not capable of doing it; you're the smartest little Jew I've ever seen. I know you'll get the money. I obtained the ration cards for you so you can take the time you need, but mind you," he said, pointing his finger, "it won't be a pfennig less."

He exhaled deeply, as if he had just relieved a tremendous burden. He bowed to them slightly. "Trude, thank you for another charming evening." He winked at her then purposely looked her up and down again before returning his stare to Johannes. Her husband said nothing. Gunther smiled as if satisfied, then turned to the door, whistling as he stepped into the night.

CHAPTER NINE

Belgium
May 10, 1940

Erik and his group broke into a loose jog in the darkness. It was not yet dawn. Low-hanging branches clawed at his face, and he could hear muffled swearing behind him. He commanded them to silence in the lowest whisper he could manage, then turned and continued.

In the distance the rat-a-tat of an MG 42 broke the silence, echoing through the forest like staccato thunder. Erik almost mistook the booming thuds of his heart for the pounding percussion of artillery. He hadn't fought in eight months. A lifetime. An eternity. All the fears were here. An old enemy returning home.

The hot whistle of bullets flickered through the trees. The enemy was out there somewhere. He wasn't sure whether they were here in force or if this was some lonely outpost delivering a parting embrace before retreat.

His group spilled out of the forest and into a field, now semi-illuminated by the ever-lightening sky. In the distance a farmhouse loomed, a lonely sentinel in a field of hay. He gestured for his men to follow him.

They spread out and sprinted in a wild zigzag fashion. He waited for the bullets to come. Expected them as always, but they didn't arrive. The farmhouse filled up the horizon. Thirty meters out, then less. Soon just a few footsteps. He finally slammed against it. Too hard. Erik's shoulder flared in pain, but he didn't care. He hugged the protective shield that would hold back the bullets, at least for a little while.

He counted heads. Everyone had made it. A surge of relief. Where had the gunshots gone? The Belgians must have retreated. If they were Belgian. They could be British or even French. They'd been told not to expect any of the primary allies here, but intelligence was often faulty. He crept along the wall of the farmhouse until he was near the edge. He motioned for his men to remain where they were. He peered cautiously around the corner. Fragments of stone and dust exploded around him, long before he heard the crackle of a machine gun. He sputtered and pulled back, throwing himself against the wall. He sat for a moment trying to catch his heart. He ran his hands up and down searching for wounds. There were none. He was safe for now, but the machine gun was still out there.

More of his men were coming up now through the field. The farmhouse must have blocked the gunners' view, he realized—as no shots were coming his way. He traced the angle in his mind, calculating the rough trajectory and location of the gun entrenchment. An officer landed hard next to him. He looked over and was surprised to see Captain Vogel. The whole company must be here.

"Sergeant, what do you know?" he asked.

"Not much, sir, but there's a gun entrenchment out there. Automatic. Likely something like our MG 42."

"Did you see it?" he asked.

"No, sir. I think it might be about there," he reported, gesturing at an invisible line through the farmhouse wall.

"Any idea of the distance?"

Mueller shook his head.

"Where is Sauer?" the captain asked. A hand flew up a few meters down the farmhouse wall. It was the lieutenant. Vogel motioned for him, and Sauer moved mechanically toward them—cool in combat as ever, his *Stahlhelm* clutched under his arm and his sun-bleached hair a burning match in the dawn.

"Jawohl?"

"Sauer. There's a gun out there in a fixed position. Mueller thinks it's about there," said the captain, echoing Erik's gesture through the wall. "It's not going anywhere and neither are we. I need your platoon to take it."

Sauer nodded and paused for a moment, considering the situation. Finally, he looked up at Mueller.

"Sergeant. Move your group out and take that position. I want Messer and two others to lay covering fire from that corner. You lead the assault with the rest. Go on now."

Erik absorbed the order from the lieutenant. One of their few interactions these last eight months. They'd never spoken of the train or the promotion. Why the lieutenant selected him for this now, he didn't know. Perhaps to give him a chance to redeem himself. Or maybe to get rid of him. It didn't matter. An order was an order.

Erik called his group over and gave quick commands. He knew what he wanted to try to do, he just didn't know what he was dealing with out there. The machine gun was a big problem, but he had no idea what else was waiting for them. Messer and two others moved into position near the corner of the farmhouse. He would lead the other five men with him on the main assault. He slung his machine pistol over his shoulder and removed an M24 *Stielhandgranate* grenade, a "potato masher," gesturing for others to do the same. He waited a few more moments, arming the grenade as he did. Messer aimed around the corner from a standing position while the other two men leaned around in a crouch. They all fired simultaneously, and at the same instance Erik sprinted out from behind the farmhouse and into the field.

The sky was bright now, and the land in front of him jarred up and down. He could hear the bullets chipping stones around him. He strained to see the gun emplacement ahead of him, no more than thirty meters in the distance: a mound of sandbags arranged in a semicircle abutting a burned-out car. The nest rested at the edge of the outlying buildings of a small town. As Erik sprinted on, he hurled the grenade with all his strength and watched the great metal mace spin through the air over and over in a high arch that faded away and sliced downward toward the car. The grenade bounced off the dirt and skipped up, blowing apart a few meters short of the target.

More grenades flew in from behind him, but none seemed to be hitting the mark. Erik sprinted toward the nest, running a little to the right to provide a more difficult target and because he wanted desperately to look over the area and see what other potential threats awaited him. He knew he could be hit any moment, and everything had to be focused on the gun position. He could see the barrel flaring and the crew's eyes intent behind the shroud of smoke, tilting the weapon slowly to the left and ever closer to him and his hard-charging group. He could hear screams echo behind him. He threw a glance over his shoulder and watched as first one of his men, then another toppled over as the bullets found their mark. He turned his head forward again and rushed onward, slinging his weapon around. The barrel edged ever closer to him now, but he was closing the distance fast. Twenty meters, then fifteen. The screams behind him filled his ears. The barrel was almost on top of him. He wasn't going to make it. He raised his machine pistol and fired wildly into the gun nest, unable to aim. Figures in the position jumbled in and out of his vision as he poured fire toward them, continuing to charge.

He leaped over the sandbags and in among the enemy. He smashed the butt of his weapon into the nose of one of the soldiers. A metallic flash ripped across his face, and he felt the burning tear of his cheek. A scarlet fountain erupted from the wound. He turned his weapon and fired in the direction of his attacker. The enemy jerked and then slumped onto the ground. He stood panting, turning his weapon back and forth, but all the men in the machine gun position were wounded or dead.

He waited for a counterattack. Death surrounded him. One moment passed, then another, but nothing happened. He raised his hand tentatively to his cheek. The cut was long. He reached into his tunic and ripped out a handkerchief, pressing the white cloth against his wound. Harsh hands grabbed him from behind, jerking him down to the ground. He flinched, waiting for a blow, but he was staring into the face of a corporal in his platoon, his expression a shroud of grave concern. His lips moved, but Erik could hear no sounds. He didn't know what the man was trying to say to him.

The soldier reached out again, pulling Erik to his feet. He looked down; there were five bodies in the nest with him. None of them moved. They were Belgians. Erik steadied himself, reaching out to remove the corporal's hand from his back. He was a little better and could stand on his own. He was shocked by the close-quarter carnage. He'd killed all five of these men in the attack.

He kept the cloth pressed tightly on his cheek and took deep breaths, trying to compose himself and obtain his bearings. He looked around for his men. Two of his group mates were coming up through the smoke of the field, but he saw with horror seven figures twisted and silent on the ground. He'd lost almost his entire group.

Before he could deal with his emotions, Captain Vogel was there clasping his shoulder, speaking warm words of congratulations. Sauer was there, too, scowling fiercely.

Vogel looked him over, pulling the cloth from his face to stare in concern at the wound.

"Get that attended to, Mueller," he said. "That was a brave piece of work out there. Maybe the most courageous I've ever seen." He turned to Sauer. "He's making lieutenant this time, and I don't want to hear a word about it." Sauer didn't respond, but stared at Mueller for a moment and turned to walk away. Vogel clapped Erik on the shoulder again, and then turned to attend to other matters. Messer came forward and congratulated him, all smiles. The corporal escorted his commander, his friend, back toward the original line, in search of the company medic.

⸻

As the days of May passed, Lieutenant Mueller grew used to his new rank and command responsibilities. He oversaw a platoon now, a much larger group, although their company was devastated by combat, and significantly understrength. He had barely twenty men, but the battalion promised reinforcements soon.

As combat continued day after day, Erik still expected death at any time. Miraculously, he never seemed to be hit. Again and again, a man would fall right next to him. Sometimes they were wounded, sometimes dead. The enemy somehow missed him, as if he carried a charm or wore a cloak of protection.

He was reporting directly to Vogel now and was on an equal basis with Sauer. His fellow lieutenant and former commander seemed none too pleased with the promotion or the equal footing. He avoided Erik, turning away during company command sessions or gazing coldly and arrogantly at Erik, a haughty snake ready to strike.

The war continued with miraculous fortunes for the Germans. The German panzer armies crashed through the enemy lines and into the open countryside. The Belgians, Dutch, British, and French reeled back in retreat, their defenses sundered.

As May faded away, the worst seemed already over. Erik's unit rumbled north, riding on the backs of panzers in a moving battle with the British. The unit drove east and then north into France, ripping through the feeble defenses and driving the British closer and closer to their ports on the channel coast. Erik knew the Germans had achieved nothing like this in the last war. Nobody had expected this, perhaps least of all the Germans. Erik had expected to live on the western front for years perhaps, away from his family, if he wasn't killed outright. Now it seemed that in weeks, perhaps even days, the war might be over. The men they captured were dejected and had no fight left in them. They came in droves, their arms up, wanting only safety, food, and protection.

That morning Erik and Messer traveled to the company headquarters for a briefing on their plans for the day. During the discussion, he learned there was a British unit in front of them, entrenched in a nearby village with possible armored support. The Royal Air Force, so vaunted, failed to materialize in the skies over Belgium or France. Anytime Erik heard the roar of a piston engine overhead, he saw only German Stukas with Messerschmitt Bf 109s arcing across the sky in escort. How could the British compete in this war without armor and air support? he wondered. They were hardly any better than the Poles.

He returned to his command station in the shadow of a Panzer II tank. Sergeant Messer was there, his trusted friend also newly promoted to lead one of Erik's groups. He was Mueller's right-hand man, and he depended on his straitlaced friend.

"Good morning, sir," said the sergeant. Erik saw the NCO was reading the Bible. He smiled to himself. The SS might frown on the Christian religion, but as far as he was concerned, they could use the Lord's help. Just because they were winning didn't mean they were invincible. He knew his whole platoon could be killed within a few seconds under the wrong circumstances. A whisper and you were in heaven.

"How are the men?" asked Erik.

"They're well enough. What's up ahead?" Sergeant Messer asked.

"Trouble for sure. But I'm not sure how much."

"Any idea what type?"

Erik nodded. "Brits. Lots of them. Perhaps a tank or two."

"Hurricanes or Spitfires?" asked the sergeant, referring to British airplanes.

"I doubt it. They've made themselves scarce."

The sergeant grunted. "I'll prepare the men. Is it just us or the whole company?"

"It's all of us, but we're in the lead."

Messer chuckled. "As always. Tanks coming up with us?"

Erik shook his head. "They want us to flush the armor out first."

"Lovely. I enjoy being the bait."

Erik laughed in return. "Agreed, but what can we do? Might as well get it over with. You take the first group up. I'll be behind you on both sides, moving a bit slower and firing in the village."

The sergeant nodded. "Sounds about right. We have any air cover ourselves?"

"Could be. Captain is checking into it."

Erik watched as Messer spread the word, bellowing not only to his group but throughout the platoon. Erik checked his weapon, the same machine pistol he'd carried all the way from Poland. He had a full clip and three reserves in a pouch connected to his belt. Vogel had told him to lose the machine pistol; he should be concentrating on tactics and leading the men. But Erik never felt comfortable with the idea. He would do his own fighting. He didn't want other people to die for his mistakes. Of course, he knew this had already happened many times. But that was part of war.

The time to move was fast approaching. Sergeant Messer had his group at the ready. They were tucked behind the Panzer II tank just inside a line of trees and out of sight.

Erik caught Messer's attention and gave him the signal. The sergeant sprinted from behind the tank and was followed quickly by his group, spreading out rapidly in a wide arc, with the men several meters apart from each other so that when they hit the clearing they would make no single target for anyone. The other two groups moved quickly out of the trees, following behind the lead group. Erik expected to see the telltale flash of rifle fire and hear the whistle of incoming artillery, but there was nothing. Perhaps the intelligence was wrong.

Mueller shouted an order, and the two reserve groups picked up their pace, struggling to catch up to the assault group that was outdistancing them.

As they ran, Erik kept straining at the horizon, looking for any sign of the enemy. Perhaps the British had waited, holding back, knowing more men would advance, giving any tanks that were waiting fat, rich targets to lay their shells on. Heartbeat after heartbeat passed, and still there was no fire. He searched for targets in the village. He realized he could make out the forms of men among the rubble of the building, but they were not shooting, not aiming.

Then he knew why. The British in the village were standing among the rocks and the crumbling houses, arms to the heavens, surrendering without a fight. He'd never seen this before, not like this. Some units had given up without too much of a fight, but always in the past they'd encountered at least some resistance and often fierce fighting before anyone waved the white flag.

They crossed the remaining distance quickly and soon were a bare ten meters from the British. Dozens of them stood at the edge of the village, hands up. As the men reached the first buildings, Erik ordered his men to move forward carefully and take the enemy soldiers into custody, keeping an eye out for any possible counterattack.

Minutes passed and soon the whole company was up. Vogel arrived, congratulating Erik on his courageous advance and the capture of the British. "Mueller," he said, "take your platoon through town and look for any tanks or stragglers."

Erik moved his men into the cluster of buildings, immediately spreading out among the houses of the village, moving from wall to wall, looking for the enemy and the tanks. Eventually they reached the other end of the small collection of houses, but there were no more enemies.

Finally, he breathed a sigh of relief and brought his men back together. He congratulated them on a fine assault. "Let's head back. We will get something to drink and grab some rations." The town was quiet. Erik couldn't hear any explosions in the distance or the drone of airplanes overhead. He couldn't remember a moment in the past month more tranquil this.

The peace was torn suddenly by the ripping thunder of machine gun fire. Erik jerked in response and threw himself against the wall, his men scrambling for cover. Erik thought the sound was coming from behind them. He couldn't tell for sure. In the enclosed space the rattle of fire cracked from every direction.

There was a counterattack coming from somewhere, that was for sure. They needed to get back to the company. He quickly assembled his platoon, giving rapid orders. They spread out into groups and moved back cautiously house to house, returning to the front of the village. In the distance Erik was surprised to see Germans standing casually. Why weren't they taking cover? His platoon moved closer. Some of the men were clumped as if in a crowd. Others were facing away, toward the village, wearing strange expressions.

Then Erik knew. He sprinted forward the last few meters and into the assemblage, shoving his way through until he saw the nightmare in front of him. At the base of a small rise right before the village the bodies of dozens of British soldiers lay. An MG 42 rested no more than ten meters away. Smoke still billowed out of the barrels. Sauer stood directly behind the gun, hands on his hips, examining the dead. He pointed with his pistol at a still-moving form in the mass, and a soldier fired a few more rounds into the moaning figure. The British soldier's body leaped into the air, jerking for a few moments before it was still.

"What the hell are you doing!" demanded Erik, screaming across the distance between the two lieutenants.

Sauer looked up, unfazed, and stared coldly at Mueller for a moment, his mouth curling in a slight grin. "I'm doing the Führer's work," he responded unabashedly.

"These are innocent, unarmed men! They surrendered peacefully!"

"They are enemies of the Fatherland," retorted Sauer.

"This is murder!"

"No, Mueller, it is merely war."

"Sauer, what the hell have you done?" A new voice snapped sharply in the morning air. Erik looked over. Captain Vogel stared with wide eyes at the carnage in front of them. "Answer me!"

Sauer turned to his commander with the same impassive face, his lip twitching in disdain. "This is nothing, Captain, just disposing of a little vermin."

"Lieutenant Sauer, you are under arrest," shouted Vogel. He pointed to one of his own men. "Take the lieutenant into custody. I have to report back to battalion headquarters. I'll return within the hour." He approached Erik, pale. "I'm putting you in charge of the company for the time being, Mueller. I'm going to take this monster back to headquarters. They will deal with him there. Spread the men out in the village in a defensive position. Do not advance until I return."

Erik acknowledged Vogel and gave the orders. The men started to spread out, and Erik detailed a duty group to inspect the prisoners. "If any of them are alive, get them medical attention as soon as possible."

Messer nodded. "Don't worry, Lieutenant Mueller; we're not all like that. We are Germans. We have honor. That coward will soon be forgotten."

Vogel got in his command car. Two guards moved into the back with Lieutenant Sauer between them. The vehicle rolled into motion, headed down the road toward the woods.

Everything was quiet again, but only for a moment. Erik heard a sputtering rotary engine above. A fighter must be returning home. He craned his neck for a glance but was shocked to see the brown outline of a British RAF Hurricane racing ever lower. He saw the flash of the wings followed by the machine gun shells as they thudded down the road in parallel paths, ripping through the command car in the distance. The vehicle lurched this way and that before disintegrating in a belch of fire and smoke. The awful sounds echoed in his ears as he watched the fighter rise above the tree line, arch to the left, and disappear, leaving the billowing wreck behind.

CHAPTER TEN

Königsberg
May 1940

Trude stood in the kitchen, listening to the war news on an old radio she'd found in a back closet. She washed the dishes as she kept one ear on the news. She opened her cupboards, placing porcelain plates next to pots and pans she'd purchased at a used furniture store. The commentator claimed glorious victory for German arms against the French and British. She hoped the arrogant voice was lying and the British and the French were stopping the Germans cold, or better yet pushing them back into Germany as they'd done in the last war. She did not delude herself, however. Nothing could stop these people. It was as if the rest of the world had aged somehow, grown weak and complacent, whereas the Germans had grown stronger on a diet of retribution and hatred. Or perhaps it was that these Germans had devolved to a state of barbarianism—had grown primitive and warlike while aged, cultivated Europe decayed around them.

She finished the dishes and made her way into the sitting room where Johannes and Britta played. She watched them for a moment as he sat on the hardwood floor, rolling a ball back and forth to Britta, too intent on the game to look up. He had come so far back to her she realized. Each month more himself. Not the same as before, but much more like the man she had fallen in love with and who had loved her in return. He didn't leave the house, except to take Britta to the park. He couldn't. They had their false papers, but Johannes was not exactly unknown. He always ran the risk of being discovered.

Trude was the one who left the house as frequently as she could risk. She traveled to the grocery store. Then there were the more terrifying journeys. Visits to old friends of Johannes's father, all gentiles. Any one of whom could pick up the phone, denounce her, and change their lives forever. Or they could be turned in by any of their neighbors simply for being Jewish. Danger filled their every moment.

Somehow, time and time again the Gestapo did not come. Some old friends had refused them, but only a few. Little by little they gathered the Reichsmarks until finally, miraculously, they had the enormous sum demanded by Gunther. He collected the money in April and told them he would be in touch as soon as arrangements had been made. Now they waited anxiously day by day, hour by hour for the Nazi to return with word of the escape plans.

Britta paced the room. Trude was surprised to see her daughter had grown so tall that her head was above Trude's shoulder. Soon Britta would be the same height as Trude; perhaps she would be even taller. She thought with hope of their future in Britain. A childhood far away from all of this with school, music, bright young men coming to call. Everything was possible for their daughter in another land where their religious past and racial background would mean little.

She wanted to get out of the house. "Let's take her to the park," she suggested.

Johannes looked up, thoughtful. He shook his head.

"I've got a bit of reading to catch up on, my dear. I'm also packing, which is what you should be doing as well," he said, waving a finger her direction. "Remember, no more than we can carry."

She realized she had not begun the process of packing. Had she not believed this would ever happen? Perhaps it was her distrust of Gunther. How could they truly trust that man? Johannes thought he was mostly harmless. He'd known Gunther in and out of social circles for years—a lazy, jovial, almost clownlike figure waltzing around the edges of Königsberg society. A relation of a rising star in the SS, but little more. Johannes still thought of him that way. Trude disagreed, and she wondered if her husband understood just how dangerous this clown might well be.

Upstairs, she drew out her suitcase, a small weekend-sized bag. As much as she could carry a long distance. She began to fill it with clothing and a few mementos: a picture of her parents, a porcelain figurine she had from her childhood. They had so little left to connect them to the past. Outside on the street she heard the squeal of brakes. Her heart sank. She made her way cautiously to the window, flicking the curtains back a fraction to inspect the street below. A car had parked at a jarring angle a few houses down. Close enough. Doors opened and four men quickly climbed out of the vehicle, staring sternly this way and that, up and down the sidewalk. A fifth figure tumbled awkwardly out of the vehicle, wrapped in a leather trench coat. It was Gunther. *He's betrayed us,* she thought.

Gunther shambled toward their door, trailed closely by the additional men. He strode out of view beneath her, and she heard a sharp rap on the door.

"Get the door, Trude," yelled Johannes from down below. Her mouth closed and dry dust filled her heart. She tried to breathe, but she felt unable to gather enough air. "He's betrayed us," she repeated in a whisper.

Nothing could be done. There was no time to flee, and where would they run to? She pulled herself together and willed her limbs forward, one agonizing step at a time down the stairs toward the looming door. Halfway down there was another crisp, staccato bang on the door.

"Trude!"

She reached the landing and stood a couple of steps from the handle. She glanced to her right. Johannes's face was buried in a book. Britta ran past her and into the sitting area to stand next to her father, gazing over his shoulder at what he was reading. She took another step. The pounding resumed. She laid her hand on the handle and unlatched the door. Gunther strolled in past her, the four men wedging in behind him, then spreading out like fierce hawks at the hunt. Johannes finally looked up, and she saw the fear and surprise in her husband's eyes.

"Gunther," he said, his voice stretched tight with uncertain twang. "What is the meaning of this?"

"You know why I'm here."

"You betrayed us," she accused, her voice dripping venom. She didn't care anymore. What difference could it make if she was rude now?

He looked at her sternly for a moment and then broke into a wild laugh, tipping his head back and clutching at his stomach.

"Whatever do you mean, my dear?" asked the agent. He glanced back at his men and then jerked a thumb at them. "Do you mean these? How silly of you. Just a little extra security because of the war." He puffed up a little. "At headquarters, they think I'm important these days." He motioned to the closest man and whispered in his ear. The stranger stared at them fiercely for a moment, then motioned, and the other men followed him out of the home.

"Don't bother yourself with those precautions," Gunther said dismissively. "A lot of good those automatons do me. They are too full of their beliefs of party and duty to be any real use to anyone. But they'd stop a bullet perhaps," he joked.

"Then you're not here to arrest us?" she asked, still not believing him.

Gunther laughed again. "Arrest you, my dear?" His face assumed a wounded look. "How does such a pretty little head come up with such things? How can you even think such a thing after all that I've done for you? Do you think I would just take the money and desert you? I know it was a great sum, but it is paid off now and I've made the arrangements for passage. She will sail three nights hence in the early morning." He pointed his finger at Johannes. "You must be ready, my friend, and I cannot escort you. Leave everything except the smallest of luggage. Even that is a risk. If a policeman sees you with luggage in the streets, they will ask many questions, and your false identifications might not be enough."

"But you promised a truck," protested Trude.

Gunther shrugged "What can I do, my dear? Plans change. I've done the best I can, but I cannot pick you up and I cannot get you there. You must make your way to the harbor. You must be there before two a.m. The ship will depart at three. The captain will be waiting for you at two o'clock sharp. Walk directly to the docks, to the gangway. They will escort you on board. Twenty-four hours from that moment you'll be in Stockholm."

Gunther reached into his pocket and pulled a small roll of Reichsmarks back out. "Here," he said, handing them to Trude. "You'll need a little money where you're going."

She was taken aback. Was this really happening? She had never quite believed it. And now Gunther was giving them money so they would have resources where they were going? She had expected they would have to sell the remaining jewelry in Sweden for food and lodging. Now she would have cash immediately. They could find a hotel in Sweden and send a telegram to the family to try to arrange for transportation to England.

Before she knew what she was doing, she embraced him. He froze for a moment and then put his hands on her back, patting her gently.

"Now, now, my dear." Gunther released her and bowed slightly to Johannes. He waved at Britta and silently departed, leaving behind a miracle and the first real hope they had had these many months.

⟞⟝

The three days passed slowly. For so long, they had grown used to the fear of discovery, of sudden arrest, until the sensation eroded away to a kind of constant, dull anxiety. Now the fears returned sharply. Each moment Trude expected the Gestapo to burst in, guns drawn to arrest them all, taking away the future that was growing so close. She found herself strangely hoping that Gunther would return. If for no reason other than to reassure her that this escape was real. She could've at least spent a little of their time packing, but as Gunther had explained, they could take so little with them. It would be strange enough to find a family walking the streets of Königsberg after midnight. They would take only a couple of satchels they could sling over their backs, as if headed out for a hike. Even this would arouse suspicion up close.

Trude had carefully sewn their jewelry inside the seams of her dress and overcoat. She also brought with her the tiny porcelain doll given to her by her mother before she could even remember receiving it. She placed this fragile object in the right pocket of her coat and fastened the button above so she did not accidentally lose it. She also had the small stack of Reichsmarks. She divided this equally between her and Johannes so they would both have resources even if they were separated.

Finally, the night came for their departure. She cooked a splendid meal, using up their ration cards for the occasion, knowing if all went well she would not need them again. There were bread and butter, even a little sugar to go in their coffee. For once there were plenty of potatoes and cabbage to make a thick broth. She looked around at her family as they ate. They'd all lost a little weight in the past few months. The standard-issue ration in Germany was insufficient to sustain the daily needs of a person. She wondered about this even as Germany mounted victory after victory. Was there something the government wasn't telling the people? She realized she would know soon enough. In Stockholm, she would buy papers from a free press, the first access to real information they would have in years. She hoped when she learned the truth it wouldn't be as bad for the Jews and the rest of Europe as the Nazis were telling them.

She thought again about the evening that lay ahead. Their whole life would be at risk for a couple of hours before they were safely onboard. Even at sea there would be some danger. There was always the possibility the ship might be attacked by a British submarine. However, Gunther had assured her the risk was slight. If all went well, they would be free tomorrow, safely in a neutral country and already proceeding toward contacting her family in England. She had no idea how they would get from Sweden to England, but she couldn't worry about that now. One step at a time.

She looked at their still-full plates. She had no appetite, and her family clearly felt the same. She sternly commanded them to eat. They would need all their strength for the journey ahead. When they were finished, they did the dishes and put them away. She laughed at this empty gesture. What difference did it make? Still, she couldn't bring herself to think of leaving their home out of order.

They gathered in the sitting room with all they would take with them. They tried to talk or read, but nothing kept their attention. They all sat in silence, alone with their individual thoughts as the moments ticked slowly by. After an eternity, Johannes finally rose and checked his watch. "It's time," he said. She checked the clock—it was past midnight.

"Remember," he said, "follow closely behind me. Walk casually as if on a stroll. If we are stopped by anybody, let me do the talking." He looked sternly at their daughter. "Britta, you must say nothing. If you are questioned directly, pretend to cry. I will explain that you are too shy to answer. Our lives may depend on that. Do you understand?" he asked. She nodded, but her eyes flickered with fear.

"I know I haven't been myself these many months," he said. "I've done my best since the arrests—but it hasn't been enough." He looked at Trude. "I know I've put far too much on you, my love. I will confess I gave up hope, but now I know we will make it." He smiled. "We are going to get to that ship tonight, and we will escape. When we get to Stockholm let us start over with this past forgotten."

Trude felt a shudder, and hot tears ran down her cheek. This was so much like the old Johannes. He was asking her forgiveness and promising to return to his old self. That was everything she had ever wanted: the safety of her family and the return of her husband. She nodded gratefully in answer. He kissed her on the cheek and drew her and Britta to him, holding them both close for a moment.

"Let's go," he whispered. He opened the door a crack, looking out. Then he pushed it open a bit farther, poking his head out and staring for a moment up and down the street. He turned back to them. "It's safe. Let's go."

He stepped into the street. Trude and Britta followed closely behind him. The night was dark, the moon hidden behind clouds. The air was warm but would not be hot for another month or two. Trude was thankful that the streetlights had been extinguished at the beginning of the war. The city was dark so it would be difficult to mark their passing, with their muted clothing.

Johannes headed out on Yorckstrasse, turning north to travel toward the Rossgarten District and onward toward the port. The old feeling rose in her again, experienced on so many journeys at night. This one took on so much more urgency and anxiety because it was the last. She waited for the sharp command of an officer emerging from the shadows, demanding their papers.

Minute by minute time passed, but nothing happened. She didn't know how long they'd been traveling, but she knew they were making good progress through the darkness. Once Johannes stopped them, rais-ing his hand and turning, a finger pressed to his lips. Straining, she saw in the distance a dark shadow walking no more than fifty meters away from them down the street in the opposite direction. Fortunately, the figure turned the corner and disappeared. They waited there, frozen, not sure who it might be, or whether they'd been spotted. Was it a police officer or merely an eccentric pedestrian taking a late-night walk?

After long minutes Johannes motioned them on and they began to pick their way forward. They reached the intersection, keeping to the shadows. Johannes searched up and down the street. Trude did the same. She could see nothing. The figure had disappeared. They crossed the intersection rapidly, rushing down another street. She held her breath the entire way, waiting for a scream or a whistle, but again God seemed to be on their side and they were safe. *God.* There was that word again. Something she didn't even believe in but somehow a powerful image of salvation here in the darkness.

They journeyed on. She wondered what time it was, but she didn't dare call out to Johannes. She wasn't even sure where they were. She hadn't traveled very often in this area near Königsberg's port. The streets were filled with shops and warehouses and the salty stench of the harbor.

Then they were there. Johannes motioned for them to stop. Trude stepped near him. They were across the street from what appeared to be an empty lot bisected by railroad tracks. A few hundred meters away she could see the port itself. Docked immediately in front of them was a huge merchant ship. *Their ship.*

"Let's go," she whispered. She could feel their freedom just a sliver away. He motioned for her silence and checked his watch. He nodded to her. They had made it.

She felt a surge of relief. They weren't too late. "Let's go," she repeated. She squeezed his hand; her fingers were shaking, she realized. She started forward, but he stopped her to pull her back behind him.

"I'll go first," he said.

"What do you mean?" she asked.

"You wait here. In case something is wrong. I don't want all of us to be there. Think of Britta."

"No!" she said, her voice too loud. She didn't want to wait here in the darkness. She wanted to go forward and get on the ship. She wanted an end to all this torment. They were so close.

He stared at her intently. "Listen to me. We can't all go out there together. If this is a trap, I don't want them to get us all."

"I don't care," she said. "I don't want to face this without you."

He shook his head. "I can't let you come. I know I've not been much of a man these past months, but I will be now. You will stay here with Britta and you will wait. When I make sure everything is in the clear, I will come back for you."

She wanted to resist, to fight him, but he pushed her back again, holding her firmly. This was the Johannes she had married: determined, sure he was in the right, brave and powerful.

She embraced him, kissing him on the lips. "I love you," she said.

"I love you, too." He lifted her up and kissed her. Holding her tight before gently letting her down. He looked at her a moment longer, then turned and walked briskly toward the ship. His form faded out of her sight. She watched carefully, waiting for his outline to reappear under the lights of the harbor. She was not breathing, expecting the worst at any moment. She saw him again as he stepped up a slight incline and crossed the railroad tracks, then he disappeared again from view. He was gone for long seconds and then emerged under a solitary streetlight near the gangway of the ship. She saw him speaking to another man at the base of the dock. They shook hands.

She breathed a deep sigh of joy. They were going to make it.

From the darkness figures appeared. Her soul filled with horror. Johannes turned to confront them. She could hear the shouts back and forth ripping through the night. He turned in their direction and screamed. A man grabbed him; Johannes struggled but was seized by several others. They wrestled him to the ground. Now there were lights behind her. She could see a car driving down the street, then another. They were looking for her, she knew. Searching for her and Britta in the darkness.

"What's wrong, Mommy?" Britta asked.

"Nothing, nothing," she murmured. She steeled herself. They were trapped, but she had to try to flee. "Everything is fine. You must come with me; we are going home."

"But what about Daddy? And the ship. You promised me we were going on a ship!"

She slapped her daughter across the face and grabbed the front of her jacket, pulling her close. "Look at me, Britta. We are in danger. Terrible danger. We must go right now. You can't talk, you can't cry, you must follow me where I go. Do you understand? Our lives depend on it."

Her daughter was ghost white, but she nodded. Trude removed her satchel and Britta's, placing them on the ground. She led her daughter back through the vacant lot, her eyes darting back and forth down the street where they had come from. Fortunately, there were still no vehicles there. She broke into a run, crossing the road onto the first block away from the harbor. Britta followed close behind her. She tried to move as quietly as she could, but her shoes clumped loudly on the concrete. Trude was sure they would be arrested any moment, but she had to try. She reached another intersection and approached slowly. A vehicle raced down the street from the other direction. She pulled Britta into the shadows. The car passed without stopping.

She grabbed Britta's hand and sprinted across another street. Somehow they made it. They kept going, step by step, drawing farther away from the port. Soon there were no cars at all, only darkness. She couldn't think, didn't know where to go. She knew home would not be safe, but she still led them in that direction. She needed time to think, to determine what they should do. They kept walking as the early morning slipped past them. Kilometer after kilometer they retraced their steps, always waiting for the police to stop them. They would be looking for them now, she knew. Looking for a woman and a child.

She lost her way several times, but she kept heading as best she could toward the south. In the east, the sky was beginning to lighten imperceptibly, and this aided her in her directions. She gradually drew nearer more familiar surroundings. They reached the Sackheim District as dawn began to soften the darkness. When they finally reached their street, she led them onto it a few blocks away from the townhome. She stared down the street, searching for vehicles that might be patrolling or parked out in front of their dwelling. There were none. This didn't necessarily mean anything. The Gestapo could be hiding inside, or they might arrive at any moment. She was desperate; she didn't even know what they would do when they arrived. She walked carefully down the street, passing one house, then another. Britta was pulling on her sleeve, urging her to continue.

"I'm so tired," she whispered.

"Trude, what are you doing out there?" came a voice. She turned in surprise to see Frau Werner, the old widow who had warned them so long ago. She stood on her front steps, watching them walk by. The kindly woman motioned for them to come up. Trude hesitated at first. Then she grabbed Britta by the hand and walked quickly up the stairway and into Frau Werner's home.

"What are you doing?" her neighbor repeated. "There have been cars outside your house all night. Men coming and going!"

Trude put her finger to her lips and then closed the door behind her. She hoped against hope that none of the other neighbors had seen them come in.

"The Gestapo is after us," she whispered. "We were trying to escape. They've arrested Johannes."

The woman's eyes widened. "Whatever do you mean?"

"You know we are Jews. We've been in hiding for almost a year. We had a plan to get to Sweden, but it was a trap. We were betrayed by the Gestapo. They have Johannes. Britta and I fled. We have no place to go."

Frau Werner stared at both of them, her face a mask of shock. Trude could see a conflict waging inside the elderly woman. She started to speak several times but stopped. Trude saw her expression harden resolutely.

"You are wrong, Frau Bensheim. You do have a place. You will stay here."

CHAPTER ELEVEN

Königsberg
July 1940

At the celebration dinner for Erik, the excited chatter of his family did nothing to calm the storm in his mind.

"You'll never believe the Officers Club," said Corina. "I've never seen such expensive decorations, and they treated me like royalty. I made a reservation there on Saturday at seven. Karl might join us. He's so excited to hear about all your adventures."

"Let the boy catch his breath a little," admonished Peter. "Give him a few days before you worry about that nonsense."

They weren't really squabbling, Erik noted. Even their traditional irritation with one another was glazed under the varnish of his promotion and decoration. An air of giddy excitement permeated the dinner.

"Show me your new medal again," said Greta, beaming at her father. She held her hands out greedily. Erik passed her the Iron Cross First Class and she held it up, closing an eye and holding the object close, as if inspecting a scientific specimen.

"I never won one of those," said Peter. "Second Class was the best I ever achieved. They handed those out in the last war like breakfast." Greta passed him the medal, and he examined it, turning it over and over in his fingers like a happy child. "But First Class, now that's something else. Now we have a real hero in the family."

"Your new uniform will be here in just a couple days," said Corina excitedly. "I ordered it right away. I can't wait to see you in it and to pin your new decoration on. Think what they will say at the club."

His mother reached over to the middle of the table, grabbing a large bowl of potatoes and spooning several onto Erik's plate. She was silent, but he could see the pride and happiness gleaming out of her. None of them understood. He felt no pride, no accomplishment. He'd done his duty, nothing more. Worse, he struggled now with the pain of what he'd witnessed. What Sauer had done.

He stumbled to his feet.

"What's wrong?" asked Corina.

"It's nothing," he said. "Just a little indigestion." He patted his stomach. "I'm not used to all this rich food."

"Sit back down," she demanded. "I made this meal especially for you."

Erik knew his mother had made the meal, but he didn't bother to correct her.

"Let him go," said Peter, helping himself to another serving of meat. "Plenty of time to celebrate."

Erik stepped swiftly out of the kitchen and into the sitting area. He unbuttoned the top of his shirt and sat down heavily, out of breath, trying to collect himself. He felt the sweat drawing in beads on his forehead.

"What is it, my boy?" Peter entered the room and took the other chair. Erik observed concern from his father. He didn't answer right away.

"Tell me what's on your mind," said Peter finally.

"It's worse than you said."

"The fighting?" said Peter, shaking his head. "I told you I couldn't really tell you how it would be."

"He killed them. Dozens of them. All unarmed. Nobody stopped him."

"What are you talking about?" his father asked.

"The lieutenant. Sauer. At the end of the fighting in France. He rounded up a couple dozen prisoners and had them shot. English. Right in front of all of us. We let him do it."

Peter was silent for a moment. He took out his pipe and lit it, taking a few deep puffs and leaning back, closing his eyes before he responded.

"You're right. I never saw anything like that. Surely he won't get away with it."

"He did. Captain Vogel placed him under arrest. I thought there would be justice, but the command car was strafed and Vogel was killed." Erik's voice shook as he described the incident. "Sauer was in the car, too, but he survived. Nobody else has come forward to accuse him. I don't know what to do."

"That can't be the end of it," said Peter. "Sounds like plenty of people saw what happened."

Erik nodded. "Lots of folks dead center, but no one is going to come forward. I was the highest-ranking person there. It's my responsibility to do something. I just don't know what to do."

Peter puffed away a little longer this time, then he nodded. "That's murder. You have to report it."

"You will do nothing of the kind." Erik looked up to see Corina standing in the doorway. She had overheard the conversation.

"This is none of your business," said Peter. "You don't know anything about the military."

141

"I may not know a thing about the army, but I know plenty about life," she said. "Erik was just promoted and decorated. Now you want him to go and report his former commander? What do you think will come of that? Look at where we are now. My husband is an officer. We are making our way in the world. We can't risk that for nothing." She placed her hands on Erik's shoulders, her slender fingers digging into his back.

"The death of all those men was nothing?" asked Erik. He was shocked at his wife's words.

"How is it any different than anybody else that dies?" she asked, releasing her hands. "Thousands of people died in those battles. A few seconds before, any one of those men would've gladly killed you. I'm not saying what he did was right, but it's not your responsibility to risk our lives and our future." She turned to him. "You need to keep quiet."

"I can't believe you," said Peter, shaking his head in obvious disgust. "Always looking after yourself."

"Someone has to," she snapped back, taking a step toward her father-in-law. "I'm the only one that looks after this family. A fine pair you two were, unemployed, sitting in this room just a few years ago wondering aloud what you would do with yourselves. I was the one who acted. I brought Erik to Karl, and look at where we are now. We aren't going to risk everything I put together."

"All you can do is chirp about everything you've done for us!" shouted Peter. "You think of yourself and nothing else." He half rose out of his seat.

"I think of this family, that's true." She turned to Erik, her voice calm and pleading. "Dearest, I know how hard all that must've been," she said. "I understand how you feel, and I think you do need to do something, but don't talk to the military. I have a better idea. You should go see Karl. I know that he will be able to give you the best advice on who to report this to, what action should be taken. He only has your best interest at heart."

Erik hadn't thought about Karl. His wife's friend was in a different branch of the SS, but he had many connections and was much more familiar with the party than Erik.

"You might be right," he admitted. "Perhaps I should talk to Karl first."

"Of course you should," she said. "He'll make sure this is dealt with in the proper way, and he'll also make sure there are no ramifications against you."

"I don't agree," said Peter. "That Gestapo agent has nothing to do with the military. You need to report this up the proper command. It's the only honorable thing to do."

"Stay out of this," she hissed. "This is a decision between a husband and wife."

Peter started to retort, but Erik raised his hand.

"She's right," he said. "Although Karl will probably tell me the same thing, that I need to report this up the chain of command. But it doesn't hurt to get his thoughts on this first." Erik could tell that his father wanted to say more, but he stopped himself. He also observed a flicker of triumph on Corina's face. He had grown so tired of their constant fighting, this struggle for power in his own house. "I will make the decision," he said firmly.

Erik spent the rest of the evening with Greta sitting on his lap, sharing stories with the family about the places he'd seen and the things he'd done. He glossed over the bad parts, focusing on the beauty of the landscape: the dikes of Holland and the fields of France. He didn't talk about the fighting, the blood, the death. He tried to put on the bravest face. He knew how happy they all were, delighted he was home and that he had done so well for the family; he didn't want to destroy the mood by brooding. If only he'd thought of Karl in the first place, he could've saved his family the stress.

He lay in bed that night, unable to sleep, wondering if he was doing the right thing. The images of dying English prisoners still flashed in his mind like a picture, as they did each night. He struggled for hours until sleep finally found him.

———

Erik sat in the waiting area of the SS offices in Königsberg. Unlike during his last visit, the building teemed with activity. Black-clothed minions scurried this way and that like so many busy ants. He looked at his watch. His appointment was supposed to be at six, but it was already seven thirty. He wondered if Captain Schmidt had forgotten about him and whether he should announce himself again to the front desk. He decided he would wait.

Finally, Karl appeared, a blond giant wading against a current of black.

Erik rose and delivered a stiff salute. Karl returned the gesture. "I'm sorry I had to leave you waiting, but as you can see we've so much to do these days. So many new regulations and countless people to follow up on." He motioned for Erik to follow him, and they retraced the familiar steps to his office. Erik remembered the last time he had visited here, just days before the fighting started. He'd asked for a transfer Karl was not in a position to provide. Today he sought advice, not favors.

"How are things at home?" Karl asked. "The wife certainly seems to be enjoying her new standing in our community." Erik noted Karl's flicker of a smile.

"We're both very appreciative of everything you've done for us," said Erik.

"Oh, but I didn't do anything. You're the one who did all the work. Look at you coming back a hero and an officer," he noted approvingly. "You've exceeded all my expectations."

There was a knock at the door. "Come in," said Karl.

In came a middle-aged man clothed in ill-fitting SS regalia. He slumped heavily into a chair. Erik hadn't expected anyone else at their meeting, so he eyed the stranger curiously.

"Gunther, I want to introduce you to somebody. This is Second Lieutenant Erik Mueller. Erik, this is First Lieutenant Gunther Wolf. He's my number two here." Karl turned to Gunther. "You don't know Mueller, but you know his wife, Corina."

Gunther's face brightened, and he rubbed his chubby hands together. "*Ach, ja,* you're the famous war hero. You and your wife live over on Yorckstrasse, *nicht wahr?*"

"You know the neighborhood?" asked Erik.

Gunther's eyes took on a glint. "I've been there once or twice."

"Erik here was trying to find a home in our office before the fighting started," explained Karl. "Who knows, he might still be interested. What do you think, Gunther?"

The Gestapo agent sized him up, looking Erik over for a few moments, his mind clearly clicking away. He whistled. "A strapping young hero like this? I'm sure we could find something for him here."

Karl dismissed Gunther with a flick of his hand. The aged officer bowed slightly to Erik and slogged out of the room, closing the door behind him.

"That's Reinhard's cousin," whispered Karl conspiratorially. "He's the one who nipped your spot in the first place. He's not nearly the administrator he thinks he is." Karl shrugged. "I would have preferred you, but Gunther does have his uses."

Karl's pupils sharpened, and he rested his elbows on the table, studying Erik. "How about you, Erik? You were looking for a transfer before. Are you still?"

The question surprised him. He had come seeking advice about Sauer; he wasn't here begging for a job. How should he answer? If there was a position available to transfer, that would solve all his problems, wouldn't it? He certainly would be relieved of the responsibility of dealing with the massacre. Could he just let it pass? No. He realized that didn't solve anything. Sauer would go on to commit new atrocities, with or without Erik's presence. He couldn't allow that without trying to do something. He had to speak up.

"I'm . . . flattered you brought that up, although that's not my reason for coming to you today."

Karl frowned, leaning toward him. "What is it then? Why are you here?"

"Corina thought I should come to you with something."

Karl sparked with interest. "Tell me."

Erik related the significant events that had occurred in the past year. He started haltingly, uncertain of himself, but soon the details rattled off as he described the first incident in Poland, his discussion with his father, the terrible murderers in France. Then Vogel's arrest of Sauer, and Vogel's untimely death. Karl listened with rapt attention. He did not interrupt. Erik finished his story. He had spoken for more than a half hour.

Karl was silent for a few minutes more, and then he nodded his head as if deciding what to do. "Thank you, Erik. Thank you for trusting me with this. You were right to come to me. I will need a day or two to consider the circumstances. Please don't tell anybody else the story, even neighbors or friends." He gestured toward the downstairs. "What do you think all those busybodies are doing? They are following up on reports made by neighbors, by family. Things have changed since you've been gone, my friend. Nobody is trusted these days. Arrests are made. People disappear.

"Some might look at what you're telling me as an act of patriotism. Others would look at it as a betrayal of the party. This is a very delicate matter. Go home. Spend some time with your family. I will contact you in the next couple days, and we can talk further."

They both stood and shook hands. Erik departed feeling tremendous relief. Thank God he'd talked to Karl before he spoke with anyone else. He had no idea what was going on at the home front. Were they truly arresting people in droves? Neighbors turning each other in? Family? He felt terribly disconnected from the situation. What had happened while he was gone? Germany was victorious. This was a time for celebration, not for pointing fingers. How strange that in the midst of victory his people could be turning on each other.

Erik returned home and spent the next several days relaxing as best he could and spending time with his family. He took Corina and Greta to the park each day. He was surprised to see his daughter had grown so much in the past year. She was in the awkward stage between being a little girl and a young woman. He cherished every moment he could spend with her.

He expected to hear from Karl by the second day but did not. After the third and fourth day passed, he started to worry. Finally, on the morning of the fifth day he received a telephone call from SS headquarters. Karl summoned him back for an appointment that afternoon.

Erik arrived a little early and was surprised to be ushered immediately into Karl's office. Both Karl and Gunther were waiting for him. He saluted Karl at the door, but the major did not return the salute. Instead, Karl simply pointed to the chair and directed Erik to sit down.

Without any small talk, Karl launched into his response. "I've made some inquiries into your situation." His voice was clipped and brisk.

"Thank you for that. What should I do?" Erik asked.

"You should do nothing."

Erik shook his head. "I can't do that."

Karl raised his arm and pointed a sharp finger. "You'd better keep your mouth shut and do exactly as I say. You're going to grow up, and you're going to do it now."

Erik was shocked. Karl had never spoken to him like this. "My honor will not allow me to keep silent on this, sir."

Gunther chimed in. "Your honor will get you killed and maybe your family as well. I made some calls on Karl's behalf. The SS is well aware of what Sauer did. Just like you, he's a decorated hero. They have no interest in punishing him, and they want the situation to go away. By bringing this up, you've become a bit of an embarrassment for them."

"What?" demanded Erik. "How can that be?"

"That's not the worst of it," said Karl. "Sauer is furious. He's demanding your arrest for insubordination, cowardice, and failure to follow orders."

"Let him try me," said Erik, his blood up. "I've done nothing wrong. Cowardice? How dare he! He knows the truth."

"You think the truth will save you?" asked Karl. "How naïve. I thought you might be right for our office, but I was clearly mistaken. I have nothing here for you; that is obvious now. But for your wife's sake, let me give you a little advice that might save your life: you need to put away your romantic notions of the past. This is a new world, a new order. The party is the future. Germany will do whatever it takes to earn our rightful place in Europe. In this new world, there is no place for sentimentality and weakness.

"I've intervened on your behalf. Captain Sauer and I had a long talk about you. I assured him that I could make you understand. I put my own reputation on the line to save you." He glared at Erik. "Don't make me a fool. This is the last time I will step in on your behalf, and you had better take advantage of the gift I just gave you.

"Captain Sauer has agreed to drop his case against you. He will let you serve beneath him as a platoon leader at your current rank, but you must commit yourself to follow all his orders without question and without hesitation. If you fail to do so, make no mistake, you will be prosecuted to the full authority of military justice. At that point, there will be nothing anyone else can do for you. Even me. Do you understand?"

Erik nodded, stunned. He didn't know what else to say. He could hear Gunther chuckling quietly to himself.

Karl exhaled deeply as if in relief. His voice softened slightly. "*Gut.* I hate to say those things to you, Erik. But I do so for your own good. You're a decorated officer of the SS. Act like one. You're dismissed," he said, waving his hand. Neither of the men looked up or saluted.

Erik rose and stalked out of the office, his mind a whirlwind. What kind of a world did he live in? Sauer wasn't punished but instead had been promoted and decorated? Erik was the one in trouble? If he spoke out again, it would be the end of his career, perhaps worse. He stumbled home in a daze. One thought echoed in his mind over and over: *What has happened to mein Deutschland?*

CHAPTER TWELVE

Königsberg
May 1940

Trude stayed up through the dawn and into the morning. Through a slit in the drapes she watched one leather-shrouded monster after another tromp through the front yard, searching for her. Frau Werner sat on a sofa nearby, Britta's head on her lap. Her daughter was asleep, blissfully unaware of the evil lurking just a few meters away.

Trude whispered to her gray-haired savior, "You shouldn't have taken on this danger. We will only stay here until it's dark, then we have to leave."

"You'll do nothing of the kind, child," her neighbor responded sternly. "Your death is out there. Both of yours."

"You risk too much—your life."

"My life is my own to gamble. You don't get to decide for me, Trude. I can't call myself a German and let them come and take you— these worms who crawled out of the sewers and took over our country. Someone has to stand up to them."

"My husband thought that way, and look what happened to him."

"Tell me everything."

Trude told Mrs. Werner about meeting Johannes. Of their life together, the birth of Britta, her work in the music conservatory. Then the coming of Hitler. The new racial laws that resulted in the loss of both of their jobs. The departure of their parents, the loss of their beautiful home, and the move to the middle-class town house in Sackheim. Johannes's defiant role with the organization and her growing anxiety. Her constant pleas to secure their departure. The arrests, Gunther, his demands, his conduct, and his betrayal.

"You are so brave," said Frau Werner. "You are a remarkable woman. Here I was thinking I was courageous, offering you shelter, after everything you've gone through."

A sharp rap interrupted them. They froze. Mrs. Werner nodded toward the upstairs. Trude stepped over as quietly as possible, lifting Britta up. Her daughter was dead weight, almost too heavy for her to bear. She labored up the stairs, her heart racing. She reached the bedroom door and closed it just as she heard another loud banging on the door. Even with her ear to the wood, she could only make out muffled voices below. She heard a loud, demanding male voice, almost shouting, followed by Mrs. Werner's quieter, measured responses. Her heart leaped out of her throat. She waited for the thunder of boots on the stairs. The Gestapo probably already knew she was here. Minute by minute passed, and there was a soft tapping at the door.

"Are you in there?" whispered Mrs. Werner.

"Ja, in here," she responded. Frau Werner entered.

"That was the Gestapo, as I'm sure you've already guessed. They are searching the neighborhood for a Jewish woman and her child. A neighbor. He told me you've been dealing in the black market and are wanted for questioning. Of course, I don't believe that rubbish."

"Did he say anything about my husband?" she asked.

"Nothing. I wanted to ask but, how could I?"

Trude nodded. "You did the right thing. I just wish there was something I could do. I'm so worried about him." The tears, held back throughout the night, finally released, and she buried her head in Frau Werner's shoulder, sobbing.

"Hush now. You cannot think about that right now. It will do you no good."

"What are we to do? We can't stay here. I can't use those ration cards or identification papers again. They will be looking for them. We can't buy food, and I would never let you use yours to try to feed all of us. We would all die. We have to leave here tonight."

"You're not leaving. At least for a few days. I'm going to go out and see if I can learn anything about what's going on. I want you to stay upstairs and out of sight."

"There is someone you can visit. Someone who will want to help us."

"Who is that?"

Trude told her about Captain Dutt. She explained her visits to his house and the help he'd provided them.

"Where does he live?"

Trude gave her the directions.

"That's too far for me to walk. I will call a cab." Frau Werner picked up the phone, speaking to an operator and then to a cab company. They sat quietly for about a half hour, until a car arrived for her.

"I will be gone for a few hours. Remember, stay upstairs and out of sight, and for Gott's sake, don't open up the door for any reason."

Trude nodded. Frau Werner hobbled down the stairs and out the door. Alone now with her daughter, Trude was terrified. She had heard such horror stories about what the Nazis did to prisoners, particularly the Jews. She shook her head, trying to clear the thoughts. It was too much for her to think about. She heard a stirring yawn. Britta twisted and turned on the bed. She looked up sleepily. "Where are we?" she asked.

"Mrs. Werner's house."

"Where's Daddy?"

She knew the question would be coming, but she still struggled to control her voice when she answered. "He's gone away for a few days on business. I don't want you to worry about it. He will be back with us soon."

"But what about last night? Why did those men attack him? What about the boat ride? We were going on a big trip."

"We're going to have to wait a little while longer before we do that now, dear. We will be staying with Mrs. Werner for a few days. I need to talk to her alone for a while, but before I do that, there is something you need to listen to. Do you understand?"

Britta assumed a serious expression and she nodded.

"We mustn't leave the house. Also, you are not to walk in front of the windows downstairs unless the curtains are closed. Do you understand?"

"But why, Mommy?"

"Don't you worry about that right now, but you must promise me."

Britta agreed and then told her mother she was hungry. Trude was terrified to even go downstairs. She did not know when Mrs. Werner would return. She could be gone for hours.

She decided she would have to risk it. She opened the door a crack and peered down the stairs toward the front door. She was relieved to see that the drapes were closed in the sitting area. Gently, she made her way, trying not to make any noise. She wasn't sure how thick the walls were with the adjoining homes.

Step by cautious step, she lowered herself down the stairs until she reached the landing. Her heart stuttered when she noticed a slight gap in the sitting-room window curtains. She could see outside. The full morning sun was out. A car passed by on the street, then another. She couldn't tell from her limited vantage point whether it was regular traffic or something more sinister.

Trude made her way through the shadows to the kitchen. She opened the cupboards searching for something to eat. She felt guilty taking any food from Frau Werner. But they were starving. They hadn't eaten since dinner the night before, and they'd covered so many kilometers since then their bodies screamed for sustenance.

The first couple of cupboards were bare, but in the next she found some rough black bread and a half-empty jar of jam. She chopped rough slabs off the loaf with a nearby knife. She started the stove and toasted a couple pieces over the burner, gently waving the bread back and forth over the flame until it was well browned on both sides. She spread a thick red coating of jam onto each piece. Trude took the food back upstairs as quietly as she could. Soon her daughter was making happy smacking sounds as she chewed away at the toast. Trude looked over, surprised to see the black-and-white wooden toy top resting on the crumpled blankets of Mrs. Werner's bed.

"Where did you get that?" she wondered.

"It was in my pocket," Britta answered, her mouth still full of bread. "I carry it with me everywhere."

Trude fought back tears. Johannes had made the toy for Britta with his own hands. She always seemed to have it with her, perhaps because her father was so often gone in the old days. Trude wondered again what the last year had been like for Britta, tucked away inside most of the time, no school, her father home more than ever but strangely distant. She must've felt the tension. They did everything they could to keep the fear away from her, but there was so much of it. They could all sense the Nazis reaching out with giant claws to clutch them.

Britta finished her meal, looking around for more. Trude assured her that's all there was. She had gone without, giving her daughter both slices. She daren't take any more food without asking. She tried to ignore the knots in her stomach. Britta lay back down, still tired, begging her mother for a story. Trude told her about the old days, growing up just after the first war. The huge house, the trips all over Europe, stories of the grandparents that Britta hardly remembered any longer.

In the late afternoon, she heard a rustling at the door. She held her breath for a moment and then heard the door open. She cracked the bedroom door a fraction and was relieved to see Frau Werner struggling up the stairs. She hobbled into the bedroom and let herself gently down on the edge of the bed, her arms shaking a little under the effort.

"Did you see the captain?" Trude asked. Frau Werner nodded, still catching her breath.

Trude was relieved, but she also felt terrible. She realized what a tremendous strain traveling just a few blocks must be on the elderly woman. Even with the help of the cab, the trip had clearly exhausted Frau Werner. She looked like she might pass out. She was pale, and she closed her eyes, taking another deep breath.

"Let me get you some water," said Trude, starting to head downstairs. Mrs. Werner motioned for her to stay.

"I'm fine. I just needed to catch my breath. I have met with Captain Dutt. He's quite the man, and he cares deeply for your family."

Trude nodded. "He's one of the best men I've ever met. What did he say?"

"He was shocked, as I'm sure you can imagine, with what transpired, although he said he was not surprised that Gunther betrayed you. He said he'd warned you all along."

Trude nodded. "He did, but we had no choice. Nobody else was willing to help us escape. Can he do anything for us now?"

Mrs. Werner shook her head. "He's not sure. He said providing a little money was one thing, interfering with police business is another. The least he could do was to make inquiries about Johannes. He said he'll try to do everything he can, but he has to think about things. He said you would understand."

Trude nodded. "Anything he can do is a great relief."

"I'm sorry I couldn't find anything out about Johannes. Perhaps the captain can at least do that."

"Yes. That would be a blessing. I just wish we had our ration cards still."

"That's the one good piece of news I have brought," she said. "He told me he receives substantial allotments of food because of the size of his household and because of his status. Everyone in his household receives the ration card of a heavy industrialist worker, which means extra portions of everything. He said he would have a delivery of food brought by this evening after dark, and he would try to send more each week if he is able."

"Each week? What do you mean? I told you, we can't stay here."

Frau Werner reached over, clamping her spindly fingers tightly around Trude's wrist. "You have to stay here, my dear. They will kill you otherwise. Captain Dutt agrees. There is no other option."

"I can't risk your life along with ours."

"I told you, it's mine to risk. Besides, what can they do to an old woman like me? They wouldn't dare."

They both knew that wasn't true, but Trude accepted this greatest of gifts. She had found another German to trust. In this forest of enemies, she had found a friend. Trude felt the relief wash over her. At least they wouldn't starve, and for the first time since she watched her husband's arrest she felt a flicker of hope. If anybody could find out what was going on, it was Captain Dutt, and perhaps he might still find some other way to help them out. If by some miracle she could secure Johannes's release, there was still a chance that they might escape. Until then, miraculously, she had a place to stay away from all her enemies. A tiny raft of light in an ocean of darkness.

As the days passed, her sense of peace dwindled and her anxiety for Johannes increased exponentially. Trude knew dreadful things must be happening to her husband, but she didn't know exactly what, or whether he was even alive. It tormented her that she couldn't tell him that she and Britta were safe in hiding.

Trude watched the world passing by on the street each day through the partly open curtains. Occasionally she would see a uniformed police officer or a gentleman in plain clothes walking up and down the strasse. She didn't know if they were there for routine reasons or if they were searching for her.

Britta grew ever surlier, denied the opportunity for even an occasional trip to the park and forced to be quiet at all hours. She was simply too young to be in such cramped, limited quarters day after day with nothing to do.

The front bell rang, knocking Trude out of her reverie. Hot panic scorched through her. She grabbed Britta by the wrist, dragging her upstairs as quickly as she was able. Before she made it to the bedroom, she heard the door open below and the sound of muffled voices. She was surprised to hear Mrs. Werner calling out for her to come down. Had she been betrayed? She couldn't fathom that her protector would have turned her in, but she couldn't think of another explanation. She went down the stairs reluctantly, straining to see who was there. A young man stood near the door, not in uniform. He watched her come downstairs without saying a word. She'd never seen him before, but she felt the panic rise again. She shook her head. If it was the Gestapo, they wouldn't have sent this wisp of a boy to come collect her. As she reached the last step he clicked his heels and introduced himself as Friedrich Mauser.

"Who are you?" she asked tensely.

"I'm Captain Dutt's driver. I am here to collect you. The captain wishes to see you."

"Can't he come here?"

Friedrich shook his head rigidly. "Too risky."

"Can I bring my daughter?"

"I was instructed to bring you, and only you."

"I can't go without her."

"Nonsense," said Frau Werner. "She'll be just fine here with me."

"What if she misbehaves while I'm gone? She is so bored. I understand why, but she wants to go outside. She doesn't understand."

"I can keep her under control. She listens to me."

Trude wasn't sure. She hadn't left Britta's side since Johannes's arrest. If something happened while she was gone, she could never forgive herself. Still, she knew the answer she needed to give. The captain was their only point of contact with the outside world, their only possible salvation. He was demanding to see her, and she must comply.

She nodded to Mrs. Werner, thanking her with her eyes. "I'll only be gone a little while," she said.

Friedrich opened the door. She followed him apprehensively into the sunshine, trying to adjust to the brightness after so many days inside. Friedrich stepped up to the black car and opened the back door for her. She sat, letting the black leather envelop her, hoping to disappear from sight as quickly as possible.

Friedrich stepped around to the driver's seat. He turned the key, and the car gave a stuttered cough and then erupted in ignition. They started off through the streets. The day was bright and warm. There were many cars on the street and people walking up and down the sidewalks. She looked out in wonder at the world she had left behind. A world of markets, cars, walks, friendship, and family.

"You're that Jew, aren't you?"

The question startled her.

"My family is Jewish, that's true," she responded.

Friedrich grunted.

"Is that a problem for you?" she asked.

He shrugged, not answering. "I follow orders from the captain, that is my duty. I don't have to like them."

"Why aren't you in the army?" She was curious how a young man like this had avoided service. As soon as she realized her question might produce an uncomfortable answer, she blushed slightly, feeling embarrassed.

She expected a sharp response. How would a Jew dare ask that kind of question of a German? But he answered with no trace of anger in his voice.

"I have an illness," he explained. "Anemia. I was found unfit for duty. Captain Dutt was kind enough to find me employment. My father is a friend. In any event, I don't know why we are in this war. The Jews caused it in the first place, if you believe the stories."

"You don't believe that, do you?"

"I don't know. If it isn't true, why would they tell us that? My father said the army didn't lose the last war. They were still in the trenches with plenty of ammunition, food, and everything else they needed. Then suddenly the fighting simply stopped. If the Jews didn't betray us, then who did?"

Trude could feel Friedrich's hard stare in the rearview mirror, boring into her. She was afraid; she realized there was something about this young man that was very unsettling. Mrs. Werner had told her stories of neighbors reporting neighbors. All it would take was one member of the captain's household to turn her in.

A long silence followed as the car rolled through the streets of Königsberg. Finally, Friedrich wove up through the narrow driveway and into the carport attached to the captain's home. She was ushered out of the car, up the back steps to the kitchen, and then through a hallway she'd never traveled to the familiar library.

Friedrich delivered her to the chair in front of Dutt's desk and departed without saying good-bye. He did not offer coffee or tea. She sat alone for a few minutes, looking around again with admiration at the elegant collection of books, paintings, and mementos. She was struck at how much the room reminded her of her father's study. His had been smaller, but in its own way just as charming. She heard a door open, and she turned to see Captain Dutt in the doorway. There was a look in his face she'd never seen before: a sadness and perhaps something else.

"Have you been made comfortable?" he asked.

"Yes, thank you," she responded, not wanting to say anything about Friedrich's lack of hospitality.

"Don't you have anything to drink or eat?"

She shook her head.

The captain shouted and Friedrich quickly reappeared. "Didn't you offer our guest anything?" he asked sternly.

"You instructed me to bring her here."

"You know full well I want every guest to be furnished with refreshment. Bring it now. We will talk later about this."

Trude saw the young German flush. He turned sharply and stormed out, returning a few minutes later with a tray of small sandwiches and tea. He placed them on the desk and bowed to the captain before departing. He refused to look Trude's way.

"I apologize for my driver," he said. "I see there are some elements of his education that I will need to restructure." He motioned at the food. "You need to eat, my dear. You look like you've lost weight. Not that I'm surprised."

She reached out with shaking hands and picked up a sandwich. She'd had so little to eat in the past week that she struggled to maintain her dignity and eat slowly. Her body screamed inside, desiring to shove the delicate food into her mouth. She chewed carefully, setting the food down between bites, and sipping some tea with composure. Captain Dutt sat back, watching her silently, letting her finish before he asked her any questions.

"You're withering away," he said at last. "Why don't you stop with all your manners and eat." He motioned to the food, then called out for a servant to order more to be brought.

Trude abandoned her decorum and reached out with both hands, shoving a sandwich into her mouth. She didn't know when she had tasted anything better in her entire life. In a few minutes, she had consumed all the sandwiches and a full cup of tea filled with cream and sugar. She then set to work on the new tray of food, continuing to eat until her stomach finally felt full. The captain kept insisting she continue, but finally she shook her head, unable to eat anymore. Satisfied, he rang a bell on his desk, and the servants came back and whisked the tray away.

"Now," he said, leaning back and pulling out his pipe. "I want to hear from your own lips, is what Frau Werner told me true?"

She told him everything about the terrible night. Captain Dutt listened intently, interrupting here and there to ask a question. He registered surprise and then deepened into a greater sadness.

Finally, she was done. He leaned back farther in his chair, his eyes half-closed.

"You're a brave woman," he said.

"Not as brave as you," she responded. "You've taken terrible risks on our behalf. I have no right to ask for anything more from you."

He waved his hand in dismissal. "There are still true Germans in Germany," he said. Then he broke into a slight grin and chuckled to himself. "Well, at least there is Mrs. Werner and me. Perhaps we are the only two. I'm sure you enjoyed your ride with Friedrich. Don't worry about him; I trust him completely, even if he has some interesting ideas about Germany and the Jews."

She hoped he was right and decided not to press things too far about the driver. "Have you been able to learn anything or come up with a plan?" she asked.

"Nothing specific at this point, Frau Bensheim. I've been racking my brain this past week, trying to come up with something, some idea or option. I told you I have friends out there, but that they must be approached with caution. What was true a year ago would be doubly true now: no one is willing to put their life on the line. There is always the possibility of a betrayal. Still, I'm not without connections. I just need some time to consider this matter. We must proceed carefully in the meantime. You need to stay put. I'll be able to drop food off at Mrs. Werner's for you. There should be enough to keep you going, although I can't provide a feast. Stay there and stay safe. Do not leave until I come for you and for your daughter."

She was disappointed but so thankful there was at least some hope of a plan to rescue them. She was grateful that he was risking so much for her. She rose and cautiously stepped around the desk. She placed her arms on his shoulders and embraced him. He stiffened in surprise and awkwardly raised a hand to pat hers.

"Remember what I told you, child. You cannot leave your house for any reason. I will be in touch as soon as I know anything."

He rang the bell again and Friedrich reappeared.

"Drive her home," the captain ordered. "And, Friedrich, you will treat her with the respect that I afford her."

Friedrich stiffened. He glanced at Trude for a moment and then marched out. She turned to follow him.

"There is one more thing," said Dutt. She looked over.

"I've heard news of Johannes." He hesitated. "It's not good. They've taken your husband deep into Germany. I don't know where or what has happened to him. I'm so sorry."

CHAPTER THIRTEEN

German/Russian Border in Poland
June 1941

They waited in the early morning darkness. Erik's platoon was in the lead of the company, spread out among the trees. He had ordered total silence, but here and there he could hear the crackle of a brushed branch or the snap of a twig under a heavy boot.

The forest erupted in fire and light. Artillery shells shrieked above them. Erik shouted for the men to advance and he stormed forward, rushing from tree to tree, taking his first steps into Russian-occupied Poland.

Tracers raced by; he could hear their whistling echo as the enemy returned fire. He raised his machine pistol and fired a blind burst into the darkness ahead. He couldn't tell if he had hit anything or what was in front of him. From behind he could hear the rumbling of the panzers as they jolted forward, cannons roaring, adding their fire to the weight of the artillery attack.

As the morning passed, the platoon streamed onward. Kilometer after kilometer passed as they progressed. Resistance was surprisingly light. The last briefing they received told Erik to expect at least a division in front of them, so heavy fighting would be likely from the moment they invaded. But so far they had run up against nothing more than a company of badly surprised Russians who made only a token of resistance before retreating. How strange to be here in the first place. They'd signed a treaty of friendship with the Russians less than two years ago, and now they were invading them with no warning. *I won't think about those things.*

By noon they rumbled into the center of a village. There were no Russians in sight. Shortly thereafter Captain Sauer rolled into the collection of houses in a new command car. He exited the vehicle looking this way and that, his back straight, scanning the town for threats. After his gaze settled on Erik, he strode rigidly over.

Erik saluted and received a stiff response. "Lieutenant, what's the status?" asked the company commander.

"No Russians in this place," responded Erik. "Doesn't look like they were ever here."

"Nonsense," said Sauer. "We've been told the Poles avidly collaborated with the Russians. Round up the village leaders for questioning."

Erik hesitated.

"Are you disobeying a direct order?" demanded Sauer.

"No, sir, I'm not."

Sauer glared for a moment, his eyes narrowing. "Get to it then, Lieutenant," he ordered, waving a dismissive hand before returning to his command vehicle. He directed his Polish interpreter to follow Erik. The two went from house to house knocking on doors and demanding information. They asked who the mayor of the town was and the location of the principal officials.

Eventually, they were directed to a home on the edge of town. The house was slightly larger than the others in this modest village. Erik banged on the front door and waited. No answer. He banged again, harder this time, and he heard the release of the latch on the other side.

The door opened a reluctant crack. A middle-aged man stood inside, a woman behind him clutching a couple of children.

Erik asked through the interpreter if he was indeed the mayor. The man stood frozen for a moment before nodding. Erik reached out, and over the screaming objections of the man's family members, he half carried, half dragged him into the center of the village. Sauer was there, a makeshift table of crates and a plywood board serving as a command center as he examined the maps. He issued orders tersely to runners, who took off in different directions. Captain Sauer looked up with grinding satisfaction as Erik approached with the mayor.

"Good work, Lieutenant," the commanding officer said. He turned to Erik's captive. "Where are the Russians?" he demanded. The mayor waited, listening for the interpretation before answering.

"I do not know what you mean," he said through the translator. "There are no Russians here. There never have been. We are too small, too poor. They would visit now and again to collect some taxes or to investigate some crime or misdemeanor. Other than that, we hardly saw them."

"You're a liar," said Sauer. He drew his pistol from the holster, cocked the trigger, and aimed it at the head of the mayor. "Where are the Russians?" he repeated.

Erik could feel his heart beating out of his chest. He thought of the mayor's wife, his children. Waiting in fear and silence a few hundred meters away. What could he do? He'd been warned. He would put his own life at stake if he interfered.

The moment continued. The mayor begged, telling everything he knew about the Russians, where their headquarters were, when the last time was they visited. Sauer was unmoved. He took a step forward and slapped the man across the face. The Pole crumpled to the ground, his hands over his head, whimpering. Sauer stepped forward and placed the pistol barrel against the man's temple.

An explosion rocked the village, then another. Erik threw himself to the dirt, covering his head. Sauer and the others did the same. The rat-a-tat of machine gun fire ricocheted off the stone houses. Sauer rolled a few times until he was hiding behind one of the houses. He called out orders. A panzer nearby rumbled to life and advanced toward the sound of the fire. The company spread out, a few men hiding behind each house, slowly working their way toward the enemy rifles blazing away at them. Erik watched Captain Sauer scream orders at a couple of men near him and then disappear around the corner.

Erik seized the mayor. The man resisted, but Erik slapped him again and shook him until the mayor made eye contact. Erik grabbed the man by the shirt and pulled him backward, away from the attack and toward his house. The mayor continued to resist until he realized what Erik was doing. He raised his hands in supplication and then shook himself free and nodded. Now the Pole took the lead, scrambling between the houses as Erik followed. Finally, they were back at the man's home. He knocked on the door and shouted something several times in Polish. The door opened on his wife and his children. They ran into each other's arms, holding each other tightly. The mayor turned around, thanking Erik silently.

Erik nodded and sprinted back toward the fighting. He found some members of his platoon and led them forward, but the battle was already dying off.

Captain Sauer returned from the fight, heading to his command vehicle. He leaped up, standing on the front seat, calling out orders as several more panzers rolled into the village center. Soon the entire company was back, unscarred, in secure control. The counterattack had been repulsed.

June turned into July, and Erik's company stormed through Poland and into Russia proper. Their enemy seemed stunned and totally unprepared to resist, just as in the attacks on Poland almost two years ago. There was hardly an enemy airplane in the sky. Stukas ranged at will over the battlefield, strafing enemy formations and dropping bombs on the armored vehicles that hadn't already been wiped out by the powerful panzer formations. Russians surrendered in whole units, smiling and surprisingly good-natured. Erik was amazed at the progress of the war as they stormed with abandon hundreds of kilometers into Russia.

Still, everything was not perfect. Occasionally they came across a unit fighting desperately, even to the last man. Hundreds of Russians would come charging out of the woods, as if ghosts materializing from the trees. The panzers would mow them down, but they kept on coming. Erik's company took casualties, far more than they took in Poland, Belgium, or France. Perhaps even more alarming, a month into the battle they had covered more territory than in either of the previous battles, but they were still nowhere near their objectives. Intellectually, Erik knew that Russia was far bigger than France or Poland, but to walk the actual steps, to see the kilometers, seemingly unending, pass by was another thing altogether.

Even more disturbing were the stories circulating among the troops. Bloodthirsty Russians sneaking into camps in the middle of the night to slit the throats of German soldiers. Captured SS men found hanged or even crucified. Each rumored atrocity was met with fierce retribution by the German army or the SS, but this did not seem to deter the Russians, who kept on fighting when it was so obvious the war was already over.

This Russian will to fight, to take massive losses and yet keep going, was something Erik and his comrades had never experienced before. They whispered about this around the campfire at night and during their long marches over the endless kilometers. Erik felt a tinge of panic—just a spark, but it seemed to grow with each passing day.

As they pushed on, farther and farther into Russia, the men moved faster and faster, trying to find the end, becoming more desperate, more uncertain at a time when victory seemed assured.

Erik received a boost in his morale when Sergeant Messer reappeared in his unit as July turned into August. Messer had been injured in a training exercise a few months before the Russian invasion began. The sergeant was his right arm, his compass. He was entirely reliable and a great source of strength for Erik.

As usual, their division was in close support of a company of panzer tanks. Over time the Panzer I and II's had been replaced by the more powerful Panzer III. This tank was more heavily armored and possessed a 50-millimeter cannon and two 7.92-millimeter machine guns. The machines proved unstoppable across the Polish and Russian plains. Erik's platoon oversaw finding appropriate cover for the tanks to stop each night. This was typically either a wooded area or within a town or village.

This evening they traveled far, fortunately without engaging the enemy. Except for periodic airplanes overhead, the day had been eerily quiet. They had moved forward more than thirty kilometers, and Erik and his men were slopping over in exhaustion. As the sky began to darken, he spotted a collection of houses a few thousand meters down the road. He halted the platoon and heard the tanks behind him rumble to a stop. Straining through his field glasses, Erik inspected each house one by one, looking for anything suspicious—a rifle, a face, anything.

After about ten minutes he was satisfied there were no visible risks.

"Sergeant Messer!" he called.

"Yes, sir," said the sergeant.

"Take your group and check out those buildings ahead. If everything is safe, give me the all clear, and we will set up camp in there for the night. Mark the best houses for sleeping quarters and for cover for the panzers."

"Yes, sir," said the sergeant. Messer called his group together and gave them brief orders, then the men spread out and made their way down the road, rifles drawn.

Erik watched them through his field glasses, anxiously making sure they were safe. Soon the men disappeared behind the buildings. Erik waited, first five minutes, then ten. He couldn't see anything. There was no movement, no sound from the village.

Something was wrong. They should have had an all clear by now. Erik called the rest of his men together along with the panzer commander to express his concerns. He ordered the men to spread out and approach the houses cautiously.

He watched the peace explode into chaos in a moment. Flashes spurted from every window in the village. Bullets ripped by, slamming into flesh. Several of Erik's men were hit. Erik's ears rang as a panzer near him opened fire, sending a shell into a house that exploded in a cloud of smoke, fire, and rubble. The panzer rumbled and accelerated, storming down the road. The men filed in behind it, sprinting to stay close to the armored protection. More panzers rolled out into the fields on both sides of the road, their cannons blazing.

They reached the first houses in what seemed an eternity. Erik darted his head back and forth behind the turret, firing with his machine pistol toward the windows. The lead panzer rolled between two houses. A young Russian peasant, no more than twelve, streamed out the back door of a house, a bottle in his hand. He threw it even as his body was riddled with machine gun fire from the tank. The bottle exploded, spewing fiery liquid all over the panzer. Erik could hear the screaming within. The turret opened and men scrambled out, their bodies on fire, writhing in agony and stumbling about before tumbling to the mud.

The remaining panzers entered the village moments later, their machine guns spewing bullets. Erik ran past the burning tank in the first row of houses. He fired this way and that, spraying in the general direction of the flashes he saw in his peripheral vision. He ran past the still body of the young Russian boy. He couldn't glance down.

Bullets danced around his feet, and he knew any moment he would be hit. He charged forward as fast as he could and dived through the front door of the house directly in front of him. He hit the ground hard and tried to rise, taking in the interior of the Russian house, looking for threats. His gaze rested on Sergeant Messer, sitting on the dirt floor a few meters away from him staring back at him with eyes wide. Behind the sergeant was a Russian girl, no more than fifteen. She held a huge knife against Sergeant Messer's throat. She was screaming at Erik in Russian.

Erik raised both of his hands slowly, trying to speak to her as calmly as possible. Outside the battle raged on, but he kept his focus on the scene in front of him.

The girl's hands trembled. A rivulet of blood dripped down the sergeant's neck.

"I'm sorry, sir," whispered Messer.

"Everything is going to be fine," said Erik, his eyes never leaving the Russian. "She won't hurt you." Erik placed his hands on the dirt floor and pushed himself up to his knees. The girl screamed at him again, but he ignored her. He maintained eye contact, speaking soothingly in his most reassuring voice, knowing she did not understand but trying to calm her.

Her trembling increased, but her voice seemed to soften just a fraction. Erik continued to rise, his hands in the air, speaking softly to her.

The Russian girl ripped the knife across the sergeant's neck. Scarlet liquid washed over her hands as Erik's friend slumped into the dirt. His body writhed in silent agony.

Erik's mind exploded with rage. He reached down to retrieve his pistol, taking a couple of steps toward the girl. She looked down at the sergeant's body still twisting back and forth beneath her feet. She seemed to realize what she had done. She dropped the knife and fell to her knees, placing her hands on her head.

Erik raised his arm and fired, shooting the girl in the head. He did not hesitate or think about what he was doing. He only knew this girl had killed his best friend. The Russian girl fell backward, blood splashing the wall behind her. Her body jerked once and was still. Erik ran forward to help Messer, but it was too late.

Tears streamed down Erik's face. His closest companion was gone. And something else, something worse: he had killed someone in cold blood. Not even a soldier, just a girl.

"It's about time." He heard a familiar voice. Captain Sauer stood in the doorway, nodding approvingly. "You did the right thing, Lieutenant. I didn't know if you had it in you." He stepped over and grasped his shoulder. "Now you are the man I needed you to be." The captain slapped him hard on the back and walked from the room.

Erik stood there in the fading gunfire for a moment, alone with his grief and his shame.

CHAPTER FOURTEEN

Königsberg
December 1941

Trude sat in the front room of Mrs. Werner's townhome, thread and needle passing back and forth through torn fabric. *How many more times can I mend this shirt?* she thought. Captain Dutt still dropped off food on a weekly basis, but he could do nothing about clothing. Fabric had been strictly rationed in Germany since the war began. From everything Trude had heard from Mrs. Werner and from the radio, people were making do with the clothes they'd had before the war. This was a problem for everyone, but doubly so for Trude, since she had come to Mrs. Werner's house in the middle of the night with only the clothes on her back. Several times she chastised herself for not keeping the luggage they had with them that night so long ago now, when her husband was arrested at the docks. Still, that wasn't realistic. They'd needed to get away quickly, and there was no way that she and Britta could have run all the way back with their satchels and still escaped. Frau Werner had a spare dress she was able to use, and she'd been able to modify a couple of outfits for Britta, but there would be no more.

She couldn't believe that night was now about a year and a half ago. In some ways, she was so thankful; here she was, still alive, still with her daughter in safety thanks to the courageous efforts of Frau Werner and Captain Dutt. At the same time, she'd heard nothing more about her husband's whereabouts. Whether he was alive or dead. She and Britta had been prisoners in this home, unable to go out for risk of capture.

She glanced over at Britta, sitting nearby. Her daughter was spinning the wooden top. The black-and-white paint had faded and chipped now with no way to repair it, and no father to do so. Her daughter was so pale; she hadn't seen sunlight in all this time. Trude felt guilty. At least every now and again she could escape to Captain Dutt's house when he summoned her to give her an update on his efforts to locate Johannes. While this was only every couple of months, at least she'd been able to leave the tiny townhome on a few occasions. She could breathe the fresh air and look out at the sky. Frau Werner was afraid to even part the curtains, lest a neighbor spot them and call the Gestapo.

Time passed so slowly. There was little to do except the basic functions of the day. Cooking, cleaning, sewing, laundry, and listening to the radio at night for the news. Trude had hoped after all this time that something in the world would go right, but she had been sorely disappointed. The Germans continued to rack up victory after victory. First in France, then in the Balkans, now storming through Russia. The German army was within a few kilometers of Moscow, and the radio predicted a swift surrender and the end of the war.

More alarming were the stories of captured Jews and the Germans who harbored them. There were nightly lectures from radio broadcasters about the strict prohibition of hiding this unwanted population. All Jews in Germany were being collected and relocated. It was a severe crime to harbor them. Trude discussed this periodically with Mrs. Werner, telling her that they should leave, that she could not risk her life for them. But Mrs. Werner would not be moved. She refused to even listen to Trude's discussions on this point.

Trude thought of her husband again as she did so many times each day. What had happened to Johannes? Was he safe? Was he even alive? She just wished she knew something about him. She didn't want to hear that he was dead, but if it was true, she would rather know, and then the anxious, agonizing waiting would finally be over.

Escape was the other thought that filled her mind hour after hour. Captain Dutt had promised, without much hope, to consider the issue. He still had connections at the docks and among the various ship captains. But a year and a half had passed with nothing. She wasn't surprised; there were so few places that were safe to go. Even if she could find a ship, what port would it reach that would get her away from the Nazis' grasp? Germany was at war with Russia now. Norway was controlled by the Germans and so was Denmark. She might escape to Sweden and somehow make her way from there to England, but even if she miraculously found a ship, there was every chance it would be sunk by one enemy or another on the way. Still, some chance was better than nothing. She felt the Germans closing in on her with each passing day.

A ring at the door jolted her out of her reverie. She looked up in alarm to see Mrs. Werner mirroring her fear. "Britta, go upstairs as quietly as you can," she whispered.

Her daughter rose without making a sound and tiptoed rapidly toward the stairs. Trude followed right behind her. It had been so long since they'd had an unannounced visitor. Captain Dutt always called ahead before he sent Friedrich with food or to collect her.

Trude reached the top of the stairs and went into the bedroom, closing the door except for a crack so she could listen to any conversation below. She heard the door open and Mrs. Werner greeting someone.

A woman's voice answered. She heard the clip-clop of heels on the landing. Relief washed over her. It wasn't the Gestapo; it was some neighbor or another probably making a social visit to check in on Frau Werner.

"Frau Mueller, what a pleasant surprise," said Mrs. Werner loudly. Trude froze. Could this be Corina Mueller? She hadn't thought of Erik in ages, but he was in the SS, wasn't he? She recalled her conversation with Johannes; her husband had said Erik was in the wrong kind of SS. What did that mean? Did that mean they were safe?

"Frau Werner, how delightful to see you," Corina responded.

"What may I do for you?" asked Mrs. Werner, still standing near the doorway.

"May I come in and sit down for a moment? This will not take long."

Trude felt her anxiety rise again. She knew Mrs. Werner must feel the same because she hesitated before answering.

"Certainly, please come in."

Trude heard the clip-clop of Frau Mueller's heels stepping into the sitting room where they had been just minutes ago. "Please sit down," said Frau Werner. "Is there anything I can get you? Some tea perhaps?"

"I see you're doing some sewing," said Corina. "But whoever are you doing it for? You would swim in this shirt."

"Oh, it's not for me. It's . . . for my niece."

"I didn't know you had a niece in town. What's her name?"

"It's Helga," said Frau Werner.

"Helga. I see. You must bring her by sometime. I have so few guests from the neighborhood. Although you must hurry."

"Why is that?" she asked.

"I'm looking for a new place in the Steindamm District. Erik has done quite well in the war, you know, a decorated hero and an officer. We are just waiting for his promotion to captain before we take the leap."

"Your husband is safe, I hope?"

"Oh yes. I don't think he's even in the fighting most of the time. He's in charge of everyone else. I think he just sort of sends them in."

"And you don't worry about him?"

"Certainly I worry, but he's done so well for himself. We seem destined for great things, you know. Was your husband in the last war?"

"Oh no, we were far too old for that."

"I suppose so. Well, talking about Erik was not the purpose of my visit. I've been asked to organize a neighborhood patrol."

"What sort of patrol?"

"I'm sure you've heard all about it on the radio. There are Jews hiding everywhere. Right here under our noses."

Trude felt her skin crawl. She tried to hold her breath, not wanting to make a sound.

"That sounds silly," said Frau Werner. "There can't be any more Jews in this neighborhood! Didn't they all leave ages ago?"

"Oh, you couldn't be more wrong, Frau Werner. They're rats. You walk through the house and you think they're not there, but they are, hiding in the cracks and the crevices. My friend Karl told me just the other day that there could be five thousand Jews or more left in Königsberg, hiding in the cellars, the basements, the attics."

"What would you like me to do?" she asked.

"Well, obviously, we can't have you marching up and down the street," said Frau Mueller, laughing. "I'm just going door-to-door asking people to keep an eye on things. If you see anything suspicious—a person who's not supposed to be here, strange sounds at night, even people moving around in your neighbors' houses who you wouldn't expect to be there—please just give me a call. Here's my number." Trude heard a rustle of paper.

"I . . . I will certainly do so."

"Why, what's this?" asked Corina.

"That's nothing. Just a toy." Trude's heart froze. Britta had left her top behind when she'd run up the stairs.

"Does your niece have a child?"

"Yes . . . She does. She must've left it behind."

"So strange. You know that feeling when you've seen something before? I'm certain I've seen something just like this. Silly me, I can't remember when. Well, I will remember eventually."

Trude could hear the determined heels move again across the floor. "Thank you again for seeing me today, Frau Werner. It was a great pleasure."

Trude heard the door open and close. She sank to the ground trying to catch her breath. The danger was closing in.

—◆—

For agonizing days Trude waited for the Gestapo to come. She anticipated the moment that Corina remembered she'd seen that same black-and-white wooden top when they ran into each other that fateful August day in 1939. Erik's wife seemed very sharp and obviously had no qualms about turning in a Jew, child or not.

No one came. Mid-December became late December. The Germans were on the verge of capturing Moscow. Leningrad was surrounded. Soon the Russians would be out of the war, and the Germans would rule Europe and perhaps the rest of the world. At some point, they would look inward and ferret out the rest of their perceived enemies. The door-to-door searches would increase, and even an honest German like Mrs. Werner would be subject to a thorough search. At that point there would be nowhere else to hide.

She again raised with Mrs. Werner that she and Britta should leave. Frau Werner was insistent. "I'm not going to let that callous blond wench push me around," she said. "If she remembers and the Gestapo comes, it is God's will. I've had a long, full life, and I will not sacrifice you and your daughter for another year or two. No true German could do anything less."

"I'm afraid most of the true Germans have gone over to the Nazis," said Trude. "You are a true human."

There was a loud bang on the door. The sound jolted Trude, and she saw Mrs. Werner flinch. She grabbed the bread and raced up the stairs as quietly as possible, knowing it would do no good to hide upstairs if the Gestapo was here for her. This was the end.

She heard the door open below and the sharp voice of a male.

"Trude," Frau Werner's voice called up the stairs. "You'd better come down."

She steeled herself. This was it. She motioned for Britta to stay there. Perhaps they would just take her and not search the house.

She opened the door and started toward the stairs, searching for the group of men in leather coats who would be here to take her. She was shocked to see it was only Friedrich, Captain Dutt's driver. He'd never come before without calling.

She breathed a sigh of relief and came down the stairs quickly. "Friedrich, what can I do for you?"

"I've come to collect you," he said gruffly, not meeting her gaze. A year and a half of deliveries and the occasional trip to the captain's home had not altered his icy demeanor. He seldom spoke to her in their drives back and forth to the captain's home. She knew his feelings about her, about the Jews. Another worry that had haunted her. Another person who might betray her at any moment. She knew only his loyalty for Captain Dutt kept him from immediately turning her in.

"Why didn't you call ahead?"

He grunted. "No time."

She didn't know what that meant, but she remembered Corina's words about watchful neighbors.

"Do you have news?"

"Yes, urgent news."

"Well, I can't go now. Can you come back later, after dark?"

The young German shook his head. "We have to go now."

Urgent news? What did that mean? Had the captain finally found some way out? She would have to risk it.

"All right," she said. She turned to Mrs. Werner. "Can you watch Britta for a little while?"

"Of course, dear. But be careful," said Mrs. Werner, eyeing Friedrich doubtfully. "And you, mister, make sure she gets there and back safely."

Friedrich nodded sternly to Mrs. Werner, a flash of disapproval slipping across his face. He turned stiffly and marched back out the front door toward the car.

Trude set a foot on the porch and looked up and down the street. There was no one out for a walk and few cars. She strode as swiftly as possible toward the open door. She was certain there were eyes on her from every house. Some people might even recognize her. She was putting everything at risk, but she had to know what news the captain had.

Friedrich whisked her through the streets of Königsberg. She hadn't been outside during the day in all this time. She was surprised by how light the traffic was and how many stores seemed to be closed even during the day. Many were boarded up. She also saw alarming signs of anti-Semitism. Store windows with giant Stars of David and insulting statements painted on the glass. Broken windows, boarded-up doors. She felt her fear rising.

"They hate the Jews," said Friedrich. "I told you so."

She was surprised. He rarely spoke to her. "We haven't done anything to you."

Friedrich grunted. "I never knew a Jew before I met you."

"Do you still believe all the trash about us?"

He was silent a moment. He pointed out the window at another boarded-up store. "The Fuhrer has taken everything away from them. The captain says the Jews are a scapegoat."

"What do you think?"

He turned his head for a moment, staring at her. "You're the only Jew I know."

He was quiet then. She wanted to ask him more, to press him, but she wasn't sure what to say. He was so stern, he scared her.

179

They arrived a few minutes later at Captain Dutt's home without incident. Friedrich led her into the captain's study and then politely pulled a chair out for her. She sat down, a little surprised. He never did that. He turned and left the room.

Captain Dutt was already at his desk waiting for her. He looked older and frailer than ever. So strange that the two people who were helping her so much were so elderly. She wondered at this. This elder generation seemed to have a conscience that was missing from those who'd grown up after the last war. Or perhaps it was because they had so much less to lose? She didn't know.

"Good afternoon," said the captain, smiling up at her, his stern countenance aglow and flashing like a lighthouse. "Have a seat."

"Friedrich said you had something urgent."

"I do. News of your husband."

She couldn't believe it. She'd heard nothing for a year and a half now. Finally, something. But then she realized the seriousness of Captain Dutt's face. *Johannes is dead,* she thought, *he's gone.*

"Tell me," she whispered, bracing herself. "Is he dead?"

"No."

"What then?"

"Perhaps worse."

"What can be worse than death?"

"He's in a prison. Perhaps 'camp' would be a better word. There have been rumors. Labor camps where they are collecting Jews and other undesirables. These camps are run by the SS. People go in, but no one ever comes out. I don't know many details, but your husband is in one of these camps. The conditions, I'm afraid, are terribly harsh. There's little food and much labor. There are even . . ."

"Tell me."

He hesitated. "There are even stories of executions. Mass executions." He raised his hands toward her. "Don't put too much stock in this. I heard this from someone who heard it from someone else. The stories may be just that—only rumors. But I know that your husband is in a camp and that he is still alive."

The news was terrible, but she felt joy surging through her. If he was alive, there was a chance. After the months and months of uncertainty she felt tremendous relief wash over her. The emotions welled up inside and the tears cascaded down her cheeks. She covered her face with her hands and sobbed, unable to stop herself. It was long moments before she could continue.

"Is there anything you can do for him?" she asked.

"No. Outside of Königsberg I have some friends, but no one in the SS. I'm afraid I cannot help you, at least right now. But I will keep trying to find a way out for you and to see if there's any way to help your husband."

She thanked him again for everything he had done for her.

The captain called Friedrich back and directed him to return Trude home as soon as it was dark and with a load of groceries.

Friedrich nodded without responding, then busied himself with loading the car while Trude visited a bit longer with the captain. Darkness was falling already as this was one of the shortest days of the year. She stepped through the slushy, snow-covered courtyard, picking her way carefully to avoid slipping, and took her seat again in the back of the captain's automobile.

Friedrich drove away and into the now-darkened streets of Königsberg. On the drive back, again she was shocked by the deadness of her town. Her home city had always been a bustling metropolis with cars and people traveling even in the evenings here and there. Now they were one of the sole cars on the street. A few travelers on foot were bundled up with heads down walking briskly to their destination. Otherwise, Königsberg was a ghost city.

Thoughts of Johannes flew through her mind. Her husband was alive. She imagined him emaciated, working backbreaking labor, starving, beaten. She shook her head. She couldn't think of such things just now. At least there was a sliver of hope.

"The captain told you about your husband?"

"Yes."

"He is a Jew also, yes?"

She nodded.

"Do you love him?"

The question caught her by surprise. "Of course. He's my husband."

Before he could respond they were turning on her street. She couldn't wait to tell Britta that her father was alive. But the thought froze in her mind. Three dark cars were pulled up in front of Mrs. Werner's house. Figures stood in front of the townhome. Gestapo, she knew right away. She reached for the door. Her daughter was inside. They would take her daughter. She must not leave her. She felt a strong hand on her arm pulling her back.

"No!" said Friedrich.

"Let me go!" she demanded.

"No!" he repeated. His eyes flared with violence. She'd never seen him like this before. "Get down!" he demanded. "They'll kill you!" His voice was desperate and sharp.

She complied without thinking. Her heart tore itself into pieces. She just wanted to die. They were taking her little girl, and there was nothing she could do about it.

Friedrich pushed the accelerator, and she felt the car sliding by. Her head was down and her mind numb. She had to be with her daughter, but she was frozen with guilt and terror, every horrid emotion haunting her as they slipped into the cold darkness of the night.

CHAPTER FIFTEEN

Russia, 50 km from Moscow
December 1941

Erik rode along with several members of his platoon on the front of
the Panzer III. They were rumbling down the dirt pathway frozen solid
with snow. A white landscape covered as if by an icy quilt. The men
were huddled together, pressed tightly against the tank, trying to draw
heat from the machine and each other.

Erik could not remember ever having been so cold. Königsberg, in
East Prussia, at the extreme northeast end of Germany, often experienced frozen, snowy winters. But while the temperature there hovered
at or slightly below zero, here he'd experienced a real Russian winter.
His unit was totally unprepared for the weather. They'd received no
winter clothing and were still dressed in their summer uniforms with no
overcoats, gloves, or winter boots. They had taken blankets from villages
and stolen gloves or made crudely crafted mittens out of socks or anything else they could find. They discovered that stuffing newspaper into
their boots and around their legs and arms helped keep out some of the

biting cold, but the materials they possessed were woefully insufficient for their needs, and the men suffered from frostbite and other ailments.

Worse yet was the effect of the cold on their machinery. Tanks refused to start. The men lit fires underneath them in order to get the engines to turn over in the morning. Airplanes were grounded or froze in the air, crashing to the ground. The biting cold brought one blessing: the slogging fall mud finally solidified. After storming across much of Western Russia, the autumn rain stopped them cold. The rain churned the dirt roads into a river of mud that would sink a tank up to the turrets. Now the ground was frozen, and the German army was swarming forward once again.

Erik looked around, his men riding the various tanks as they rumbled along. He had scarcely twenty soldiers left. Less than half his original platoon. Sauer's entire company was less than fifty. Headquarters kept promising them new replacements, but their casualties exceeded the fresh troops by a ratio of two to one.

Still, they were making rapid progress. The Russians on the eastern front had died or surrendered in the millions. They were reportedly on their last legs. Sauer informed the company if they captured Moscow, Stalin would surely surrender and they could all go home.

As if invoking his commander to materialize by thinking of him, the captain pulled up next to the tank in his command vehicle, motioning for the tanks to stop. The panzers rumbled to a halt for a midday break. Several of the steel monsters rumbled off the highway and into the field to form a defensive perimeter. Other men removed the field cooking equipment from a nearby truck and prepared a hot meal, the first in days.

"Lieutenant, come over here for a second," commanded Sauer.

Erik jumped stiffly down from the tank. He worked his arms and legs, trying to restore circulation as he made his way to his captain. Sauer withdrew a metal cylinder from his command car. He unscrewed the top and poured coffee into a cup, taking a sip himself before handing the same to Erik.

"How are you doing, *mein Freund?*" Sauer asked.

"Frozen," said Erik, his teeth clicking together as he stomped his feet, waiting for the hot liquid to warm him.

Sauer chuckled. "The whole German army is frozen," he said. "Hopefully these Russian bastards are about the same. Like the Führer said, one more kick and the whole rotten structure will fall in."

"We've kicked them awfully hard, and they haven't quit yet," Erik said.

"An animal is always most desperate when it's wounded and in a corner."

"How much farther to Moscow?" asked Erik.

"Fifty kilometers at the most. One more push ought to do it. Anything I can do for the boys?"

"Do you have coats, and food, and ammunition, and boots, and gloves?" Erik joked.

Sauer laughed and clapped Erik on the shoulder. "I have all those things in Berlin, my friend. We just have to get back there. Don't you worry; I think the whole show will be over in a few days."

"This hot meal will help. It won't solve all the problems, but it will make a difference."

Sauer nodded approvingly. "You make quite an officer."

"Thank you, sir."

Sauer saluted him and turned to attend to his other platoon commanders, leaving Erik alone with his thoughts. Erik felt the hot, churning mix of emotions rifling through him again. Sauer was an excellent combat commander who took care of his men and fought fiercely and courageously. In many ways, they were perfectly matched, and Erik was proud he could keep up with his commander. But on the other hand, Sauer was a ruthless killer fully indoctrinated into the Nazi cause with no remorse for the torture and killing of civilians and unarmed prisoners. His newfound respect for Erik grew from the mistaken belief that Mueller's feelings on this issue had changed. But Sauer had merely witnessed a moment of weakness on Erik's part that haunted his every hour awake and ran through his dreams each night.

By some miracle, in these many months of fighting Erik had avoided any other incidents. Sauer had fortunately not called on him to do anything Erik would struggle morally to perform. But he knew that moment would come again, and he did not know what he would do.

With frozen fingers, he removed a crumpled letter from home and read it again. Corina wrote that word had reached her through Karl that Sauer was pleased with his performance. There was talk of another promotion eventually. Sauer said the same to him directly. Corina's letter was full of praise and excitement, plans for a new home and their future after the war. Karl told her that the next promotion would open even more doors. Erik's position in Königsberg as a leader in postwar Germany was assured. Perhaps they would go even higher, she hinted. Karl was on his way up, recently given command of SS activities in East Prussia. Now after a period of disappointment, Erik was apparently back in his good graces, and Karl hinted he might wish to bring Erik onto his staff. With the war almost over, their future seemed assured.

Erik folded up the letter and closed his eyes in prayer. He prayed that the war would end in the next few days. He prayed for the safety of his men and that he would not be called on by Sauer to do anything that would ruin his career or destroy his soul further. He prayed for protection for his family, and that when these battles were over peace would come to the world. He smiled at the thought. He'd dreamed of Germany taking its place once more as one of the world's mightiest, freed from the humiliation of the last war. He had been reared on stories from his father of the kaiser's Germany when the great nation stood poised on the brink of empire, when anything seemed possible for his country and his family.

Would Germany be great, or would it be the Nazis'? His father believed that after the war the rhetoric and propaganda would cool and Germany would return to the peaceful civilized nation full of artists, scholars, musicians, and industrialists that he had fought for. A new Germany would rise with all the resources of Europe open to it, taking its rightful place in the sun. But if the leaders of the new Germany were like Sauer—and his darker self—men forged in such hatred and hardship, could his country ever move forward into lasting peace?

⟞⟝

The company did not move again that day. The men ate their hot meal for lunch and another for dinner. Captain Sauer decided to check in with battalion and regimental headquarters before proceeding forward for the last push to Moscow. He left Erik in charge of the company while he was gone. Erik made sure the panzers were properly positioned and that each man had a full share of the hot meals. He sent a runner back for what ammunition could be spared and made what seemed like his hundredth requisition for winter clothing.

Captain Sauer arrived back at the company early the next morning before the sun had risen. He brought with him a reserve of gasoline and some additional rations but not any warm clothing.

"I gathered what I could," he explained. "Ammunition supplies are dangerously low. I only have enough fuel to get us to Moscow. No real room for maneuver. I guess we must take what the Russians leave us when they retreat." He outlined regimental plans for the final push: the entire division would stream forward beginning at eight a.m. on a five-kilometer front. This attack would represent not only a divisional effort but the entire army and indeed the army group. High command was throwing everything available into the last effort to capture the capital and hopefully end the war.

"They expect us to be in Moscow by the end of the day, or at least by the end of day tomorrow. They say this will be the end of them," said Sauer.

"They've said that before."

Sauer laughed. "I know, but this time it might really be it. There's been very little resistance in the last week or so. I think they are at the end of the rope."

Erik was doubtful but kept his mouth shut.

"Make sure the gasoline is distributed equally and that the cold rations are picked up by each group. There should be enough for three days for each man."

Erik nodded and turned to issue the orders. Soon the quiet morning was interrupted by the coughing motors of the panzers as they struggled to life in the subfreezing temperatures. Erik noted the crews were getting better at coaxing the machines back to life out of the stunning cold. They were marvelous at adjusting to the extreme conditions, and he was proud of them.

Soon the tanks were sufficiently warmed up, and Erik briefed his men. They would be in the lead today as they so often were. Erik chuckled to himself. He used to take point because he thought Sauer wanted to get rid of them. Now he drew the same duty because his commander depended on him.

He checked to make sure his machine pistol was armed with a full clip of ammunition. He only had two in reserve. If they ran into any real fighting, he would run out quickly. He shook his head. The entire platoon was dangerously low on bullets.

He pulled himself up onto the lead Panzer III and helped two of his men up behind him. Soon they were rumbling down the road ever eastward toward Moscow. Throughout the morning and into the afternoon they rolled onward, encountering no resistance. Perhaps Captain Sauer was correct. Perhaps the Russians were done this time. He couldn't imagine they would let their capital city go without a fight unless they had truly exhausted all their resources already.

"Lieutenant!" One of his men was shouting to him enthusiastically and pointing. Erik looked down the road to the horizon. For long moments, all he could see were pastures covered with snow, the fences and the farms. Finally, he sought the extreme horizon and could make out a glint of red: the very top of a tapered tower far in the distance. He realized with growing elation he could just make out the tip of the Kremlin. They'd made it. They'd traveled more than a thousand kilometers into enemy territory. He couldn't believe after all this time, all this struggle, they were nearly there.

"Come on, boys!" he exclaimed excitedly. "A few more hours and we will have dinner in Moscow!"

The cheering of the men was harshly interrupted by the long, shrill arcing whistle of incoming shells all along the horizon. Erik strained to see. Flashes of light popped in and out all along the borders of his vision. There were tanks out there and artillery, he realized. Dozens and dozens of them, perhaps more. They had moments to react.

"Spread out!" he screamed, even as the first shells landed among them. A tank nearby exploded in a furious ball of fire. Hot shrapnel flew in each direction as the tank disintegrated. He'd never seen anything hit that hard, and he wondered what sort of weaponry the Russians had brought to bear. He dropped off the panzer and sprinted behind the tank as the machine rotated its turret to return fire.

Shells sprinkled their position like deadly raindrops. Erik was covered in frozen mud. A sliver of hot metal landed on his neck, burning him. He screamed and frantically clawed at his uniform, trying to remove it. The fiery steel stuck to his skin—too hot to handle with his fingers. He tore at it and ripped the shrapnel away. He nearly bit through his tongue from the pain. He fought down the agony, trying to concentrate on the chaos exploding around him.

Panzers blasted apart. He felt the flashing roars and the heat. An explosion knocked him back away from the lead panzer and into the mud. He stared up at the heavens, blinking for a moment, as he tried to remember where he was. He ran his hands over his body, feeling for wounds. Miraculously, he hadn't been hit. He rolled over, striving again for a glance of the enemy.

He was stunned by what he saw. A massive tank rolled down the road toward him rapidly. He'd never seen one like it before. Two angular protruding fenders jutted up above the treads. A giant cannon, probably a seventy-five-millimeter gun, sprouted out of the raised turret. The tank stopped for a moment and belched fire, rocking backward. Another round rocked the ground behind him. Erik realized most of the German panzers were already burning. He crawled backward away from the fighting, clutching his machine pistol. He sprayed wild bursts toward the enemy. Probably fruitless, he realized, but he had to do something.

After an eternity, he reached the last row of panzers. He found a few members of the company huddled with a couple of the black-uniformed tank crew members. They hid behind a burned-out panzer, firing sporadically at the oncoming Russians. Captain Sauer was among them, his pistol drawn, his pale Aryan features smeared with mud and smoke.

"What are those tanks?" he shouted.

"Don't know, sir, I've never seen them before."

"I've heard rumors," said Sauer. "There are stories about them at headquarters. Some kind of new supertank. They said they might have a few in production but that they would make no difference in the fighting."

"Looks like headquarters was wrong," said Erik.

Sauer pointed to some woods behind them no more than a half kilometer away. "Let's try to get out of here," he said. "That's our only chance of escape."

Erik shook his head. "Too far."

"You have a better plan, Lieutenant?"

Erik didn't. The shells still exploded around them. He knew in a matter of minutes they would all be dead. The woods were impossibly far away. He was going to die today. The thought didn't scare him for some reason, although he mourned for his family at home—his parents, Corina, darling Greta. He nodded to Captain Sauer and cocked the bolt of his machine pistol, slamming in his last clip.

Sauer waited a moment, wincing a little from the blast of a nearby shell. He smiled and nodded. They turned and ran, waving for their men to follow them and bolting from behind the tank toward the woods. They tried to use the line of sight from the burning tanks as cover. After thirty meters they turned into the field and sprinted through the ankle-deep snow. So far they had not been spotted, but their field-green uniforms stood out mightily against the white backdrop. Erik heard the whistle of an incoming shell. An explosion landed a few meters away. Another shell quickly followed suit. Soon they would have the range. They were five hundred meters away from the woods. Too far, he knew; they'd never make it.

CHAPTER SIXTEEN

Königsberg
December 1941

The automobile slid through the streets of Königsberg. Friedrich whipped the steering wheel around violently with both hands as if he would tear it off the console.

"Let me out!" screamed Trude. She leaned forward from the back seat, pounding on his back, screaming, begging, pleading. The world was a blurry, misty haze through the torrents of tears flowing down her cheeks.

"You bastard!" she shouted. "Take me to my little girl!"

Friedrich slowed the vehicle down and moved to the shoulder. He turned the car off and turned to her, rage in his eyes. He raised his hand as if to strike her. She flinched, pulling back.

"Now listen here!" he shouted. "I can't take you back there. They'll kill you."

"I don't care! They have my little girl!"

"I know that. But you won't do her any good if the Gestapo have you. I can't drive with you beating on me. We must get to the captain. He'll know what to do."

Her mind was a ravaging storm. She heard the logic in his voice. If they went back to Frau Werner's house, they'd arrest her along with Friedrich. That would lead them to Captain Dutt as well. They would all be in jail, tortured, or killed. If there was any hope for Britta, they had to get away. If there was any chance of helping her daughter, she must go see Captain Dutt. She nodded and closed her eyes, leaning her head against the seat.

"That's right, Frau Bensheim," said Friedrich, his voice grating steel. "Sit back and let me take care of this."

Friedrich started the automobile again. He pressed the accelerator and the vehicle lurched into motion, sliding slightly back and forth before gaining enough traction to proceed down the icy road.

They'd been lucky, she realized. If it was daytime when they returned, they would surely have been spotted and arrested immediately. But in the darkness, they were just one more pair of headlights, a steel-enclosed vehicle shrouded in darkness.

Her mind all these months had been alive with blazing pain, but now those feelings seemed a laughable frolic compared to this. She didn't think she could take this for one more instant. She knew it would be hours, days, or even worse before anything could be done. All that time they would have her little girl. What about poor Frau Werner? She realized guiltily she hadn't even thought of the elderly German woman. They would have arrested her, too. She'd sacrificed herself to try to save them, and now she was paying the price.

The car rolled on through the icy streets. She closed her eyes again, praying, opening her heart to God, begging for a miracle, for anything to protect Britta.

The car slowed down and turned, winding up a slight incline, and she knew they were at the captain's home. Friedrich ordered her to stay put. He left the car running and opened the door, and she heard his quick footsteps clattering on the driveway. An eternity later her door was opened, and she heard the captain's voice. Hands reached for her, pulling her slowly from the car. She couldn't see, tears swallowing the world around her. There were people on both sides of her, helping her to stand, to lurch reluctantly into the captain's home.

They took her to the study, setting her gently down in a high-backed upholstered seat. Someone handed her a cloth, and she dabbed her eyes, trying to focus them. Finally, she could see. She was alone in the room with the captain and Friedrich.

"What happened?" asked Dutt. He sat on the edge of his desk, near her, his heavily lined temples creased with anguish.

Friedrich explained in slow and shaky words what had happened on their drive back to Mrs. Werner's home, the appearance of the Gestapo and the race back to his house. His hands clenched and his knuckles rippled white.

"*Gut Gott!*" said the captain. He rang his bell, and a servant swiftly appeared. "Tea and food," he ordered, before returning his attention to Trude. "I'm so sorry. I didn't expect this. Of course, we always knew it was a risk, but it has been so long now. I believed the danger had largely passed."

"Mrs. Werner knows about me," said Friedrich. "She knows about you, too, Captain. I assume the girl does also."

"No," said Trude, shaking her head. "We've been careful not to discuss your name or anything else in Britta's presence. She doesn't know anything. At least not enough to lead them here."

"It may not help us. Frau Werner could betray all of us."

"She would never do so willingly," said Trude. "I've put you all in danger." All the way to the captain's house she had thought of only Britta. But there was so much more to this. Not only was Mrs. Werner in immediate danger, but she had placed Captain Dutt's life and the lives of his household at risk as well. Why had she ever gone to any of them in the first place? How selfish of her to put others in harm's way.

Captain Dutt squared his shoulders, pale but resolute. "I knew the risks when I got into this. If she talks and they come, that is God's will." He turned to Friedrich. "I should never have involved you or the rest of my household."

Friedrich stiffened and clicked his heels in salute. "I'm glad you did, sir. I would do anything for you . . . and for Frau Bensheim."

Trude looked up in amazement. Had she just heard him correctly? He'd never said a kind word to her. She thought he considered her vermin, an Untermensch. Now he was putting his life on the line willingly for her and the captain. She smiled gratefully, feeling an unexpected flicker of warmth and hope amid the ocean of anguish.

Dutt nodded to his driver approvingly and then turned back to Trude. "What's done is done. We will wait and see. If Mrs. Werner is half the tough old bird I think she is, she may resist them for a long time, perhaps forever. In the meantime, I will find out everything I can about her and your daughter."

"I thought you didn't have any connections with the SS?"

"I don't in Germany at large, but here in Königsberg it is another thing. I cannot promise you a miracle, child. I may be able to obtain knowledge, but I'm not sure what more I will be able to do. If there is anything, no matter how remote, I will try."

She rose and took his hands in hers. "Thank you, Captain, for everything. You put far too much at risk for me."

"I will set to work immediately," he said.

"What can I do?" she asked.

"You can pray."

The days dribbled by at Captain Dutt's home. Trude, who was put up in grandiose and spacious accommodations on the second floor, spent most of her time in the captain's study, a book or magazine absentmindedly resting in her hands. She looked up hopefully with each passing sound, praying for news. She had hoped intense anguish would fade at least a little as time passed, but if anything, her anxiety only intensified.

The captain had taken to dosing her with liberal glasses of sherry. She gulped them greedily, the fiery liquid burning her throat and numbing her emotions, at least a fraction.

She would punctuate moments of extraordinarily desperate waiting by listening to the radio. The news reported heavy fighting around Moscow. Although there was no news of any losses by or defeats of the Germans, she noticed the announcers no longer predicted victory any day. After two long years, finally something was not going exactly as the Germans desired. Was it possible the Russians still had some fight left in them? How could they after so many millions had been killed and captured?

She had never really known any Russians. She wondered what they were like. The Germans called them Bolsheviks and Jews. How many Jews were in Russia? She didn't know. She felt a strange sense of pride, however, that perhaps some people with the same blood as her were standing up to the Germans. Were fighting and killing them.

When she thought about Britta, she was bombarded by horrible premonitions: gray concrete, bare bulbs, and grim, uniformed Nazis. She shook her head. These nightmares raced through her sleep and crept in to every waking moment. She could not think about it long without going mad.

Friedrich brought in lunch. He quietly took the captain's chair, setting down the silver tray containing a basket of bread, fresh apples, and some sliced cheese. She stared at the food for a moment and shook her head.

"You must eat," said Friedrich sternly. When she made no move toward the food, he took a plate himself, stacking it with bread, cheese, and fruit and stepping around the desk to place it gently in her lap. "You must try to eat something," he repeated, softly this time. "If you do not have any strength, you will be unready when we need to take action."

He was right, of course. She placed the white aged cheese onto the still-warm bread and forced it up toward her lips. She bit down, nearly gagging, but she pushed herself to chew the food. It tasted like ashes in her mouth, but she swallowed, took another bite, and swallowed again before she set the food aside.

"That will do for now," said Friedrich, "but you must have more. Do you promise me?"

She nodded. "I want to thank you," she said.

"For what?"

"For driving me. For saving me. For caring about me as a human."

He watched her with those intent, almost fanatic eyes. A face that had so frightened her at first. He wrung his hands, looking away.

"I should've told you before."

"You showed me. Your actions are greater than the words of dozens of people who said they would help. You don't owe me any explanation."

The door opened and she looked up. Captain Dutt hobbled into the room. His face was red and splotchy. He walked with slow deliberate paces. *He knows something,* she realized.

"What is it?" she asked.

He did not answer. Instead he went to the desk and poured a tall glass of sherry, handing it to her.

Trude shook her head, her soul engulfed by darkness. "I don't want that."

He stepped forward again. "Drink it down and then we will talk."

Bad news, she realized. Perhaps the worst. Unconsciously she took the sherry, moving it slowly to her lips. Her hand shook, and some of the liquid splashed out onto her wrist. She tipped the glass back, gulping down the fiery liquid. Even as she drank she prayed. She feared the worst. *My little girl is gone.*

"I have news of Britta," he began, his normally strong voice shaking and tenuous. "She was arrested as you feared. She was interrogated by an SS officer named Gunther Wolf."

"No!"

"Hold on," he said, reaching for her. "I understand there were no physical methods used in the questioning. Since then she's been kept in a cell, but she's receiving adequate food and water. There are strict orders from Gunther that no one is to touch her."

Trude felt the relief welling up inside her. Britta was safe. But Gunther had questioned her? She was revolted by the picture of the old letch standing over her daughter, alone in some cell. But he hadn't used any physical force. He was protecting her, she realized. She would've never believed it. She questioned his motivations, but for now, her little girl was safe.

She rose and rushed into Captain Dutt's, arms, thanking him. It was a few moments before she realized there must still be something wrong. He had made her drink a whole glass of sherry to steel herself for the news. She remembered the look on his face when he came into the room. She stepped back, watching him closely.

"What is it?" she asked.

Captain Dutt looked down. "We don't have to worry about betrayal anymore."

"Then you mean . . . ," she started, her veins full of ice.

"She's gone."

"Frau Werner?"

"Yes."

"How?"

"They tortured her. She wouldn't talk. She was too frail, but perhaps also too strong . . . They went too hard on her, and her heart gave out."

Trude fell to her knees, clinging to Captain Dutt's legs. She held him so tightly he nearly tripped. "Frau Bensheim, please, you're hurting me."

She let go, dropping to the carpet. Tears pooling onto the thick silk weave.

"It's all me. All my fault!"

"No, Trude. She made her own choice. She was a true woman, a true German. She chose to help you for her own reasons, her own beliefs. Just as I have. You mustn't blame yourself for her misfortune."

"What are we doing to do?"

"We are going to survive. We are going to find a way to get your daughter out—if such a thing is possible. We are going to live."

She tried to hear him, tried to believe the words, but it was all too much. She had directly caused the death of a poor, kind elderly woman. Her daughter and husband were in prison. There was no hope, no future. Only the darkness of her heart and mind.

CHAPTER SEVENTEEN

Kharkov, Russia
February 1943

Captain Erik Mueller rode near the turret of the Tiger tank through the open fields of the Russian steppe. He was bundled warmly in new winter clothing, camouflaged white to blend into the snow. The massive 88-millimeter cannon loomed overhead as he jolted along through the field.

How different from the last time I was here, he thought. He thought back to a time not much more than a year ago when his unit and the entire division were mauled by Russian forces on the outskirts of Moscow. He would never forget the agony of that frozen retreat. He remembered their shock and surprise when massive numbers of Siberian Russians appeared out of nowhere with new equipment, new tanks, endless divisions—fierce, angry, and vengeful.

Through sheer courage and determination, they had somehow stopped the furious Russian counterattack, but to do so they had had to give ground. The spires of the Kremlin disappeared, and they had never seen them again. Slowly, kilometer by kilometer, they'd abandoned their gains.

He smiled, through gritted teeth, thinking of the day he'd learned they would leave the eastern front and refit in France. He'd had a glorious month at home, a promotion, visits with his wife and family. He was a hero now, somebody important.

Despite the disappointment at Moscow, everything had pointed to victory in the spring of 1942. But he did not have to be part of that push as his unit refitted and restructured in France. He remembered the luxurious time among the French people, so different from the Russians. The people he encountered were timid, passive, for the most part, if aloof. He'd drunk wine, eaten his fill of food, and lived largely free of danger. During this respite, he'd trained his company of men and incorporated replacements until the company, *his* company, was back to full strength, with new equipment, fully supplied with ammunition, and outfitted with the new panzers, including the massive Tiger like the one he was riding on now.

He'd hoped the war in the East would be done before they ever needed to come back, but this was not to be. In the summer, the Germans again were streaming almost uninterrupted into Southern Germany toward the oilfields of the Bolsheviks. They had gone so far again, so fast, their progress almost greater than the gains in 1941. Then came Stalingrad. At first the city seemed like it would fall in a day or two. But the Russians put up a stubborn resistance. Days became weeks became months. Then the Russians counterattacked, cutting the German 6th Army off. The end of the war, which had again seemed so close, fell away, and a new specter appeared, the first shade of defeat. Just a hint, a glimmer, but it was there.

Instead of heading home for a victory parade, Erik found his unit called back up to active duty on the eastern front, traveling by rail out of the occupied territories, across Germany, and finally back into the dreadful expanses of the Soviet Union. They'd arrived here near Kharkov only a few days ago. Now they were roaring forward again toward combat, his old enemy, and he faced the ever-present possibility he would never see home again.

The Russians were out there. Millions of them. Not the disorganized, frightened mob of 1941, but an army increasingly well equipped with superior tanks, air support, and endless ammunition. He knew when one matched the ferocious nature of the Russian with proper equipment they would be a formidable force indeed.

Still, there was hope. There were virtually no SS units fighting in Stalingrad. In Erik's opinion, only the valiant fanatic spirit of the SS could match the Russians' passion and power. Now he and his men were not only reequipped but provisioned with new materials, new tanks. This infusion of new men and equipment should turn the tide.

Erik rolled off the tank and into the snow, stumbling a bit and falling to his knees before he pulled himself up. He dusted his pants off and headed back into the column. Eventually he found Major Sauer, now a battalion commander, rumbling along the tanks in an armored car. Despite their history, Sauer had become the closest thing to a friend Erik had in the army since the death of Sergeant Messer. The major looked up from a map he was studying, smiled on seeing Erik, and motioned for the captain to climb aboard.

Erik jumped in and then looked out the back to see a long line of tanks spread out single file along with an endless train of covered trucks, huddling on the sole ribbon of the road.

"What's the situation, Major?"

"Good question. No telling exactly what's ahead. There's supposed to be a batch of Russians coming in against us."

"No idea how many?"

"Plenty. There's a couple armies out there somewhere. Question is how much of it's right in front of us. No doubt we get warmed up. I hope these Tigers live up to their reputation . . ."

"Can't be worse than those Panzer III's. The shells bounced right off the T-34's like the rounds were made of paper."

Sauer nodded. "That was quite a shock. Here we thought they were done, then they show up with a whole new tank, better than any of ours."

"Village ahead," announced Sauer's aid, scanning the horizon with binoculars. As if in answer, Erik observed flashing lights and drifting smoke. Moments later a sharp report thundered across the sky followed by the whistle of incoming shells. The panzers returned fire, a massive echoing boom of the 88-millimeter cannon sending shockwaves through Erik's ears. He covered them with his hands.

Incoming shells rained down in random fury. Erik saw with satisfaction a shell directly strike a Tiger and bounce off the armor. The steel behemoth kept moving forward as if nothing had happened.

The panzers rained fire down on the village, and in but a few moments the firing from the enemy had ceased. *There must not have been more than a tank or two in there*, thought Erik. It was suicide to attack this column, but that was typical of the Russians.

The Tigers accelerated, closing the distance with the burning village. The tanks stopped less than a hundred meters from the first houses.

"Better secure the place," said Sauer. "I don't want any Molotov cocktails destroying my panzers."

Erik nodded and jumped down from the armored car. He called his company together. The men assembled in just ten minutes. He noted with approval that his company looked cool and collected, the handful of veterans helping the new men keep their composure under this baptism of fire.

"Pay attention, everyone. Listen up. We've got a village or a small town ahead. I don't know what's in there, but you can figure at least a few Russians are holding out. There may be some snipers. Everyone stay low and spread out!" He sent two platoons in at a rapid charge, with the third in reserve along with his headquarters support group and mortar unit. He did not bother to set up the heavy machine guns. There wasn't sufficient time, and the Tigers would fulfill that role if necessary.

The men closed the distance quickly, and Erik was relieved to see no return fire. The tanks must've operated alone. His men occupied the village within a few minutes and waited for him to come forward. He jogged through the snow, his breath providing a foggy cloud in front of him as he ran. He noticed he was breathing heavily. Too much time in France.

He saw that his men had done an excellent job securing the location. The sole T-34 tank stood near the front cluster of the village houses. Smoke rose from the crumpled unit. A few dead Russians lay inside. Without exception, the village seemed deserted. Even the peasants were gone.

———

Erik explored the village further and soon realized this was something of a small town. They'd glimpsed the narrow outskirts from the plains beyond, but there was a rolling ridge that gently declined into a shallow valley below. The small cluster of houses his company occupied led to more houses dotted down the rolling hill and widened into a thicker cluster a few hundred meters away. This cluster contained a small downtown with several larger buildings and a significant church. Erik scanned the buildings with his field glasses carefully but could find nothing. The whole town seemed empty.

He heard the rumbling of panzers behind him, and soon the main body of the battalion rolled into the village. Major Sauer's car pulled up and Sauer himself jumped out, his head hawkishly scanning the horizon.

"It's much bigger than I thought," he said.

Erik nodded.

"Sent anyone down there yet?"

"No, but I've scanned the area pretty carefully with these," he said, motioning to his binoculars. "The rest of the town seems as quiet as this part."

Sauer scanned his watch. "It's almost three. Might be nice to give the boys a hot meal and a warm place to sleep tonight. Orders are for us to keep pushing forward." Sauer grinned and gave Erik a wink. "I think I might ignore those for now. Captain, issue the instructions."

Erik called a few men together. He sent a lead platoon into the main part of the town, a couple of panzers rolling after them. In a few minutes, he received the all clear, and the rest of the men made their way to the main part of the city. The downtown was only one street, barely two blocks long. This was full of abandoned storefronts with broken windows.

In the very center a two-story brick building with a large portrait of Stalin towered above the rest of the structures. This must be their city hall, Erik realized. The building was composed of light sandstone. The exterior walls were pitted with rifle bullets and tank shells, proof positive of heavy fighting in this area before. Erik wondered how many times the small town had changed hands, what it would've been like to live here, through it. There had to have been fathers, mothers, children, elderly—all gone now. Most of them probably dead. The Russian civilian casualties in this war were in the millions. Erik knew they had to be. He thought back to some of the things he had seen. Thankfully, he had been spared direct responsibility, the promise he made himself. Except that one time.

The soup wagons were set up in the courtyard in front of the government building. Erik gave further orders for a series of outposts in each direction. He smiled as he heard the men who drew this assignment grumbling. They would have to dig foxholes or find other cover and stand for hours in the freezing cold while everyone else had a warm meal and found shelter in the various houses. What a strange life he lived, where a little hot soup eaten outside in subzero temperatures and the chance to huddle in a dirty, unheated, windowless home felt like the pinnacle of luxury. He wondered if there might be any extra food hidden around somewhere, or, even better, vodka. He doubted it. The town looked picked clean.

He waited while the men lined up and made their way to the food. When everyone had eaten, he took his own bowl and took a portion of the thin, watery soup. He mopped the lukewarm liquid up with stale bread and munched away, sitting with a group of replacements who nervously asked him questions about the war in Russia. So few men had survived 1941—only nine out of a company of well over a hundred. Most of these privates were mere boys, eighteen-year-olds who were still in the middle of high school when the war began. He was thankful, though; at least these were real Germans. Some of the SS divisions were filled out with French, Dutch, and any other foreigners that Himmler could scrape together.

Major Sauer came over and sat down in the snow, warming his hands and feet at the fire the men had constructed. "How are you doing, Captain?" he asked.

"Well enough."

"Enjoying the feast?" Sauer joked.

"Never better," said Erik, grinning in return.

"Look at this." Sauer handed Erik an envelope.

Erik blew on his hands to try to work out some of the frozen stiffness, and then he unwrapped the paper. It was a letter written to Sauer from his wife, and inside was a photograph. The picture depicted a middle-aged blond woman and two children, a boy and a girl. The girl looked about eighteen, the boy, in a Hitler youth uniform, about sixteen.

"That's my family," he said. "My oldest just graduated this last spring. She's quite the dancer." Sauer smiled. "You should see her."

"What is she doing now?" asked Erik.

"Getting ready for university. She took a year off to help my wife with the household. It's a lot to manage when I'm never there."

Erik nodded. "My wife lives with my parents so she has a lot of help." He'd never thought of the burdens that might fall on a wife whose husband had left for war. His parents, at times an added responsibility, nevertheless provided tremendous support.

"My boy there, Peter," said Sauer pointing to the picture. "He's quite the football player. Plays forward most of the time but sometimes mid. In another time, he might've played professionally, but now I don't know. If this mess isn't sorted out soon, he'll be called up."

"Surely you can pull some strings?"

"Oh sure, I can get him into the SS, probably with a commission. That's hardly a delay. A little extra training. But does that help him? Lieutenants die out here faster than the privates."

Sauer was right. Of the three lieutenants in their original company, Erik was the only survivor. More than that, he'd seen a half dozen more come and go since then. He thought about his own girl, Greta. Almost twelve now. As tall as her mother the last time he'd seen her. On her way to becoming a beautiful young woman. Thank God he would never have to worry about sending her to war. But Gott forbid if they lost this one.

"What will you do when the war is over?" asked Erik.

Sauer chuckled. "Would you believe it if I told you I teach little kids at the gymnasium? Before all this mess I spent my days teaching eight-year-old boys and girls: grammar, music, history, and math."

Erik was surprised. He assumed the major had always been a soldier. He was stern and martial at all times. He tried to imagine Sauer in the classroom attending to the young children, but he couldn't make the image fit.

"What will you do?" Sauer asked.

"I don't really know. I taught history before the economy fell apart, and I lost my job. I came across this by chance, a friend of my wife's."

"I know," chuckled Sauer. "I thought you were too soft for the SS. Remember?"

Erik started to answer, but the head of a private across the fire burst apart in a hurricane of brain and bone, a flash of scarlet rain. Instinctively, Erik fell toward the snow as his senses absorbed explosions and the bullets landing swiftly among them.

CHAPTER EIGHTEEN

Königsberg
February 1943

Trude woodenly ran the soap over the cloth and dropped the shirt again into the sudsy warm water. She perched on a stool in the protected courtyard behind Captain Dutt's home. A tall hedge blocked prying eyes from access to the massive stone enclosure. She came here often, performing chores, trying to keep her mind off the past, the present.

More than a year had passed, and she hadn't seen her little girl. Poor Britta, locked up in a Gestapo prison cell, protected by Gunther from the worst of what might happen to her, but still caged, alone, afraid. Trude died a little each day since then. At first, she had contemplated suicide—a swift end to the anguish she couldn't escape. Eventually she'd decided to live. To survive for her little girl. If there was any chance of saving Britta, she needed to stay alive.

In the past year, Captain Dutt had risked everything to secure Britta's release. He had contacts all over Königsberg, but in every case, he was met with a sympathetic but firm refusal. Gunther was only interested in one deal for the girl: he wanted the location of the mother.

The SS officer knew she was out there somewhere, and that she must have a powerful connection. For each contact made, there was a stab back. A grasp at information from the Gestapo. Captain Dutt gambled with his life. Someday, Trude knew, he would go too far. He would trust someone he shouldn't. If that happened, the Gestapo would materialize abruptly, and they would arrest not only her, but everyone in his household.

She lived with that irreconcilable guilt. She had to risk the lives of everyone who protected her, to save herself and her daughter. At least there was some hope because she continued to receive some updates about Britta. She had heard nothing else about Johannes in all this time. They'd tried to find out more, but Dutt's only source was gone, on the eastern front now. Everything was silent.

She pulled the shirt back out and scrubbed it again sharply against the metal washboard. She didn't need to do this. Captain Dutt had a machine for washing. She didn't care. The chore kept her busy. The pain from the blisters and the bloody hands dulled the scorching agony of her mind. She ran the cloth back and forth vigorously, the grooves tearing at her flesh, letting the physical pain burn through her, cleanse her.

"That's a waste of time." The gruff voice drifted over her shoulders. She turned. Captain Dutt held his cane in both hands, leaning heavily, watching her intently. She didn't know how long he'd been there.

"It feels good to be out here."

"It's freezing. You're out of your mind."

"I'm allowed to be."

He took an unsteady step toward her, placing a hand on her shoulder. "I've some news."

She looked up, dropping the shirt. "What do you mean?"

"A contact. A hope."

"For Britta?"

He nodded. "I have just discovered one of my friends has a nephew that works at Gestapo headquarters. This nephew was recently placed on guard duty in a row of cells that contains, among others, a young Jewish girl. A rather special prisoner who is protected by a middle-aged Gestapo agent. A fat one. Sound familiar?"

"Can he help her escape?" She was too afraid to let her hopes rise. They'd been dashed too many times.

He placed his hands out. "Not too hasty now. He's only a nephew of a friend. I don't know anything about him. He could be another one of these maniac believers. If so, it will be for the worst for all of us."

"I put you in too much danger."

"We aren't going to discuss that again. We need to make contact, but we have to do so carefully."

"Why would he betray his country? Certainly not for a Jew." *The captain is going to bribe him,* she realized. "I can't let you pay him. That's what you intend, isn't it? No. You can't. You've done too much already."

"Nonsense," he said. "I don't even know if he'll do it, but if he will, it's not very much money. Far less than your friend Gunther wanted. I still think we should contact them directly."

"No! You can't trust Gunther. He'll pretend to negotiate. He'll take your money, and then he'll arrest us all."

"You don't know that for sure. He has protected Britta all this time."

Trude knew this and hated it. Hated having any sense of gratitude. He didn't deserve it. She knew Gunther held Britta as bait. He wanted Trude. But why not torture her daughter? Why protect her? She'd tried to understand this so many times in the past year, but she couldn't come up with an answer.

"How soon can you contact him? The guard, I mean."

"We've already started. I may know more tonight."

"Who's going to talk to him?"

"You don't want to know."

"It's Friedrich, isn't it?" she asked.

Dutt hesitated then nodded. "I don't know who else to send."

Trude's heart sank. If the guard refused, he might arrest Friedrich on the spot or call for help. Again, she was so helpless. Everyone else was putting their lives on the line for her.

"When will he leave?"

"He's gone already. They're meeting for a drink after the guard gets off duty." He looked at his watch. "They might already be there."

"Thank you," she said, dunking her hands back into the warm water to retrieve the shirt.

"Trude . . ."

"I'm all right," she said, not looking up. She returned to washing the shirt, then wrung it out over the bucket, twisting the cloth over and over to remove the moisture before hanging the cloth on a line attached to the corners of the stone wall of the house. She had a basket full of clothing, and she cleaned each item one by one, trying to work through the minutes and the hours before Friedrich would return.

Eventually she made her way inside and sat through a quiet dinner with Captain Dutt and several members of the staff. The captain had a huge dining room that would seat more than twenty people, but he never used it except on formal occasions. Typically, he would eat at a small table in the kitchen with the staff. Tonight, he instructed the cook to take the night off, so they ate cold sandwiches and soup while they quietly sipped white wine.

The captain made a few attempts at conversation that Trude found she could not answer. Soon he stopped trying, and the minutes ticked by in silence.

They were cleaning the dishes with even Captain Dutt chipping in when the kitchen door abruptly flew open and Friedrich stepped in. She was relieved to see he was safe. The young German's cheeks were splotched white and red from the cold. He poured himself a cup of coffee from a nearby container, warmed his hands on the mug, and took a couple of sips before he spoke.

"Good news," he said.

Trude felt her heart explode in joy. "Tell us," she said.

"He's sympathetic. He grew up with Jewish friends. He doesn't believe all this garbage the Nazis are peddling. He lost an older brother on the eastern front. He hates the war and just wants all of it over. But he's terribly afraid of what might happen if he is caught."

"Did he take the money?" asked Captain Dutt.

Friedrich shook his head. "Not yet, but I think he will. He said he needed a day to think things over."

"When?"

"He said to meet him again tomorrow night and to bring the money. If he will do it, he plans to try to take her out tomorrow evening. He said he didn't think it would be too difficult if things went well. He works the night shift tomorrow night. There are only two guards, and he said they take turns sleeping sometimes. He should be able to sneak around while the other guard is taking a nap. He's afraid of the ramifications, but there's been an escape one time before. The guards that time got in trouble, but nothing long-term."

Friedrich looked at Trude. "He's very fond of Britta, you know. He talks to her at night sometimes. He said she is very brave."

Trude felt the tears welling. It was a miracle. A miracle from God. After a year of nothing, she was hearing real things that were happening to her daughter. Friedrich had met with somebody who saw his daughter every day. Someone willing to help.

"I need more money," said Friedrich.

Captain Dutt nodded. "That is not a problem. Whatever the amount we will pay it." Friedrich stepped over and put his hands on Trude's shoulders.

"I know this will be an agonizing day, but you've waited so long already. Tomorrow night, I'll bring your daughter home to you."

She turned and put her arms around Friedrich, burying her face in his chest. "God bless you all," she said.

The next day was worse than the last. The new sense of hope vied with an intense sense of urgency she had not felt since Britta was arrested. Now the potential of an escape raised new fears. What if the plan failed? Would Gunther punish Britta? Would she be relocated? The guard would be tortured probably. Did he know who Friedrich was? Would that lead them back to Captain Dutt? It was a strange feeling that this new possibility brought intense despair at the same time.

Captain Dutt tried to keep her busy all day. He was teaching her chess, a game Johannes enjoyed but that she had never picked up at the university. She listened patiently while he explained the roles of the various pieces and how they moved, and they played game after game as he walked her through the strategy. She didn't want to tell him she wasn't listening. Then again, he must have known. Her clumsy moves. She was too bright to need to learn the basics over and over. She was grateful for his effort. It helped if only a little to pass some of the time.

Time. An enemy as formidable as the Nazis. Since the loss of her husband and her daughter, time was the only thing she always had too much of. She realized the last three and a half years of war were one long exercise in endless time. Time and fear, her other constant companion. She could hardly remember her life before the war. Her childhood, the happy times of the university and with Johannes. Even losing their jobs and their rights under the racial laws seemed a pleasant holiday compared to what she'd endured since the fighting started.

Now it was time again. Time for Friedrich to leave with the money, with her future in his hands. He would not be back for hours, perhaps not until morning. When he returned, there was every chance he would bring her daughter home to her finally. If this miracle happened, perhaps she might one day see Johannes coming through the door. Perhaps this war would end and they would be free again.

She allowed herself another thought: What if the conflict resulted in a Nazi defeat? Though she had not dared consider that idea until this fall, when the Germans started suffering enormous losses, first at El Alamein, in Egypt, and then at Stalingrad in Russia. The invincible now seemed mortal. And while the end seemed an eternity away, no longer was it certain the Germans would win the war.

Friedrich dressed in dark clothing, putting on a heavy black wool overcoat. Captain Dutt handed him a satchel stuffed full of Reichsmarks. Bribes were a reality of her life during the war. Some Nazis, despite their high-and-mighty ideology, could be bought because of that pettiest of human emotions: greed.

Friedrich turned to Trude, taking her hands in his. A flicker of a grin crossed his lips. "I'm going to go get your little girl," he said.

"I know you will," she said, smiling encouragingly, not feeling the confidence she tried to portray. "Thank you for everything, Friedrich, you've been like a brother to me."

"Does that make me an honorary Jew?"

She looked sharply at him, but he was smiling, and she realized he did not mean it as an insult. She nodded.

"I could live with that," he said. He stepped forward and embraced her briefly. "I'll be back as soon as I can."

Then he was gone out the door. She heard the automobile cough alive and stutter off into the night, and she was left again with hours to wait, the terrible fear and anxious hope returning. Her entire life depended on what happened tonight.

They finished a cheerless meal. Trude picked at her food, unable to eat. She felt like she might be sick. The minutes stacked up, collecting slowly into hours.

Evening became night as they held their vigil. Midnight passed. Trude and Captain Dutt went through the motion of playing chess hour after hour until her hands trembled from weariness. Her eyes were bloodshot, her vision blurred; she could hardly make out the pieces any longer.

The jiggle of keys in the door froze her breath. She stared at Captain Dutt for a moment and then rose, running to the kitchen with arms out, ready for her daughter. The door swung open to reveal Friedrich. He was winded, ashen faced, sadness in his every movement. Alone.

"He refused," she said. "He won't help us."

"No, no. That's not it," he said, stepping forward.

"What then? What happened to my little girl?" She drew her breath in sharply. "Please don't tell me they were caught."

He shook his head. "She's gone."

"What do you mean? What are you saying?" Her head exploded in pain and confusion. She tried to beat her fists against his chest, but he held her wrists, holding her back.

"Calm down and listen. I met the guard and paid the money. No problem. He left and I waited with the car running, for his return. He was back about a half hour ago, but he was alone."

"Then he did refuse."

Friedrich shook his head. "No, she was gone. When he went to his shift, she'd been transferred from the cell. He doesn't know where."

Trude felt her knees giving way, and she struggled to maintain her consciousness. "What do you mean transferred? Where is she? We have to find her!"

"Don't worry, Trude," said Captain Dutt. "It will be all right. This is a temporary setback. So, they moved her? We will find out where. We have someone on the inside. It's a delay, perhaps a day or two."

Trude shook her head, unable to answer. She didn't believe him anymore. What good would it do to locate her again? She couldn't believe there would be another chance like this. If this guard no longer had direct access, who else would risk their lives on her behalf? Her girl was gone. She might not even have Gunther's protection anymore. She had lost her like she had lost Johannes.

She wanted to scream out to the heavens. All this time waiting, hoping was but a cruel hoax. She felt what little life she had clung to falling before her eyes. The fragile glass of her soul shattered, the cruel fragments slashing her apart. She felt sanity slipping away; her tears flooded the hard stone floor of the kitchen. She flung herself to the ground and pressed her face against the surface, closing her eyes, clinging, praying, and then with all the force she could gather she drew her head back and smashed it as hard as she could against the tiles. A blinding fire flashed and there was darkness.

CHAPTER NINETEEN

Near Kharkov, Soviet Union
February 1943

Erik looked up from the snow, his hands over his helmet. Ice and mud flew as bullet rounds crashed into the ground around him. Two more men across the fire were quickly hit even as they attempted to scramble out of the way. Erik rolled, clutching his machine pistol with one hand.

Even as he moved into position, he scanned the street, taking in what was happening. He completed his roll to his stomach and cocked the bolt of his weapon with one motion. He was facing away from the fire and across the street toward the government building. He saw out of the corner of his eye that Sauer was here, too, hugging the frozen ground.

"Where are they?" said Sauer, shouting through clenched teeth.

"I don't know," Erik responded, but even as he said that he saw a flash from the second story of the town hall across the way. A sniper, he realized. He must have hidden and been missed in the first sweep of the buildings. Erik watched flashes up and down the street coming out of various buildings. This wasn't a single Russian but a team of snipers working in concert.

An ambush. It was suicide to attack a battalion, he thought. Not that the Russians were incapable of insane actions. Still, there had to be more to this. As if in answer, the screeching of incoming artillery shells rained down to join the whistling bullets. There were Russians out there in some force, attacking the town. This group of snipers was working with them.

Another shell erupted near him, and he knew he had to move again or be hit. He reached out, grabbing Sauer by the shoulder, and tugged on his uniform. He dragged himself to his feet, slipping in the icy snow.

"Let's go!" he screamed to his commander. He jerked the major up, and the two of them dashed through the snow, bullets crashing into the ground around them as they rapidly closed the distance to the government building. In a few moments, they made it and kicked open the wooden door. It was just Sauer and him. They were armed with his machine pistol and the major's 9mm. He gestured silently, mimicking a grenade. Sauer shook his head. They would have to make do with what they had.

Erik rapidly scanned the downstairs of the town hall. There were a few offices ringing a large central hallway leading to stairs rising up about five meters before turning sharply to the left. He looked around for another way upstairs, but there wasn't one. The sniper or snipers upstairs assuredly knew they'd come into the building, and there appeared to be only a single way to reach them. They were walking into a trap, he realized, but there was nothing he could do about that.

He motioned toward the stairway. Sauer nodded in grim approval. They spread out, keeping a few meters apart as they moved forward as silently as they could toward the landing of the staircase. Erik's eyes darted this way and that. He did not know if the offices were empty, whether other Russians were hiding downstairs. Agonizing minutes passed as they picked their way slowly to the stairs, weapons aimed at each successive office doorway. Erik hoped their silence and their patient progress toward the stairway would confuse the people upstairs, who would've expected an immediate attack. Of course, the snipers were professionals, and they could not expect to take them easily.

Three quarters of the way across the hallway he heard a clatter on the steps, a click-clack, click-clack. He and Sauer both stepped backward quickly; he recognized that sound. A small metal ball appeared, bouncing down the stairs. A grenade. Erik drove himself to the ground as it exploded, showering the room with shrapnel. He waited for the hot metal to tear into his body, but he felt nothing. He was unhurt. He'd been lucky. He lifted his head. Sauer was still on the ground. The major smiled and gave him a wink; they were safe.

Erik motioned for Sauer to remain still, and they trained their weapons on the stairway. He hoped the sniper would come downstairs to investigate the grenade. They waited, but the Russian did not come. Outside the sound of the shelling increased, along with the staccato trill of machine guns. The battalion was fully engaged in combat with a force of unknown size. He hoped his junior officers were rallying the men in his absence. If they did not put up an adequate defense, the Russians would overrun their positions and they would all be captured or killed. There was nothing he could do about that right now. He had to focus on the immediate danger.

He waited a couple of minutes more and motioned for Sauer to rise. They both cautiously moved to their knees and pulled themselves up into a standing position. They did so in perfect silence. Erik retrieved his weapon, checking it over to make sure it was functioning and still armed.

Sauer made eye contact again and motioned with his head toward the stairs. Erik nodded and resumed his silent movement toward the landing. Sauer followed, but Erik motioned for the major to stop. No reason for both to be killed by the next grenade. He would go first and call on the major if he needed to cover.

He placed a boot on the first stair and took a tentative step up, lowering his weight onto the concrete in gentle intervals so that there would be no sound. Another step, then another. He tensed himself, ready to spring backward if another grenade came tumbling down. Each step was an eternity. He was midway up the first set of stairs. He kept going, one stair at a time. Finally, he reached the corner. This was the most dangerous part. If the sniper was at the stairway with his gun aimed and sighted, he would kill Erik before he even had a chance to look up the stairs.

He removed his Stahlhelm. He lifted the steel helmet slowly into the field of view around the corner, expecting a bullet to rip through the metal and tear the helmet out of his hand. Nothing. This meant the sniper either wasn't there or was too smart for the trick. He cursed himself. If he only had a grenade, this would be so much simpler. Still, there was nothing he could do. He had to take the sniper out.

With his next move, Erik gambled everything. He stormed across the landing to the other side, slamming himself against the wall, hoping the sniper would miss. Again, nothing happened. He looked up the remaining stairs. The Russian wasn't there. He must have moved back to a safer position or determined the grenade had done its work and there were no threats from below.

Erik motioned for Sauer to come up to the first landing. The major moved a little more swiftly, and soon they were back together again. Sauer raised his pistol to aim at the top of landing, prepared to provide cover fire if necessary. Erik knew the pistol would have little value in a real gunfight, but it was better than nothing. He started his slow ascent again, first one step, then another. Soon his head was nearly even with the top stair. Now he faced the same danger. Again, he lifted his helmet above the rim, waiting for the telltale bullet, but again nothing came. He took another step and quickly a second, so his eyes were now slightly above the floor landing that gave way to a hallway and an office door across the way. The hallway and the office were full of rubble and dust.

He didn't see any Russians. He motioned to Sauer again, who moved up the stairs and joined him. Sauer pointed to the hallway and the door and made a running motion with his fingers. The major wanted to sprint across to the hallway and into the open office. Erik shook his head in disagreement—too risky. But Sauer insisted. Erik finally nodded and took a tenuous step and then another until he reached the top of the landing. Sauer followed right behind him. Erik drew in a deep breath, leaned slightly forward, and sprinted across the hall. Sauer rushed tightly behind him. He felt his commander crash sideways before he even heard the rifle report. Instinctively, he spun around, sped back into the hallway, and sprayed his machine pistol up and down the long corridor even as his body flew horizontal and slammed into the ground. Erik held onto his weapon with all his strength, pulling himself as quickly as possible into a prone position, but it was unnecessary. His first burst had made its mark. Down the hallway at the end he saw the slumped body of a Russian, riddled with bullets. Blood pooled greedily underneath him. The sniper's rifle lay on the floor in front of him. Eyes stared vacantly and his mouth hung cavernously open in a silent scream.

Erik stayed a moment longer to see if anyone else would attack and turned to attend to the major. Sauer was on the floor behind him, his body twisting in pain, a fountain of red gore spurting from a shoulder wound. Erik tore a handkerchief from his pocket and pressed down on the hole, desperately laboring to stem the flow of blood.

Sauer looked up at him with gritted teeth, smiling. "You're right," he said. "It was too risky." He clutched a bloody photograph of his family, fingers trembling.

"Got him, though," said Erik.

Sauer bent his head, staring down the hallway. "You did good, Captain, as always."

"I'm going to leave you just for a second," explained Erik. "I'll be right back." He pulled himself to his feet, ignoring a lancing fire in his back, and stumbled over to the window. Looking out he was shocked at the chaos in the courtyard below. Blood and bodies mixed everywhere with the churned mud and snow. Shells were still exploding in the street. Men ran in every direction. He looked out across the horizon and was stunned to see what looked like thousands of Russians and dozens of tanks rumbling toward the town. A smattering of Germans faced them at the outskirts, returning fire, but they were hopelessly outnumbered.

Erik spotted a medic running down the street carrying his equipment bag and kneeling to assist a wounded soldier. Erik screamed to the man, shouting until his chest nearly burst. It took several tries among the explosions to get his attention.

"I need you now!" he screamed.

The soldier hesitated, looking down at the man he was tending to.

"That's a direct order!"

The medic nodded and ran into the building, arriving at the top of the stairs in less than a minute.

"Major Sauer is wounded," Erik explained, meeting the medic at the stairs. "It's a shoulder wound. A bad one. He needs immediate attention." The medic moved to Major Sauer, and Erik squatted down to assist as best he could. He held Sauer's hand, squeezing it, trying to take his commander's mind off the wound.

The major grimaced as the medic set to work. Sauer shifted under the pain until a shot of morphine calmed him. He lay his head against the floor, drawing a deep breath.

"What's going on out there, Captain?" he mumbled through the drug-induced stupor.

"All hell's broken loose," said Erik.

Sauer waved his arm at him. "Don't worry about me," he said. "Get out there. Take charge and run those bastards off." His family picture slipped from his fingers. He groped for it frantically.

Erik picked up the picture. He slid his fingers across the slick surface, doing his best to remove the blood before he pressed the photo into his friend's hand. *Sauer is my friend,* he realized. Something had happened somewhere along the line. He rose and ascended the stairs, preparing to take over this desperate battle for survival.

———

Erik raced down the stairs and out of the building. He hesitated in the doorway for a moment, taking in the chaos around him. Most of the square was now empty except for the wounded and the dead, splashing the snow crimson. The salty-sweet smell of burnt and bloodied flesh seared his nostrils, but he shook his head, pushing through a brief flicker of nausea to concentrate on the task at hand.

Erik made a mental note of what he'd seen from above. The battle seemed to be shaping up at the outskirts of town. What might be happening behind him, he didn't know, and now wasn't the time to find out. A private ran past him, fleeing the battle. Erik grabbed the soldier by the chest and shook him until his wild expression calmed and he turned to the captain.

Erik motioned to the courthouse with his head. "I want you to head to the other side of town and see if anything is going on. If there are men there engaged in combat, find out who's in charge and what the situation is. I'm going this way," he said, turning his head the other direction. "When you find out what's going on come back to me and report immediately. Do you understand?"

The soldier hesitated, staring past Erik. Mueller shook him again. "Did you hear what I said?"

The private nodded.

"Then do it and get back to me!" He let the soldier go and turned his attention to the street in front of him. He sprinted across the road as quickly as he could, slipping and sliding, struggling to keep his balance in the sloshing, bloody snow. He didn't know if any of the other snipers were still active, but he made it safely across the street and under the cover of the next buildings. He kept on moving out of the downtown and into the jumbled, sporadic houses near the outskirts.

The roar of explosions and the whistle of bullets drew near as he passed one house then another. Now he could see a couple of tanks, nestled among the houses, one a smoke-belching pile of twisted metal. An active panzer rocked back as it expelled another round from its cannon. Erik moved behind it and slightly to the left. When he saw a narrow opening between the tank and the house, he wedged between them and past the vehicle, advancing into the storm.

He had reached the main line of resistance centered on the ragged edge of town. The tattered remnant of a German company spread out a hundred meters or more in both directions. The men huddled behind low-hanging eaves and pressed against the back walls of the Russian houses. At the extreme edge of each house, two or three men were positioned, firing around the corners for a second or two before stepping back to let other men take over. Several panzers were also wedged among the houses, firing their cannons and machine guns.

He called out to a lieutenant whom he didn't recognize, demanding an update.

"We're trying to stop them, but there are too damned many!" shouted the lieutenant. "There's got to be at least a brigade out there, maybe a whole division!"

Thousands against a hundred, thought Erik. "How many tanks?"

The lieutenant shrugged. "I don't know, fifty maybe." Erik grunted. Their nine Tigers had been reduced to seven by the fighting, and they had just a dozen Panzer V's.

"Lieutenant, we have to hold this line, do you understand?"

The lieutenant looked stunned. He clearly expected an order to withdraw. He nodded. "I'll do my best, sir."

Erik saluted in return and headed back to the center of town. He dragged a couple of privates with him and hurried them to the north and the south to reconnoiter. His heart beat against his rib cage. He expected the Russians to pour in from every direction.

Three quarters of the way to the other side of town he found the original private he'd sent for intelligence, who informed him there was no fighting in the west. Erik drew a breath of relief. There was some hope. He sprinted in that direction to see exactly what was going on.

He found his own company spread out in position, idly standing by with nothing in front of them. Should he leave them here to guard the rear? He shook his head. He couldn't spare them. He screamed to his lieutenants, ordering them to abandon their position and move into the fight. He was evening the odds a little, giving his men the best chance to survive the day. He wanted to run, to get them out of there, but there was nowhere to go, only the endless kilometers of steppe. If they fled the town, they would all die.

He raced back to the center of town. Captain Sauer was resting, still groggy under the influence of the morphine. Erik hunched next to him, hands on knees, gasping for breath. He examined Sauer's injury. The bleeding was under control. He might make it if they could get him to a surgeon in time.

Erik drank a cup of coffee from an abandoned field canteen, gulping down the lukewarm liquid quickly, then turned back toward the fighting. Back at the main line, he took full control of the battle. In his absence two more Tigers and three Panzer V's had been destroyed by the Russians. He still had fourteen operating tanks and several hundred men. His side had the advantage of cover and a well-entrenched position. Would it be enough against these odds?

He found a relatively open observation point across the street from the first row of houses in the second story of a Russian home. The window was small but afforded him a 180-degree view of the battlefield, except the portion directly beneath him, which was partially obscured by the roofs. He set up a system of runners and a radioman to assist in communication.

Now that he finally had things in hand he realized they were not as bad as they had seemed. The Russians attacking were clearly inexperienced. They came on in waves, clumped together, subject to massive casualties from tank and machine gun fire. The tanks themselves were another thing—T-34's. Not quite the threat these tanks had been two years ago, but still formidable.

As he watched, a line of several hundred Russians jogged through the snow, clustered among three or four tanks. The armored vehicles poured machine gun fire into the buildings.

First one T-34 exploded, then another. The Russians following were cut down by MG 42 fire, the heavy machine guns planted on the rooftops, along with the panzer guns, which strafed the attackers over and over. Another Tiger was hit; he heard screaming and the bellowing of smoke and fire. His men were taking casualties but at an acceptable level.

The battle continued. Another wave came and then another. Two more Tigers and four more Panzer V's were knocked out, leaving him only eight operating tanks, but the Russians seemed spent. He counted three dozen burning enemy tanks. Russian dead and wounded lay in mounds like hewn wheat in the field below him.

Erik decided it was time to act. He ran down the stairs, gesturing for his men to follow him. He clutched a radio and shouted instructions, directing the remaining panzers to sweep out in a wide circle to the right and left, with the infantrymen charging in between. The orders were crisply followed; he watched with pride through field glasses as his men surged through the blood and snow. The Germans took rapid casualties but they kept charging on. Soon the tanks outdistanced them. He watched the panzers overrun the Russians, knocking out the last two enemy tanks and spraying the infantry with machine gun fire.

His men surrounded the Russians within minutes. After some sporadic additional fire, all was silent as the Russians threw their arms up and dropped their weapons in surrender. Erik hastened out of the building past the burning husks of several panzers and out into the field beyond. He did his best to ignore the screaming wounded, calling out to him in German, until he reached the surrounded Russians.

He called one of his lieutenants over and ordered the enemy prisoners to be taken back to the town square. He drew out his field glasses and anxiously scanned the horizon, looking for more threats, but he could see no more enemies. The battle was over.

For another half hour, he stood in the field, making provisions for the wounded and dead and ensuring his men kept up an active defense in case any additional enemies approached. The Russians had attacked in brigade strength, and he worried his men might stumble on the rest of the Russian division. But there were no new threats on the horizon. He finally called for the rest of his men to return to the line of defense at the outskirts of the town, and he escorted a group of them back toward the city hall.

He arrived in the center of town a few minutes later. Major Sauer was sitting up now, his back supported by some coats rolled behind him on his stretcher. He directed men, pointing in various directions and organizing the battalion.

When the major looked up to see Captain Mueller approaching, a grim grin crossed his face.

"You've done an amazing job," he said. "I'll get you the Knight's Cross this time for sure."

Erik beamed. Germany's highest medal would take him another step on his path to security in postwar Germany. "Thank you, sir," he said gratefully.

"Quite a bag of prisoners, Captain."

"Where are they, sir?" asked Erik.

Sauer nodded behind him. "I had them stuffed into the church," he said, gesturing at the structure Erik had observed when they first arrived in the center of the town.

"Have you interrogated them yet?"

"A couple. Sounds like they were an independent command. I don't think we have anything to worry about, at least at this point. Is the town still secure?" he asked.

Erik nodded. "We're down quite a few men and we need more tanks, but we can hold a bit if they hit us again."

"Excellent, Captain. Then there is just one more order of business. Burn the church and let's clear out of here."

"Excuse me, sir?"

"Those Untermenschen ambushed us. With snipers. They deserve no quarter."

"Those troops had nothing to do with the snipers, sir."

Sauer raised his hand. "Nonsense. That attack was too well coordinated. They were all part of it, and I want them dead. Burn it."

Erik was stunned. He didn't know what to do. The adrenaline and the excitement of the battle swiftly left him. "I . . . I can't, sir."

Sauer frowned, his expression hardening. "Mueller, don't make me order you."

"Please, sir," pleaded Erik. "I can't do that. Don't make me. For our friendship."

Sauer stared at him with surprise, his eyes gradually filling with disgust. "I can't believe you. I can't believe it's coming to this. That wasn't a suggestion. I'm giving you a direct order, Captain. Burn that church."

Erik nodded. He faced the building and took a couple of steps, conflicting emotions battling within him. This was the moment he had dreaded. Everything hung in the balance. He was a hero, an officer, about to receive another commendation. These Russians had attacked them, ambushed them. If they'd succeeded in overwhelming the town, they probably would have killed all of the Germans. There was no mercy on the eastern front.

"Captain. Now."

He took another few steps. *You have to do this. Your future depends on it.*

He hesitated, taking a few deep breaths.

"Now!" the major repeated.

Erik turned and bowed slightly. "Sir, I must respectfully refuse."

Sauer stared at him incredulously. "Erik, don't do this." His voice pleaded. "Please, my friend; this is nothing, a simple order."

"I'm sorry, sir, I can't."

Sauer stared at him for a moment more and then turned to a private standing nearby, tears running down the major's face. "Place the captain under arrest," he said.

CHAPTER TWENTY

Königsberg
February 1943

Trude woke in the darkness, disoriented. She lay in bed. Her head burned with a scorching pain beginning at the temples and lancing all the way through her back as if a spear had pierced clear through her.

Her mind chased elusive memories. There was something important she couldn't quite remember. And then it struck her like a stone wall: *They've taken my daughter. We missed our chance. After more than a year, we missed her by one day.*

As she struggled to rise, she realized she couldn't move. She was immobilized. She fought again and became aware she was restrained. Someone had tied her to the bed. Had the SS caught her? She calmed herself. That didn't make any sense. Then she remembered slamming her head against the pavement. *They think I'm going to kill myself,* she realized. *My friends tied me to the bed to stop me from hurting myself.*

They needn't worry. Or should they? If she had a gun right now, would she use it? She didn't know. Much of her wanted to give up, do something extreme to take away the pain, the worry, the fear, and the responsibility of all these lives at risk on her behalf. But her daughter was out there, alone, afraid, under conditions Trude hoped were still safe, but there was no way to know.

Things had changed. Under Gunther's protection Britta had lived a relatively safe existence in the Gestapo jail. Now who knew what might be happening to her, where they had taken her, or what her future was.

What had changed? Had Gunther given up on ever finding Trude? Was he washing his hands of the whole situation? She determined that she would not kill herself. Not while there was the slightest chance her daughter might survive. If she had confirmation that Britta was gone, well, that was another thing.

She yelled, trying to get someone's attention, but her voice came out in short, clipped, guttural spurts. She was hoarse, probably from the crying. She tried again and this time made a louder sound. Minutes passed. Her door opened and the light flipped on. Her eyes burned for a moment, adjusting. Captain Dutt stood over her, full of care and concern.

He looked at her forehead and lifted what must have been a bandage, peeling it back to peer carefully before returning it to place. He shook his head. "You've done some wonderful work there," he said gently. "It's a wonder you didn't finish yourself off. You've a nasty bruise and some cuts. I'd bring the doctor here, but unfortunately we can't risk it. So, you're stuck with my feeble ministrations."

He sat at the edge of the bed and clasped one of her hands. She tried to sit up, but the restraints held her.

Captain Dutt coughed uncomfortably. "I see you've discovered our little . . . precautions."

"I don't need them," she said.

"Well, I would love to believe you, but after last night . . ."

"Look at me," she said, her voice gaining an edge. "I won't do anything stupid. Where's my daughter?" she asked. He didn't speak for a moment. She realized he must know something.

"Tell me," she insisted.

"I sent Friedrich back out yesterday morning after he returned. He met up with the guard again. He returned the money, by the way. He's quite a man, my friend's nephew."

"What did he say? Why did Gunther let my daughter go?"

"He didn't."

"I don't understand."

"Neither did I, but now I do." He explained, "Gunther's been transferred out of Königsberg. Or rather should I say he's traveled to his new promotion?"

"Where?" she asked, her heart falling.

"I have good news on that issue. He hasn't moved very far. It's a place called Soldau. It's only a few hours away by train or car."

"Why would Gunther move to Soldau?" She'd been near the place a time or two as her family traveled around in the summers all those years ago. "There's nothing out there."

"There is now. A big prison of some sort, and Gunther's been placed in charge of the whole thing. He took Britta with him. Apparently, he's grown rather fond of the girl."

Trude froze. A new idea she had never considered creeping into her mind. She knew Gunther's character, what he wanted from Trude. What if those feelings extended to other women, a younger woman? The thought was too terrible to even consider. "We have to get her out of there," she said.

"I don't know if we can," said the captain. "I'm out of options, unless . . ."

"Unless we deal with Gunther directly."

The captain nodded.

She shook her head. "I told you, you cannot trust anything he does. He is the most diabolical man I've ever dealt with. He'll make initial contact in a friendly manner, he'll arrange a payment, and then he will arrest all of you and still get me. No, there must be another way. What about this guard? Could he be transferred, too?"

The captain raised his arms in exasperation. "I don't know how that would happen, Trude. We don't have any control over his future, and probably neither does he. Plus, you'd be asking him to move, perhaps permanently, away from home, just so he could execute a life-daring escape for someone he doesn't know." The captain shook his head. "Even if he had the power to do it, he wouldn't. There's too much at risk."

Trude laid her head against the pillow. Of course, the captain was right. But what could they do? She felt dizzy. Her injury burned. The room spun round and round.

"You need more rest," he said. "We'll talk more about this later." She tried to rise again, but the spinning in her head defeated her.

"Take these restraints off," she pleaded.

"I . . . I'm so sorry, child. I will, but not just yet. I wish I could stay with you while you rest, but I have to attend to some matters. Get some more sleep and we'll talk at dinnertime."

She lay in the darkness, her mind whirring, trying to come up with some kind of solution, some miracle, anything that would help her achieve her daughter's freedom. With new realization and new fears, she no longer felt the comfort of Gunther's protection. She had to get Britta away as soon as possible. She tried to think of some way, but she was too exhausted. Soon she slipped back into a restless, painful sleep.

She woke hours later to a bright, stabbing light. Dutt and Friedrich sat on the side of her bed, tugging at the straps, untying them. "How are you feeling?" asked Friedrich.

She didn't respond. The room was no longer moving, but the stabbing pain had not relinquished in the slightest. They helped her rise out of the bed. She saw she was still dressed in the same clothes she'd worn the night before. They pulled her to her feet and then slowly lowered the pressure on her arms, letting her find her own balance. When they were sure she would not fall, they left the room, giving her privacy to change. She shakily removed her clothing and put on a dress from a nearby wardrobe before heading down to the kitchen.

Dinner was already waiting. There was hot soup, bread, and a roasted chicken. She realized she was ravenous, that she had not eaten in a day. She hoped this would restore her energy and clear her mind. She helped herself to a heaping bowl of soup, a slice of chicken breast, and several crudely cut slabs of the bread. She wolfed down the food.

"I like to see you eating like that," the captain said jokingly. "Perhaps we should knock you on your head more often. You could stand to gain some weight."

She smiled, trying to indulge the comment, but she felt no humor. With each bite, she felt a little better. Within a few minutes even the stabbing pain in her head seemed to recede some. She looked up and saw both Friedrich and Captain Dutt watching her intently.

"What is it?" she said. She realized there was something new they needed to tell her.

"I need to talk to you about something," said Dutt.

"What is it? What do you know?"

"You won't be happy with me. I've taken the only step I believe is left to us."

"You don't mean?"

The captain nodded. "I've been in contact with Gunther." He raised his hand as she began to protest. "Not directly. He doesn't know who I am or how to find us, but he knows someone out there is asking about Britta and is interested in finding her."

"I told you, you can't deal with him. He'll find us, he'll find you."

"Trude, be silent," said the captain, his voice stern. "There's no other way at this point."

"What did you learn?" she asked, her desperation for information overruling her significant reservations.

"We confirmed what we'd heard. He's the commander of some sort of camp or jail out at Soldau. He took Britta with him. She's safe still in a cell and protected. Gunther says he'll make a deal for her, but it will cost us dearly. He said you Jews paid heavily already and you'll pay again."

"He's lying. He doesn't want money. At least that's not all he wants. He wants me."

"What do you mean?" asked the captain.

She told them everything about Gunther, his statements, his hands on her, his threats, the secret shame she'd held back all this time.

The captain looked at her in stunned dismay. "What kind of a scoundrel would grope a woman in front of her husband? Does this man have no honor?"

She shook her head. "I told you, he has none. He'll take your money and mine, and when he's done, he'll arrest all of us."

The captain stared at her in confused disbelief. Friedrich started to say something and then stopped himself. Dutt leaned back in his chair, stroking his chin with his fingers. Finally, he turned back to Trude.

"At the end of the day, I don't think it changes anything. I don't know what else we can do. We must be cleverer than this man. For now, we will play this game and see if any other answers appear. We'll find out how much he wants. I will figure some way to get Britta when we get him the money. If we're smart enough, we can do this."

Trude did not answer. Captain Dutt, an honorable man, did not understand. You could not outmaneuver Gunther. He would never give up Britta no matter what promises he made, no matter how clever the captain was. She knew the situation was hopeless. But at this moment she didn't know what else to do. Her head still hurt, affecting her thinking. Finally, she nodded her agreement.

"Be careful," she said. "Make no move that gives a hint of who you are. If you do, he will find you."

The captain nodded in agreement, and silence fell over the room, each of them picking at their food, no one knowing what to say or what to do.

—◆—

After dinner, Friedrich escorted Trude back to her room.

"I'm going to have to ask you to lie back down," he said. She didn't understand him for a second and then realized he was going to tie her to the bed again.

She shook her head. "No, Friedrich, that's not necessary. I'm not going to harm myself. I promise."

He looked uncomfortable, but he moved forward. "Captain's orders," he said, reaching for her hand. She slapped it away and took a step back, fire in her eyes. "I said no."

He started to move toward her again, and again she slapped his hands away. "Friedrich, we've known each other so long now. You can trust me. I swear to you I will not harm myself."

He stood there a moment longer, clearly undecided about what to do. Finally, he shrugged and then looked at her sternly. "I have your word?" he asked.

"Of course. I will do nothing to harm myself."

Apparently satisfied he stepped slowly backward and then left the room, closing the door gently behind him.

Alone again, she was better able to collect her thoughts. Captain Dutt was wrong. She knew there could be no deal with Gunther. He would betray them no matter what, and even if by some miracle the captain was smart enough to protect himself, Gunther would never let Britta go, no matter how much money was paid.

Was there any benefit in the captain negotiating with Gunther? A week or two would ensure Britta's ongoing protection while they pursued discussions with the guard, no matter how unlikely or farfetched. And there was always the possibility of some other miracle taking shape, although after more than a year she didn't know what that might be. She sat up for the endless hours of the evening, turning ideas over in her head, trying to determine what could be done. Finally, as dawn rose again she came up with a plan. She felt peace wash over her as she realized exactly what she had to do.

At breakfast, she took another heaping plate of food: eggs, sausages, and boiled potatoes. She would need her strength today, assuming she could convince Captain Dutt to acquiesce to her plan. She realized she would have to do battle with him this morning. This would not be easy. He could be an immovable mountain, particularly when it came to protecting her. She would have her hands full getting his agreement.

He was watching her closely, she realized. She smiled at him, and the curtain rose on her performance.

He smiled back, taking the initial bait. "You seem much recovered this morning," he noted, his eyes searchlights, carefully probing her face.

"I got some rest," she lied. "I feel a little better and so does my head."

He reached over, peeling back the bandage and looking carefully. He removed the rest of it and crumpled it in his hand. "I agree," he said. "It looks much better. I don't think you'll need this anymore."

"I think you're right, that we should pursue things with Gunther."

He smiled. "Thank you, Trude, for your vote of confidence. I can't think of anything else to do."

"I can," she said. "I have another idea." He looked at her with interest and so did Friedrich, both leaning forward.

"What is it?" asked Friedrich.

"We should meet with the guard again."

Dutt shook his head. "That's a dead end. I told you he won't risk it."

"He might if we can put a human face to it, a mother's face."

The captain's eyes widened in alarm. "You can't possibly be suggesting you would meet directly with him?"

"Yes, that's exactly what I want to do."

Dutt sputtered his response. "Absolutely not! He'd have to arrest you on the spot. You might not even make it to him. They are checking papers everywhere."

"We must do this," she said. "Listen to me. I told you, with Gunther there is virtually no chance. I think all we do by communicating with him at a distance is buy ourselves some time. He'll never let Britta go willingly. He will take your money, and he will stall until he finds out who you are."

"This guard won't risk his whole life for you. You ask too much."

"Probably not," she agreed, "but at least with him there's a chance. If he can see me, put a face to Britta's mother. If I can tell him my story. You said he had friends who were Jews, that he doesn't believe the Nazi ideology. There's a small chance he might be able to do something for me. What if he has contacts in this Soldau camp? Another guard, anything. If he sees my pain, sees me as a human, I think he will do anything for us that he can."

"She's right," said Friedrich to Trude's surprise. "I don't like this at all. But she's right. I don't trust this Gunther a bit. If she says he will never let Britta go, then I believe her."

Dutt glared at Friedrich for a moment, clearly feeling betrayed. "We can't let Trude go," he said. "She'll be arrested or turned in."

"I don't know what other options we have," said Friedrich. "If Gunther is as clever as she says, he will find us out. We will all be arrested, and we won't have helped at all. On the other hand, this guard could have betrayed us already. He took the money, but he returned it.

He's an honest man. I think the worst that might happen is he will say no. If Trude meets with him, I think there's a better chance he will help us. He's already sympathetic because of Britta, but if he sees both sides of the story, there's a chance he will do even more."

"I don't like it," said the captain, shaking his head. Trude smiled to herself, knowing she had already won. She looked at Friedrich, with a small smile of gratitude. He stared back at her with a surprisingly cold countenance. *He doesn't trust my motives,* she realized. *Well, I have the very best intentions, you will come to see.*

"I need to think about it for a little while before I agree. If I do, do you think you could arrange a meeting tonight?" he asked Friedrich. "I want a public restaurant, a big one where they won't be noticed but with lots of people around. I want you nearby, Friedrich. If anything happens, you get her out of there and bring her home."

Trude breathed deeply in relief. Although the captain said he needed time to think, she knew she already had her answer. She would meet with the guard tonight if it could be arranged. She had won.

After breakfast, she made her way into the courtyard. The day was cold but sunny. She sat with a blanket around her, the sun warming her face in spite of the frigid air. She closed her eyes and turned to the light directly, letting the warmth and rays shine deeply into her. She felt more at peace than she had in all the time since Britta's arrest. Finally, she had a course of action. Something she could directly do to try to bring her daughter to true safety.

She heard footsteps. Friedrich came out and affirmed that the captain had given his agreement and the meeting would take place that night. She nodded and thanked him, already knowing all of this would occur. She thought about God, about the supernatural and the unknown. She felt his power strongly today. She remained outside for the rest of the afternoon until the sun sank behind the trees.

She'd enjoyed her time in the brightness, the illuminated sky and the beautiful clouds. The birds chirping, giving the first hints of spring, which was but a little way off. She sat that night with Captain Dutt and Friedrich as they ate dinner. She sipped tea without eating anything. She was too anxious now for food. Finally, it was time. The captain stood in front of her at the doorway, both his hands on her shoulders, staring intently at her.

"Now you listen, child," he said. "Keep your wits about you and your eyes in every direction. If anything happens that's suspicious, you stand up and make your way quickly to the exit. Friedrich will be waiting for you. Watch the guard carefully. If he makes any sudden hand movements or starts looking around the room, you don't wait a second, you get up and leave. You understand me?"

She nodded, basking in the warmth of the love of this elderly gentleman who was like another father to her. "Thank you for everything you've done for me," she said, stepping forward to embrace him.

"Now, now," he said, "no need for any of that. I'll see you back here in a couple of hours."

She stepped out of the house and into the car. Friedrich took his traditional place behind the wheel, and they motored out into the darkness. During the short drive to the restaurant he talked endlessly, giving her tips and repeating Captain Dutt's instructions. She nodded without listening. She was looking out the window, noticing some of the snow had melted. She wondered again at the darkness and the abandoned feeling of her beautiful city. *So much joy is gone out of our lives. All in the name of nation.*

They arrived at the restaurant, and Friedrich found a convenient parking spot directly in front of the main entrance.

"You heard everything I said."

"Yes," she answered. "Thank you for everything, Friedrich." She grabbed his hands for a moment and smiled at him gratefully. She stepped out of the car and into the restaurant. The maître d' was waiting, and she gave him the name of the guard who was already there. She was escorted to the table.

The guard was young and, to Trude, looked almost a boy. His close-cropped hair was night itself, covering bright-blue eyes and eclipsing a soft, kindly face.

"Frau Bensheim," he said, whispering. She could hear the respect and decency in his voice. "It is an honor to meet you."

"I'm the one who's honored, and thankful for everything you've done. Please, tell me about my little girl," she said, her voice breaking. She steeled herself, knowing she had to keep control.

"She is well," he said. "Or at least she was." His face darkened a shade. "I don't know why, but Major Wolf has strictly ensured she is taken care of. She received the best food and was even allowed, under supervision, to play an hour or so a day in the prison courtyard."

"Did he . . . Did he see her himself?"

He shook his head. "Not to my knowledge. I don't think he ever went to visit her. That was one of the curious things the other guards discussed. He protected her but didn't seem to have any interest in questioning her."

Trude felt relief wash over. This wasn't definite confirmation, but it was good evidence Gunther had not turned his attention to her daughter—yet at least.

"But now to the task at hand," he said. "I wanted to meet you. I can answer any questions for you but . . . I'm afraid I don't know what else I can do."

"I do."

She watched his jaw set, and his body became more rigid. *He's prepared for this. He's worried I'm going to put his life on the line and he's afraid he won't be able to say no.*

"Don't worry," she said. "I only have a simple thing to ask of you."

"I'm sorry, Frau Bensheim," he whispered. "I don't know what else I can do."

"You can take me to Soldau."

His eyes widened in shock and surprise. "What do you mean? You can't possibly. They would arrest you."

"I want to be arrested."

"You're mad." He started to rise, his face flushed.

"Please, sit back down, let me explain."

He hesitated, then returned to his seat.

"I want to be arrested," she continued, "but not just by anyone. I want you to arrest me, and I want you to take me to Major Wolf."

He shook his head. "There is no way I can do that."

"Listen to me," she said, straining to keep her voice as quiet as possible. "You don't know Gunther like I do. Even now he's seeking out the truth. He will find Dutt and Friedrich and eventually you. He's caught the scent of this plot, and he won't stop until he has all of you. You'll be arrested and probably executed as traitors. None of that will help Britta, and none of it will help me. If I go to Gunther, I can protect all of you and I can protect my little girl."

"I don't understand," he said. "What does the major want from you?"

"That is between Gunther and me," she said. "I have considered everything, and this is the only way. Outside in the front Friedrich is waiting. We must leave by the back door. You must take me, and when you're done, you must give this letter to Friedrich for the captain. It explains everything and exonerates you."

He hesitated, shaking his head, not knowing what to do.

"Listen to me," she said. "You don't really have a choice. If you don't do as I say, I will stand up and announce myself, and I will turn you in for collaborating with me."

His expression hardened. "You wouldn't dare."

"Look at me carefully. I'm desperate, and I'm out of time. The only small chance I have to save my daughter is to go to Gunther. I want to save you and everyone else, but one way or another I'm going to Britta."

He realized he was trapped. His eyes showed it. He hesitated for a minute longer, and then he finally nodded in approval.

It was done. They would sit for a few more minutes and then they would leave. She felt terribly for Friedrich, but soon enough they would understand. She had protected the only Germans who had ever helped her. Well, those who were still alive, in any event. She was saving her daughter for now and giving her a chance for survival. It didn't matter what sacrifices she was going to make. The only way Trude would ever see her daughter again was to survive whatever terrors awaited her. She was ready to face her crucible.

CHAPTER TWENTY-ONE

Near Kharkov, Russia
February 1943

Erik sat in the frozen snow, his hands bound tightly behind him. Two guards stood over him, weapons drawn. He was turned facing the church. Major Sauer had ordered that he watch what was about to happen.

He could hear the screams from inside. The desperate pleading in Russian that didn't need translation. Members of Major Sauer's staff were busily stacking wood all around the base of the structure. Others doused the walls with jerricans of gasoline. Sauer stationed himself directly in front of the structure, calling out orders and sharply barking commands. Throughout the process he never looked Erik's way.

Finally, the preparations had been made and Sauer gave the order. A sergeant lit a homemade torch consisting of a long wooden broom handle with a rag wrapped around the end, soaked in gasoline. The torch ignited immediately, and the sergeant tossed it onto the stacked wood, which burst into a roaring flame. At first the fire merely licked at the foundation, but soon an inferno swallowed the building.

The screams inside deepened from begging to terror, to the shrieking agony of pain. The prisoners screamed in a bloodcurdling symphony, their cries reaching a terrifying crescendo before fading off to silence. The fire belched out a sweet, cloying fragrance. The battalion stood in silence, the flames flickering in the growing darkness. In less than an hour it was over. The church collapsed in on itself and soon devolved to glowing embers, the sole remaining evidence that the building or the lives of those hundreds of Russians within had ever existed.

Only when the fire had burned low did Major Sauer return his attention to Erik. The major's face was red from the heat. His blue eyes threatened to burst out of his skull with a fanatical euphoria as he strode swiftly back and stood in front of Erik. He jerked a thumb back at the crumbling embers.

"You see this!" he shouted. "Nothing you did changed anything. They're all dead. None of them can hurt any of us ever again. I just made room for another German family to farm these lands. I took another step for the future. Our future."

Erik shook his head, not knowing what to say.

"Why did you refuse me?" said the major. He softened. "You are my friend, Erik, my only friend here." He stepped closer, his voice a whisper. "Take it back," he said, his voice pleading. "Say you were exhausted from the battle. Apologize to the men. If you do, all will be forgiven. I can make that happen. Please, I beg you. You saved my life. Let me save yours."

The major was offering him everything. His life back. His future. What should he do? Could he condone what had just happened? Feign a moment of weakness? He knew what Corina would tell him to do. She would be furious with him. How could he destroy everything over a few dead Russians? What would his father say? He wasn't sure. Certainly, he was only following orders. But to kill hundreds of unarmed people? He looked around. Nobody else in the entire battalion had hesitated to follow the major's orders. Why should he be different?

He'd made his compromise long ago. He would not stand up to atrocities, but he would commit none himself. Now the major was giving him an out even for that. He had taken no part in this; all he had to do was make these excuses and all would be well.

He was ready to acquiesce. The words were on his lips. But something stopped him. This was too far. He didn't know what the difference was, but he couldn't remain who he was and take this final step. Without thinking further, he shook his head.

The major's eyes grew wide in surprise and his cheeks flushed. "I can't believe you. You've been my brother. I would've given you the world. And now for this," he said, motioning to the burned church, "for nothing, you give up everything." He tilted his gaze to the ground. "I'm sorry, Erik, I cannot help you further." Sauer walked slowly away, his shoulders hunched in defeat.

Erik wanted desperately to call him back, to beg forgiveness, to take the offered excuse, but he could not force himself to do so. He sat that way into the night, watching the stars come out above the remains of the church still glowing in embers. He watched the men busy themselves with their evening meal and then go off in small groups into the deserted houses to find some rest. He was freezing in the snow, but he could not rise, could not move. The church no longer gave out any warmth, and he shivered in the darkness. He couldn't sleep or think. He didn't know what would happen next.

At dawn a car arrived and an SS officer he didn't recognize stepped out. The officer spoke with Sauer for a few moments, turning to glance at Erik before saluting to the major. He stepped over toward Erik. His face was hard, almost angry. He was flanked by two guards with machine pistols held at the ready.

"You are the prisoner Mueller?" asked the officer in crisp, clipped Pomeranian German.

"Jawohl."

"Don't look at me!" The officer snapped. "You are a traitor to the Fatherland. My name is Lieutenant Messerschmidt, and I'm taking custody of you. You will do what you are told when you are told. Do you understand?"

Erik nodded, staring at the ground.

"Get up, we are leaving now."

"Where we going?"

"Keep your mouth shut!" ordered Messerschmidt. He motioned to one of the guards, who stepped forward and kicked Mueller in the face with his jackboot. The blow sent Erik spinning, and he hit the snow hard, his chin and nose scraping against the mud and ice. As his body twisted and jerked itself, his back, which had not recovered from the fall yesterday, wrenched again and sent searing pain through his body.

The guards roughly grabbed his arms, pulling him to his feet. His back exploded and he screamed in agony.

"Silence," ordered Messerschmidt. "Blindfold this worthless dog!" A dark piece of cloth was tied tightly to his head, and he was pushed and dragged, then roughly shoved into the back seat of the car.

The automobile was still running, and he felt the motion as the vehicle lurched to life. They traveled over bumpy roads for what seemed an age. For the most part it was quiet, punctuated by whispered conversations he couldn't quite make out. Erik could hear the dull thud of artillery in the background. He asked about it but was told again that he was not to speak. Time passed slowly.

It must've been hours until finally the vehicle slowed and he felt the car turn off the main road. The vehicle stopped, the engine was turned off, he heard the door open, and rough hands ripped him out of the car. He felt a new rush of pain, but he gritted his teeth, clenching his jaw, and managed not to make a sound.

He was walked slowly a few dozen meters and then pulled up some stairs and shoved into a seat again. He felt the handcuff being clipped tightly to his wrist and then connected to something next to him.

"Prisoner Mueller, can you hear me?" said Messerschmidt.

Erik nodded.

"You're being transported to Berlin to await trial. I'm your escort. We are on the train. You are not to speak until spoken to. If you must go to the bathroom, you will ask permission. That is the only reason you may talk. Do you understand?"

Erik nodded. "What's going to happen to me?" he asked.

A stinging slap ripped across his face. His mouth filled with liquid and he spat, tasting blood.

"You may be used to giving orders instead of receiving them, but I assure you that time is past. If you open your mouth again, you'll wake up in Berlin, if you ever wake up at all."

Erik sat miserably in the silence. He wished he could talk to Sauer again. Not to relent, but to ask him to reconsider. But he knew it wouldn't do any good. They had been close friends, but always the gaping rift existed between them. A difference in idcology that could never be bridged.

Erik felt the train lurch into motion and soon gather speed until he felt the familiar clip-clap as the car sped over the rails and away from the front. For days, they traveled that way. He would doze off and on. Occasionally he was handed a slice of bread. He religiously followed the lieutenant's instructions only to speak when requesting to go to the bathroom and thereby avoided any further blows. He was alone with himself, his mind racing, fear swallowing the beats between the aching agony of his back and the occasional fitful nap. He was moved once, from one train to another, shifting from the wide gauge of the Russian line to the narrower German rails. The seemingly endless journey continued.

Finally, the train stopped and he was pulled to his feet. He didn't know how many days they had been traveling. Each had merged into another in the dreadful and eternal agony.

He was moved down the narrow corridor of the train. He felt so weak he could hardly walk, but hands were all over him, pushing and pulling. He was thrown into another car and whisked through the streets. He hadn't heard the sound of wheels on pavement in some time. The smooth surface was so unlike the endless mud and icy dirt of Russia. The vehicle traveled for about an hour and then came to a halt. His blindfold was removed, and for the first time in days he could see where they were. At first the light was too blinding, but as he adjusted he could make out the inside of a building of some kind.

He blinked painfully, trying to get his bearings. The room was no bigger than an average office, with a single bare bulb hung from the ceiling. He was surrounded by SS in black uniforms, the skull and crossbones of the *Totenkopf* embossing their caps.

Lieutenant Messerschmidt stood before him. The officer reached up and with scorn tore the insignias of rank off Erik's uniform. He ripped off Erik's medals, throwing everything to the ground and stomping on them. The men jeered and mocked Erik as he endured this humiliating ceremony.

Messerschmidt looked back to his men, nodding and apparently sharing some kind of joke. He spun violently around and flailed out, punching Erik in the face. The blow caught Erik by surprise, landing hard on his cheek. The force knocked him backward and he fell over, still in his chair. He rolled out of the seat and curled up as blow after blow rained down on his back, his stomach, and his head.

He felt sharp, wrenching pain from so many different directions he was unable to process it. He felt a hot blackness covering him and all was dark. He awoke later, disoriented. His body ached everywhere. He was naked, lying in the fetal position on the hard concrete floor.

Looking around groggily, he realized they had moved him into a tiny cell. A heavy iron door covered the entrance with a tiny glass window. He tried to rise, but the pain was too great. His back hurt worst of all, along with his right arm. He stared down and saw, horrified, that it was broken. His eyes were puffy and felt like they were spilling out of his skull. His lips were cut in several places. He was freezing. He closed his eyes again and lay there, shivering and in wretched pain. He could not remember ever feeling such agony, even on the freezing steppe of Russia. The darkness spun around him and soon he was overwhelmed again, and he lay there unconscious, alone in this wretched place, a hell on earth.

—◆—

He woke abruptly later. He wasn't sure how long it had been, but the agonies had dulled to a throbbing soreness all over his body. His arm and back still burned, but otherwise the pain was bearable. As he struggled to get his bearings, a tiny slat at the bottom of his cell door was unlocked and a tray of food shoved into the cell. There were some cold beans smeared on the tray along with a small piece of bread. He grabbed the crust and sopped it through the beans, hungrily gulping down the food in a few greedy bites. The meager portion was gone quickly and hardly satisfied the first tinge of his hunger, leaving him almost more ravenous than before. The door swung open, and an SS guard stared down at him with contempt.

"How pathetic," the stranger said and threw a couple of articles of gray cloth onto the ground, slamming the door shut harshly behind him. Erik fumbled gratefully for the tattered, coarse trousers and faded rank-less tunic. The clothes were several sizes too large, but Erik didn't care. He was thankful to feel less vulnerable and to have something to assuage the freezing chill of the cell.

He pulled himself up to a sitting position and rested his back in the corner farthest from the door. His back and arm seared in pain from the effort of moving, but the food and clothing had perceptibly improved his condition. He found he could think.

So much had happened so quickly he hadn't considered his condition in any detail since he refused the final plea from Sauer. He'd had time on the train, but he'd felt too distant, too numb. Now that he was able to think clearly he was terrified about what might happen. However, he was not without hope. Although it was true he had refused a direct order, it was also a reality that Major Sauer had committed mass murder and ordered him to do the same. How could the SS possibly try him for refusing such a command?

Erik knew that there were many instances of atrocities on the eastern front. He had seen many and heard of far worse. But none of it was condoned officially or discussed publicly. In fact, not only did the government deny any of these atrocities even occurred, the Nazis had even gone out of their way to prosecute a few soldiers who had committed them. Could he be tried on the record for refusing to burn hundreds of unarmed Russian prisoners in a church? No, they might demote him, transfer him, or quietly punish him, but if he launched an official protest and demanded a trial, there was some hope he would be vindicated and ultimately released.

Here was the problem, though: How to make his situation public? Nobody even knew he was here. He had to reach out to the outer world. Otherwise they might quietly execute him in a cell and nobody would ever know. It would be the easiest thing in the world to simply inform Corina that he had been killed on the eastern front fighting the Russians. A part of him realized perhaps this might be for the best. Then they would not take away his rank and humiliate his family. Corina would become a widow, respected in the community. The wife of a dead hero. Perhaps he should even request this?

No! He wanted vindication. He wanted to live. If he allowed himself to be killed, the world would never know what he stood up for, what he defied. He wanted justice.

The door opened again abruptly, jolting him out of his thoughts. He looked up. Lieutenant Messerschmidt was there. "Bring him!" he shouted.

Two burly SS privates forced their way into the cell. He tried to resist them, but he was far too weak. The guards grabbed him by the arms, jerking him onto his feet, wrenching his back and arm again as they dragged him out of the cell. He was pulled out of the small enclosure and down a narrow stone hallway, passing dimly lit cells before they came to a barrier at the end of the hallway. Another SS guard unlocked it, and they pulled him through and down another long corridor with a second barred entrance.

They finally approached a door. A guard reached into his pocket and pulled out a set of keys. He tried several of them and eventually found the right one. He opened the door. Inside was a lonely table and two chairs, nothing else. The guards dragged him to a seat and thrust him down. Lieutenant Messerschmidt lowered himself into the chair opposite Erik across the table. The guards stood behind Erik on each side. Messerschmidt tugged on the bottom of his tunic as he sat, straightening the cloth until it was tailor fit. He scanned his decorations for a moment, making sure all was in order before looking back to Mueller. The lieutenant's face was a mask of cold, calculated fury.

"Talk," he said.

"I don't know what you mean."

Messerschmidt nodded, and Erik felt a hard crash on the back of his head. One of the guards had struck him. He felt the bright flashing lights and he blinked several times, trying to maintain his balance on the chair. Finally, he could refocus on the lieutenant.

"Talk," Messerschmidt repeated.

"I need to reach my family."

Messerschmidt nodded again. Another crushing blow landed on the back of Erik's head.

"Talk."

"I . . . I was ordered to set fire to a church full of hundreds of Russians. Ordered by Major Sauer. I refused."

Messerschmidt looked at him for a moment and then scoffed. "You lie."

"No, I don't. That's what happened."

"Nonsense. I have Major Sauer's report right here," said Messerschmidt, picking up a brown folder and opening it to scan the contents. "Sauer was wounded and unconscious. When he came to, he saw you commanding the burning of the church over his protests. He directly ordered you to stop, but you merely laughed at him and continued. He was too weak to stop you."

"That's not true!" exclaimed Erik. "He gave the order to kill the Russians. I was the one who refused!"

"Funny. That's not how the rest of the battalion saw things. Major Sauer's report is countersigned by three other officers and a dozen enlisted men. They all agree under oath that Major Sauer's recitation of the facts is *richtig*."

Erik was incredulous. He would never have anticipated this strategy. Sauer had turned everything on him, and other officers and men had apparently gone along. Of course they would, he realized. The cowards—they would do anything Sauer told them to do, particularly after what had happened to Erik.

Erik shook his head. "That's not what happened. Sauer was the one ordering me to burn the church."

Messerschmidt nodded and the guard struck him again.

"Stop it!" yelled Erik. "I'm telling the truth."

Messerschmidt leaned forward across the table, putting his lips almost against Erik's ear. "It doesn't really matter, you know. Truth, lies. No one will believe you. No one will want to. You want to take down a decorated battalion commander with stories of murder. How could we ever let that out? You're an embarrassment to the party, to the SS. You will never leave here alive."

He reared back, reached out, and pulled Erik to him by the shirt, then slapped him hard with the back of his hand. He dropped him into the chair and turned to leave.

"Remind Captain Mueller of the truth," he said as he departed.

The guards went to work on Erik, striking him over and over on the head and shoulders. He tried to protest, to put his good arm up to protect himself, but nothing helped. The blows rained down. He slumped out of the chair, landing on the hard concrete. The ground was almost worse; now they were kicking him as well. Soon the darkness overwhelmed him again.

He woke and found himself in a hospital bed. There was an IV attached to his arm. Through the fog of his emotions, he could tell he must be heavily sedated. A white-garbed gentleman stood over him, a doctor's coat over his SS uniform.

"Captain Mueller, you're awake. You've been out almost two days. I was afraid we'd lost you. But you've improved." A flicker of sadness passed the doctor's face. "Not that it will do much good."

"I need your help," said Erik, taking a chance. "I've been framed."

The doctor looked down at him for a moment and then shrugged, shaking his head. "There's nothing I can do for you."

"Please, listen just for a moment. I'm asking you to contact SS Lieutenant Colonel Karl Schmidt in Königsberg. You don't have to say anything else. Just tell him that I'm here."

The doctor scoffed. "You have to be kidding me. Do you want me to join you? Sorry, my friend, but I cannot help you that way. I can do this for you, though." He reached into his pocket and pulled out a syringe, placing it into the IV. "I can keep you comfortable, and give you oblivion for a while."

Erik tried to protest, to rise, but the medicine was already washing over him, and he felt himself fading again into darkness.

"Hush now, my friend. All of this will be over soon enough. You need your rest." He depressed the remainder of the syringe. Erik struggled to keep his eyes open, to protest, but soon he was out again. He was pulled away groggily sometime later. He had no idea how long. A nurse was removing the IV from his arm.

Guards dragged him out of bed. He tried to resist, but he was still in so much pain, so weak. They carried him down the hallway and into another, larger concrete enclosure, where a single chair rested against the wall. He was pulled to the chair and flung down; his arms were wrenched behind the chair and he was tied tightly. He sat there for a moment, dazed, disoriented.

The door to the room was flung open. Lieutenant Messerschmidt strolled in arrogantly, along with two guards with machine pistols. The guards stepped up in front of him, and Messerschmidt moved aside.

The men raised their weapons, pulling back the bolts in unison and aiming the barrels at Erik.

Messerschmidt puffed himself up, unfolding a single sheet of paper and beginning to read. "Captain Erik Mueller, I regret to inform you that you've been sentenced by tribunal to death for disobeying a direct order from your superior officer, and for the killing of innocent prisoners of war. Do you have anything to say?"

Erik was stunned. His mind tried to work slowly through his drug-induced fog what was going on. He couldn't formulate any words, and he shook his head. He couldn't believe it. He was going to die right here, right now.

"Nothing?" asked Messerschmidt. "Good, then you accept our verdict and we will proceed. Guards, prepare."

The men raised their weapons, fingers on the triggers. Erik felt his heart beating out of his chest. He could see the order to fire dancing on Messerschmidt's lips. He closed his eyes, bracing for the bullets to come.

CHAPTER TWENTY-TWO

East Prussia
March 1943

The rolling farmland passed Trude by, tidy, patched squares of the Prussian countryside. She was surprised she'd been allowed to be a passenger in the train, and she had relative freedom to stand, use the bathroom, or walk around a bit without restraint. Her two guards were friendly, although they kept a close eye on her and would not speak to her about any details of the trip, where they were going, or what was in store for her.

Of course, she knew the answer to all of that. They were headed for some sort of camp—Soldau, where Gunther had an important position. This was also supposed to be the location of her Britta, so although she was terrified about her future, she was also, paradoxically, thrilled by the prospect of seeing her daughter again. The first part of her plan had worked without a hitch. She had maneuvered Captain Dutt into allowing her to meet with the SS guard. She'd convinced the guard to take her into custody and turn her over to Gunther. Now she prepared the hardest part: facing Gunther and convincing him of what she had in mind.

She had feared she would be tortured for information about who had assisted her, but that had not happened. After a brief time of confusion where she was largely ignored, a noticeable change had come over her captors. They'd become polite, respectful, and ensured she received ample food. They hadn't asked her anything, and they certainly hadn't tortured her. This conduct gave her further comfort that Britta may have been treated similarly all this time. This also gave her some hope for the future.

The train whisked by another nameless station, not even slowing down as it rumbled through. The car was relatively empty. Just her and her guards along with a smattering of civilians: an elderly gentleman traveling by himself; a young family with two small children who kept running up and down the aisle. Another young couple sitting close, the husband obviously on leave, wearing his tattered Wehrmacht uniform. They all eyed Trude and the SS guards curiously, clearly wondering who they were and where they were going, but keeping their distance.

As the train kept rolling down to the southwest, they passed the old Polish border. The signs had been taken down, but the purpose of the buildings and the platform were obvious as they whizzed by.

"How much longer?" asked Trude.

The guard stared at her for a moment, and then one of them answered. "Not long now." He shrugged. "Perhaps a half hour."

Thirty minutes. She closed her eyes, trying to compose herself. She had another role to play. The most important part of the performance. Captain Dutt and Friedrich were strong, intelligent men, but they were also honest and straightforward. They could be manipulated.

Gunther was another matter. He was every bit as bright if not smarter, and he was full of cunning cynicism. Over and over, she worked the scenarios she'd crafted. Tweaking them, trying to throw in unexpected events to feel how she would react. Trying to see everything from Gunther's point of view. The scenarios occupied her mind and quickly passed the time. She felt the train slowing down for the first time since they'd left Königsberg. She opened her eyes and one of the guards nodded to her.

"This is our stop," he said.

A sign at the station said "Soldau." Underneath were other words, faded and in Polish. The train lurched to a stop. The guards waited a moment and then stood as one, motioning for her to follow them. She could feel her heart rate rising. She willed herself to remain calm. They stepped off the train and walked along the old wooden planks of the platform before stepping down a short flight of stairs.

A car was waiting for them. One of the guards hurried forward to open the back door for her. She took a seat inside. Another SS soldier was at the wheel along with the lieutenant in the passenger seat. A guard stepped into the car on either side of her and closed the doors. There was nowhere to go, no place to escape. Not that she intended to.

The vehicle took off and began weaving through the streets of Soldau. "Where are we going?" asked Trude.

The lieutenant turned and stared at her for a moment. "Llowo," he responded. The name meant nothing to her. They drove out of the town and back into the familiar fields. She could see no difference between this land and the farms dotting East Prussia. How strange that they fought, creating arbitrary borders and naming the lands "Germany" and "Poland," when there was no real difference.

The car drove for another half hour. She started to see buildings dotting the horizon. They turned off to the left down a road, heading toward a train track and a large fenced enclosure. The car came to a gate guarded by watchtowers, SS men with machine pistols at the ready. The car stopped, and one of the guards asked them some questions.

The driver responded and showed his papers. The guard looked into the back seat, staring at Trude for a moment, and then nodded. The gates were opened to allow the vehicle to drive through toward the largest building, a great brick two-story structure with white-framed windows. The roof was flat except for a central gable tapering upward toward the sky.

The car pulled up to the front doors. Her breath caught in her throat. Gunther awaited them. She hadn't seen him in two years. He eyed the car curiously, clear anticipation painted on his pudgy face. He was a little older, perhaps a little fatter. He was still shoved into a crumpled SS uniform, now bearing the insignia of a major. He rubbed his hands together against the cold, or perhaps in expectation, as the car rolled to a stop. He ducked his head down and peered into the back seat. Their gaze met. She saw the flash of recognition as a clever grin creased his mouth.

He stood again as the guards removed her and feigned disinterest. He spoke directly to the lieutenant.

"I see you brought Frau Bensheim. Nice to finally tidy up that piece of business. Her husband was a little Jew who thought he was a big shot in Königsberg." Trude flinched but remained silent.

"He worked the system before the war, getting other Jews out under fake passports and visas. The little shit waited too long, though, and got his own family caught in the bargain. I nabbed him in '40 and the daughter in '41, but I needed this one to complete my collection. She sacrificed her daughter for her own freedom. A typical Jew. They don't even look after their own young."

Trude was stunned by the words, but she knew they were for the lieutenant and perhaps to bait her, to unbalance her for the fencing match they both knew was about to begin.

"What do you want me to do with her?" asked the lieutenant. "Should I throw her in the camp?"

Gunther pressed his index finger against his cheek, tapping it slowly back and forth as if he was considering this. "Likely, but let's drop her in my office for now. I've got a few questions for her before I throw her to the wolves."

The guards escorted her through the brick enclosure and down a cold, cheerless hallway. Gunther's office, on the second floor, was large but sparse, with a plain metal desk and a few pictures indifferently tacked on the walls. Boxes filled the corners. He was just moving in, she remembered. The guards stayed with her for a few minutes until Gunther arrived. He nodded for them to leave. They saluted crisply and walked out, closing the door behind them. He sat down across the desk, ignoring her for the moment. He looked down at some paperwork, pulling out a letter and studying it as if he had more important things to do.

"Gunther, please don't," she said.

He looked up in mock surprise. "Frau Bensheim," he said, a look of irritation falsely parading across his face. "How impatient of you. I'll be with you in just a moment. I have many pressing matters to attend to." He looked back down again, scanning the contents of the letter. He was clearly enjoying himself. This was a moment she realized he had looked forward to for a very long time, and he was relishing every second.

Finally, he set the letter down and pressed his hands together. He took a deep breath and looked up at her again with a clever grin curling the edges of his mouth.

"Now, where were we?"

"I don't know what you mean," she said.

"As I recall, you were supposed to be arrested in 1940 at the docks. Unfortunately, that husband of yours was too suspicious and you escaped my web. Not that I blame him. He sacrificed himself. He thought he was being noble, but he was only an irritation. He thought he was the big fish I was after, but the real one I was looking for unfortunately got away." He smiled at her. "I assure you he paid for it dearly."

"I don't want to know," she said.

Gunther chuckled. "I'm not surprised. You seemed indifferent. I waited for you to come to me then, but you didn't. Not then, and not even when I caught your little Britta. Imagine my surprise when even that didn't lure you in."

"I want to see my daughter," she said.

"Oh, so you do care about her? My dear, I was beginning to wonder. A German mother would've come to me immediately, but you chose to remain away," he admonished, waving a finger. "They say you are less than human, that you're below us. But sometimes I wonder. You're stronger in some ways. The way you cling to your own lives." He leered at her. "I admire that about you," he said, his eyes moving down her neck and then below, lingering on her waist. She could see his almost ravenous look and she shuddered.

He shook his head. "I'm sorry, my dear, I got a little . . . distracted. Where were we?" He tapped his finger against his temple. "That's right, Britta. Well, you will be relieved to know that she's here with me, and she's doing fine. She's remained safe all this time." He looked up with a coy expression. "Not that there haven't been some requests from my guards about her."

"What do you mean?" asked Trude, terrified.

Gunther shrugged. "It doesn't matter. What does matter is that you're here, that your daughter is safe, and that she has remained safe because of my sole discretion and power. That, my dear, places you rather exceptionally in my debt." He tapped his head again. "I wonder if I can think of any way you could make it up to me."

"I won't talk about anything until I've seen her," she said.

Gunther shook his head, snorting out loud. "Listen to you. Do you know where you are? You're in hell! The end of the world. Do you know who I am? I'm the angel of death. Yet here you are bargaining, making demands. I knew I was right about you the second I saw you." He laughed again, snapping his fingers at her.

"You know what," he said. "I'll indulge your game a little longer. Britta is right in this building. I've kept her here as I kept her there, safe and sound. I'll have the guards take you to her." He waved his hand over her. "I give you tonight with her. I'll have dinner brought in. You can have the evening . . . no, I'll go further than that. You can have the whole night with her. In the morning after breakfast, we will have a nice little chat about the future, shall we?"

Trude nodded, forcing a smile, trying to look appreciative, when all she felt was horror. She'd forgotten what Gunther was like. Or perhaps he was worse now. Perhaps as he'd gathered more power, he'd become more arrogant and cruel. None of that mattered right now. She was about to see Britta. Whatever happened tomorrow didn't matter this instant. She would be in paradise, if but for a brief time, if she could just see her girl.

"Thank you," she said, forcing the words.

"Oh, you're more than welcome, my dear. I'll just add it to your tab." Gunther rose and shouted a command. Guards entered. He spoke to them briefly and then turned to Trude, bowing slightly. "Have a good evening, my dear," he said. "I'll see you in the morning." He strode from the office and Trude was left with the guards. She was moments away from fulfilling her greatest dream of the past year.

The guards walked Trude out of the office and down the hallway to the extreme other end of the building. She passed a series of doors, all nondescript with tiny windows. She wondered what the rooms were for. Were they other offices for the SS? Apartments? She hadn't noticed any houses or barracks as they drove in.

Finally, they arrived at the end of the hall, and one of the SS guards reached for a large ring of keys in his pocket. He worked through them one by one, eyeing each until he finally came across the key he was looking for. He placed this into the hole and turned it to open the door.

Trude was awash with emotion. There was Britta sitting at a table with pencil and paper busily working away. When her daughter looked up, her eyes widened and she jumped from the chair, running into her mother's arms. Trude held her, sobbing. She'd never been happier in her entire life. "My little Britta," she kept repeating, her voice broken. They held each other tightly while the guards waited a respectful distance away. After a few minutes one of them asked her politely to please step into the room. She complied, and they locked the door behind her.

It was a long time before she could look through her tears and peer around the room. It didn't feel like a cell at all, she realized—more like a dormitory. There was a bed with sheets and blankets. A small desk rested in the corner stacked with books, paper, and pencils. A bookshelf sat to the right, filled with dozens of books. There was a window without bars, looking out through a white wooden frame onto a series of other buildings. The only thing that made the room feel like a cell was the locked door—and the distant view of the towers and barbed wire beyond.

"Mommy, how did you get here?" asked Britta through the tears streaming down her cheeks. "I never thought I would see you again. Uncle Gunther said I would, but I didn't believe him."

"Uncle? He's not your uncle."

"Oh, but he told me he is," she said. "He said he was taking care of me while you and Father were away. That's why the soldiers came to our house and took me and Mrs. Werner that night."

"What's happened to you, my love?" Trude asked, trying to ignore what she'd heard. "Tell me everything. Have they hurt you?"

"What do you mean, Mommy?" she asked, laughing. "Nothing's happened except I'm bored all day and I've missed you terribly, and Father, of course. They stuck me in this room. I must stay inside, but they let me out sometimes. Uncle Gunther comes and visits every day. The guards are really nice, too, but the food is awful. I like this new place better. The room is bigger and there's a window I can look out."

Trude's voice shook. "They didn't hurt you in any way?" she asked.

"Whatever do you mean?"

She felt the relief burning through her and the strange, conflicted feelings for Gunther. He was a monster, yet for some reason he'd protected her little girl and kept her safe.

The door opened again for the guard to bring in a large metal tray, which he set down on the desk. He turned without a word and left, locking the door behind him. The tray contained a large bowl of soup, two bowls, a pitcher of water, and a small loaf of bread. Britta stepped over to the steaming liquid and bent over, sniffing. She curled her nose up. "Cabbage again. I told you, the food isn't good here, but you'll get used to it."

Trude couldn't help but smile. She couldn't believe her daughter. By some miracle Britta had been shielded. No, not a miracle, she thought—by Gunther's will.

They ate a cheerful meal, Britta chattering away about the guards, the old courtyard at the Königsberg SS jail, and the train ride out. She showed her mother some pictures she had drawn. They were crude renderings of memories. Pictures of Trude and Johannes, of their town house in Königsberg, the streets where she had grown up and played.

The sun set. They stayed up late, continuing to talk. Trude soaked up this brief, miraculous eye of the storm. She knew it was a fantasy. She knew what price was ahead, but this moment of happiness filled her with strength.

Eventually Britta grew tired and yawned, unable to keep her eyes open. Trude would have loved to stay up all night, to wring every moment out of this sacred reunion, but she couldn't put her daughter through that. Trude lay down with Britta, her child climbing in next to her, nuzzling her head on her chest. She ran her hands through Britta's hair, tears of joy streaming silently down her face as her daughter fell gently asleep in her arms. Trude remained wide-awake in the darkness, soaking up the moments, her mind floating between her euphoria and her dread for the dawn.

The next morning, she woke heavy-eyed and exhausted. She'd caught a few moments of fitful sleep at best. A guard opened the door and dropped off another tray of food, this one with a thin tea and some more bread. They ate quietly, Britta chirping in here and there with laughter or a question. Trude answered as best she could, but she was more subdued this morning knowing what was coming. Finally, there was a knock at the door and another guard peered in.

"Frau Bensheim, may I come in?"

"Yes, what is it?"

"You must come with me, please."

She nodded, fear flooding her heart. She followed the soldier. She was led back down the hallway and then into Gunther's office. He motioned for her to sit down, and she did so. He left her alone. She looked back around, examining the contents of the office. Time went by, first a few minutes and then longer. Always time to wait. Eventually the door opened, and Gunther came in. He smiled at her and sat heavily down in his chair, as if relieving himself of a great burden. He was quiet for a moment while the guard brought in more tea and some toast with jam. He gestured at the tray. "Would you like some more refreshment?" She shook her head.

"I trust you enjoyed your evening? You've seen for yourself that I have taken care of your daughter."

"Thank you for that. At least for that."

"Well, I suppose it is time we discuss our future."

Trude steeled herself and began. "I know what you want, Gunther. I've always known. I know why you protected Britta, and why I'm here now. I will give you everything you want, but you must give me what I want in return."

His eyes narrowed. "Go on."

"I want you to give me a pass. Papers for Britta and me. I will depart here with her and take her back to Königsberg. I will leave her with some friends . . . people I can trust. When I'm done, I will come back. I give you my word."

He stared at her for a long moment, then burst into laughter, spitting flecks of toast out onto the desk. "Oh my dear, dear, I forgot how charming you can be. I've worked so hard to get you here. You can't imagine what the waiting has been like. I'm just not able to wrap my head around the concept of letting you go again. I'm sure you're completely trustworthy," he said, leaning forward with an ironic grin. "Despite *your word*, I'm unfortunately not going to be able to accept that. As for Britta, sorry, but I've grown tremendously fond of her. Plus, you'd be miserable without her. I can't have you moping around here all day long, pining for your daughter."

"I told you, I'll give you what you want."

"I'm not sure you understand me. It's not what you think."

A moment of hope flittered into her mind. What did he mean?

"I don't want your body. Well, not just that. I want all of you, my dear. I want you like a wife, and Britta like a daughter. I want us to live here like a family. I want you to go along with this with happiness and willingness in your heart. In exchange, I will keep Britta safe and sound. That's my bargain." He sat back, folding his hands behind his head, clearly satisfied with himself.

He wanted her and Britta as a family? She'd never conceived of this. She knew he wanted her, but what kind of disgusting, twisted plan was this? Didn't he understand how much she loathed and feared him? She watched him for a second. He looked at her with hope, with confidence. He was completely deluded, she realized. Yet he held all the power. He was even more dangerous than she had thought he was.

She had to push through this. "I agree to all of that, but my terms remain the same. I need to get Britta to safety. Then I will be what you want . . . I'll be your wife."

He leaned back, waving his hands in the air as if surrendering. He chuckled and wagged a finger at her. "I was not wrong about you, my dear. Look at you sitting here in this place, bargaining with me for the terms of your surrender. You still don't understand, do you?"

"I know what you want, and I know what my terms are."

He flushed red. She could tell he was growing angry as he struggled to calm himself. "You must not understand what this place is. What do you think goes on here?"

She shook her head. "Some kind of SS jail."

"No, it's something much, much worse. It's hell unimaginable. If you live long enough to see it." His face puffed up in scarlet blotches. "Why, with a word from me, you and your precious daughter would be dead, do you realize that? Before I finished my toast, I could make that happen. But there are worse things than death. Should I let you see the camp?" He leaned back, drawing his fingers to his jaw, considering the issue. "Yes. Yes, I like that. I think that's an excellent idea."

He called loudly, and the door was opened instantly. A guard appeared.

"Frau Bensheim would like to see the camp. She doesn't quite understand what we're all about. Give her the grand tour."

The guard saluted, a little grin appearing.

"Make sure she sees everything. When you're done, bring her back here."

She rose and started to leave. She felt Gunther's hand on her arm, holding her back. He stepped forward, moving his lips to her ear, touching them against her for a moment. "Enjoy yourself," he whispered. "When you return, we'll have a nice little chat about things."

CHAPTER TWENTY-THREE

Berlin
March 1943

Erik sat with his eyes closed. His body shook violently. He had mere moments to live. He heard the command to fire, and his body went rigid, waiting for the bullets to tear him apart. He heard the sharp metallic clank of the triggers. A moment passed, then another. His heart was in his throat, trying to push its way through his mouth. He couldn't breathe, and he wondered if he was in that strange limbo between life and death. Another few seconds passed. He hadn't been hit by anything, nor had he heard the explosive echoing thunder of gunfire. He opened his eyes. The guards stood in front of him, their machine pistols still aimed his direction. Their weapons must be unloaded, he realized. They were mocking him. As if to answer that question, he heard the shrill laughter of the lieutenant. Erik turned to his tormentor. Messerschmidt's shoulders bounced up and down in a furious mirth, his face a mottled mask.

"Don't worry, Captain," he said. "This is just a dress rehearsal. We want to make sure everything is in order for the real thing, which won't be long in coming, I assure you." He nodded to one of the guards, who stepped forward to stand directly in front of Erik. The man smiled a wry, bitter, ironic grin and swept the butt of his pistol across Erik's head. Erik felt the sharp flashing and his body spinning as he hit the ground, then all was darkness.

Erik woke later, his head a burning ball pressed against the cold stone floor. He had retched and he lay in the sticky, foul refuse. When he tried to rise, his head spun and the nausea overwhelmed him again. He ran his tongue along his teeth and realized one was missing. Several more were loose. A guard returned, crashing open the door, and stared in disgust at the vomit.

The soldier grabbed Erik, pulling him to his knees and then half-carrying, half-dragging him down the hallway. Erik was placed in a small stone room. The door opened and a different guard stepped in, aiming a nozzle at him to spray him with ice-cold pressurized water. The stream nearly knocked him over, and the frigid water burned him with icy fire as the jet was walked up and down over his body. The torment felt like it lasted an eternity. He was ordered to stand and follow the guard into another room.

He recognized this cell, with the solitary table and two chairs. Or perhaps there were many interview rooms like this. He looked around indifferently. A part of him wanted to fight furiously to survive, but an equal side clambered and begged for the end. He sat at the table in the room by himself for a very long time. He wondered what new torment awaited him. There was nothing on the walls, no clock, no window, nothing to see and nothing to do but to sit and wait. When the door opened again, he braced himself for more blows. He was shocked to see a familiar form stroll into the room and stand staring at him, legs spread apart, hands on hips, a grim grin on his chiseled Aryan features.

"Quite a fix you've got yourself into, Mueller."

Karl. Erik invoked the name in his mind. Was he here, or was this merely an apparition? Erik reached shaking hands out toward his friend, his heart filled with relief and a spark of hope.

Karl turned and barked at the door; it banged shut harshly behind him. He stepped forward, his eyes never leaving Erik, and seated himself at the table across the way.

"Tell me everything," he demanded. His face was impassive.

Erik told the whole story, holding nothing back. He explained about combat in Russia, the sniper he executed, the battle near Kharkov, and Sauer's order to kill the Russians. He told of his arrest, the torture, the threats, and the false allegation that he was the one who had ordered the killing of the Russians. When he was finished, Karl watched him for a few moments, waiting to hear if there was more of the story. Then he responded.

"It's about what I'd assumed," he said. "Imagine the irony I felt when I learned that you of all people were facing charges for cruelty to the enemy."

"It's all a lie," Erik said. "I know if I just could have contact with my own company, there are many men who would vouch for me."

"Are you sure? Do you think any of them would cross a major? Even if they would, do you think a couple of privates and a sergeant or two would count over the word of multiple officers and Sauer?"

"But it's the truth," said Erik.

Karl slammed his hand on the table. "Silence!" he demanded. He looked at Erik for a moment and then shook his head. "You still don't get it, do you? I thought I'd explained things to you the last time around, and judging by your success in Russia, I thought you learned your lesson. Sauer wrote to me several times to tell me how proud he was of you, that you'd embraced the party, embraced the future." He looked at Erik in contempt. "Then I hear of this betrayal. This weakness cropping up again. How could you have such stupidity in your moment of triumph? How could you do this to yourself? To your family, your wife, to me?"

Karl leaned over the table, pointing a finger. "Listen to me, you worthless little shit. I put my reputation on the line for you. For your wife. And this is how you repay me? You had a future, Erik. A future with limitless potential. This war will not last forever. Sure, we've had a few setbacks, but that won't last long. The Russians were almost finished before Stalingrad. They may have gained a moment's respite, but they can't last forever. Germany will rule the world. You could have had a part of that. I had plans for you. Not just in Königsberg, either. Instead you chose a coward's path, and you've ruined everything for yourself."

"There were hundreds of them," protested Erik.

"I'd kill a million of them without blinking," said Karl. "In fact, I have, directly or indirectly."

Erik was shocked. "What do you mean?" he asked.

"I won't be telling you any bedtime stories, Erik. I wouldn't want to give you nightmares. Let's just say I would have burned those Russians without a second thought." He stood up, taking a couple of steps away from the chair and beginning to pace. "Right now I'm not worried about dead Jews and Russians. Right now, I need to try to figure out what to do with you. Frankly, I should just walk out of here and let them finish their work. They are trying to figure you out. Do they put you on public trial for atrocities or give you a quiet bullet to the head?"

"Then you mean . . ."

"Your arrest isn't public yet. Your family doesn't even know. Perhaps that might be for the best if I could convince them to just shoot you. A private execution here, and your family lives on with honor. Your memory lives on. I talked to the commander about that, but some people in the SS want something bigger, something to show the world that the SS cares about military discipline and punishes those who commit war crimes. They may make an example out of you."

"But I didn't do it."

"Silly boy. As if that mattered. You are a convenient scapegoat. You'd be lucky to get two words in at the trial. They would shout you down, then convict you and take you out back and shoot you right afterward. That would be the end of you. That seems to be the prevailing plan for now. I'd let them do it without any thought if it wasn't for Corina. She doesn't deserve that. She doesn't deserve you, either, you simpering, weak pile of refuse. How she ever became attracted to something like you I'll never know."

"You have to tell her I'm here. She needs to know I'm alive."

Karl's disgust increased. "You would tell her of this when I'm offering you a quiet and honorable death?"

"Please, Karl, I'm begging you. Even if they do shoot me here, please someday tell her what happened. I want my family to know."

Karl shook his head. "You truly don't understand, do you?"

"Are you saying she would want me to die here quietly just for the sake of the family?"

"No. She would have wanted you to burn those Bolsheviks and come home the hero you were instead of the coward you are."

"I'm not a coward," said Erik, feeling a touch of the old courage. "I did what I thought was right."

Karl stared at him again without responding, and then he rose to leave. "I've talked to Sauer. I can't believe it, but even now he's of two minds about you. He said you saved his life, that you've been a brave comrade and a friend. He doesn't understand your weakness. He doesn't want to see you again, but he asked me to help you. Can you believe that?"

Karl shook his head. "I don't understand why anyone cares about you at this point. But for Corina's sake and for Sauer, I'll see what I can do. Like I said, it may just be a quiet bullet in the head. I'll speak to the commander on your behalf. I will pull this one last string for you, Erik, and then I'm washing my hands."

Erik rose to thank him, but he felt the dizziness overwhelm him again. He thrust his arm out in the Hitler salute.

Karl stared in surprise and then chuckled. "A little late for that, don't you think?" His eyes softened a little around the edges and a look of sadness filled his face. "So much waste. I don't know if I'll see you again, Mueller. Fare thee well." Karl walked slowly from the interrogation room, leaving Erik again in the gray dim solitude.

Erik was eventually taken back to his cell. He noted the guards handled him less roughly. Perhaps it was only his imagination, or maybe his meeting with such a high-ranking influential individual had made some sort of impression. He didn't know if he was grasping at straws, but he prayed for a miracle. Another thing changed after Karl's visit: the beatings stopped. He was left alone. The only marker of time passing was the twice-daily delivery of stale bread and water. Three days passed. Long and full of boredom, anxiety, and uncertainty for the future.

On the morning of the fourth day after Karl's visit, the door opened. He looked up hopefully, wishing for Karl, but it was the lieutenant, cold and passive.

He gestured and guards pulled Erik out of his cell and marched him down the cold gray dark corridor. They went through first one security door then another. He had never been to this part of the jail, he realized. They reached a set of wooden double doors at the end of the hallway. One of the guards reached out and knocked. An answering sound emanated from the other side of the door, and it opened widely. He was led into a large windowless rectangular room. At the front, several steps led up to a small platform where a huge table dominated. At the table three SS officers sat, staring out at him sternly. The men were flanked by guards, standing, weapons at the ready. He was in a courtroom, he realized, and his spirits sank. There was to be a show trial after all.

Immediately in front of the stage was a single hard wooden chair, facing the officers of the court-martial. He was led to this chair and ordered to take his place. He blinked against the harsh light of the room. His judges stared at him, three muscular statues with sharp blue eyes. Unmovable.

The center officer, a full colonel, was older than the other two. His light-brown hair was tempered with gray. He leaned forward, addressing Erik.

"Tell us your story. Everything. Now." His deep voice bellowed through the courtroom, filling the space.

Erik thought for a moment. What should he say? Should he lie? Should he admit the charges and beg for mercy? He realized it would make no difference. He'd heard of these trials. They always ended the same way. The best he could do was tell these men what happened; his fate would be in their hands. He began speaking, telling his story identically to what he explained to Karl only a few days ago, although he went all the way back to Poland and filled the men in on what had occurred there and in France.

The officers listened attentively. He'd expected they would shout him down as he'd been warned. Instead they sat back, taking in the information, interrupting him politely to ask a question here and there. When he was done, the colonel asked if there was anything more he wanted to say. Erik shook his head. The officer then reached down and opened a briefcase Erik had noticed resting near his feet and pulled out a folder of paper. He reviewed it for a second and then said, "I will now read the statement from Lieutenant Colonel Sauer."

Lieutenant Colonel. That was a surprise. He must have had another promotion.

The colonel cleared his throat. "This is the sworn statement. 'Near the city of Kharkov our battalion was supporting a company of tanks when we were attacked by both snipers and a full brigade of Russian infantry supported by fifty T-34 tanks.

"'Our men were just settling down for a meal and were caught by surprise. Captain Mueller and I rushed into a building and neutralized one of the snipers. In the process, I was wounded. Captain Mueller assisted me back into the street and arranged for medical care. He then took over command of the battalion and successfully fought off the attack, capturing several hundred Russians in the process. By all reports, the captain performed brilliantly. I was treated with morphine, and when I awoke, to my dismay I realized that Mueller, apparently flushed with victory, was packing the Russian prisoners into a large wooden church with the intent of setting it on fire. I immediately ordered him to desist, but he refused. I commanded him again, but I was unable to rise because of my wound, and he simply laughed at me and walked away, directing for the building to be lit on fire. I was distraught, but there was nothing I could do. Ultimately I was able to call over a couple privates, and I ordered Mueller to be taken into custody and sent away so that these crimes could be addressed. I've attached an affidavit with the signatures of additional officers and men, all of whom attest to the facts as I've described them.

"'I must say formally how distressed I was by Captain Mueller's conduct. He has been a brave officer and a friend. I never expected him to disobey a direct order. I know he must face the consequences of this action, but I would ask the court to consider Captain Mueller's prior service and bravery, which I've outlined below, along with his decorations. I leave this matter to the judgment of the court.'"

The colonel watched Erik closely as he read the statement and the confirming statements of the fellow officers. When he was finished, he turned back to Mueller. "Lieutenant Colonel Sauer is well known to the SS. He is a rising star in our military. He not only made this statement under oath, but he's gone out of his way to defend you despite your conduct. Now I will ask again, and think closely before you answer: Are you still prepared to tell me in the face of all of this evidence that it was Sauer and not you who ordered the Russians to be burned?"

Erik knew he was in an impossible situation. If he changed his story now, he proved his own guilt plus he would be lying, something he had never overtly done in his entire life. If he continued to assert his story, then in the eyes of the men in front of him he was betraying a brother officer, a superior who still displayed loyalty to him even after such heinous actions.

"I stand by my story, which is the truth," he said.

A hint of color grew in the colonel's cheeks and his expression hardened. "I see," the judge said, shaking his head slightly. He exchanged glances with the officers to his left and right before returning to Erik.

"You may return to your cell while we deliberate." The guard stepped forward and removed Erik from the room, walking him swiftly back to his cell. There was lunch there, a meal they didn't normally serve. He was surprised to see that there was not only bread but a little meat on the plate.

Perhaps this is a good sign? Then he smiled to himself. *You truly are naïve. This is a last meal.* He ate the food, not tasting it as he felt his nerves coursing through his body. He wondered how long he would have to wait. When the door clanged open again just a few minutes later, he was surprised. The guard sternly motioned to him, and he was rushed back down the hallway to the courtroom. The officers were still there, staring impassively as he was dragged into the middle of the room and shoved down into the chair.

The colonel addressed him. "Do you have anything else you wish to say before we pass sentence, Mueller?"

Erik responded. "I simply hope that whatever sentence I receive will not be extended to my family."

The colonel responded. "That is not in my jurisdiction, but I would point out that is something you should've considered before, Mueller, and it is not for you to decide now."

The colonel cleared his throat. "I've rarely seen a case with so many witnesses, particularly one of such a high rank, who have all sworn

under oath concerning an event where the responding party continued to deny their involvement. The only thing that surprised me in
this case is that anyone would speak on your behalf. Yet you had not
only Lieutenant Colonel Sauer requesting leniency for you, but another
influential member of the SS. You have powerful friends you perhaps
do not deserve.

"The original intention of the SS was for you to be publicly tried.
An open humiliation which, in my opinion, you richly deserve. Based
on the pleas of these others, we decided to utilize this more private
process, although I can't imagine why you are entitled to it. That said,
it is the unanimous position of the judges in this matter that you are
guilty not only of the murder of hundreds of prisoners of war but more
importantly of refusing not only once, but twice, to follow the direct
orders of your superior officer.

"For this reason, this tribunal sentences you to death by hanging.
This sentence will be executed tomorrow at dawn. You are also to be
stripped of all rank and all decoration, and you will be expelled from
the rolls of the SS. Do you have any questions?"

Erik was stunned. He knew this was a possibility, but somehow
he thought the truth would be believed or perhaps some other miracle
would happen. He realized now that would not be the case. He stared
at the men silently for a few moments. Death was all around him.

CHAPTER TWENTY-FOUR

Soldau
March 1943

Trude was escorted by the guard out of Gunther's office and down the long corridor and the stairs. He led her out the back door toward a barbed-wire gate guarded by a single SS sentinel, machine pistol at the ready. The guard nodded at Trude's escort, eyeing her curiously before he opened the gate and motioned them through.

Trude stepped into a world she would never have believed existed. Her senses were assaulted from every direction as they walked past row after row of what looked like military barracks. The buildings and sur-rounding area were teeming with women, scarecrow like, with shaven heads and ratty striped uniforms. These living corpses shambled to and fro, under the watchful eyes of SS guards, who screamed at them to hurry along. Most of them were barefoot, and they shuffled along through the snow and dirty slush, stares vacant and hopeless.

The guard led her to one of the barracks, opening the door and pushing her inside. The stench was overwhelming. Trude nearly passed out from the pungent smell. Row after row of wooden bunks lined the interior. There were no mattresses. The barracks was almost entirely empty except for a few wretched souls, too weak to move, laid out on the hard wooden beds. Their bodies rocked back and forth slowly. The barracks was ice-cold, and she could see no blankets.

"Do you know what these women did wrong? Why they are here?" asked the guard.

Trude shook her head.

The guard laughed. "They are Jews. Just like you. They are here for that crime and that crime alone."

Trude stared in horror as that truth sank in. These women were Jews just like her. They were here only because of their race. She shook her head again, not able to grasp what she was hearing. Surely the guard was lying. He must be taunting her. Gunther had probably put him up to it. A thought struck her suddenly: Johannes was sent to some special camp in Germany. What if it was the same as here? She couldn't imagine her poor husband, beaten, weak, and emaciated. Suffering in a camp just like this.

I can't think about that right now, she told herself. The guard motioned, and she followed him back out the door and onward until they reached the kitchen. Inside other inmates were cooking a soup in large iron kettles. The guard took her over to inspect the contents, and she saw it was little more than hot water with tiny globs of cabbage.

"This is what they live on," he said, chuckling. "They get a half bowl of this slop twice a day. That's it. Nothing more."

"No one can live on that," she said, almost to herself.

The guard snorted again. "They don't. Not for long anyway. They end up like those wretched sticks lying in the barracks. But there's plenty more where they came from. Trainloads of them every week." He walked out of the kitchen and into the fields, where Trude saw hundreds of women at work, on their hands and knees, lifting rocks of all sizes and carrying them slowly on weak and unsteady legs until they dropped them into waiting wheelbarrows. Guards stood by, talking to each other, ignoring the inmates. Now and again one of them would turn and scream for a woman to hurry up. The inmates would flinch and push themselves a little faster.

Trude observed a girl who could not have been more than fourteen. She hobbled along and then fell face first into the field. The guards ignored her. Trude watched the girl for long moments, but she didn't move. Trude cringed. The guards would notice the girl any second, then she would be beaten, or worse.

Her own SS soldier followed her gaze and laughed again. "Don't worry about her. She's a goner." Trude saw it was true. The girl wasn't moving. She was dead.

"Don't tell me this is your first corpse?" he said sarcastically. "Is it? You really don't know where you are, do you? We could build a wall to Berlin with the dead here. Let me show you."

She didn't want to follow him, but there was nowhere for her to run. Reluctantly she shadowed his steps as he led her around the last set of barracks, where a massive snowdrift extended off the back. The drift sloped downward, extending from the building in an arch about ten meters to the ground. The guard stood near her, waiting expectantly with a grin.

At first she didn't understand what he wanted her to see. The guard huffed in disgust and moved toward her, grabbing her harshly by the neck and turning her toward the drift. "There, you stupid bitch. Look there!" She turned her head fearfully and realized with horror that mixed in the snow were arms, legs, and faces. Corpses, hundreds of them, frozen, naked, discarded, and jumbled in the ice.

"That's just a taste," said the guard. "A little appetizer for you. A sniff of this place. I could fill every barracks top to bottom with the dead." He grabbed her by the arm again and harshly jerked her around. Her eyes were closed, and he screamed at her, "Look at me. I don't understand what kind of spell you've cast on our commander, but you better knock off your game and wise up. He's offering you your life and the survival of that little brat you call a daughter. Look around you. You wouldn't last five minutes out here."

He grabbed her by the hair and shoved her into the snow. She landed with a hard crash into the frozen bodies. She pushed herself up, horrified, nauseated, trying to regain her balance.

The guard stood there laughing at her, leaving her to struggle. She finally regained her footing and rose to her feet. "Shall we continue our little tour?" he asked.

She wondered what could be worse than this pile of poor frozen souls. She braced herself as they continued on. She felt the freezing numbness invade her body and spirit. She trembled, and she didn't know how many more steps she could take. She feared she would fall again. Thankfully the guard led her back through the camp and out the barbed wire and into the administrative building. Perhaps he'd decided he'd shown her enough. He brought her down the long hallway on the first floor. She'd expected to go up the stairs, but he stopped her abruptly at one of the doors, pulled out keys to open it, and ordered her inside.

"I thought I was going back to Gunther. What about Britta? I need to go see her."

"Orders are for you to stay in here," he said.

"I want to talk to Gunther. Please take me to him."

The guard laughed again. "Oh, now you want Gunther. Now you want to negotiate, do you? You don't get to bargain, you Jewish slut. Now get in there!" He reached for her, but she moved out of his way, stepping quickly into the room. The interior was bare except for a single cot. A framed window looked out onto the camp through barbed wire. There were steel bars fastened over the window to prevent escape. She was in a holding cell of some kind, she realized.

"Enjoy yourself," said the guard. "We will send some of the delicious soup from the camp for you. I hope you enjoyed the tour." He slammed the door behind him, leaving her alone. She stood, staring out the window for long minutes, her body shaking. Soon she was sobbing uncontrollably. She was more afraid than she'd ever been. What was this place? Why were they doing these things to people, to her people? As terrible as she knew the Nazis were, she'd never dreamed such a place could exist. A place where they murdered people in countless numbers based on their race.

She'd come to expect their propaganda, the arrests, the beatings. This was something more, something beyond the landscape of humanity. She'd come to the land of demons and devils, mocking God above, destroying his creations with a wicked glee.

—⋄—

Trude was eventually taken back to Britta's room. She was relieved that her daughter was still there. As she spent the day there in the quiet with Britta, her mind reeled. This was a camp where the living and the dead blurred. Where they intentionally starved and beat and humiliated a person, where they strove to take all humanity away. She thought of Johannes. What foolish arrogance he'd possessed to try to defy these people. To think he could control them, that he was immune to them. He'd had no idea what they were capable of. Neither had she.

After a time, she grew hungry. Lunchtime passed, and still there was no food. What was Gunther going to do to them? she wondered. He must be enjoying himself immensely, playing this game of cat and mouse that for him could never result in anything but a temporary delay of his satisfaction. For her the reverse was true. Her entire world was on the line. She felt her resolve crumbling. Should she just give in and do what he wanted? She realized it was crazy to demand that they be allowed to leave together. There was no way he could ever trust her to return, and she had no leverage, nothing to offer him in return. She racked her brain, trying to think of some way she could get Britta back to Captain Dutt short of leaving the camp. It was impossible. If she gave a name, a contact, even a street location, ultimately Gunther would find them. Besides, he would never let Britta leave. She realized that now. No, she had to insist that no matter what, Britta must be allowed to go. She had to hope that Gunther would allow this. Finally, the door jingled open and the guards brought in food, bread and soup. Her stomach grumbled and she hastened to the tray, attacking the food. She looked outside and realized light was already fading. It must be almost dinnertime. The guards turned to leave, but even as they did so, Gunther appeared.

"Hello, my dear. I trust you enjoyed your tour of the camp and had a day to think about it." She saw the insipid smile on his face as he sat down, breaking off a piece of the bread and dipping it in the soup. She ignored him, continuing to eat. She was starving, and even Gunther's presence could not assuage her hunger.

"That said, my dear, eat your fill. You need to keep up your strength. I trust you are going to put aside your silly illusions about leaving now."

She did not answer but kept eating. He took her silence as acquiescence and smacked his lips appreciably, slurping the soup.

She continued her meal, ignoring him as best she could. Within a few minutes she had gulped down a full portion along with several slabs of bread. She felt her hunger gradually dampen. She was ready. She set the tray aside, looking up at Gunther.

"I would like to speak to you alone," she said.

He smiled, misunderstanding her intentions. "Of course. Let's let Britta stay here, and we can step into my office." He rose and motioned for her to follow him. He let her out of the small apartment, locking the door, and then took her down the hallway to his office. He closed the door behind her and led her to the chair across from his desk. She sat down and cringed as she felt his hands on her back, giving her a little squeeze before he stepped around the desk and sat down, pulling out his pipe and loading it with tobacco. He lit it. Again flashing that satisfied smile, he asked her, "What can I do for you, my dear?"

She had to try one last time. "I'm asking you again to let me leave here with Britta. I saw the camp. I understand everything you are doing for us. I appreciate it very much. I'm willing to give you myself, give you everything you want, but my price is my daughter's freedom."

She saw the flash of anger followed again by a grin. "I'll tell you, you Jews," he said, wagging his finger at her. "Always bargaining even when you have nothing to bargain with. I can't believe that you saw the camp today, and you still came back asking for the same thing again. You're going to be a fun one to conquer," he said laughing to himself. She cringed. "But seriously, I told you, my dear, anything else you want, but that I cannot do for you."

"At least let her go," she asked. She was desperate. If he would agree to this, she would think of something, someplace. She could have her dropped off and give her daughter instructions. Somehow Britta could make her way to Captain Dutt.

Gunther shook his head. "I can't do that. You know better. You know that she must stay here. She's my leverage, you might say. My guarantee of your good behavior. Britta guarantees my happiness, our happiness."

She felt the tears flowing. She was trapped. There was nothing she could do. Still, deep inside she felt the flame burning. She had to protect her daughter. She shook her head again. "You have to let her go, or I will not comply. I don't care what you threaten me with, what you do to me. You will get nothing from me until you agree."

He stared at her again, his eyes widened in amazement, and then a sadness seemed to creep over him. He shook his head. "It gives me no pleasure to do this," he said, "but you have left me no choice." He stood and stepped over to the door, opening it and calling for his guards. He turned back to her. "A few days in the camp should change your mind." He looked at her, shaking his head. "I'm so very sorry."

She felt the fear welling up in her, but she stood her ground, praying this was a bluff. Surely he would not send her out among the prisoners. He was merely gambling, waiting for her to fold. But she did not bend and neither did he. Soon the guards were leading her down the stairs, through the corridor, and out into the frozen camp beyond.

CHAPTER TWENTY-FIVE

Berlin
March 1943

The guards brutally slammed Erik against the wall. He crumpled into the corner as they crashed the door closed behind him. *I'm going to die,* he realized. Not someday. Not in a few years, but tomorrow. What a strange feeling that was. He'd faced death so many times in combat, but still it was different. With combat, there was always a chance to survive. Not now. Now he knew for sure that in the morning his life would be over.

Everything was going to end. *All over a few hundred Russians,* he could hear Corina's and Karl's voices mocking him. *You threw away everything for nothing. They probably would've died in prison camps anyway, if they even made it that far. They weren't even human in the same way that the Germans are.* At least that's what he'd been told all these years.

The night seemed to last an eternity. With no clock and no stimulus except the occasional passing sound of a guard, he didn't even know what time it was. The lights went out, bedtime for those who could sleep, for people with some form of future. He lay there in the darkness, anxiety coursing through him. Every possible thought flitted through his mind as the hours ticked by, moment by wretched moment.

And then it was over. The lights flipped on in the outside corridor. Morning had come. His heart pumped viciously. They would be coming for him any moment. He wished he had pen and paper, a chance to write something to his wife, his parents, his poor little daughter. None of them would understand. Why hadn't he asked for something to write with last night? He'd had all evening. But then they would never take anything he had to say back to his family. That's not how things worked in the SS.

He heard the iron clang of boots in the hallway. The fateful clomping drew ever closer. They were coming. The end was here. He heard the jingling of the keys and the door opened. He braced himself as a guard stepped in, surrounded by the light, reaching for him.

"Mueller." He was surprised. The voice was familiar. He looked up, blinking, trying to adjust to the light. The figure wasn't a guard after all. It was Karl.

His friend was impassive as ever. He watched Erik, his eyes searching.

"Have you . . . have you saved me?" Erik asked.

"I don't know," he said. "It will depend on what you tell me right now."

Erik nodded, unable to speak again. His throat was dry and he tasted bitter bile in his mouth.

"I came as soon as I heard the judgment," Karl said. "I drove half the night to get here. I told you I'd pull strings for you one last time, and I have, but I'm not going to waste the effort unless I have assurances from you." He looked down harshly. "I'm putting my own ass on the line." He shook his head. "Not that you deserve it. Your word to me now will make the difference whether you walk out of here with me or dance on the end of a rope. Do you understand?"

Erik nodded.

"I have a place for you."

Erik looked up hopefully.

Karl shook his head. "Not the one I planned. That future is gone along with your medals and most of your rank. I can keep you in the SS, but you won't be an officer anymore."

"But they ordered me out of the SS."

"Out of the Waffen-SS, but that's not my organization. They don't have total control and they know it. I've got a job for you in East Prussia. It was the only one I could find on short notice. It won't be easy, especially for you. You may be called on to do things, things worse than you faced in Russia. That's where I must have your word. You've already balked in weakness at these so-called atrocities. You can never do so again."

Erik thought about that. If he agreed, he would be compromising everything he had fought for, sacrificed for. He shook his head.

"Don't answer so quickly. There's more than that. Your death sentence doesn't apply only to you. I don't know if you understood that. Your parents, your wife, your daughter. They are all going to be arrested. They will be jailed at best, at worst . . ."

That was it then. He had to choose between his own morals, and the freedom, perhaps the very lives, of his family.

"Choose carefully, Mueller." He reached into his tunic and pulled out a document, handing it to Erik. Karl called out and a light flipped on in the cell. Erik looked down, scanning the contents. The document was a full confession to the murder of the Russians, in exchange for a pardon and release to Karl's custody.

Erik had no choice. The only way to save his family was to sign this paper. He would have to admit to a crime he hadn't committed.

He would have to follow orders from now on no matter what, or his family would suffer the same fate he would. There was no choice. He nodded. Karl smiled, handing him a pen. Erik signed, his hand shaking as he did so.

Karl pulled the paper away, folded it, and then crossed his arms, staring back down at Erik. "That's the first sensible thing I think you've ever done. I thought when we had that conversation long ago you understood this was a new order, a new world. It has no place for weaklings. You're weak, Erik Mueller, one of the weakest men I've ever seen. Well, the weakest German at least. This war is at a crisis point. There will be no room for cowardice. You must prove yourself to me every day. I will give you no more chances, and I will not stand in the way of what happens to you or your family if you fail. Do understand me, Erik?"

He nodded. Karl turned without another word. He knocked on the door and was let out, leaving Erik behind. The prisoner slumped back down against the door. He felt the full misery of what he'd just done. He'd compromised everything to save his own life and his family. Could that be enough to justify his decision? While he and his family would not die today, he wondered if this world was worth living for. Perhaps that was the reality of this entire war: all honor and decency was gone. All that was left was survival.

Erik stood at the door of his town house, pausing for a moment to take a deep breath. He was elated to be here, to see his family after almost a year. But he was also filled with misery. He would have to break terrible news to them, and he knew how they would react. He was humiliated and bent over with guilt. He still wore the wrinkled, badgeless clothing from his captivity. Karl had driven him back this morning after he'd secured his release from the jail. They'd barely spoken a word to each other. When Karl dropped him off he did not say good-bye.

Erik paused a few more moments and then knocked at the door. He didn't even have a key. He had no money, nothing, not even his papers. Karl told him those would be sent back from Berlin in the next few days. His new papers, denoting whatever rank Karl could preserve for him. He heard a shuffling; his father answered the door. He saw surprise and shock register, and then an overwhelming happiness as Peter swept his son into his arms, holding him closely. He turned and shouted. "Erik's here! *Mein Gott!*" He clasped both of his son's hands. "What a delight! I don't know what to say. We weren't expecting you."

Erik didn't respond. He could hear a stampede of footsteps coming from every direction behind his father, along with the steady plod that could only be his sturdy mother. Greta was the first to appear, rushing past her grandfather to jump into her father's arms, kissing and hugging him. Erik was so overjoyed that his grief fell away for a moment. How tall she was now, as tall as her mother and just as beautiful.

His wife was next. She rushed out, swimming as always under the bright cotton dress, a severe scarlet scarf tied tightly around her delicate neck. She was joyful and excited at this surprise, although she scanned him appraisingly. "Where's your uniform?" she asked.

He ignored her question, as his mother materialized out of the dim light of the house. Her lips were pressed tightly but her eyes gleamed and she radiated contentment. He smiled back at her as he held Greta, squeezing her tightly, clinging to these lingering moments before the hurting began.

"What a surprise," Corina said. "How delightful. What did they give you leave for? Is it another medal? A promotion? Karl will be so excited to see you."

Erik nodded. "I'm home for a few days."

"Well, which is it?" asked Corina. She flushed with excitement. "Is it both?"

"What's wrong?" his mother asked, her steady eyes seeing something in his expression that the others had missed.

Erik shrugged. "There are things I must tell you. Important things." He glanced down at Greta. "Subjects that we should discuss as adults."

Erik saw the happiness flee his family's expressions. Corina ordered Greta upstairs. His daughter protested, but Corina shouted at her until she slumped off up the stairs.

"Perhaps we should all go sit down at the table," said Erik. They made their way into the kitchen. His mother poured tea and they all sat down. Fear stifled and choked the room.

"Tell us," said Corina, a hint of impatience in her voice. She wouldn't look at him, but instead ran a rag back and forth over the table, worrying away at an invisible blemish.

Erik started at the beginning, talking about the growing warmth in his relationship with Major Sauer, their return to Russia after the refitting in France. He explained the battle near Kharkov, the snipers, and taking over for Sauer. He described the victory, and he could see the triumph in his wife's eyes but also the confusion.

His voice broke and he hesitated. Then he launched into the story of the Russian prisoners, the church, Sauer's order, and his refusal. Corina's face fell ghostly white. She started to speak, but he raised his hand and continued.

He told of the arrest, of the threats to kill him, the trial, Karl's intervention, and Erik's demotion. Corina gasped at this news. She stood up and stormed swiftly out of the room. Erik sat silently with his parents. They didn't look at him and were clearly too stunned to talk. They sat that way for a few minutes.

"You're alive," said Peter, finally breaking the silence. "You're alive, and you protected your family. You kept your honor. I don't know what else you could have done."

Peter reached over and squeezed his son's arm. Even as his father did so, Erik heard footsteps rapidly returning. Corina was there, her face on fire, her eyes sharp and wild.

"He protected his family?" she shrieked, obviously having overheard his father's words. "How did he do that?" She turned on Erik. "You've lost everything! You idiot! We were going to move to the best part of the city. I've been invited to tea and to shopping with the very best people in Königsberg. We had a future, Erik. A future away from all this middle-class garbage. You've lost your rank, your medals, and our hope!"

"But I didn't kill those Russians," he said.

"What difference does that make? What good did it do for you? Those prisoners are just as dead. Now you'll be lucky to get a job in a shop after the war. We'll be stuck in this hellhole together forever. You've ruined our lives." She raised her hands to the ceiling. "I always knew you were soft. I thought I could fix that after we were married, but I was wrong!"

"Enough!" yelled Peter. "Enough from you!"

Corina turned. "And you!" she screamed back at him. "Worthless, unemployed. You didn't even have the sense to keep your business intact. You've sat back judging the new order, the party. You've been on your high-and-mighty horse. What has that done for you? You sat here with that son of yours, day after day, wondering what to do. Jobless and hopeless. I had to go out and find a job for Erik. There was nothing I could do for you. Who would take you?"

"I didn't need your help, and neither did Erik!" Peter retorted. "I've sat back long enough and watched you try to shove my poor son up the social ladder for your own benefit. Look what good it's done. What world are you living in? Let me say it out loud for you: the Russians are winning the war. The English and the Americans aren't far behind. It's only a matter of time until your precious party is going to burn to the ground and take Germany with it. When it's over there will be nothing left except those that survive. If he killed those Russians or not, the result would be the same. His medals and his rank won't help any of us when the Russians get here. Gott help us all."

"You'd better watch your mouth, old man," warned Corina. "They've arrested people for far less than that. I will not sit here and listen to this defeatist talk. We are winning on the eastern front, and we will win the war!"

She turned on Erik. "Karl has saved you again apparently. You are going to take whatever job he gives you. You will follow every command. You will be better than anyone else in the position, whatever the cost. You must at least finish the war in his good graces. Perhaps you can redeem yourself if it lasts long enough. If you love me and Greta and you want any kind of future for this family, you will do everything in your power from now on to save us. And I don't just mean our lives, I mean our reputation, our future in this town and in this country. Do you understand me?"

Erik nodded. He didn't know what else to do. Peter was flushed with anger but seemed cowed by Corina's harsh words. Erik looked at his mother. Anna was visibly upset, but as always she would not speak. He knew how much she hated conflict. She wanted simple peace and contentment in the house. For her sake, and for the sake of his father, he did not continue the battle with his wife.

Besides, Corina was right. She always was right. He would have to do everything that was asked of him from now on. Not only for the future she wanted, if there was such a thing, but also to save all their lives.

He didn't believe in Corina's vision of the future anymore. He knew deep in his heart they would lose the war. The Russians were piling on new men, new equipment, more tanks and planes in seemingly inexhaustible supply. The Germans couldn't hope to contend with them. They could try to hold them back. They might score some counterattack victories and even negotiate a reasonable peace, but there would be no "great German victory." No unified Europe with the SS and the Nazis in charge.

One day in the distant future, it was likely the Russians would roll through Königsberg. He shuddered at the thought. He remembered all the terrible things the Germans had done in Russia. The retribution could be dreadful, indeed.

He couldn't worry about that right now. He had to think about the immediate future. He needed to battle to keep his family from falling apart.

"I will do everything necessary," he said. "Karl has saved my life. I will work hard for him in this new assignment, and I'll make sure all of you are protected and that our future, such as it may be, is assured."

"You're going to be tested," said Corina. "They know you're weak. They will want you to fail. You can't hold on to your ridiculous morals any longer."

He nodded, but he prayed he would never find out what that meant. For now, he was home with his family and he would try to eke out a few days of peace before the new, unknown storm.

He called Greta back down, and for the rest of the evening the family visited in relative tranquility. He told stories of France and lighter subjects about Russia: the endless snow, the steppes, the charming villages and towns. The onion-domed churches. There was a gloominess to the room they all tried to hide, but the air was thick with it.

The evening wore on until it was time for bed. Erik took his daughter up to her room and prayed with her before tucking her in. She held his hand.

"I'm so happy you're home," she said. She squeezed his fingers before drifting off to sleep. Erik sat there for a long time, praying to

God, hoping for a miracle, for a future for his young daughter. He thought of the Russians again and shuddered.

He rose and tiptoed out of the room, heading toward his bedroom. He paused outside the door. He'd dreaded this moment alone with Corina. He took a deep breath and entered. She was already in bed, her back to him. She didn't speak when he came in. He undressed and put on his pajamas, then climbed carefully into the bed.

She did not move. They hadn't lain in bed together for so long. He placed a tentative hand on her back. There must be some way to feel close to her again, to say he was sorry. She bristled, moving away.

"Don't touch me!" she hissed.

"Corina, please, I'm only going to be home for a couple of days."

"Don't touch me," she repeated. "You are no man. I'm repulsed by you."

He tried again and she whipped around, facing him. "I mean it, Erik. Don't ever touch me again until you redeem yourself. If you become a man again, then I will treat you like one. For now, I can't stand to look at you, let alone let you touch me. Now go to sleep!"

She jerked back around and rolled over.

Erik said nothing but flipped over on his back, staring up at the ceiling. Things had gone about as he had expected. His father and mother shocked and sad but understanding. Corina angry, blaming him, demanding that he fix their future. Maybe she was right, he thought. Maybe he was weak. Karl had said the same. Look at Sauer: ruthless, single-minded, he never let petty things like morals get in the way. He'd risen all the way to the top. A lieutenant colonel now with a future. If there was a future. Karl was the same—same morals, same future.

Erik hadn't grown up that way. His father and mother had ingrained right and wrong in him from the time he could understand them. You didn't prey on the weak. You didn't torture and kill people. Hitler had come along and challenged all their beliefs.

The Führer had conquered half the world. Erik thought they were going to lose, but he didn't know that for sure. He'd been wrong about so many things. He'd brought near ruin on his family. He knew he had no more chances left, that everyone would be watching him in his new assignment. He would not be coming in as a hero, as an officer. He was a marked man who would have to do what he was told or risk losing everything. He lay there for hours in the darkness, unable to sleep, his thoughts a cauldron of boiling turmoil.

CHAPTER TWENTY-SIX

Soldau
March 1943

Trude was awakened harshly by the clanging of metal on metal. She opened her eyes, blinking warily in surprise. What was going on? Then she remembered. She was inside the camp. Gunther had made good on his promise. She was in hell.

They'd taken her from Gunther's office to the barber, where her beautiful hair was shorn off roughly. She remembered the ripping, the pain. It felt like they were tearing each strand out by the roots. They tore her clothes off until she was naked. The men stared at her, leering and mocking her. She was forced into an icy shower and then doused with a stinging powder. They shoved clothing into her hands. She was still blinded by the powder, but she fumbled through the material, dressing in the ill-fitting, coarse pajamas. She slid on thin slippers that she knew would do nothing to protect her feet against the frozen snow and the cold.

When they were finished dressing her, they dragged her out of the administrative building and into the camp. She was pushed into a barracks not far away. A woman was there, dressed in a striped uniform, another Jew. She was middle-aged and she stared skeptically, perhaps angrily, at Trude as she was brought in. A guard stepped forward and whispered to her in hushed tones, jerking his thumb back at Trude. The woman's face hardened into stone. The guard turned, smiled at Trude one last time, and the SS men left. Trude was disoriented and afraid. She looked around, trying to get her bearings. The middle-aged woman stepped over to her, moving in close, too close. Trude could smell her hot, fetid breath. She smiled and Trude saw she was missing many teeth. The grin of a malevolent clown.

"Well, what do we have here?" she asked. "The guard tells me you're Gunther's special toy but that you've been a bad little girl." She shook her head. "Tsk, tsk. We can't have any of that around here. Well, that's where I come in. You've been naughty, and it's time for your punishment, correct?"

Trude shook her head. "That's not true. Well, it's partially so. He's been after me for years. I only . . ."

The woman stepped forward and struck her hard across the face. Trude's head snapped back and she reeled in surprise. She felt the metallic, bitter bite of blood flowing in her mouth. The pain was stinging in the cold. She was in shock. She'd never been hit before, not even by her parents.

"Shut up, you little slut," said the woman. "My name is Frau Dauch." She stepped forward again, standing a hair's breadth away. "This is my barracks day and night. I run the show." She looked Trude up and down with disgust, shaking her head. "To think I don't have enough problems already without getting a piece of Jewish tart dropped on me. A stupid one at that. You think you can tell the *Kommandant* what to do?" She grabbed Trude roughly by the front of the shirt. "You listen to me. You're going to play the game for the next couple days. You're going to work hard and keep your mouth shut. You're going to suffer with the rest of us, and when we're done you will go back to

Gunther. You will do whatever he says. Otherwise we will all suffer, and if that's the case I'll take care of you myself. A knife in the night and no one will be the wiser. Sure, Gunther will be upset, but not for long. All these Germans seem to have a taste for Jewish skirt, but it's not love. That's what you better learn very quickly. Forget about the stories they told you about right and wrong. Your life and all our lives are at stake. You do what you're told with a smile, or you'll be dead before you know it."

"I have a daughter," said Trude.

"What?" asked Frau Dauch.

"It's not as easy as you say. My daughter's here. Gunther has her and he's threatening her, too."

She looked at Trude in disbelief. "Do you think I care? Do you think anybody here does? I had two children, girls twelve and ten. We were all taken together along with my husband. I was pulled off the train here, they weren't. They're gone. They're dead. Most of the women here are in the same boat. Everyone's dead but us. We've all lost everything and everyone." She pushed Trude backward, letting go and pointing a finger. "You keep your mouth shut about your little girl. If you care about her at all, you do what you need to and survive. Now go find a bunk. You're in luck. We had a few fatalities today, so you have plenty of choices."

Trude made her way down the long corridor between the bunks. A few women stared out at her in curiosity, anger, surprise, every possible emotion. She knew that word would travel quickly among these women. She would be hated, pegged as a favorite of the Nazis. A pariah among the prisoners. She wanted to scream. How on earth could she be put into that position after all she had been through and everything she had done to defy them? She found an empty bunk and pulled herself up to lie down on the hard, dirty wood. The stench was unbearable: sweat, sickness, and fear. She didn't know if she could stand it. As she lay there she could feel her skin crawling. She realized to her horror the beds were teeming with lice. She pulled one off, trying to crush the insect in her fingers. The woman next to her cackled.

"No sense in trying that, sweetie. Soon you'll have thousands. They'll eat you alive. Best to make friends with them." The woman let her head back down, giggling to herself.

Trude did not respond. She lay there twisting in itchy misery, staring at the ceiling. Soon the lights were turned off and she was in the darkness with the coughing, the moaning, the tears.

What was she to do? She had to put up with the suffering. She knew there was very little chance, but if Gunther somehow relented, she could send her daughter away to safety. There was nothing here in the camp. She knew what the ending would be no matter what promises Gunther made for her safety. She spent the agonizing evening twisting and turning, catching the briefest snippets of sleep before the morning came. Everyone scrambled as best they could in their emaciated, weakened state to pull themselves out of the terrible torture chambers and hobble out into the snow and the cold to line up for roll call.

They stood there shivering. It was still dark out. The guards and the capos (the camp name for prisoners who assisted the guards) walked among them, counting, tallying. They stood for more than an hour. Trude wondered how early it was. She was freezing. Her body shook from the cold. A woman fell to the snow, then another. Nobody helped them or even looked their way.

Finally, they were dismissed, each person rushing back into the barracks. Trude followed behind them, wondering what was next. She lingered near the back of the crowd, pressing to get through the barrack doors. When she finally was inside, she realized her mistake. In the center of the room was a wood-burning stove. Apparently during roll call, someone had cooked some soup and brought in a few tiny loaves of bread. Now the women fought each other, tearing at each other and the bread, stuffing the crumbs into their mouths and slurping up the soup. By the time she could get to the front there was nothing left to eat. Frau Dauch spun Trude around, laughing at her, her voice dripping with mockery.

"Look at you, so strong but hanging in the back with skeletons. You won't last long like that. You'd better learn to fight your way to the front, or you'll be weak as a chicken before the month is out." She reached out, pointing to a couple of wretched forms lying in the bunks, still. They hadn't even made it out to roll call. "Some of these ducklings won't survive the day. But don't you worry about that just yet. I wager Gunther won't let that happen to you. He has other plans." She laughed to herself, shaking her head back and forth and holding her sides. "But until then, I've been ordered to show you the ropes around here. Come with me."

Frau Dauch led Trude out into the snow. Her feet were already frozen and sopping wet. Each step was a slippery agony. Trude was led through the barracks and out into a field toward the forest. The other prisoners were coming out in groups, each led by a woman wearing the same special markings of a capo. "I have a special job for you," said Frau Dauch, guiding her into the forest. She reached a crumbling building in a clearing. The building looked like it had been hit by bombs, perhaps during the Polish war. There were bricks everywhere, many broken, but others intact. A long line of women stood with wheelbarrows, clinging in clear exhaustion, even so early in the morning. Other women laboriously picked up the bricks with great effort and shuffled over to drop them into the carts. When they were full, the women turned and started pushing the heavy wheelbarrows back down the pathway and through the forest toward the camp.

"We are constructing some new buildings," explained Frau Dauch. "We don't have enough bricks from this building, but it's a start. Now listen here, you will run one of the wheelbarrows. You will help the other women load it up, and then when it's full, you will bring it back to the camp. You better move quickly," she said. "Everyone knows about you. There will be eyes on you in every direction. If you stop or if you drop your load, you'll be beaten, or perhaps worse."

Trude, terrified, nodded in response. Frau Dauch moved away, and soon Trude was among the women, lifting the bricks and placing them in the wheelbarrow, one after another. At first the work was relatively easy, but soon her back was throbbing, and her arms shook with weakness. The worst part was pushing the wheelbarrow itself. The tires were aged and flattened so that the wheel rumbled along through the rubber, stalling behind each twig and pebble of the pathway. The cart was so heavy she could almost not push it. Her arms trembled. Where before she had been frozen, now she was roasting. Her body shook and sweat trickled down her forehead and neck.

Finally, she made it back to the camp. Trude pushed the wheelbarrow over at the location designated, piling up the bricks with so many others. She wanted to take her time on the way back to the forest, but guards shouted for her to move faster. She was so exhausted after a single trip she did not know if she would be able to take another. The sky was just beginning to lighten. She was desperate. The day had barely started and she felt she couldn't take another step. There was no way she could do this until evening.

She willed herself to continue, starting the pattern again: first one brick, then another, then the terrible crucible of pushing the burden back to the camp. Over and over and over she repeated the cycle. She was dizzy. Her vision blurred. Her body shook. She alternated between freezing cold and stifling heat at the various steps of her journey. All she could see was the snow and the gray feet around her. She heard the screams of the guards at the edges of her nightmare, a reality that threatened her sanity.

She heard a sharp report. Trude saw, out of the corner of her eye, a body crash to the snow in a scarlet pool. She was stunned. A guard had shot a woman right there in front of her. The inmates nearby moved on, increasing their pace, struggling to remain anonymous, she realized.

Nobody wanted to attract the special attention of the Germans, who were quick to beat and kill.

On and on the day went. Trude thought she would die, but somehow she kept moving. She no longer felt her feet or legs. Her arms were one throbbing mass of pain. And then it was over. More screams and shouting, and they were herded back to the camp. The capos lined them up again in the snow. They stood at agonizing attention, a near impossibility after the backbreaking day of labor.

Another torturous hour of roll call. She could barely stand, but at least she was not bending over picking up the bricks or carrying that wretched cart. When the guards shouted for them to return to their barracks, she was ready. This time she sprinted as best she could, elbowing several women out of her way. She was at the front of the line and reached the soup and bread at the center of the barracks first. She helped herself to a bowl of the watery liquid and a full loaf of bread. She stepped away and glared at the women coming after her, growling at one who came too close, ensuring that nobody tried to take what was hers. She chewed as quickly as she could, gulping down the soup and stuffing the chunks of bread into her mouth before anyone came after her. In one day, she realized, they'd made an animal out of her. She didn't care. She was still alive, and she'd had something to eat. She could rest, if only for a little while. Before the torment began again.

The next night of sleep was even more impossible than the last. Her muscles were knotted with pain. She was so exhausted she couldn't sleep. Her moans joined the symphony of coughing and crying. Only the smell had lessened. Probably, she realized, her own odor had joined the rest. Hour after horrid hour she tossed and turned until she eventually gave up even trying to sleep. In the morning, the frozen roll call was repeated, along with the battle for a little food.

After breakfast, however, she was abruptly marched away by guards and was returned not to the forest but to the now-familiar red brick administrative building. She realized with relief her ordeal was over. At least one aspect of it. She was brought into Gunther's office and shoved into the familiar seat across from his desk. He was not there yet, and she sat listlessly for an hour before he arrived.

When he walked through the door and glanced in her direction, his whole body jerked in surprise. She saw his cheeks fill with a fiery red. "What the hell did they do to you?" he demanded. He screamed and the guards appeared again. They stood at attention, their eyes wide. Gunther paced back and forth in front of them, apparently too angry even to speak at first.

"Who authorized her hair to be cut?" he screamed. One of the guards stammered, managing to spit out a few words, but Gunther had no interest in the explanation. "Get out of here now!" he shouted. "I will deal with you later. Bring her hot food immediately." He turned with concern to Trude, his eyes softening. "I'm so sorry, my dear," he said, taking a couple of steps toward her. "That was not supposed to happen to you." He extended a hand, and she flinched as his fingers ran along her scalp, lingering on her temple.

"My daughter," said Trude. "Is she safe?"

Gunther snorted, obviously taken aback. "What do you take me for, a monster? Of course she's fine. She didn't share your punishment, if that's what you're asking."

"My punishment. How did I deserve that?"

He threw his arms up in exasperation. "Don't blame me, my dear. This was your choice. I told you there's a world out there that you cannot imagine. That I've done everything to protect you and your daughter from that."

"For your own selfish reasons," she said.

"Nothing for nothing in this world, my dear." He chuckled. "Look at you, still defiant. A whole day spent at death's door and still you want to argue with me." He reached out, pulling her head up toward him by the chin. "That's my girl," he whispered, beaming proudly at her.

Gratefully, the door opened just then, and a guard brought in a tray overloaded with food. Trude's stomach rumbled, the rich, overwhelming smell of sausages and hotcakes assailing her senses. Her stomach almost jumped out of her throat as the guards set the tray down on the desk. He bowed and quickly left the room.

He turned to Trude. "Eat, eat," he said, motioning to the food. She wanted to stuff the food into her mouth more than she'd ever wanted anything, but she hung back, clinging desperately to her final hope.

"I won't eat anything until we've talked." She wasn't sure that was true, but she held herself back for a few moments, praying for a miracle.

"What do you mean?" he said, his voice full or surprise.

"I still need your agreement."

"Don't worry, I won't send you back out there again. You've learned your lesson, I'm sure."

"I have. And I know you will protect me from all of that. But I still need you to let Britta go."

He was incredulous. The words stammered out of his mouth as he responded. "Are you seriously asking that?" he asked. "You have to be joking. After everything you saw, you still think you can bargain with me?" She heard the hint of steel in his voice. She was angering him now. She had to be careful. There was no telling what he was capable of if she pushed him too far.

She turned her head slowly and raised her eyes, ignoring the pain, the intense, burning flavor of the food so close. "That's all I'm asking. Just for Britta. You can have me. All of me. Everything you want."

Gunther stared at her for a moment and then shook his head. He reached down, picking up a sausage. He put it to his lips and took a bite. He watched her carefully.

Her hands shook. She could feel her mouth filling with water. The smell overpowered her.

"Are you sure you don't want one of these?" he asked. "Come on, my dear, let's quit playing this game." His voice was kind, gentle, pleading. "You know I can't let your daughter go. Just remember, I protected her for more than a year. No harm will befall her. I have everything here for you, for both of you." He grabbed her hands, holding them tightly with his. "I have the keys to the kingdom. Clothes, food, protection, safety. All you have to do is say yes. You can have a life here. You'll be able to read and play. You can teach your daughter." He let go and raised his hands as if in surrender. "Good Gott," he said, "I'll even get you a violin. You can play for her, for me. We will be our own little family right here. But no." He shook his head. "I can't let her go."

She hesitated. He was promising her the world. At least a paradise compared to what she'd seen in the last day. But he would not bargain with her. If she continued to defy him, how long would she last? A day perhaps? A week? How long did it take for your body to fall apart with no food and hours of backbreaking labor? With no sleep. She didn't know, but it couldn't be very long. Every part of her wanted to give in. But she knew she only had this last slim chance to save her daughter. She stared at the food for a moment longer, then shook her head. "I agree to everything, but Britta has to go."

Gunther scoffed. "I can't believe you," he said. "Now you've done it. Do you know what you're forcing me to do?" He rose and turned away. He shouted and the door opened again. Gunther motioned at the table, and the guard swept the food away. Gunther stepped to the door and gave more commands. Soon the guards were returning. They stepped in and stood behind her on either side, granite hands on her shoulders.

"Take Frau Bensheim back to the barracks," he ordered. "She apparently misses her friends there. Order that bitch capo in here as well." He turned to Trude. "I'm sorry, my dear," he said reproachfully. "You've left me with no choice. Apparently one day wasn't enough for you. I'll check back with you in a week, perhaps in a month. If you're still alive." He glared at her, angrier than she'd ever seen him.

The soldiers lifted her out of the chair and dragged her from the room. Every ounce of her body cried out to stop them, to turn to Gunther, to beg him for anything, for everything. She knew she could not. Britta had only one chance for true safety. *Gunther is bluffing,* she told herself. *He'll never wait a week. No, he will come to me and give in to this one small demand.* She was dragged back into the camp and into her barracks. The guards stayed with her there for about an hour. Eventually Frau Dauch returned from her visit with Gunther. She looked like she'd aged ten years. Her face was ghostly white. One of the guards shoved her to the ground, and then they turned and marched out the door, leaving the two women alone together in the empty barracks.

Frau Dauch picked herself up from the ground, dusting herself off, her gaze on the floor. She took several deep breaths and then looked up, locking eyes with Trude. Her pupils burned with an intense fury. She stepped forward and struck Trude across the face, first once, then twice, driving her down. The capo kicked her hard in the stomach, knocking the wind out of her.

"You stupid little whore," she screamed. "What did I tell you? I'm not going to let you harm me and these other women. I told Gunther to have you taken out back and shot, with that little brat as well, but he refused. I don't know what kind of spell you've cast on him, but it won't last long. You're mine for the next month. I promised I'd break you. When I'm finished with you, he won't want you back. He'll have no interest in a scarecrow, and I promise you will be nothing but a bag of bones in a week. If you think yesterday was hard, you're dreaming. I have more plans for you today. I'm going to attend to you personally. Now get up!"

Frau Dauch grabbed her by the ears, pulled her to her knees, and dragged her viciously to her feet. She pushed her outside into the snow, prodding her along until they traveled the familiar path past the barracks and out into the forest. The capo took her to the same crumpled building as the day before, only this time she did not leave. The rest of the day was something out of Trude's deepest nightmares. Frau Dauch dogged her every step. Screaming at her, striking her, forcing her to work double time. If she stumbled, the capo rained blows down on her head until she forced herself back to her feet.

When the wheelbarrow was full, she was compelled to run with it, the bumping cart jarring, tearing at her muscles. On one trip, she upended the wheelbarrow midway and Frau Dauch was instantly on her, beating her over and over as she scrambled to pick up the bricks and pile them back into the cart.

Hour after hour the trial continued. The screaming and the beatings soaked into every fiber of her existence. Time lost all meaning. The world was a blur. The last day in the camp seemed a pleasant vacation compared to this. She prayed to God to end the agony. Let her heart give out. Perhaps one of the guards would mercifully shoot her. She didn't care anymore; she just wanted it all to end.

Somehow she made it to the end of the day. Frau Dauch dragged her back to the barracks and shoved her into the frozen line. When everyone was assembled, the capo announced loudly that because of Trude, they would all have to stand in roll call twice as long. They would be punished for her bad behavior. Trude could hear the grumbling and saw the looks of hatred from up and down the line. God knew what would happen next. She might be murdered in the night. They stood there in the frozen snow, conducting the roll call hour after hour. Finally, they were released, but Frau Dauch held her back.

"No food for you. You will stand here during dinner as well." Frau Dauch kept her out in the cold, forcing her to stand perfectly still, striking her each time she moved. Trude's legs shook so badly she did not know how much longer she could make it. Eventually she allowed Trude to return to the barracks. The lights were still on when they came through the door. There was utter silence.

She saw the stares from the angry women, the accusing looks. She understood. She could not blame them. She'd added one more misery to this hell they were all living. How could they do anything but hate her. She started toward her bunk, but Frau Dauch stopped her again.

"Stay there," she said. "I have a little surprise for you."

What could it be now? What new torment? She just wanted to collapse into her bunk.

The door opened. Guards dragged in another prisoner, head shaved, in the familiar striped uniform. She realized with horror it was Britta. Her daughter looked up, not recognizing her mother for a moment, fear and anxiety capturing her eyes. When she realized it was Trude, her daughter ran to her, throwing her arms around her, burying her head in Trude's chest and sobbing. Trude looked up and saw Frau Dauch's cruel smirk. She felt her heart dying. She'd lost. The game was over.

"I want to see Gunther," she said. "I want to see him now."

Frau Dauch rolled her head back and bellowed out a loud guffaw. "That Gunther's a clever one. He told me that's exactly what you would do when your little brat arrived here."

Trude ignored her. "I want to see him now."

"Still think you're calling the shots? I'll take you to him . . . in a week."

"No. I want to go now."

"You will stay until I say so, you little bitch."

"I'll tell Gunther."

The capo laughed. "Go ahead. Those were his orders. You are both to stay here for a week, no matter what you say. He doesn't even want a report. You're going to spend some time with your daughter." Her mouth wrenched up in a crooked smile. "You wouldn't deprive me of the opportunity to get to know her, would you?"

Trude fell to her knees, grabbing the hem of the capo's pants. "I can't," she said. "Please just take me to him now. I'll do anything he wants."

"I'm glad you finally get it. Of course you will do anything, you little slut. What did I tell you? That's how things work around here. But you must learn your lessons first. You don't get a second chance and you don't bargain with the Germans. Now shut your mouth and go to bed. You'll stay until I say so. I'll see to your comfort. If you survive, Gunther will meet with you then."

Trude clung to Britta. She could feel the hostile stares boring into her. She could expect no sympathy from these women. No mercy from mothers, sisters, and daughters who'd already lost everything. A week, a lifetime. She had to focus on that. They would have to survive somehow. She would protect her daughter. They would work hard, double time. They would make it through this torment. Someday she would have her revenge. She swore it there on her knees to her God, to the universe. She would have vengeance for herself, for her daughter, for her people.

CHAPTER TWENTY-SEVEN

Königsberg
March 1943

Erik Mueller reported to duty at SS headquarters in Königsberg. He wore a plain sergeant's uniform, black now, rather than the gray of the Waffen-SS. There were no decorations. He'd lost those. His past was scraped clean. He expected to meet with Karl, but he was informed that the lieutenant colonel was not available. Instead he was tersely handed some documents providing him orders for his new assignment. He read the materials carefully. He noted with surprise he would not be stationed in Königsberg as he'd hoped. Instead he was assigned to work in another part of East Prussia.

After returning home to pack, he was driven to the train station by a low-level orderly and summarily dropped off without ceremony. As he waited for the train he reflected on the last couple of days. The icy tension of his home. Corina's cold, careless stares. At least there'd been no more explosions between her and his father. He had been able to spend time with their daughter, the one joy in an otherwise trying visit. This morning he breakfasted with his parents, but Greta was not yet awake and Corina refused to come down. She did not bid him farewell or good luck. Perhaps he did not deserve it. He'd hoped to have some words of encouragement from Karl, anything that might give him a path to redemption, but he'd been denied even this. Well, he knew what he must do. He must work hard and follow orders. Whatever was asked of him, he must perform without question. If he did this, there was a small chance he could redeem himself and perhaps restore a portion of his future.

The train arrived and he took a seat in third class, riding with the other soldiers and noncommissioned officers. He was struck by the small portions and the poor quality of the food on the train. Things had clearly changed in the last year. He knew from speaking to his parents that the rations had been cut back to less than half of what they had started the war with. There was still plenty of food coming from the occupied countries, but not all of it was making its way to the average civilian apparently. He sat by himself, not knowing the strangers around him. One soldier, a corporal in the Wehrmacht, tried to strike up a conversation but gave up after Erik responded with a couple of terse answers. He was in no mood for conversation.

The train chugged along, hour after hour, stopping at the various stations. As darkness fell they arrived at the town he was assigned to. He disembarked. He left the platform and was greeted by an SS corporal who saluted smartly and took him, after examining his papers, to a waiting car. The vehicle roared off into the night. Erik looked around him curiously, not knowing this place or the countryside. However, there was little he could see. Soon they had pulled up to a barbed-wire fence gate. His papers were reviewed again, and then they were admitted. The car drove down the road a few hundred meters, coming to rest in front of a large red brick building with white frames on the second floor. He was ushered inside and up to the Kommandant's office. When he knocked tentatively, a voice inside ordered him to come in.

Erik entered and was shocked to see that the major in command was someone he knew. He gave a salute, and the commander beckoned him forward.

"Hello, *Sergeant*, we meet again," said Major Wolf, his voice stressing Erik's diminished rank.

Erik couldn't believe it. He'd been assigned to work for Karl's old assistant. He still stung from the lashing Karl and Gunther had given him several years ago, when he'd come to his friend about his concerns with Sauer's conduct in France.

"Sit down, Mueller," snapped Gunther, watching him sternly. He took a seat while the major reviewed some documents in front of him. Finally, he looked up again. "I heard about all of your little adventures. So, they sent you to me," he said, "as if I needed more problems."

"I won't be a problem, sir. I've—"

"Keep your mouth shut," he barked sternly. "I don't want to hear it. Karl told me all about you—the whole story. Let me start by saying I don't give a damn about a few hundred Russians." He leaned forward, his eyes black as coal. "What I do care about is men who are loyal to the party and to Germany. You've displayed none of that. Instead you disobeyed orders from a superior commander. And that after you'd already been warned. Do you remember that? I was there when Karl told you what you had to do. You ignored him, so you failed your party and the SS." Gunther leaned back. "And now I have to deal with you."

Erik listened, not sure if he should respond. He decided against it.

Gunther nodded approvingly. "Well, at least you're keeping your mouth shut now. Perhaps you can learn something after all. We shall see. Do you know what this place is?"

Erik shook his head.

"This is a labor and transit camp. Do you know what that means?" he asked.

Erik shook his head again.

"We collect Jews here, along with Russians and other undesirables." He waved his hand negligently. "Some stay for a while; most move on to bigger camps."

"What are the camps for?" asked Erik.

Gunther laughed. "Why, for extermination, of course."

"What do you mean?" asked Erik, his horror rising.

"This is why Karl sent you here. To find out whether you have anything inside you worth saving. You've come to the bottom of the heap, my boy. Let me tell you what we're about. Very few people outside these camps know what's going on.

"As you know, the Führer has spoken for a very long time about the evils of the Jews. They cost us the last war. They won't cost us this one, though. We've been tasked with special duty. The SS is eliminating the Jews from Europe."

"All of them?" asked Erik, stunned by the news. "There are millions of them."

"There were," corrected Gunther. "I don't know how many are left. They hide in the cracks and crevices of society. But we are rooting them out, and soon there will be none."

"That can't be possible," said Erik. "You're testing me."

"Oh, it's all too possible, my friend. We started right after the invasion of Russia. We were shooting them at the time, but that's messy and expensive business. We experimented and found a better way."

"What does that mean?"

"Gas chambers. Stuff them in and seal them up. Twenty minutes"— Gunther snapped his fingers—"and they're gone. They gas them, yank the gold out of their teeth, sort through their valuables. Bodies go up the chimney. Rinse and repeat. Easy."

"We're gassing Jews here?"

"No," said Gunther, a trace of sadness passing his face. "We're too small-time for that. Although I've advocated for them to build a chamber here. No, here we're stuck working and starving them to death. It takes much longer, but you'd be surprised how the numbers mount up over time. Pretty impressive really.

"That's not our main business, though. Mostly we collect them up and ship them out. We've got some people here doing labor. Inmates, if you want to call them that. They mostly grow a little food, do some repairs, a little construction. None of them make it long. A month or two and they're worn out."

"You're working them to death?"

"*You're working them to death,*" mocked Gunther, repeating the words in a shrill voice. "Just so. Karl wants you in the thick of things. He told me to give you the toughest assignments. I disagree. I'm not about to create more problems for myself. Weakness is a sickness like fear. It invades not only the man but everyone around him. I cannot have a soft hand in the camp. So, good news for you. Our supply sergeant was recently promoted and has moved on. I don't think you can do too much harm in the warehouse. I hear you're smart, too. You should be able to handle things. There's a corporal there. He'll show you the ropes. It's mostly food and supplies and the valuables we collect."

He opened a drawer, drawing out a piece of paper and handing it to Erik. "Here is a list of certain items you will set aside. These are to be brought directly to me, do you understand?"

Erik nodded, folding up the paper and tucking it away. He would read it later.

"I'll expect a report each week. I want detailed records. Everything must be accounted for. The last thing I need is an audit." Gunther ran his hands through his thinning hair.

Erik started to rise.

"Look at me, Mueller."

Erik turned back to Gunther. "People die here, lots of them. I'm not going to call on you to be directly involved. I don't think you have the stomach for it. But you've already shown a propensity for squealing. This is a difficult task the SS has taken on. Not even the whole organization knows what we're doing. I don't need problems from above. Do you understand me?

"Karl placed me in charge because he knew I could get the job done. The same can't be said of you. He sent you here because he knows I can handle you. I want to remind you what you signed. What's at stake if you do anything wrong. I won't hesitate a moment to crush you and your family if you step a toe out of line. This is your last chance. You're hanging by a thread. If you do your duty, if you serve me loyally without complaint, without any problems, I will write you a commendation at the end of the war. Who knows," said Gunther shrugging, "perhaps you'll even be promoted again. But do one thing wrong and it will be the end of you. There will be not a breath of a second chance. Do I make myself clear?"

Erik nodded.

"Then get out of my office," Gunther said. "Ask one of the guards to show you to the warehouse. It's a bit of a trip. I'll see you here once a week for your report."

Erik saluted stiffly. Gunther did not look up or return the gesture. He walked out, dazed at what he'd just heard. They were intentionally putting millions of people to death? Innocent, unarmed civilians? Women and children. He thought back to the Russian front, what Russians and Germans did to each other. As terrible as all of that was, it at least was war. What was this? He couldn't think about that right now. He had to get his bearings. He had to follow orders and struggle to survive.

⸺⸺

Erik reported to the warehouse, where he found an SS corporal who stood and saluted him as he arrived. The corporal stepped forward, a scrawny figure no more than 60 kilograms with a thin mustache. "I'm Corporal Schaefer," he said. "You must be the new supply sergeant." He sized Erik up, but Erik was sure the corporal must have already heard all about him from Gunther.

Schaefer beckoned him into the rectangular warehouse and over to an old cast-iron stove belching out puffs of dense air that filled the space with warmth and a choking smoke. They both took a seat. Behind Schaefer, extending for at least fifty meters and the length and breadth of the giant building, were rows of floor-to-ceiling shelves, rising ten meters or more. Each shelf was stuffed full. The left-hand side seemed to contain food: bread and giant cans of vegetables and meat. The right-hand side was more diverse, stacked to the ceiling with suitcases, clothing, artwork, bicycles, and every imaginable product. The front of the warehouse contained a modest office with a few bunk beds. Erik assumed these were their sleeping quarters.

Schaefer leaned forward, removing a kettle. "Would you like some tea?" Erik nodded, and the corporal retrieved a metal cup and poured steaming hot water through a metal strainer into the cup. Erik, who'd never felt entirely warm on the long train ride, took the cup gratefully.

"So you've been in the war, I hear," said Schaefer. "Got into some kind of mix-up, though, and ended up here?"

Erik started to answer, but Schaefer stopped him. "No sense in explaining, sir. We're all misfits in this outfit. I was in the Waffen-SS, too. I struck my officer. Came back drunk after we found some vodka in a farmhouse. He ordered me under arrest, but I wouldn't have any of it, and I punched him right on the nose. Broke it good, too. Most of the guards here have been in trouble one way or another. Except a few that came here because they love it."

"What is this place?" asked Erik, still not believing Gunther.

"The end of the world, my friend. They bring all the peoples of the world here." He ran his fingers along his hand: "Tromp, tromp, tromp—they come in by foot or by train. A few of them stay, the rest go to God knows where. The ones who stay are luckier; they get to live a little while. They say the big trains go from here and take people right to their deaths down the railway. Some big murder factory or other. Doesn't matter in the long run, though. Whether they stay or go, the poor souls all eventually die. It's a sorry business, but it's where we've landed."

Erik felt the anxiety rising again. "I've seen some terrible things in Russia," he said. "Nothing like this, though."

Schaefer laughed. "Who has? Don't you worry about it, Sergeant. You'll settle in here okay. We're the lucky ones. All we must do is pick through the goodies here in our warm, safe warehouse. No bullets coming our way, and we don't have to deal with the unpleasant stuff going on outside. Besides," he said, motioning behind him, "you won't believe the stuff that comes in here. Gold and silver, watches, diamonds.

"Most of what arrives is just a bunch of junk. But you must keep a careful eye out. Those Jews are smart. They sew things into their clothes. You should give them a good shake, run your fingers through each part before you put it back in the sorted pile. Look back there, everything has its place. Except the good stuff. Gunther gets most of that, but we can hold back a little for ourselves, don't you worry," he whispered slyly.

Erik nodded, remembering the list in his pocket. He was sure he knew what it was for. "How can he get away with that?" asked Erik.

"Who?"

"The major."

Schaefer shrugged, his eyes darting nervously to the door. "Careful with that kind of talk, sir. He's got ears everywhere. He's a clever one. Even has a piece of Jewish skirt he keeps here against all the regulations. It's punishable by death, but nobody says a word about it. He's got connections all the way up they say, so who's going to stop him?

"Don't worry about that, though. We don't bother him and he won't bother us. And I haven't told you the best part yet. The valuables are fine. Maybe gives us something to tuck away for the future. But it's the perishables that really help the here and now: biscuits, jam, cookies, tobacco. Every kind of luxury item." Erik shifted uncomfortably but didn't respond.

"All in all it's not too bad. It gets too damn hot here in the summer, but in the winter, we got our stove. Best of all we don't have to deal with all that mess outside." Schaefer leaned forward, reaching down and pulling up a bottle full of clear liquid. "This is vodka, sir. We get plenty of it. The Russians bring it in, always hiding in a boot or a pocket. Officially we're not supposed to be doing much drinking, but nobody really cares." Schaefer folded his hands in satisfaction.

Erik was shocked by what the corporal was telling him. Looting the clothes of these poor prisoners for valuables, food, and liquor. He'd never heard of such a thing. He wanted to say something in disapproval, but it was entirely possible Schaefer was a spy for Gunther. He could be planted here to keep an eye on Erik and report if he didn't go along with the program. He had no intention of taking the bait. He would do what was required.

"Sounds good, but no stealing," he said. "The diamonds, the gold—everything on the list goes where it's supposed to. Foodstuffs and the booze, nobody's going to miss that."

Schaefer smiled in satisfaction. "No problems there, sir. We host the real guards sometimes, too. They come for the vodka mostly. It gets to them after a while if you know what I mean, sir. The killing and the dying. The prisoners are mostly women and children after all. Pretty tough."

Erik nodded. He knew what it was like to watch innocent people die.

<hr />

He slept well enough that night and the next day got to work. Corporal Schaefer proved an invaluable resource. He knew everything about the warehouse. How all the forms worked. How much was to be distributed to the kitchen each day, to the officers' and enlisted men's mess, and how everything was accounted for. Once or twice a day huge carts of goods would be brought to the warehouse. They would stop everything else and pick through piles, rifling for food and precious objects.

Erik started to help but stopped when he pulled out a photograph of a young family: husband, wife, and two little children. They stared up at him. He felt their accusations burn through his soul. After that he told the corporal to keep up the work, and he returned to the business of sorting through a new shipment of food that had arrived that day by train for the camp. From then on he let Schaefer do the sorting, always finding excuses to do something else when the carts arrived.

Day after day went by that way. The first week he hardly left the warehouse. It was too cold outside, and when he did leave not only the frigid conditions but also the sights and sounds outside drove him quickly back. He couldn't believe the condition of the prisoners: barefoot, impossibly skinny, struggling to simply move, let alone work. He thanked God he'd been assigned to the warehouse instead. Corporal Schaefer presented him with a silver flask he came across inside a coat pocket. He kept it filled for the sergeant out of a private store he held in reserve. He handed it over to Erik, who initially refused, but Schaefer insisted, pressing the flask into his hand.

"Now, Sergeant," he said. "I know what you're thinking: this place is more than a man can take. This will help you a little. I got this brandy off a Russian major. Best-quality stuff, sir."

Erik accepted the liquor. It would help. He knew his bargain when he'd come here, when he'd saved his family. He was thankful he wasn't facing more than a pile of clothing and the belongings of the dead. He knew what was outside the warehouse walls and he wasn't sure he had the strength to face it. The fiery alcohol would further dull his emotions.

At the end of the first week Schaefer helped him complete the seven-day report. He would have been lost without the corporal, but with his assistance everything tallied up perfectly. There was also an envelope, almost too heavy for Erik to carry, sealed tight, which he was to bring to Gunther personally.

He set out that evening from the warehouse to make his report. He looked at his watch; it was near seven o'clock and he was running late. He quickly walked the half kilometer from the warehouse to the administrative building. Fortunately, he didn't have to go through any checkpoints as he was on the SS side of the camp, away from the prisoners themselves.

He had to walk along the fence of the camp, though. Thankfully, the prisoners were all inside, one of the reasons he had chosen to make the report at night. He tromped along as quickly as he could, trying to fight the bitter cold. It was late March now. He wondered when it would begin to warm up. Finally, he reached the administrative building, traveling down the long corridor then up the stairs to the second floor. He knocked at Gunther's door. There was a moment of hesitation, and then he heard a voice ordering him to come in. He stepped into the room. Gunther was at the desk, a half-eaten tray of food resting on a stack of paperwork. Gunther sat in his chair puffing at a porcelain pipe. Erik caught movement in the corner of his eye and glanced across the office. He was surprised to see a woman and child sitting on the sofa. Was this his family? He didn't even know Gunther was married.

Something was out of place with them. It took him a moment to notice that both the woman and the girl had very short, almost shorn hair. There was something else, but he couldn't quite place it.

"Sergeant," said Gunther, his voice pulling Erik away from his scrutiny. "I see you brought my report. Come on in and have a seat." The major seemed to be in a good mood and treated Erik with a joviality far different from their first meeting at Soldau only a week before.

Gunther turned, addressing the woman and the child. "I've got some business to attend to, if you could please excuse me."

They rose and walked quickly and quietly out of the office, closing the door behind them.

"Let's see what you have," said Gunther, rubbing his hands together with apparent anticipation, like a greedy child waiting for a plate of hot cookies.

Erik handed him the heavy envelope, which Gunther hefted appreciatively, and then the report. Gunther leaned back and made a great show of reviewing the paperwork, although his eyes kept flicking over to the envelope. "Everything looks to be in order here. Good work. I've heard you're getting along just fine. I must admit I was worried about you, but so far so good. I'll make a good little SS soldier out of you yet.

"Which reminds me. I have a friend of yours here. I think you remember Frau Bensheim? Jewish woman? She was a neighbor of yours. She was in hiding for a couple years, but we finally nabbed her. Corina called in a tip that brought us to her daughter."

Erik was in shock. That's what was out of place with the woman and her child. It was Trude and her daughter. He had no doubt. She'd looked so different with an almost shaved head. And she was so out of place in this hellhole. *He has his own Jewish skirt.* Erik looked up, realizing that Gunther was watching him carefully. He quickly composed a neutral expression. It was too late.

"Just as I thought. I wanted to make you aware she was here so we could avoid any unpleasantness," Gunther said. "It wouldn't be prudent for you to interject any prior friendship into this situation."

Erik nodded, trying to act as indifferent as possible.

"Listen to me," said Gunther, his voice imbuing a hint of steel. "You are not to talk to her; you're not to look at her. If she attempts any communication with you, you are to report it to me immediately, do you understand?"

He nodded again.

There was nothing Erik could do. There were so many questions he wanted to ask. How did she end up here? What was she doing? Trude would never voluntarily submit to something like this. She was married, and besides, Gunther was a fat old lecherous slob. Whatever Trude was enduring, it was like the things happening outside the warehouse. He could not control them, and anything he did endangered his own life and that of his family.

Gunther was still watching him with a skeptical eye. "I want to hear it from your mouth," demanded Gunther.

Erik turned and clicked his heels, coming to attention. "I will not speak with Frau Bensheim or the child. If she tries to speak with me, I will immediately report it to you, sir."

Gunther nodded with approval. "Good monkey. I may train you yet. If you keep this up, I may have a treat for you. Now get out of my office!"

Erik flushed with anger at the reproach. He was unused to being treated this way. He took a couple of deep breaths to calm himself, then rotated and departed, his head spinning.

CHAPTER TWENTY-EIGHT

Soldau
December 1944

Trude sat on the edge of the bed sewing a tear in one of Britta's dresses. She hummed an old song to herself absentmindedly as she worked, realizing after a while that it was a tune from her old university days. How many lifetimes ago, she realized. It felt like a thousand years. Britta sat across the way at a table. She was working on mathematics formulas with pen and paper. Fourteen now, she was stunningly beautiful, Trude thought. No longer a girl but a young woman.

How long until she's given away to one of the guards? Trude wondered. Or perhaps Gunther himself would take an active interest. More and more, she noticed his gaze lingering on her daughter. She told herself it was paternal, a semifatherly affection that had grown out of almost three years together. But she couldn't be sure. If it came to that, she'd claw his eyes out. Somehow, she'd stop him. If only Johannes were here. Her husband. She hadn't thought of him in months now, she realized guiltily. She'd never heard again what might've happened to him, but after experiencing the camp she had no doubts her husband was long dead.

She shook her head. Even if he was here, what would he do? He had hardly stood up to Gunther before, but in the camp, any defiance would bring a swift bullet to the head. No, it's better he disappeared long ago, that he knew nothing of what had become of his wife and daughter. She heard what sounded like distant thunder on the horizon. *They are coming,* she thought, hope streaking across the barren sky of her emotion. Why wouldn't they hurry? The guards whispered the rumors to her. She'd grown to know them all, and some of them shared information with her. She knew from them that the long agony was almost over. The Russians had swallowed up all their own land and now were spilling over into Poland, Hungary, and even Germany.

These same guards predicted dire circumstances when the Russians arrived. A terrible retribution against the Germans. But what did she care about that? She was a Jew, a victim just like her soon-to-be liberators. Wasn't it said by the Germans that Russia was full of Jews anyway? She imagined the soldiers arriving, the Germans dropping their weapons, the butchers becoming the victims themselves. She would find a Russian who understood German. She would tell them her story. They would capture Gunther. She imagined him standing there in chains. She felt the triumph soar inside her. The elation of victory, mixed with confusion and a measure of guilt. He'd saved her; he'd protected her and Britta. Didn't she owe him something for that? *No,* the other part of her answered. *He's taken more than full payment from you.*

Her mind moved on. To a new future after liberation. After Gunther. She allowed herself to dream the impossible again, to think of England and her parents. Even Johannes's parents were there. She'd had no word from any of them in more than five years. She prayed they were all safe. She imagined disembarking from a ship, all of them waiting for her and Britta. Poor Johannes. He wouldn't be coming home.

The door opened abruptly. It was Gunther. He stepped in and the guard followed quickly behind him, dropping off a tray of lunch.

Gunther smiled at her, then approached her daughter. Again, the lingering gaze. A moment too long. "What are you working on, my dear?" he asked, laughing. The voice of a father.

"Mathematics," she answered.

He walked over and examined the work, whistling in amazement. He shook his head. "That's more than I can understand. Keep it up and we'll make a university student out of you yet. But for now, my little one, even students need to eat."

Britta giggled, standing up and waltzing over to the table, sniffing at the food, which was piled with fruit, bread, and cheese. She picked a few slices of apple and a bit of cheese, then strolled over and dropped heavily onto the sofa. Gunther stepped over and loaded up two more plates with food, bringing one over to Trude. He handed it to her. She did not look up, pretending she didn't see it. She forced the creases of her lips up, mimicking a smile. At least they were safe, fed, warm.

"It's lunchtime, my dear. Set that down. Why are you even doing that? I told you I can have others handle it."

She continued sewing, ignoring him.

"Set it down," he said, enunciating each word. She heard the rising tide of anger in his voice. She sighed and set the material aside, looking up to give him a forced smile. He watched her for a moment and then passed her the plate, sitting down on the bed next to her. He set his own plate down and reached down to remove his boots, groaning in the process.

"*Ach, mein Lieber,* you would not believe the day I've had today. It started at five a.m. with a pile of paperwork. All day long it's been meeting after meeting. Everybody's got a problem, and nobody thinks it can be solved without my direct approval."

She nodded without responding, keeping her head down and picking at her lunch. Usually he only dropped in during the evenings. She had a difficult time eating in his presence.

He sighed, and she could hear the frustration in his voice. "Why won't you talk to me?" he said. "Do I have to bring it up again every time?"

She still didn't respond, and he threw his arms up in the air.

"Fine. Have it your way. Remember who I am and what I've done for you. Remember also what I can do to you."

"Thank you," she said, her voice flat and emotionless.

"You are welcome," he said, his voice dripping reproach. "That reminds me," he said, snapping his fingers. "I should call Colonel Schmidt. You never met him, did you? He knows Mueller and his wife, Corina." He cracked into a smile. "I know you remember her.

"Anyway, we had a long talk about logistics and the war. We're starting to get in rather a tight spot here. We may have to make new arrangements soon, my dear. Our stay here in Soldau, no matter how pleasant, may be coming to an end."

Trude looked up sharply. She felt the joy rising inside her. So, it was true. The Russians were almost here. She quickly attempted to hide her expression, feigning disinterest, but he'd clearly seen her emotions on her face.

"So that brings some life to you, doesn't it?" he asked, his grin widening. "I'm sure you've heard the little boom boom from our eastern friends. Oh yes, those are Russian guns, my dear. No more than fifty kilometers away, I would think. They'll be here in a few weeks, if that long. It certainly won't do for us to be here when they arrive."

She felt the horror and the disappointment. She'd been hoping for months that exactly that would happen. She stiffened, feeling a little of the old defiance. "I don't have anything to be afraid of," she said.

"Oh yes you do," he said, leaning closer. "You don't know the Russians. Do you think they will come as saviors? They're monsters, every one of them."

"And the Germans aren't?" She saw a hint of color flicker on his cheek. She enjoyed it, reveled in a tiny flare of power. She knew she had to be careful, however; he could snap at any moment.

"Perhaps you're right," he said, to her surprise. "Some could call us that. But that won't help you when the Russians get here. There have been such terrible reports as they've stormed into East Prussia. They've already crossed the border in some places. They've done such things: raping and killing. In one town, they crucified naked women to barn doors."

"That's awful," she said, not sure she meant it. "But surely they're killing Germans?"

Gunther shook his head. "Not only Germans. They've been killing and raping everyone: Germans sure, but French and Dutch laborers, Poles, even Jews they've come across. Anyone they can get their hands on." He smiled knowingly. "Don't take me for a fool. I know that's what you've been dreaming all about the last few months. Waiting for your Russian knights to arrive and save you." He chuckled to himself. "At first I wondered about your happy little mood. I'd hoped you'd finally accepted our circumstances. Then I realized what was going on. I'm sorry to have to dispel that myth for you, my dear. You let the Russians get their clutches into you and you'll be dead by the end of the day—and it will be a bad day for both you and Britta."

What was he talking about? Then she realized it, and she felt her face flush. She felt a fool, too. He'd known all along. She thought she'd kept her hopes secret, but he'd read her so easily. Of course he did. He always knew.

"What does he mean, Mother?" asked Britta, tears of fear brimming in her eyes.

She shot Gunther a look of venom and turned to her daughter. "He's just teasing. Don't worry about it."

Gunther's face registered understanding, and he turned to Britta. "I'm sorry. Don't listen to me. I'm just joking with your mother a little bit." He turned back to Trude. "But like I said, I'm making arrangements for all of us."

"What sort of arrangements?" she asked.

"We are going to be leaving very soon, the whole camp. It's not going to be pleasant. I've received orders to march everyone out on foot."

"Where?"

"West. Away from the damned communists."

"You can't mean the prisoners," she said. "It's winter. The snow is knee-deep. They're all starved or half-starved."

He shrugged. "Orders are orders. I agree with you, though; it's going to get messy. I argued against it. I said we should just let the poor souls stay here and wait for the Russians. Nobody listens to me."

"So we're going to march out of here?" Trude imagined them on the road, tromping through the snow, Russian planes hovering overhead.

Gunther shook his head. "That's the plan for the camp, not for us."

"What do you mean?"

"I've had my own plans laid for a very long time. The war's over. We've lost. Anyone who says otherwise is a fool. It's time for people to start looking after their own." He looked back and forth between Trude and Britta.

"Listen," he said, lowering his voice to a whisper. "I want you and Britta to come with me." He stepped forward, taking her hand; she tried to pull it away, but he held her. "Look at me. I know you probably hate me. You think I've taken advantage of you. Don't you know everything I've done for you? I saved Britta. I saved you. I've protected you for two years now. You know why, don't you?"

"You've shown me why plenty of times," she said, whispering through clenched teeth. She hoped Britta didn't understand.

"Britta, I'd like you to go for a walk for a few minutes, please. Your mother and I have something to discuss." He stood up, knocked at the door, and a guard appeared. "Take Britta out for some fresh air," he ordered. He waited until the guard escorted her daughter out before he turned back to Trude.

"You think all of this was for your body? Because I wanted you? How could you believe that? I could have anyone I wanted in this camp. The pick of any crop." He shook his head. "You've never understood me," he said, a trace of sadness woven into his words. "I love you. Haven't you ever understood that? I've always loved you. I adored you from the moment I set my eyes on you. You are a wife to me, and Britta is my daughter. I want you to go to Germany with me. We will get new identifications, new names, a new future. I want to marry you and spend the rest of my life with you. I have money. Gold, diamonds, plenty for us for the rest of our lives. I had to give most of it up to headquarters, but I've kept a little out each time." He stepped closer to her, taking her hands again. It was all she could do not to recoil.

"We can forget all of this, all our troubles. Let's start fresh and let the past be the past. I know you may hate me, but remember: I protected you, Trude. That's all I've ever wanted to do."

She was shocked to hear the tone of his voice and see his pleading expression. He was serious, she realized. In his twisted, adulterated world, all of this made sense to him. He saw himself as her protector. He saw the last two years as a quasi-marriage and the three of them as a family. Didn't he understand what he'd put her through? What she'd endured at his hands to protect her daughter? *He doesn't,* she realized. *He thinks he actually loves me.*

She was stunned. *Could he really hope that I could love him, too?* She realized just how dangerous this moment was. She had to stall him, to give herself a chance to recover. "Thank you for saying those things," she managed to say. "But I . . . I need some time to think about all of this."

She saw the excitement in his expression and her dismay increased. He squeezed her hands. "I understand," he said, his voice quivering. "Please take as long as you need. I have some places picked out. I could show you on a map. I don't think we would have any trouble getting there. I have a car and all the necessary papers. We could buy a little farmhouse with some property. Maybe an animal or two. You could grow vegetables. I'll find a new job somewhere. They will need bureaucrats in Germany after the war no matter what. I have plenty of connections."

She forced a smile of encouragement. Grinning through clenched teeth.

"I'll leave you, my dear," he whispered, squeezing her hands again. She saw the sparkle in his eye as he pulled himself up, sliding his feet back into his boots. He tucked his trousers into the muddy jackboots and then looked down at her, smiling. He bowed slightly. "I'll be back later to check on you." He turned again and strolled contentedly away, a light whistle on his lips.

When the door was closed behind him she rolled over on her stomach, burying her face in the blankets. Her mind whirled and she fought to control the tears. She had to think quickly; there was no time to lose.

Britta returned soon. Thankfully Gunther did not for many hours. Her daughter worked on her math assignment, and Trude then set her to work on writing an essay based on an oral history she'd given her on the Napoleonic Wars. She corrected the math homework, marking the mistakes she would have her daughter work through again later. As Britta labored through the assignments, Trude pondered her future and tried to process the stunning revelation Gunther had sprung on her.

What future was there for her and Britta? She didn't know now. She had prayed for months that the Russians would arrive any day, that they would roll into camp and liberate them. In her heart, she'd always doubted Gunther would allow that to happen. Now there was a new fear. This was the first she'd heard about Russians raping and killing everyone. How could that be? Certainly, she would expect them to retaliate against the Germans, but why harm allies? This camp was full of Russian prisoners. They would be able to tell the incoming Soviets everything that had happened here. Even if Gunther was telling the truth, which she didn't want to believe, wouldn't that make a difference? Gunther had lied to her so many times. Still, what if he wasn't fabricating this?

There was something else. Even if the Russians were inclined to help the prisoners, would that also apply to her? Her special status here, even if it was against her will, certainly put her life in danger. She'd seen the looks of the women in the barracks that short time she'd lived in the camp. They hated her. She was the Kommandant's girl, whether it was voluntary or not. She realized that the inmates themselves might turn her in as a German sympathizer, or take retribution against her directly. She couldn't stay here. She would have to leave, with Gunther if necessary. As far as the future, she would have to figure that out on the fly.

She wished there was something she could do now, but what was there? It was impossible to escape with scores of guards, perhaps hundreds, crawling through the camp. The entire perimeter was surrounded by barbed wire. Tall towers with machine guns dotted the circumference, sweeping the area with spotlights during the night and watching over the camp closely during the day. She had one asset alone: she and Britta looked normal. Their hair had regrown, and they wore civilian clothing. But that was it. Most of the guards knew them at a glance. They couldn't simply walk out.

Her contacts might help her if she could get outside of the camp, but she knew that was impossible. Gunther had trapped her again, she realized. That must be why he'd told her about the Russians. To take any hope away. To force her to leave with him. She sat there for a long time, feeling the despair, watching the camp through her window as the evening faded into darkness.

In bed that night as Britta lay next to her, sound asleep, she stared up at the ceiling, her mind racing. She kept trying to come up with some solution to the problem. There had to be something she could do, even a small chance to get away from here safely. Then it came to her. A whisper, a tiny pinprick of a plan. She realized how desperate it was. They would surely be caught. Still, did it matter? She spent the rest of the night preparing. She went over each detail, her excitement rising. Once she was satisfied she rested for a few hours.

The next morning, she woke feeling at peace. Gunther returned, and she was even able to face him with a cheerful composure.

She asked him about his day, something she rarely did. His expression brightened immediately. He told her all about his problems: piles of paperwork, ever-increasing limitations on trains, and the overwhelming details of preparing to evacuate the camp. He let slip they would be leaving within a couple of weeks. She kept asking questions, not listening to the answers.

Two weeks. She had less time than she thought. She would have to act immediately. Fortunately, she thought she knew what she needed to do.

"I'm doing laundry today," she casually interjected. "And ironing. Is there anything you need to have done?"

He looked up in surprise. She'd never offered to help him with his clothing before. "Why, you are unusually magnanimous today," he said, laughing to himself. "That's a first. I've got a few shirts that could be laundered and ironed. Extra starch, please," he said, his eyes brimming with joy. He left, swiftly returning with a white cloth bag full of crumpled shirts.

"Have you thought any more about . . . ?"

"I have."

"If you need more time . . ."

"We are coming with you."

She saw the shock and then the happiness in his eyes. He pressed the shirts into her hands, giving them a squeeze. "My dear, you have no idea what this means. I know all this horror has been awful for you.

For all of us. But you know I've protected you every step of the way. I've done everything I can for you and Britta. Now I want to do more."

"I know," she said, forcing the words out. "I appreciate it so much."

Gunther positively beamed. "Thank you," he whispered. "Thank you for taking care of the shirts. Thank you more for your words." He leaned over and kissed her on the cheek, something he'd never done in front of Britta before. Her daughter didn't look up, didn't even seem to notice. Gunther had been such a part of their lives the last two years, almost like a father, Trude realized with surprise and revulsion.

She chatted with Gunther for a few more minutes before he departed. She gathered up her own laundry and Gunther's, then knocked on the door. A few minutes passed and a guard opened it a crack.

"Hello," she said. "I need to be escorted to the laundry room." The guard nodded. This was a weekly event. He led her down the corridor and the stairs, and finally out of the building itself. The laundry and ironing room was in a separate structure a few hundred meters away. They reached the entrance and the guard stayed at the door, facing the outside while she went about beginning the laundry process.

She washed all the clothing and placed it in a large electric dryer. The entire project took two hours. When the clothing was dry, she removed the loads and organized everything into neat piles. Then she started the work of ironing, starting with dresses and moving on to the shirts. She worked from a large box of starch. The container was three-fourths full. She ironed one of Gunther's shirts, applying extra powder the way he'd suggested. She replaced the shirt with another, then looked up to see if the guard was watching her. He had long ago stepped away from the door and was sitting on a chair tucked against the wall. She saw his head was facing downward. He'd nodded off. Keeping a close eye on him, she reached below her, pulling out a garbage can that rested beneath the ironing table. She looked up again, making sure the guard hadn't awoken, and then she turned the starch box over, emptying its contents into the can until only a little dust remained in the bottom. She hurriedly pushed the container back under the table and stepped away, bringing the starch box with her until she was standing in front of the guard.

She cleared her throat and he jerked in surprise, opening his eyes to stare up at her. "I'm all out of starch," she said, turning the box over so he could see inside. "The Kommandant likes extra. Can you take me over to the supply room where I can get some more?"

The guard looked at her in irritation for a few moments, then exhaled loudly and nodded. He rose and led her out of the building, and they walked together toward the supply warehouse. The laundry room was about midway between the administrative building and her destination. They moved quickly in the bitter cold.

"I'll be just a few minutes," she said, walking ahead so that she reached the door first. This was an important moment. If he went in with her or retrieved the starch for her, there was nothing she could do. Her heart nearly beat out of her chest, but she was able to enter the building first, and she saw with relief that her escort merely stepped inside from the cold but made no effort to follow her farther into the building.

She blinked to adjust to the dim light within the building. When she was finally able to do so, she found a skinny SS corporal working away at a table, scribbling figures into a large book. He looked up after a few moments and recognized her immediately.

"May I help you?" he asked. His voice wasn't unfriendly.

"Hello," she said. "I need to speak with Sergeant Mueller, please."

The corporal eyed her curiously. She'd never asked to see the sergeant before. She'd only been to the warehouse a handful of times to collect an item or two for Gunther.

"Why?" he asked.

"It's not anything important," she said. "I just have a couple things to talk to him about, that's all. A private request from the Kommandant."

The corporal still hesitated, but she knew he couldn't cross Gunther. He rose, motioned for her to follow, and led her a dozen steps over to the office. He knocked at the door, and she heard a muffled voice in response. It was Erik. She felt her nervousness rise again. She knew he'd been prohibited from speaking to her. Other than a couple of awkward glances, they hadn't exchanged any communication the entire time he'd been in the camp. She felt a little sting of anger about that. He must know her predicament, yet he'd done nothing to help her.

"You have a visitor," said the corporal.

She heard steps. Erik appeared in the doorway. She saw his expression register a startled surprise, and he hesitated for a moment before he spoke.

"What can I do for you?" he said finally.

"Nothing much," she said. "There's a couple of things Gunther asked me to get for him."

He watched her closely. Would he refuse to speak with her? She watched him closely, and she could tell he was thinking about what he should do. To her relief, he nodded and motioned for her to follow him into his office. She stepped inside, and he closed the door behind her.

"Have a seat," he said. He sat down as well. "I'm not even supposed to be talking to you, but then I'm guessing you already know that. Whatever you must say to me, you better say it quick. I'm taking a tremendous risk."

Trude started talking rapidly, the words pouring out. She filled him in about Johannes's arrest, their hiding, Britta's seizure, and her own eventual surrender. Her voice trembled as she explained the last two years, the nightmare she'd endured. Finally, she told him about the camp evacuation and what Gunther was offering her.

Erik listened, his forehead creasing in concern. "He's telling you the truth about the Russians," Erik said. "Maybe he didn't even tell you everything about them. You can't be here when the Russians arrive. They will exact revenge, particularly on someone like you."

"What do you mean someone like me?"

"A collaborator."

"Do you think I've chosen this life?" she demanded. Her voice rising—too loud.

Erik raised his hands. "I'm not saying you did. I don't know your situation. It doesn't matter, though. The Russians won't draw that distinction. There's more than one guard who would be happy to tell them your role here, not to mention the inmates. They all know you are Gunther's girl, and the Russians would assuredly treat you so."

Trude was not surprised. She'd suspected that Gunther was telling the truth, and now Erik confirmed it. "I can't stay then."

Erik shook his head. "You should go with Gunther."

"I can't." She leaned forward until her lips were just a few centimeters from his ear. "I have to get out of here, and I need your help."

Erik looked both surprised and wary. "What do you mean? What do you think I could possibly do for you?"

"I need you to get me and Britta out of the camp."

Erik laughed, shoving himself back from his desk as if trying to put distance between them. "You can't be serious. How on earth could I do that? I don't have any special powers here. If I walked out with you two, we'd all be arrested immediately."

"I don't know how yet; you have to be able to do something."

Erik's face clouded. "Even if I wanted to, I can't help you."

"You mean you won't help me."

"No, I don't mean that. I can't put my family's life at risk. You don't understand my situation any more than I understand yours."

"What do you mean?" she asked.

Erik told her as quickly and as quietly as he could the whole story. Trude was surprised. She didn't know any of this, although nothing about Karl, Gunther, or the Nazis surprised her anymore. Now she understood why Erik had avoided her all this time, why he had done nothing to help her and why she feared he would do nothing now.

"I still have to ask you to help me," she said. "Please, for my daughter."

Erik stared at her helplessly and finally shook his head again. "I can't do anything for you. If I could, I would. I've risked too much just talking to you. If I help you, we will be caught, and my whole family will suffer. You must hate Gunther. I understand that completely now. Still, he's your best chance for survival. Go with him."

She tried to argue with him, but he cut her off.

"You are a selfish bastard," she said. "What happened to the man I knew at university?"

"He's long gone," said Erik quietly, his eyes cast to the ground.

That was it then. She'd tried her only chance and she'd failed. She turned and left, a blanket of stifling hopelessness smothering her.

CHAPTER TWENTY-NINE

Soldau
December 1944

Erik spent the rest of the evening with the door closed to his office, sipping away at his flask, the fiery vodka inside burning his throat and numbing his emotions. He'd long ago worked through the brandy and now helped himself to whatever cheap liquor was available.

She wanted his help to escape. Was she mad? He'd risked too much even talking to her. Corporal Schaefer was his friend, but would he risk his own neck for Mueller? He might have already reported the incident to Gunther. Certainly, the guard who'd accompanied Trude owed him nothing. As he sat there, he waited for the summons to the Kommandant's office.

He felt wretched. For nearly two years, he'd spent most of his time in a stupor. The liquor helped him survive this hell on earth. That and the corporal, his only friend in this horrid place. He'd received infrequent letters from home, cold and disappointed in tone. They were filled with complaints, of the dwindling food supply, the ever-increasing bombing by the Russians, the death of the future they had planned before he failed Corina so spectacularly.

At first she had pushed him about new promotions. Was he doing everything he needed to do to make that happen? But with the crumbling fortunes of the war, she had stopped even trying. He'd had several leaves, but she told him in no uncertain terms that she had no wish to see him.

Now the Russians were knocking at the door. On the other side of Germany, the British and Americans had invaded this past summer, and were already nipping at the borders. The radio still proclaimed ultimate victory but focused more and more on the heroic defenses of towns and cities in an ever-shrinking circle around the Fatherland. In the past few weeks, the dull thudding of artillery erased the need for news reports. He didn't need to try to figure out anymore what was happening; the Russians were close.

Erik had already received several briefings from Gunther. They would vacate the camp soon. The prisoners were to be marched westward into the heart of Germany. Erik shook his head, thinking about that prospect. The ground was frozen and snow covered. The temperatures outside were below freezing. The prisoners were already starving and practically naked. They would die by the thousands long before they reached their destination. Even the guards had no proper equipment and little food. *What is the point?* he wondered. *Why not just leave these wretches here and let the Russians take care of them?* In Erik's opinion, they should all go home to their families, for the war was clearly over.

But then did Erik have a family to go home to? Corina was terribly afraid of the Russians and was planning to evacuate. Karl had a plan to get her and the family out by a ship through the Baltic Sea. The route was dangerous, filled with submarines and enemy aircraft. But Karl assured her they would have German navy protection, and there was a good chance they would be able to get through.

Always Karl. Erik felt strangely jealous. Corina's letters were filled with references to the colonel. He shook his head. He shouldn't feel that way. Karl had saved his life. Karl and Corina were friends, nothing more. The colonel was in a position to help his wife and daughter, and Erik must be grateful.

Erik took another deep drink of vodka and poured himself another full glass. The liquor warmed him. The office was far from the stove. He stomped his feet and pressed his hands together before returning to his thoughts.

Trude. He couldn't shake her from his mind. Why should he care about her at all? Just because he'd known her at the university? Sure, he'd found her fascinating, even attractive. She was mysterious, intelligent. They'd shared a meal or two. He'd attended a couple of her musical performances; she had talent. They'd never even held hands. He wasn't sure she'd even been interested in him. Then she'd found another Jew. This Johannes. They'd started to date, and Erik moved on. His interest faded, and eventually he lost contact with her entirely. He'd never seen her again until she appeared that day in his neighborhood, just before the war.

They had no real connection. Now she was asking him to put his life on the line for her. What about all the rest of these people here? What made her more important? He had no problem with Jewish people. He didn't believe the propaganda about the Jews and the Russians, or the rest of the Nazi nonsense.

He just wanted to go home and try to protect his family. He thought of the Russians arriving at his door in Königsberg. He knew what they would do to Corina, even to Greta. They would probably kill them all. He was SS after all.

Didn't he deserve whatever happened to him? He wondered if any of the other staff at the camp thought of the thousands of people coming and going from Soldau. He thanked God again he'd never been forced to work directly with the prisoners. But did that make him more innocent? He knew everything that was going on, but he'd done nothing to stop it. Instead he'd ignored the truth as much as he could, drowning himself in alcohol and waiting for the end.

He walked out of the office and into the warehouse. Corporal Schaefer huddled near the stove. He looked up at his commander and nodded by way of greeting. Erik acknowledged him, stepping over for a few moments to warm himself. He looked out over the warehouse and approached one of the carts spilling over with possessions.

For two years now he'd stayed away from the sorting. He'd let Schaefer conduct that task, always finding a way to stay busy with paperwork. The corporal never complained; perhaps he understood.

Now he stood over the cart, looking down at the contents. He stuck his hand in, pulling out a jacket. He ran his hands over the fabric, searching it. There was a watch, a biscuit, some twine. He dropped the coat and picked up another item, continuing his search. He went through article after article, setting aside an object here and there. Finally, he had enough of what he was looking for. He looked down at his hands. He held a stack of pictures he'd gleaned from the clothing. Without looking at Schaefer, he returned to his office, closing the door behind him.

He sat at his desk, pouring himself another tall glass of the clear Russian drink. He took a deep gulp and then leaned back in his chair, setting the glass aside and thumbing one by one through the pictures. He stared at the images. There were young families staring out at him, elderly couples, a reunion. He looked at them for hours. These were real lives, humans who had perished all around him as he'd sat day by day inside the walls of his sanctuary.

Tears ran down his face. He'd allowed all of this to happen, he realized. He'd come here, intent on saving his own family. He'd protected himself in this warehouse, insulated from the world outside. He'd allowed thousands to perish here, simply to save his own life, his own family. Why did he have more of a right to live?

He'd felt himself more noble here, a step away from all the death. But was he? He knew if they'd placed him in the camp, he would have had no choice. He'd made his bargain. He would have committed atrocities under orders. He would have done anything to save his family. He sat that way, thumbing through the images, gulping the fiery liquid, drowned in his shame.

⊶

When he was jolted awake the next morning, his head was buried in his arms and he was lying across his desk. His back and neck were wrenched with pain and his head swam with a wretched hangover. His bones were frozen. A blanket was slung over his back. Schaefer had placed it there. He looked over and saw the corporal lying down in his bunk, under a pile of blankets.

Erik felt ill. He lurched up, stumbling over to the waste bin where he threw up loudly, his stomach jerking back and forth in waves of nausea.

"Are you all right, Sergeant?" Schaefer's head poked up from behind its pillow.

Erik nodded and tried to raise his hand, but the movement made him ill again, and he returned his head over the pail.

"Now we've talked about this before, sir," said Schaefer. "There is such a thing as too much of a good thing." Erik felt a gentle hand on his back and looked up into the concerned eyes of his corporal.

"Are you all right?" Schaefer asked again.

Erik nodded. The corporal helped him to his feet and back over to his chair, pouring a tall glass of water for Erik to drink.

"I'm going to get the stove going, sir. Come out when you're feeling a little better."

Erik was grateful. He was freezing and could use the warmth. Schaefer departed, and he took sip after agonizing sip from the water. He was worried the new liquid would make him throw up again, but his stomach seemed to be settling down, and he was terribly thirsty. After a few minutes, he felt a little better. Even the spinning was starting to subside, although his pounding headache gave no sign of relief. Well, he'd known what he was getting himself into when he'd kept going last night; he had drunk far too much.

He hadn't felt this ill in a very long time. He opened his drawer and pulled out a hard biscuit he'd found in the bin yesterday. He took a couple of bites, washing the stale bread down with water, and then he pulled himself slowly to his feet and stumbled out of the room, closing the door behind him. Schaefer was at the stove. He'd already started a sizable fire, and he was feeding pieces of wood into the greedy, licking flames. Erik could feel the warmth emanating from the hot iron, and he pulled himself gently into a chair, soaking up the heat.

"That feels splendid, Schaefer," he said. "Thank you so much."

"Think nothing of it. I don't want us to catch our death of cold. Speaking of not catching something: What was Gunther's girl doing around here yesterday?" he asked, eyeing Erik curiously.

"She wanted my help," he said.

Schaefer snorted. "Why on earth would she expect to find help from you? Besides, it seems like she can get anything she wants from her precious Gunther."

"She's worried about the Russians coming."

"Ha!" said Schaefer, slapping his knee. "And well she should be. The Bolsheviks won't look too kindly on a piece of Jewish skirt that sold herself out to the SS."

Erik grunted in agreement. "She's in no better position than we are. Maybe worse. She told me Gunther's planning on taking her away from here by himself. Her and the child. Do you think that's true?"

"Who knows?" said Schaefer. "He certainly put enough at risk just keeping her around in the first place. If word had ever gotten to his superiors, he would have been arrested on the spot. Frankly, I don't know how he's pulled it off."

"He's well connected, don't forget it. He's Heydrich's cousin."

"Heydrich's been dead for years. I'm not sure that carries as much weight as it used to. Still, Gunther's a shrewd character. Who knows who he's threatened and bribed? He's a survivor, that's for sure."

"He certainly is. And he's dangerous."

Schaefer shrugged. "I don't like him much. But I must thank him for leaving me here all this time. Three square meals a day and duty inside this warm warehouse. I couldn't ask for much more, particularly with you at the reins."

"She wants to escape the camp," said Erik.

"Is she out of her mind? She'd never get out of here. Even if she did, where would she go? She has no papers. She's in the middle of hostile territory. Any German worth their salt would turn her in immediately." Schaefer shook his head. "Fool of a woman. The only protection she's got is Gunther; if he is truly planning on leaving with her, she better go and be thankful she has the chance."

Erik mused over that for a moment. Schaefer was right, at least as far as he could be, but Erik knew the price Trude was paying. Schaefer assumed the arrangement between Trude and Gunther was voluntary, but it certainly was not.

"What if I wanted to help her?" he said quietly, his eyes on the floor. He knew he was taking a tremendous risk, but he'd grown to trust the corporal implicitly.

Schaefer was quiet for a few moments. "Why would you want to do that?" he asked finally.

"I know her."

"What do you mean you know her?"

Erik explained their history, the university, the neighborhood.

"Why are you just telling me this now?"

"I don't know. It didn't really seem important before. Gunther made me swear to never speak with her. I wasn't willing to risk my family or myself, at least until yesterday."

"You shouldn't have spoken with her then, either. If you refused, that would have been the end of it. What's changed? The risk is still the same. Your life and your family will be sacrificed if you're caught, which you most assuredly would be. So, what, you went to school with her? You went to a couple concerts. You flirted. I don't care if you slept together for three years. That was then and this is now. She's a Jew. Your life's on the line. Look at her; she sold her own people out. You don't owe her a damned thing."

Erik looked up, seeing the lines of care creasing Schaefer's face. He appreciated his friend's loyalty and concern for his well-being, but he couldn't agree with everything he'd said.

"Maybe I don't owe her anything," Erik explained, "but maybe I owe myself something. I did a lot of thinking last night. This whole war I've seen awful things happen. Everyone told me to stay out of it. I did everything I could to do so. Finally, the terrible things and I ran afoul of each other. I refused to commit them. I risked my life to disobey an order. I was proud of that. Proud, too, that I came here and stayed out of the worst of things here. Look at me, I've even refused to go through the carts," he said, nodding over toward the stacks of articles. "Haven't you ever wondered why I'm always busy when it comes to the sorting?"

"I know why you don't go through it, sir," said Schaefer. "You didn't fool me. I knew from the start you were a good man. I've tried to protect you because you're decent and kind. I respect you. You've taken care of me, of us. You've protected me, kept me here away from all the horror outside. You say you've never done anything in this war, but you've spared me, and I'll never forget it."

Erik looked up, surprised and thankful. But he shook his head. "Those words mean a lot to me, but it's not enough. While I protected you and my family, thousands have died around us. I was thankful just to not be directly involved, but I realized last night I'm still responsible. We all are. Even if we haven't directly done it, we've let it happen: all the killing, the torture, the destruction of mankind. All of us are responsible, not just the ones who pulled the trigger."

"You're being too hard on yourself. What could you do differently? If you stood up, you'd be dead and so would your family."

"I realize that. But last night, I started to wonder if it matters if I am killed. Even if my family is. If enough people stood up, they wouldn't be able to continue all this. We've all been too afraid. We all stood by and let it happen. We let these monsters in the door. They promised to protect us. They named our enemies and drove us to destroy them, but in the process, we've destroyed ourselves as well."

Schaefer reached over and grabbed Erik's hand, giving it a squeeze. "Maybe you're right, sir, but we can't do anything about it. You did do something. You protected us. You've saved our lives and your family."

"It's not enough. I have to do more," he said. "I have to help Trude and her daughter escape, whatever the cost."

Schaefer shook his head. "It's not possible, sir. You'll never make it. If you get caught, she'll still suffer, and they'll kill you and your family, too."

"I have to try. I can never make up for what I've done, or what I've failed to do. But I have to do something to try." He stared at his friend for a moment. "Will you help me?"

Schaefer paused for a moment, then nodded, a tear running down his cheek. "Anything for you, sir."

"Think carefully. If you're caught they will kill you, too."

"What else do I have to lose?"

Erik reached into his pocket and pulled out a slip of paper and a pencil. He set the paper on his knee and wrote in shaky handwriting a short, scribbled note. He folded up the note and handed it to Schaefer. "I need you to get this to Trude," he said. "She won't come back here, and there's no way I can get to her in the building."

"They won't let me in, either, sir. Not into her room."

"She needed starch yesterday. Bring her some more. They'll let you. She was ironing Gunther's shirts so he knows she's using it. Even if he saw you, he wouldn't be suspicious."

Schaefer nodded, his hands shaking a little as he took the note. "I'll do what I can."

"Are you sure you want to do this?" Erik asked.

"Like I said, sir, I would die for you." Schaefer bowed slightly, then turned and rapidly departed from the warehouse. Erik sat warming himself at the stove. His headache was gone. He felt a strange peace he hadn't known in years, since perhaps before the war. He was taking a terrible risk, gambling not only his life but the lives of many others. Somehow that didn't seem to matter anymore. For once he was doing the right thing, the just thing. He was striking a pinprick blow for humanity. His mind raced. He was trying to work out the details of a plan to whisk Trude and Britta away. He wasn't sure exactly what he would do yet, but the outline of a plan was beginning to form.

An hour passed and the door opened. Schaefer returned; his face was pasty white. He hurried to the stove, warming his hands and his body near the fire.

"Did you see her?" said Erik. Schaefer nodded. "What did she say?"

"She didn't say anything," said Schaefer. He reached his hand into his coat and pulled out a folded slip of paper, handing it to Erik. He carefully unfolded the contents and read the letter from Trude. The note contained information and an idea. Something that might help them. He refolded the paper, sat back in his chair, and closed his eyes, his mind wandering through a field of possibilities. Finally, his plans crystallized and he opened his eyes again, leaning forward to Schaefer. "Thank you so much, my friend. I will never be able to repay you."

Schaefer shook his head. "I'm not done, sir. I know you need help, and I'm here for you."

Erik wanted to decline the offer. But he did need Schaefer's help. Erik leaned closer, his voice dropping to a whisper. "I will need you to visit Trude one more time, then here's what we're going to do . . ."

CHAPTER THIRTY

Soldau
December 1944

As they planned, they realized that one of their greatest advantages now was turning into a significant liability: they had everything they would ever need in the warehouse, but that also meant that they rarely set foot outside of it. They couldn't move freely through the camp without attracting attention to themselves. Worse yet, they did not know the gate guards well, and they had left the camp only a few times on official leave. They would have to come up with some excuse to get them out of Soldau.

This would be manageable if it was just the corporal and himself. However, how could they get Trude and Britta out as well? Even if they managed to somehow free them from their locked room in the administrative building, they would have to get them out of the gate. Hour after hour they pored through various options, raising new ideas, working through the logistics and ultimately dismissing them. But they gradually perfected each step of the plan, until they settled on an overall set of steps that might, if they were lucky, get them all out of the camp.

As they finished the final points, they realized it was already evening. They hadn't eaten all day or left the confines of the office, even to use the bathroom. They rose and stepped out of the office, restoking the stove and cooking up some hot soup and bread, to be washed down with a fiery vodka.

That night Erik lay tossing and turning in his bunk, hardly able to sleep, knowing tomorrow he would risk everything. He woke sandy-eyed and depressed, starting to feel he was wasting his time, that they would surely be caught. Should he call it off? Nobody was forcing him to do this. Schaefer certainly wouldn't make him do anything that risked his life. He shook his head. No, he had to do something. This measure could not make up for the past. It was something, though, an act of defiance he had to make.

He warmed himself at the morning fire and ate some breakfast Schaefer had already prepared. When he was finished, Schaefer and he loaded up a cart with supplies for the administrative building. They weren't due to make any deliveries today, but he hoped nobody would notice.

They set out from the warehouse into the frozen air of the camp. The cart was their largest, a double-layered structure with wobbly wheels and a long wooden covering. The cart was designed to carry items both underneath and above.

They pushed and pulled the poorly made structure out the door and into the snow. It was slow going; the cart was top heavy, threatening to roll over at any moment. Both were forced to squat down, pushing as hard as they could to shove the cart through the snow.

They only managed to move the cart a meter at a time, and it took nearly an hour to reach the paved pathway barely two hundred meters from the warehouse. From there it was much easier going. Erik felt his heart race. He was nervous, although there was no reason to be so at this point. They could hardly be arrested for smuggling office supplies.

At the worst they might be chewed out by Gunther if he wondered why they were bringing such large quantities at one time into the building.

They finally made it to the headquarters and shoved the cart through the door. They pushed the unwieldy structure down the hallway until they were near the stairs directly below Gunther's office. Each of them took a load of supplies, stacking as much as they could carry, and then worked their way up the steps to the second floor.

When they reached the Kommandant's office, Erik knocked, waiting a few seconds for a response. There was none. Erik opened the door to the empty room. He beckoned for Schaefer to follow him and they entered, closing the door behind them and setting the load of supplies down on Gunther's desk. Schaefer stood watch. There was no window, so he would have to listen, and would only be able to give Erik a moment's notice if Gunther returned.

Erik set to work immediately, opening drawers to Gunther's desk. Fortunately, it was unlocked. He ran his hands through the jumbled drawers, thumbing through logs and journals, under a handkerchief and through a group of pens. He found nothing.

He opened the second drawer down to his left. It was full of paper and files. He lifted a file and sifted through the paperwork. Again, he did not find what he was looking for. Erik quickly searched the rest of the drawer but came up empty.

The third drawer to his left was empty, except for a stack of paper pads. He moved to the right side of the desk, searching methodically. In the bottom drawer, he finally found what he was looking for. He wrapped his hands around the tiny object, looking up in triumph to Schaefer.

He watched his friend's look of approval shift to concern, and he saw the door handle of the office start to turn. Erik shoved the desk drawer closed and moved the desk chair back into place as Gunther entered the room, red faced, glaring around suspiciously.

"What the hell are you two doing in here?" he demanded. They both stood at attention, flashing the Hitler salute and clicking their heels.

"Answer me!" Gunther shouted.

"We're just delivering supplies, sir," said Erik, pointing to the desk.

"I didn't order any supplies. Look at that mess. What would I do with all of that?"

"It's my fault," said Schaefer. "The sergeant told me I was crazy, but we're overstocked in the warehouse with paper, so I suggested we deliver some supplies to every office. Of course, we started with you."

Gunther's suspicion turned rapidly to annoyance. He waved at them dismissively. "Get that garbage out of here! Don't let me catch you in my office again without my permission. Do you understand?"

They nodded and then fumbled for the supplies; Erik dropped a stack of paper that went flying all over the floor.

"Clumsy fool!" shouted Gunther. "Just leave it and get out!"

Erik reached down, grabbing as much of the paper as he could, and then they bolted from the office.

"That was a close call," he whispered to Schaefer after they were outside the office.

"It's not over yet," said the corporal. "If Major Wolf discovers what's missing, he'll have to know it was us."

Erik nodded. He'd hoped they would get in and out of Gunther's office undetected, but he'd caught them. Thank God Schaefer was there to give him a half moment's warning; otherwise he'd have been caught red-handed.

They returned down the stairs with their piles of paperwork. They set the paper down carefully on the top of the cart and then moved it all out of the way, as much against the wall as possible. They looked up and down the corridor. There was no one there. They walked away from the supplies, heading back to the warehouse. They had what they'd come for.

For now, things were going as smoothly as they could. As they left the building Erik clapped Schaefer on the shoulder. "Thank you, my friend. Thank you again, and I want to say something to you," he said, stopping Schaefer in the snow. "You've done enough. I can take it from here."

Schaefer shook his head. "You saw how that cart moves in the snow. You're going to need my help. Think about Gunther's office. Without my help, you'd be under arrest already."

"Fine," said Erik. "You can help me with the cart, but that's it. After that I want you to go back to the warehouse. You can blame me for the whole thing. I don't want you to risk yourself and your family."

"I told you I'm in all the way. There's no going back now." They returned through the snow to the warehouse, warming themselves at the stove and chatting away through a lunch of canned cheese and biscuits. They worked away as busily as they could the rest of the day, a little apprehensive, waiting moment by moment for Gunther to storm through the warehouse door with guards to arrest them. But he didn't.

Dinnertime came and went. Then they sat by the stove, passing around a bottle of vodka. Erik took little sips. He needed to be alert. They lay in their bunks with the lights off, swapping stories and reminiscing about the last two years. Finally, they faded away into sleep.

The next morning, Erik and Schaefer rose together and prepared themselves. A long day awaited them. Tonight, they would strike.

The door unlatched in the predawn darkness. Trude opened her eyes. The room was dark, but she saw a pinprick of light dancing in the blackness. She followed the brightness, wondering what on earth the person was thinking. Someone would see them.

The light moved toward her and then flashed in her eyes, burning them. She blinked, trying to see. "Shut that off," she hissed.

"As you wish," a voice responded. Her heart sank. It was Gunther.

"What are you doing here?" she asked as quietly as possible, trying not to wake up Britta.

"I need to talk to you. Come here," he whispered.

She climbed reluctantly out of the bed, making her way toward the light.

"Stop shining that," she said. "You'll wake up Britta. Why don't you come back at breakfast time? It's too early."

He shook his head. "I can't come to breakfast today," he said. "Too much to do." He grabbed her hands. She felt the repulsion course through her. It was worse now than it had been when she was so close to leaving him forever.

"I have urgent news," he whispered. "The Russians have broken through. They are no more than forty-eight hours away. But don't worry, my dear. I have secured an escape for us today. We are leaving at noon. You need to be prepared. I have a car waiting. I'll come get you and Britta at about eleven. Don't worry about bringing anything; we will take care of all of that later."

"They'll never let me leave here," she said. "Even for you."

"Don't worry. I have special orders signed by Colonel Schmidt. You're wanted in Königsberg for questioning."

"Why would the colonel sign that?"

Gunther shook his head. "He didn't; it's forged." He rubbed her hands back and forth, massaging her wrist. "In a few hours, my dear, we will be free of this place. Safe from the Russians and on our way to Germany. I have maps, I have travel papers. I know where we're going."

"I don't want to go. Why can't I just wait until the camp is liberated?" Her mind reeled. She couldn't believe she was going to be whisked away, when her escape was planned for tonight.

"I told you they'll kill you," he said with irritation. "After they've raped both of you. You don't understand: I'm your only chance." He squeezed her hands again. "I told you I'd always take care of you, my dear. Now listen, I need you to get up right now. As soon as I leave, pack your things and be ready. Someone will come back to get you in the next few minutes. It may not be me. Follow them. Whatever you do, go along with the plan."

He pulled her close and embraced her, kissing her on the lips. "Soon we will be together forever. I will always protect you." He clung to her for a moment, engulfing her. She held on limply until he released her. "I promise you after the war, my dear, we will be equals. One man, one woman, one child."

He squeezed her shoulders one more time. "I'll see you in a while." With that he turned and left. She stood there in the darkness, panic racing through her mind. What was she going to do? She was locked in this room and would be until Gunther came for them. There was no way to get a message to Erik, and even if she could, what could he do?

There was nothing she could do, she realized. She would have to go with Gunther. Maybe he was right; perhaps somehow they would be safe going into the mouth of the monster. But so many things could go wrong. Gunther would have no power where they were going. Germans were always on the lookout for false papers, for hiding Jews. They could be snatched up again and imprisoned, or perhaps even shot on the spot. Worse yet, she was confining herself to a lifetime with Gunther . . .

She sat there in the darkness, her brain wheeling around the problem, trying to find an answer. There wasn't one. The darkness faded and the light slowly covered the heavens. There was a knock at the door.

Trude made her way over. "Come in, please," she said. The door opened, and an SS guard carried in a tray of food. He smiled thinly and placed the tray on the table. Trude suddenly knew what she had to do, slim chance that it was. She allowed herself to fall forward, crashing her head against the table and then hitting the ground. The blow nearly knocked her out, but she could feel the hot blood streaming.

She heard the guard gasp and felt his hands on her, reaching down to try to help her. She heard Britta's screams and the guard's shouts.

There were more footsteps. She kept her eyes closed. Several Germans were there now, and they were calling for help. She fought nausea and unconsciousness. She had to stay awake. Ages seemed to pass, and then she heard another voice, one she recognized as a camp doctor's. She felt hands on her, fingers touching her skin. The digits felt like a lit match, burning her wound. She cried out in pain.

More hands on her. She was moved over onto a stretcher. She felt herself lifted into the air. They jostled her along with an uneven gait, the guards carrying her from the room, their boots clopping along on the hard tile floors of the administrative building. A burst of light; her lungs gasped in the frosty air. They were outside.

The hospital was one building over. She heard the crunch of their boots in the snow as they carried her along. More doors, slapping open and closed. Through her eyelids, she could sense the dim lights of the hospital. This was what she wanted, but she hoped Britta was coming with her. She didn't hear her daughter's voice, but it was difficult to tell among the shuffling footsteps whether she was following or not. After what seemed an eternity she was lowered and then moved over onto a cot. She must be in the central ward.

A doctor hovered over her, and now she heard a woman's voice, a nurse, another member of the SS. They were talking about her wound. She could hear instruments clanging together. She pretended she was unconscious. She felt an intense, sharp, piercing burn at the injury and realized with horror they were beginning to sew up the cut. The pain was unbearable, a lancing, fiery sting followed by the tug of thread slicing through her skin. Somehow she endured it, agonizing stitch after stitch. She wanted to scream. She yelled in her mind, cursing and writhing, but on the outside, she didn't make a peep.

She thought she would call out, reveal herself. She wasn't sure how much longer she could handle the pain, but then it was over. She felt a cold wet cloth applied to her feverish forehead. They were cleaning her skin of the remaining blood. Then they applied a dry cloth and a bandage. The doctor discussed her wound with the nurse, the frequency of inspection and cleaning, and then finally the voices drifted away.

Slowly she opened an eye, first one, then the other. At first all she could see was the blur of the overhead lights, but soon she adjusted to the glare to be able to glance around the room. She dared not move her head for fear she would be discovered. The hospital was a rectangular stone building perhaps fifteen meters long and ten meters wide. Beds lined the length of the room on both sides. Most of them were filled with prisoner patients. Now that the agony was over she could hear the coughing and the moaning that reminded her so much of the barracks in the camp. She turned her head ever so slightly to the right and to the left, realizing the doctor had left the ward but the nurse was still there, leaning over a patient no more than a few meters away. Thankfully, her back was turned.

Trude closed her eyes again to a slit, watching with her peripheral vision as the nurse checked first one patient, then another, moving down the line and slowly away from her. Agonizing minutes passed. At any moment, Gunther might appear, having learned what had happened to her. Then it would be too late.

What was she to do? They'd left Britta in her room. She couldn't do anything without her daughter. Perhaps she should just lie here, wait for Gunther to come. At least they would be together. Something in her cried out violently against that. *You must try,* she told herself.

Finally, the nurse completed her slow tracking to the end of the building. Trude was afraid she was going to turn around and start in on the other side of the room, but to her vast relief the nurse stepped out. Trude had moments to do something. She rose to her feet slowly, vision blurred; she felt the burning agony of her forehead. She had no shoes and was still dressed in her nightgown. She had no choice; she would have to brave the frozen ground. She walked slowly with a measured pace, not wanting to raise the alarm among the patients, and moved to the far door on the other side of the building. She opened the door and peered out into a small office, probably the doctor's. Fortunately, he was not there.

She stepped through and looked around. In the corner on a rack was a long, dark wool coat. She stepped over, took the coat, and put it on. It was impossibly large on her. She shook her head; this wasn't going to work, but she had to try. She opened the door and walked out of the hospital and into the snow.

On the icy ground, her bare feet stung. She took another step, then another, marching stride by painful stride in her stolen coat on frozen feet, right through the middle of the camp. There were Nazis all around her. One of the guards passed her directly. He looked her up and down. She nodded to him, as if all of this made sense. To her surprise, he nodded back and continued on his way.

She went on. Impossibly forward. Each step was a miracle. She measured her pace, not too slow nor too fast. *You can't see me.* She saw her destination now, more than a quarter kilometer away. *I'll never make it,* she thought, but she kept going, the distance shrinking with each step.

By the time she reached the pathway, she could no longer feel her feet. She was walking along the barbed-wire fence leading into the general camp. Two SS turned the corner of the building a hundred meters away and walked in her direction. There was no way they would let her pass. She raised her head, her face passive. The SS watched her as she approached. They started to slow down, but she kept her pace. She knew them slightly. They recognized her, but they passed without stopping. She couldn't believe it.

A dog barked in the distance from somewhere off in the woods. She heard the thunderous echo of a rifle. She went on. Her feet left the path and returned to the snow. She could see the warehouse door no more than two hundred meters away. She walked on, agonizing step after step.

The door opened and an SS man stepped out, staring at her in surprise. "What are you doing?" he demanded sharply.

She wasn't going to make it after all.

"What are you doing?" he repeated.

She stood there frozen, unable to answer.

"Trude, don't you recognize me?"

She looked closer and realized it was Schaefer. The corporal rushed forward, grabbed her by the shoulders, and escorted her the last few steps into the warehouse.

CHAPTER THIRTY-ONE

Soldau
December 1944

Erik sat in his office, running some of the details of tonight's plan through his mind. He heard a commotion outside the warehouse and wondered what it was. He rose from his desk, heading for the door when it opened. He was shocked to see Corporal Schaefer leading Trude in. She was dressed in a nightgown and covered with a huge woolen overcoat. Her bare feet were blue and black. An enormous bloody bandage rested at an angle across her forehead.

"Erik," she said, "help me." She raised her hands up to him and then stumbled, falling to the concrete. Schaefer was fortunately there and softened her fall.

"What's happened to her?" Erik demanded.

"I don't know, sir. I opened the door and she was just there."

"Help me with her." Together they picked Trude up and carried her to a chair near the stove, pulling her feet up onto a small table where they could rest less than a third of a meter away from the warmth of the iron. She was barely conscious.

"Erik, help me, please," she said again. She was shaking. She seemed stunned.

"Tell me what's going on," he said.

"It's Gunther. Gunther's taking us away. We're leaving today. At noon."

"Why?"

"He came to me this morning and told me the Russians will be here any day. He moved up our departure. I didn't know what to do so I intentionally fell on the edge of our table. They took me to the hospital, and I escaped to come here. I'd hoped they would take Britta with me, but they didn't. Now she's locked up there, and Gunther will be coming any moment."

Erik looked at his watch. It was eleven thirty. Erik sat back stunned. She must have been seen by dozens of people coming here. Any second Gunther would arrive, probably with armed guards. They would all be arrested. The plan was unraveling, and they were all in danger. He racked his mind trying to think.

"What are you going to do?" asked Schaefer.

"I'm going to go get Britta, and we are getting out of here."

"I'm going with you," said the corporal.

Erik shook his head. "I need you to stay here for now with Trude."

"She's safe here for now. The danger's out there." He stepped in front of the door, blocking Erik. "I'm coming along."

Erik relented. They dressed quickly in their overcoats, and Erik slid on his jackboots, then they stepped out of the warehouse. He half expected to see parties of guards already heading their direction, but the activity outside was normal, just a smattering of guards walking this way and that. The regular sounds of the camp operating.

They hastened together through the snow toward the administrative building. Erik had no idea what they were going to do, but they had to move quickly.

"We can still use the cart," said Schaefer.

Erik thought about it as they moved through the snow. The corporal was right. It was the only way. But the plan had been to move Britta and Trude at night, undetected. Now, during the day, with Gunther sounding the alarm at any moment, the prospects seemed ludicrously slim.

They entered the building a few minutes later and stormed down the corridor and up the stairs. Here their luck held as well. The hallways were deserted. Perhaps Gunther had been delayed?

They moved quickly down to Trude's door. Erik fished into his pocket and found the small metal object he'd retrieved from Gunther's office yesterday. He pulled the key out and placed it into the door, turning the handle. He wasn't even sure it was the right one, but it worked and the door opened. Inside was Britta, sitting at the table, and a man standing over her. It was Gunther.

The Kommandant looked up sharply. "How did you get in here?" he demanded. "What are you doing?"

"The . . . the door was unlocked."

"What do you want?"

"We're still sorting out supplies," explained Erik lamely.

"I told you to knock that nonsense off," said Gunther. He started to say something and then paused. "Never mind. I can use your help right now. I've got things to attend to. You know Britta here. There's a car waiting for us. Please escort her to the front and stay there with her until I return. Her mother's had a fall. I'm going to go check on her. I'll be down shortly. Don't let the girl out of your sight, do you understand? If you do, there'll be hell to pay."

Erik nodded. Gunther grunted in satisfaction. He reached out and patted Britta on the shoulder. "Now, my dear, go with these nice gentlemen. They're going to take you to the car and I'll take care of things. I'll be there with your mother in a few minutes, all right?"

She nodded, her face red and blotchy from crying. Gunther stepped out of the room. Erik realized he would head straight to the hospital and discover Trude had disappeared. They had only scant moments.

"Britta, do you know who I am?" asked Erik.

She looked up and nodded.

"We have your mother in hiding. We must go right now. We must hurry." She stood and went with them, hurrying out the door, down the stairs, and out the front toward the car.

The vehicle was directly in front of the building, a warm exhaust billowing into the sky. They opened the door and helped Britta get in. The driver was already out hastening to assist them. Erik got in next to her and Schaefer turned, speaking with the driver. Erik could hear an argument, with Schaefer's voice rising higher and higher, and then both men got into the front seat. The driver lurched the vehicle into motion and the car drove past the vast administrative building and along the fence toward the warehouse.

There wasn't even a real road, but the car did well enough in the crushed snow. Guards and other personnel stopped and watched them in amazement as they crept past them. "Stop here," commanded Erik, at the point where the path ended and the snow deepened. He knew the car would become hopelessly stuck if it continued.

"I'll be right back," he said. He jumped out of the vehicle and ran toward the warehouse.

He reached the door swiftly and hurried into the building. He found Trude still sitting near the stove.

"What's wrong?" she asked.

"We have to go right now!" he screamed.

She stared up at him in surprise and then lurched to her feet, throwing the coat back on and starting toward the door.

"Wait!" he commanded. He stepped over to one of the carts and began furiously digging through until he found what he was looking for.

He pulled out a pair of boots; they were too large, but they would have to do. He ran them over to her and quickly helped her put them on.

The boots were huge, but they were some measure of protection against the cold. She smiled gratefully at him as he helped her.

As he pulled her up, her face twisted into a grimace. "My daughter."

"She's with us," said Erik.

Erik led Trude to the car, opened the door, and helped her in, stepping in swiftly after her.

"Let's go," said Erik.

"What's going on?" demanded the driver. "I'm supposed to be waiting for Gunther."

"Change of plans. We're meeting him outside the camp," said Erik.

"That's not what I was told," said the driver. He shut the car off and cranked his neck to the back seat. "I'm not going anywhere until I figure out what's going on."

Schaefer struck the man in the face with a heavy blow. Erik leaned forward over the seat to grab the driver by the collar and pull him backward, choking him. The driver flailed his arms and legs. Erik kept pressing his arm tighter and tighter around the driver's neck until he went limp.

The man was still alive but unconscious. Erik pulled him over the seat and into the back. They shoved him down to the carpet. Trude covered the driver with a blanket from the seat, concealing him from view.

"What do we do now?" asked Schaefer.

"We get the hell out of here."

"You drive," said the corporal. Erik opened the back door and moved to the front. He looked around nervously as he did. Several guards were stopped, staring openly at them. Fortunately, they were all relatively far away. He stepped in behind the wheel, turned the ignition to start the engine, maneuvered the vehicle around, and drove back along the fence.

Erik realized with horror that they would have to drive past the hospital and the administrative building to leave the camp. There was no other way; if they were caught, this would be the end. Erik sped along the pathway as quickly as he could. As they passed the hospital the building's door flung open; he saw Gunther stepping out, shouting at them to stop. Erik hit the accelerator and the car went into full throttle, racing past the remaining buildings. They made it by the administrative structure but were abruptly stopped at the front gate. A guard with his machine pistol tapped at the door, stepping up to Schaefer's side to review their papers.

The corporal rolled down the window, and the guard eyed them suspiciously.

"Where are you taking these prisoners?" he asked, eyeing Trude and Britta, who he clearly recognized.

"Surely you received orders about this?" said Erik.

The guard nodded. "Yes, I did. But not for you. They are supposed to be going with Gunther."

"Plan changed," said Erik shrugging.

The guard hesitated a moment and then nodded to his partner, who unlatched the barbed-wire gate and started to pull it open. From behind them a siren sounded. They could hear shouting. The guard looked up at them and then back toward the commotion. His hand had already moved to his weapon.

"Good-bye, my friend," Schaefer said to Erik. He slammed his door open, hitting the guard and knocking him into the snow. He rolled out of the car to land hard on top of him.

"Schaefer!"

"Go!" the corporal screamed. Erik reached for the handle, but the other guard was moving into action. He had only a split second to decide what to do. Shouting in frustration, he slammed on the accelerator and crashed through the partially open gate, racing away as quickly as he could. Through his mirror he could see the guards grappling on the ground with Schaefer. Other SS were closing in. The car sped down the road and away from the camp. There would be a hot pursuit at any moment, but for now they were free.

⟶⟵

Erik slowed the car about ten kilometers from Soldau. They quickly dragged the unconscious guard out of the back and laid him down in a ditch near the side of the road. Erik looked through the car, trying to find any information. He didn't have any of the maps or other things he had prepared. He had no money, no identification. They'd left everything behind in the mad scramble to escape. Even now he knew the pursuit was on. There were likely calls going out to Karl and others in Königsberg to arrest his family. He had to get to them as quickly as possible, but he knew the SS would be waiting for him so he would have to be cautious. They had to lose the car at some point and find some other way to travel.

"Erik, what are we going to do?" Trude asked.

"I don't know. We have to get into Königsberg without being detected."

"I know where we must go."

"Where?"

"I have a friend. Someone who will help us." She explained, telling him the story of Captain Dutt's friendship and help.

Erik nodded. "But how do we get there? I don't know the way from here."

"I do," she said. "When I was younger, we visited family all over East Prussia and even parts of Poland. I've been here before. We just need to keep heading north. There's an autobahn. We should hit it anytime. It will be safe."

"What if there are roadblocks? If they're checking papers?"

"I don't know," she said. "We'll have to trust our luck."

He nodded and sped on, driving down to a narrow road heading north. At least he hoped that was the direction they were going. Kilometer after kilometer passed and still they did not find the highway. He grew worried. "Are you sure we're heading the right direction?"

"Yes . . . I think so," she said.

Erik looked down at the gas tank. They only had a half tank and no money. Would it be enough to get them back to Königsberg? He didn't know. He looked up again and saw to his relief that the trees thinned out ahead of him. He could see the long ribbon of an intersecting road. It was the autobahn.

They reached the highway in a few minutes. He kept looking behind him, expecting pursuit. So far they'd been lucky. He turned right on the highway, heading east on two wide-open lanes. There was no traffic. Erik punched the accelerator, every moment putting more distance between them and their pursuers.

Kilometers were passing them by. Erik kept an eye on the gas tank. The needle slowly dipped down. First three-eighths, then a quarter, then an eighth. He wasn't sure they were going to make it, but even now in the distance he could see the outskirts of his city.

Trude took over as they pulled into the first outlying suburbs. She directed him off the autobahn and into the narrow streets, turning this way and that. Erik kept waiting for a soldier to stop them, demanding papers. Anything could stop them. An overzealous policeman might pull them over, perhaps sensing something slightly out of place.

It was late afternoon now, and the streets were practically deserted as they moved into the city. Erik was shocked to see block after block of rubble. The last time he'd been to Königsberg the city was virtually intact, having suffered only a couple of light bombings, but in the last few months everything had changed. Whole sections of the city were in ruins. Here and there a civilian walked among the rubble, picking through the bricks, looking for God knows what. Thankfully the streets were mostly clear of debris and they could advance.

"We're almost there," said Trude. "Turn left up at the corner."

They rounded a curve up a slight hill and then went around the corner. "It's right here," she said excitedly.

Erik turned into a driveway winding up an incline through the trees until they reached a clearing.

"Oh no," exclaimed Trude. The house was a pile of dust and brick. At the extreme ends on both sides, portions of the walls still stood, crumbling down in jagged curves like a mountain range. But the rest was debris.

Before he could stop her, Trude had opened the door and was out, running toward the rubble. He pressed the parking brake and then jumped out himself, chasing after her.

"No!" she kept repeating. Tears poured down her face.

He put his hands gently on her shoulder. "Trude, I'm sorry. But we can't stay here."

"They're all dead."

Erik shook his head. "You don't know that. The house is gone, but that doesn't mean anything. There's a pretty good warning system in the city. They were probably in a shelter."

She kept shaking her head. "No, I know they're gone."

He turned her toward him. "Listen to me," he said. "You don't know that. More importantly, we can't stay here. I need you to look at me. We've got to go. I must get to my family. I was hoping to change cars, but we're going to have to risk it. Are you ready? Can we go?"

She stared at him for a moment, and then he saw the understanding in her eyes. "Of course," she said. "How selfish of me. Let's go, please."

He led her to the car, and they backed their way carefully down the driveway and sped back the other direction. Erik knew where he was now and where to go. He wound his way through the streets, driving carefully, not wanting to attract any attention. He thought they would be relatively safe until they approached his own neighborhood. That's where the real danger would come.

Soon they were in his home district. They took a left on the Yorckstrasse. Erik slowed the vehicle, creeping forward as cautiously as he dared. He was only a couple of blocks from his house. He moved forward another block. Now he could see it on the left. He expected the front street to be blocked with multiple cars, police and Gestapo, but nobody was there. This only increased his suspicion. They had to be waiting for him by now. He crept the car farther forward, then made a U-turn and came slowly back down the street toward his house, stopping in front of it.

"Get into the front seat," he said to Trude. "If you see anything happen, drive away immediately."

"I have something to do," said Trude. "I just need a few minutes. I left some things hidden at Frau Werner's house. A couple rings and a gold coin, a little money. That will help us."

He hesitated then nodded. "Hurry," he said. "I'll just be a minute." He stepped out of the car. Trude drove slowly down the street. Better if she wasn't right there if the Gestapo was coming, he thought. He approached his front door cautiously, looking around. He knocked and waited, listening. There was no response. He knocked again. Still no answer. He reached down and turned the knob; the door was unlocked. He cautiously took a step inside. The front room was in disarray, chairs turned over, broken glass. Smatterings of clothing peppered the stairs. He ran from room to room calling out to his family desperately. Nobody answered. He was too late. Gunther must have gotten through to the Gestapo and had his family arrested. They would be in the SS jail; perhaps they were already dead. He fell to his knees, tears streaming down his cheeks as he beat his hands against his chest and buried his head in his bedroom mattress.

And then he saw it. An envelope addressed to him rested near the lamp on the nightstand. He tore it open. There was a letter inside, written to him, in Corina's careful, precise script. He read the contents carefully several times, and then, taking a deep breath, he tucked the note into his pocket. Gunther hadn't found them. They were gone but safe. Karl had evacuated them to escape the Russians.

There was more to the note. But he would think on that later. He sat at the edge of the bed, silent, alone. At least they were safe. That's what mattered.

—⊷—

Trude parked the car in front of Frau Werner's house. She looked carefully at the front door. She realized the house could've been inhabited again. If so, she would certainly arouse suspicion. A woman in a nightgown with men's boots and a heavy overcoat knocking at the front door. Still, she had to take the risk. They needed some money to help them escape. She had the jewelry and a little cash hidden away where nobody likely would have found it.

She turned to her daughter. "Britta, I want you to stay here. Duck down and don't look up. Don't get out of the car or make any noise. If I'm not back in fifteen minutes, I want you to leave. Do you understand me?"

Britta was clearly afraid. "But, Mother, where would I go? I can't leave you. I can't drive. I don't know anyone."

"That doesn't matter. You just get out of here and hide. Wait until the Russians arrive, then tell them you're a Jew."

She knew her daughter would have little chance without her. Still, a small chance was better than none. "Do as I say," she said sternly. Then she opened the door, closing it behind her, and walked up the walkway toward the door. Thankfully the street seemed to be deserted around her. There might be people watching her, but it made no difference. She would be in and out quickly, long before anyone could respond to a report.

If nobody lived here, she would be safe. She checked the door handle and was relieved to find it unlocked. She stepped inside, looking around cautiously. She realized immediately the house was uninhabited. All of Frau Werner's possessions were still there. She'd expected to find broken furniture, signs of a struggle, but everything looked the same as the day she had left. Furniture and books held a lonely vigil, all coated with a deep layer of dust, but otherwise undisturbed.

She took the stairs as quickly as possible and went into Britta's old bedroom. She opened the closet and saw with relief her clothes still hanging there. She removed the overcoat and the gown and quickly put on a dress, her own heavy woolen coat, and some silk stockings. She rummaged around at the base of the closet and found a pair of boots. Now she looked like any other German dressed against the cold. Her outward appearance would no longer garner any suspicion.

She kneeled under the clothing and crawled to the back of the closet. She grappled around, eventually finding the corner seam of the carpet and pulling it up. Beneath was a small section of the floor she had cut away carefully, night after night, with a pocketknife. A hiding spot unknown even to Frau Werner. She removed the flooring and reached her hand in. She pulled up and found with relief everything was still there. She removed two rings, one of them with diamonds, one gold coin, and a small stack of Reichsmarks. She tucked them into the interior pocket of her wool coat. Trude stood, reached above the clothing, and pulled down a winter hat, placing it firmly on her head.

She wanted to bring some things for Britta, too, but she realized her daughter had outgrown everything there. She smiled to herself, grabbing some of her own things for her daughter. *She's a woman now.*

She started back down the stairs and reached the landing. She was starving, she realized. But there would be no food in the house after all this time. She turned to go.

"Frau Bensheim." The words froze her blood. She turned and there he was, a waking nightmare. Gunther sat in Mrs. Werner's favorite chair in the sitting room. His legs were crossed, his hands combing casually through a magazine. His pipe unlit in his mouth. "Where are you going in such a hurry?" he asked. He looked her up and down. "And all dressed up for the weather, too."

She turned to him. "Gunther, please, I'm begging you to let me go."

"Why in the world would I do that, my dear? After everything I've done for you. Come on now, after I worked so hard to make all the arrangements, and then you desert me and even have the bad manners to steal my car?"

She took a step forward, hands out in supplication. "Gunther, I owe you my life. You've helped me survive. But it's too dangerous for me to go to Germany. I need to escape, to get away. I'm asking you, if you truly love me, I'm begging, please let me go."

He watched her intently for a moment, and then he broke into a wide grin. He shook his head. "Unfortunately, that's not the plan, my dear. You just haven't been listening well lately. I told you you're coming with me, and so is Britta. How irresponsible of you to leave her in the car. She's asleep fortunately. Teenagers. How little they know of life."

Gunther chuckled. He rose and took a step toward her. Trude took a step back. "I can't believe you would do this to me," he said, his voice growing in anger. "After everything we've been through. I protected you, protected your daughter. I've given you the world. I've loved you, yet you repay me like this!" His voice rose to a shout.

Trude felt her own anger, a defiance exploding out of her. "You gave me this?" she said. "Wrong! You stole it from me. You only protected me and Britta for your own selfish reasons. I went along all this time to save my daughter, but I've never loved you. How could you ever believe that? None of this ever came with my consent. You're a cruel, horrid monster, Gunther!" She saw the words crashing over him. His face flushed and he assumed a wounded expression.

"How can you say such things, my darling?" he said, shock in his voice. "You're not in your right mind. Poor child, you've been through so much today, haven't you?" His voice was soft. "Don't worry, everything is going to be fine. I've made some calls so my friends will be here in just a minute. I brought my things." He gestured toward a heavy bag near the chair. "Everything we will need. I have the papers for you and Britta. Don't worry, I will forgive you. Let's forget about this." He took another step forward and grasped her by the shoulders. Trude was shaking; the nightmare was washing over her again. He pulled her close, kissing her on the neck. "Don't worry, my dear," he whispered again. "We will be together forever."

"No!" she screamed. Pushing back, she shoved him hard, pulling away, but he caught her by the wrist. He slapped her with the back of his hand. She spun to the ground, crashing hard against the wooden floor of the entryway.

"You stupid bitch!" he screamed, kicking her. "Who do you think you are?" He grabbed her by the hair, pulling her to her knees. "You're coming with me. We are going now!"

He pulled her up to his waist, and her arms went around him, fighting him, trying to escape. He was dragging her toward the door.

She searched desperately with her hands, finally finding what she was looking for. She grasped an object at his belt. Pulling with all of her might, she drew Gunther's pistol out of its holster, raising it with one rapid motion and pressing the barrel against his chin. His hand came up, grabbing the end of the gun, starting to pull her away. She pulled the trigger. A thunderous roar echoed through the house. Gunther's head snapped back and his body crumpled against the ground, writhing back and forth, his blood pooling in the carpet. She took careful aim and shot him again in the chest twice. The body stopped moving. She ran over and picked up the heavy satchel near the chair, shoving the pistol into her coat pocket.

She stormed out of the house. Britta was there halfway out the car, her eyes full of fear. Trude walked rapidly toward the vehicle. There were people outside now on their porches staring at her, pointing. She jumped into the driver's seat and sped back down the road toward Erik's home. She pulled up to his town house even as she saw the black cars rolling down the street, heading toward Frau Werner's. They had no time.

Erik was already on the porch, sprinting toward her. He headed toward the driver's seat, but she rolled down the window and screamed at him to get in. He paused for a moment and then stepped around to the passenger side.

"What is it?" he said.

"Get in now!" she screamed. He jumped in and she pulled away, not even pausing for him to close the door. She roared down the street away from Frau Werner's and took a sharp turn, heading north.

"What's going on?" demanded Erik.

"Gunther was there," she said, her hands shaking and tears filling her eyes.

"Oh my God!" said Erik. "What happened?"

Trude pulled over, no longer able to drive, her heart wrenching. "He's gone," she said. "He's finally gone." She buried her head in Erik's chest and let the uncontrollable sobs overwhelm her. She felt the dizziness storming through her body, and then there was darkness.

CHAPTER THIRTY-TWO

Königsberg
December 1944

Erik took over the controls and whisked them through the streets of Königsberg. Darkness was finally falling, a blissful mask to hide them from the world. They were safer now. Certainly the Gestapo would've discovered Gunther's death, but they were no longer heading to a predictable location, and they had false papers. They could go to all points of the compass. With the Russians coming in, Erik doubted the police would be out in full force looking for them. One dead Gestapo major would not likely shut down the city.

Erik's feelings were confirmed as they drove farther and farther away, finally connecting again to the autobahn. He turned onto it, this time heading south. Trude sat next to him in the front seat, Britta behind them.

"Thank you," he heard. It was Trude, looking over, gratefulness filling her voice.

"For what?" he asked.

"For saving our lives," she said.

"I did it for myself," he said. "I've lived as a selfish observer to all the horrors around me. I was trying to protect my family. I finally realized I had to do something for someone else. Besides, it looks like my family deserted me," he said bitterly.

"You still saved us," she said. "It doesn't matter why. You did it."

He nodded, not knowing how to answer.

"What happened to your family?" she asked. He didn't answer but silently reached into his pocket, pulling out the letter. He handed it to Trude. "Read it out loud," he said.

She unfolded the note, glancing at the first few words, then started to read:

Dear Erik:

I don't know if you'll ever find this letter. But if you do, I am thankful that you are safe. Unfortunately, there is no safety left here in Königsberg for us. The Russians are coming. They will be here any day now. I cannot sacrifice our family to remain and wait for you. As I told you in our last letter, Karl has taken care of all the arrangements and is leading our family to safety.

I hope if you read this, you will find comfort that your parents, your little girl, and your wife have been taken out of harm's way.

The next part is difficult for me to tell you, but you deserve to know the truth. Karl and I have grown very close these past years. I don't know how it happened, but it did. He is strong, wise, and a good provider. I don't blame you, Erik. I know you did your best, but in the end, you failed us. If you love me and our daughter, you will let us go. We are off to a safer, better life, away from the death and the suffering.

I know all of this will be terribly difficult to hear, but I ask you to let us start a new life. Please don't try to come look for us. I wish you the very best. The world around us is falling apart. I do not think we will ever meet again. May fortune bless you, dearest.

Corina

The car was utterly silent. "How could she?" said Trude. "You've been stuck in that hellhole, and in the meantime, she fell in love with that SS bastard? What kind of a woman does that?" she asked.

"The kind of woman that Corina is," said Erik. "My wife likes safety, comfort, money, status. That's what she's been fighting for. She pushed me to achieve her dreams, and I did—well, almost. I lost everything she wanted in the snow outside Kharkov. After that, we've never had a marriage."

"But none of those things are real," said Trude. "I grew up with wealth. It's an illusion. Silver and gold and shiny cars won't bring back Johannes. It won't protect our children, or help us to laugh, or live."

He nodded. "She never understood that. I don't think she ever will."

Trude reached her hand over and grabbed Erik's, giving him a gentle squeeze. "I'm so sorry," she said. "What will you do?"

"I'll find them," he said. "I'll get you to safety first, and then I'll find them, some way, somehow. I don't care about Corina, but she will not keep Greta away from me, and I must look after my parents."

"What about after that?"

"I don't know," he said.

She squeezed his hand. "Don't worry about that right now. Let's just concern ourselves with the present."

Erik secured some gas from a lonely station on the edge of a nameless town, then they rode along in silence as the darkness deepened. The road became ever icier and more treacherous as they moved through the rolling hills of East Prussia. Within a couple of hours, they were almost back to the turnoff to Soldau, but this time they would not head south. They would continue west toward Hamburg, and then the Rhine. Erik wanted to turn them over to the Americans. He didn't know what would happen when they got to the American troops, but he knew the Russians. Their only chance was to escape into the hands of the western Allies. Hopefully they would protect Trude and Britta.

They were nearing the turnoff to Soldau when he saw it. Men stood on the highway, blocking his path, rifles at the ready. His heart sank. The Gestapo. Somehow they'd tracked them down. They would not escape after all. He started to slow down.

"Who is it?" said Trude.

He could hear the fear in her voice.

"They've got us," he said. As he grew nearer he realized his mistake. They were not Gestapo or even SS. The men wore brown quilted uniforms. They were Russians.

He realized with irony that it wouldn't help them. This was almost worse than the Gestapo. He wanted to race through, but there were too many of them, and he was already slowing down. He grasped desperately for a plan, and then he smiled, thinking of his treasured friend Schaefer.

"I'm going to get out," he said. "As soon as I do, you must get into the driver's seat." She nodded, not understanding his plan.

He came to a stop and opened the door, immediately stepping out with arms high, shouting. The Russians watched him in surprise, frozen just for a moment by his strange conduct.

He took a step toward them. "Go!" he screamed, as loud as possible. He waved his arms, shouting and jumping.

A Russian raised his rifle at him, and Erik knew he had just a moment. "Go!" he screamed again. He heard the engine rev, and the car took off behind him. A Russian raised his rifle, rotating it toward the fleeing car. Erik charged the soldier, hitting him hard in the chest and driving the man to the snow. The rifle went off harmlessly, firing into the woods behind them.

Erik felt the blows on his back and legs, the screaming in a foreign tongue. Blood was already filling his mouth. He waited for the telltale shots, but there were none. He was pulled to his feet. The men screamed. Others were shouting and pointing toward the rapidly disappearing taillights. Another soldier raised his rifle, but the car was too far away, already turning around a bend. The lights flickered and then disappeared.

One of the Russians who looked like a commander questioned him in broken German. Erik answered, "Ja. SS."

The Russian issued a command Erik didn't understand, and the men circled him again, rushing him at once. He managed to hit one of them in the face, knocking him back, but the rest pulled him down, dropping him to his knees.

He raised his hands to heaven and closed his eyes. The blows rained down on him. "Good-bye, Trude," he whispered. He fell forward into the snow, a blissful darkness overwhelming him as he lay in the cold, dark night of the winter.

<hr>

Corina Mueller stood near the front of the long line. They were next in the queue. The building was full of loud, clamoring Germans, jockeying for position, for a seat, a ticket to safety. Greta was next to her, then Karl, and Erik's parents.

"What is taking so long?" she asked, tugging on Karl's coat. "I thought we had first-class tickets." She hated waiting in lines, particularly with these cattle.

Karl turned. "Everyone must go through a pass check. It won't be but a moment longer." Beyond the yellow line a group of officials stood seated behind a wall of wood and glass. One of them motioned to Karl, and he stepped forward, waving for the others to follow him.

"Who are you, and where are you going?" asked the official.

Karl handed the gentleman their papers, and the official scrutinized them. When he was done finally, he handed the paperwork back to Karl, saluting the colonel smartly.

Karl stepped forward past the line and then led them down a hallway toward another room. He opened the door to yet a larger space, Corina saw with dismay, packed even more tightly, a throng of screaming people all with their hands in the air, holding their tickets and their passports, trying to push their way past a line of guards.

Karl led them around to the left. "Don't worry," he said. "We don't have to sit through this."

They passed a line of guards. One of them tried to stop Karl, but he showed his paperwork to the soldier. The man took one look at the documents, then at Karl's uniform, and he saluted and allowed them through.

They walked along a roped-off section past the throng and up to the gate of the gangplank. Corina saw with relief the passageway up to their ship. Finally, this nightmare would be over. Karl handed the paperwork to another guard, who inspected their tickets and the papers. He shook his head.

"I don't have five first-class spots," the guard said. "Only three."

"But we have five tickets," said Karl.

"No you don't," said the guard. "You have three first-class and two third-class tickets."

Karl looked down in dismay, shaking his head. "I told those idiots five. It looks like there is a mistake here." He turned to Erik's parents. "I'm sorry," he said, wringing his hands and shrugging. "You'll have to go back and wait. I'll make a call and get this sorted out."

"When will Erik be here?" asked Peter. "You said we would meet him."

"He's on his way," said Karl. "He was only a couple hours behind us when we left."

"Why couldn't we have waited for him?" asked Anna suspiciously.

"I told you we had to get here and secure our spots," said the colonel. "Don't worry." He pointed back at the crowd. "Just join the group there and keep an eye out for Erik. We will get on board and secure our spots. I'll get everything cleared up with the shipmaster. There's plenty of room in our cabin for all of us."

He pulled out another ticket and handed all three to Peter. "Give this to Erik when he gets here," said Karl.

Peter took the tickets silently. Corina stepped forward and hugged both briefly, kissing Peter on the cheek. "Don't worry, Papa," she said. "Everything will be all right."

She saw his suspicion, so she flashed him her best smile. They would learn soon enough that Erik wasn't coming, but no matter. They wouldn't be on this ship—the third-class line was far too long—but she had provided for them. They had tickets. They would assuredly get on one of the vessels, perhaps the next one. Karl's plan had worked perfectly. She turned, admiring him. He was so clever.

"Say good-bye to your grandparents," she said to her daughter. Greta embraced both.

"But why can't they come with us?" she asked.

"There's a mix-up with the tickets. But don't you worry; we'll be back together soon."

Greta nodded in her innocence, listening to her mother faithfully. With a final nod to her in-laws, Corina grabbed her daughter's hand and they walked up the gangway with Karl. They were led onto the deck and then up three more flights of stairs to an interior door. A steward escorted them down a long hallway, stopping at a door. He opened it with a key, allowing them to step into the cabin. The room was beautiful, spacious with a large bed and mahogany paneling. An exterior door led out to their own private deck.

"Oh, Karl," she said. "How delightful. I didn't know we would be going in such style. You think of everything."

Karl winked at her. "I promised you." They stepped outside while Greta investigated the cabin. Karl looked to make sure her daughter was busy, then he moved forward, placing his hand at Corina's back. He drew her to him and kissed her deeply, passionately. She felt the fiery excitement again. He was a real man.

"Tell me again where we are going," she said. She knew the itinerary by heart, but she enjoyed the thrill of hearing it again.

"First Hamburg and then south. I have a car waiting for us. All the arrangements are made. We'll cross the border into Switzerland the day after tomorrow. I have new names for us all, so we can stay as long as we want, or we can travel on. I have a set of Portuguese papers also, and a source for documents to Argentina. There are many Germans there already, and they are sympathetic to our way of thinking."

"How will we afford all that?" she asked.

"I told you I've been taking care of that for years. All the money you will ever need waits for us in Switzerland. I have plenty to get us there."

"We can really do anything? Have anything?"

He nodded.

She giggled in joy. Karl was so strong, blond, handsome. He was everything she'd ever wanted. "I hope we won't always have to be in hiding," she said with a pout "I want people to know who you are. Who we are."

He smiled. "Don't worry, my dear, where we're going we will be heroes. I told you, I've taken care of everything."

She moved into his arms again, kissing him. "Oh, Karl!" They embraced, holding each other closely, and then turned to smile tolerantly at the chaotic scene below them. Watching the masses battling like rats for a spot on the ship.

Corina looked up and let the winter sun stream down on her face, enjoying the warmth, dreaming of her future.

Trude drove the car cautiously down the snowy dirt road. She had traveled for days without stopping except for gas and a little food. She'd slowly made her way across smoldering, war-burned Germany.

She'd fled danger, but now she was approaching it again. She had to be careful. In the distance, she finally saw what she had been seeking. A tank loomed, facing her. She crept forward slowly, not wanting to make herself a threat. She smiled to herself. How ironic it would be to be killed now at the end. She saw the soldiers standing around the massive green vehicle. As the car approached she caught their attention; rifles were raised.

She stopped the car about fifty meters away from them. "Careful now," she said to Britta.

She stepped slowly out of the car, hands up, beckoning with her head for her daughter to do the same. They walked forward together, step by step, under the rifles of the soldiers.

One of them yelled at her. She did not understand. She took another step, then another. The soldiers spread out, walking toward them now, weapons at the ready.

One of them called out, speaking a few broken words of German. She answered them with one word: *"Juden."* The soldier turned, speaking rapidly to the others. He lowered his rifle, his face softening. He reached into his shirt pocket and pulled out a small square package. As she stepped forward, he handed it to her. She looked down. It was chocolate. The Americans crowded around them, touching them, pressing food into their hands. Laughing. "Don't worry," said the soldier who spoke German. "You're home."

HISTORICAL INFORMATION

KÖNIGSBERG

Königsberg was the historical center of East Prussia. Founded in 1255 by German Teutonic Knights, during the Northern Crusades, the city was the most important eastern city in Germany, the center of Prussia's historic past.

The city contained Albertina University (founded 1544), a fourteenth-century cathedral set on an island, and a busy Baltic seaport. Königsberg was a crossroads of German, Polish, and Lithuanian culture.

During World War II, the city was an important starting point of the German invasion of Poland, and the subsequent invasion of the Soviet Union. Königsberg was badly damaged by Allied bombing in 1944 and was one of the first areas reached by the advancing Soviet army as it invaded Germany near the end of the war.

The city held out for three months under siege by the Russians but ultimately surrendered one month before the end of the European portion of World War II. Before and during the siege, hundreds of thousands, if not millions, of citizens attempted to escape East Prussia, many by ships, including from the port of Königsberg. The effort was organized under the code name "Operation Hannibal." Those who were able to secure passage on the overcrowded ships faced substantial dangers at sea, where Russian submarines and aircraft sank dozens of German vessels. Untold thousands of Germans perished in the Baltic Sea, including aboard the *Wilhelm Gustloff*, which went down in January 1945 with the loss of 9,343 people and which left 1,239 survivors—the greatest single loss of life from a ship sinking in the history of the world.

THE SS

The SS, or Schutzstaffel, was a branch of the Nazi party, dominating substantial portions of German life under Adolf Hitler. The SS was under the control of Reichsführer Heinrich Himmler, one of the top deputies under Hitler. The organization was divided into three branches: the Allgemeine SS, the Waffen-SS, and the SS-Totenkopfverbände.

The Allgemeine SS was the general branch, dealing with administrative issues, and the security police forces, such as the Gestapo. This branch was the most numerous until the Waffen-SS expanded during the war.

The Waffen-SS was originally called the SS-Verfügungstruppe and was created as military units to supplement the German army. This branch began the Polish war with only three regiments but grew to thirty-eight divisions by the end of the war, a growth from a few thousand men to a half million. Renamed the Waffen-SS after the war in France, this military arm gained in power and influence throughout the conflict. The Waffen-SS was known for its zealous fighting spirit and for committing atrocities against civilians, political individuals, and Jews. Although these events were more widespread than any actions of the regular German army, the Waffen-SS is often mistakenly grouped in with the most insidious elements of the SS, including the Totenkopfverbände, the concentration camp guard units. Just like in this book, Waffen-SS officers and men who were punished for some transgression in duty were at times transferred to the concentration camp system to serve as staff.

The Totenkopfverbände-SS was the branch of the SS that administered the concentration camps during World War II. Although all SS branches are tainted by Nazi atrocities, this was the branch most directly involved in the deaths of over eleven million victims, including six million Jews.

Soldau Concentration Camp

Soldau Concentration Camp was established in Polish territory that was annexed into East Prussia after Germany invaded Poland. The camp was formed around buildings that had served as barracks for the Polish military. Many members of the Polish intelligentsia were liquidated at the camp shortly after the invasion of Poland.

The camp, subsequently divided into three sections, served primarily as a transit center for Jews and others moving from parts of the Reich toward Auschwitz and other death camps. Of those who stayed in the camp, thirteen thousand out of thirty thousand perished.

Soldau was evacuated by the Germans, with the remaining inmates moved to other locations in Germany. Many died during the nightmare retreat in the cold and snow. The Russians occupied the empty camp on January 18, 1945, and it was used by the NKVD (the precursor of the KGB) to hold Germans and other enemies of the Soviet Union. The camp was closed in late 1945.

Portrayal of Karl and Corina

Some readers may be bothered by Karl and Corina "getting away." Although their safety and future was not assured (see notes above regarding evacuating from East Prussia), the reality of postwar Germany is that many prominent Nazis escaped any justice. A substantial number of powerful and wealthy individuals were able to escape to neutral countries, with many finding their way to Argentina and other South American countries. Adolf Eichmann and Josef Mengele are but two notable examples. Eichmann was eventually brought to justice by the Israeli secret service, but Mengele and others lived out their lives in German microcommunities, often in the open and revered as heroes by other war criminals.

GERMANY AND THE NAZIS

Many people want the Nazis to be a unique part of history, an evil unlike any other, which could never be repeated. The reality is that the Germany of the 1930s and '40s was among the most intellectual and advanced populations in the world. The people were regular mothers and fathers, sisters and brothers, neighbors.

Perhaps the greatest crime of the German people was not committed by the leaders, the concentration camp guards, or others directly involved. The true atrocity was the responsibility of the millions who allowed it to happen, and who passively sat on the sidelines as the world burned. As nationalism begins to burn anew in the world and a new age of dictatorship appears on the rise, we must all be careful to not repeat the mistakes of the past.

ABOUT THE AUTHOR

Photo © 2016 JW Photography

James D. Shipman is the bestselling author of three historical novels, *Constantinopolis*, *Going Home*, and *It Is Well*. He was born and raised in the Pacific Northwest and began publishing short stories and poems while earning a degree in history from the University of Washington and a law degree from Gonzaga University. He opened his own law firm in 2004 and remains a practicing attorney. An avid reader, especially of historical nonfiction, Shipman also enjoys traveling and spending time with his family.